Glasgow Sun

Robert Fisher

authorHOUSE™

1663 LIBERTY DRIVE, SUITE 200
BLOOMINGTON, INDIANA 47403
(800) 839-8640
WWW.AUTHORHOUSE.COM

First published by AuthorHouse 09/29/05

ISBN: 1-4208-8570-7 (sc)
ISBN: 1-4208-8571-5 (dj)

Printed in the United States of America
Bloomington, Indiana

This book is printed on acid-free paper.

Dedicated to my family

Chapter 1

"Honest officer, that tree jumped out right in front o' me."

McNab glared at the sprawled figure on the grass verge, wrapped around a bicycle. He guessed how this man came to be inside his barracks at eleven o'clock at night.

"Get up ye Glasgow git," he growled. "And ah'm no' an officer ye ignoramus. I am a sergeant."

Sergeant John McNab of the Black Watch regiment was a strong, 5' 11' Ayrshireman from a coalmining family. Earning the rank of sergeant had been the most important achievement in his life. He often vividly recalled the reaction of his parents when he arrived home, unannounced, on a three day pass and they learned for the first time of his promotion. His mother was teary eyed as she fiddled with her apron and his father just gazed in wonder at the new stripes on his uniform. While he hugged his mother, his father finally said with typical Scots terseness, "Och son, yer Ma and me are very proud o' ye."

No-one could deny he had worked hard and deserved his promotion. Now he was ready to fight Nazis or, if the latest rumor was true, Japs. February 1941 was full of rumors, especially in Maryhill Barracks in Glasgow.

McNab's reddish hair indicated the possibility of a fiery temper; now his normally fair complexion had turned a bright red.

He knew civilians liked to buy pints of 'heavy' for the lads. He knew they reveled in the lads' exaggerated stories of their war experiences. He knew that if one of them produced a bottle of whiskey at closing time, the lads would attempt to smuggle him into the barracks. He knew all this.

He didn't condone it but he couldn't help feeling pleased knowing the vicarious thrill experienced by the common man associating with the best fighting men in the world.

Nevertheless this crumpled mass, reeking of whiskey, whining about moving trees had to be booted out and quickly. The cloth cap or 'bunnet' and filthy raincoat were typical of the average tenement dweller in Maryhill. McNab had nothing against people from poor backgrounds, he was also from just such a background, but he hated whiners. He reached down toward the person lying under the tree.

It was the last thing John McNab would ever do.

The crumpled mass moved with stupendous speed. His hand grasped the back of his cloth cap and whipped the front across McNab's throat. The razor blades embedded in the skip slashed deeply, then feet pressed into NcNab's belly, throwing him on his back and a surprisingly strong hand clamped over his mouth.

A few low gurgling sounds came from McNab as his uncomprehending eyes sought an answer.

"You should huv' been brought up in Glasgae an' ye wid know somethin' about bunnets," said the 'git'.

McNab died quickly.

His uniform was unceremoniously stripped from him; his assailant smiled mirthlessly to see that he had complied fully with regulations and wore nothing under the kilt. Having donned the uniform he ran towards the sentry box at the entrance to the barracks, making as much noise as possible. He was not concerned about the bloodstains at the top of the tunic.

The guard first heard then saw the running figure. Being trained to recognize rank he spotted the three stripes and snapped to attention. The approaching figure slowed and moved to the side of the guard, who stood rigidly, staring straight ahead.

"Why in God's name didnae ye stop him man?"

"Stop who Sergeant?"

"Don't tell me ye didnae see him. Are ye blind man? Or were ye skivin' off? That's it ye were ha'in' a smoke in yer guard box, and missed him."

By this time small beads of sweat were running down the guard's face. The 'Sergeant' was shouting in such a blustering manner that flecks of spittle were landing on the guard. All in all, guard McKenzie's face was a bit of a mess, yet he continued to stand at attention, staring straight

2

ahead. He defended himself by saying, "No sergeant, ah wisnae smokin' and naebody passed this gate."

" I am goin' doon the street tae huv' a look-see and if I find him I'll huv' yer guts for garters. Do you hear me?"

"Yes Sergeant!"

"In the meantime, you keep yer eyes peeled for him in the barrack's grounds. Is that perfectly clear?"

"Yes Sergeant."

As guard McKenzie turned to face into the barracks, the 'Sergeant' slipped around the back of him and ran down Maryhill Road. McKenzie muttered, "How the bloody hell did he know ah wis smokin?' But ah wisnae inside that box, I wis right here."

He had in fact used the time-honored method of holding the cigarette inside his cupped hand and drawing deeply on the slightly protruding tip at the back of his fingers.

"Nae matter whit he thinks, nae bugger got passed me."

By this time the 'Sergeant' had slowed to a walk and after a careful look up and down Maryhill road, turned into Blair Street. About fifty yards down the street he stopped at a 1934 black Austin 7, after yet another careful scrutiny of the area, he quickly entered the car, found the keys under the seat and retrieved a map from under the sun visor. The map indicated his destination was Bearsden; he started the engine and drove off. He gave a brief wave of his hand as he pulled away from the curb. He knew someone was there to check everything went smoothly, even though he could not see him.

Chapter 2

Once again he marveled at the flawless organization of the night's events. The car had been exactly where it should have been, the keys to the left of the passenger's seat and the engine started first time. A long coat was on the back seat along with a hat. He had stopped just outside Clydebank to put these on; perfect cover in case some insomniac was at a window. Spying on neighbors from behind a curtain was a national pastime in Scotland and no one should see the soldier's uniform. He checked the map for the location of the house before restarting the car. The house was located in Hillside Crescent, a quiet street in Bearsden, a posh neighborhood on the extreme west of Glasgow. It did not take long to drive there. He parked the car in the driveway and casually opened the front door with the Yale key which was on the same key-ring as the car keys.

The thick curtains made it safe to switch on the light. As he expected, everything was in order. His clothes had been carefully laid out and a very good whisky had a place of honor on the table. He helped himself to a decent shot and dialed a number on the telephone.

"Everything OK?" asked the voice at the other end of the line.

"Yes, I will see you tomorrow."

There had been no greeting, it was always better to be brief. Interestingly, his accent had changed from that of an uneducated Glasgow 'keelie' to a nondescript, but cultured one. Having finished his drink, he put the uniform in the thoughtfully provided large bag and went to bed.

He arose at seven the next morning, and had just finished washing, shaving and dressing when there was a loud knocking on the front door. In an instant of panic he ran to the back door and then he realized he had thoughtlessly opened the curtains, letting the light shine out. Whoever was out there knew he was inside and if unfriendly, would have every exit covered. He had to brazen it out. He took several deep breaths then opened the door. There on the doorstep was an elderly lady with a thermos flask in one hand; she offered the other in a handshake.

"Ah, Mr. Simpson isn't it; I thought it only polite to welcome you to Bearsden. I made you tea. It was so late when you arrived last night and if you are anything like my late husband, the last thing you would think of would be the purchase of a few essentials. My name is Mrs. McAllister and I live just opposite. I hope you don't mind but I noticed your light and thought you ought to have proper nourishment before starting your day."

While talking she had walked past him into the living room. Her sharp eyes took in all details. The word 'proper' was emphasized as she looked at the whisky bottle.

"I noticed the van parked outside your house these past few days. Your painters have certainly improved the color scheme, the previous one was quite, what shall I say, jarring to the senses. When you have time you will, no doubt, change the furniture."

It sounded more like an order than an observation. The 'Painters' had checked the entire house including the telephone. They had also delivered his clothes. He wondered if they realized they had been under observation.

The elite of Glasgow have a very distinctive accent. It is referred to as a 'Kelvinside' accent. They tend to draw out some words, particularly long or unusual words, to ensure the dimmer witted lower classes gain a complete appreciation of their station in life. The key is to reply with an even more impressive barrage of pomposity which lets them know you are not intimidated and then the conversation usually becomes relatively normal. He wanted to end this particular conversation.

"It was extraordinarily kind of you to welcome me in such a charming manner Mrs. McAllister. Thank you for the compliments on the decor and as you say, some other aspects could stand improvement. Unfortunately my present schedule will not permit this for some time. I am sure you can appreciate how busy one can be in these difficult days."

"Oh of course, Mr. Simpson, what type of work do you do? I am not sure I can place your accent, are you from Glasgow? There I am asking too many questions again. When you return the thermos we will sit down and get to know each other."

The emphasis appeared to be on 'will'; another order.

"Excellent idea," he lied, "actually I am a little pushed for time. Thank you again."

He escorted her to the door and watched as she marched briskly towards her house, her blue rinsed hair gleaming under the streetlights.

"Holy Mary Mother of God," he muttered. "That is one very dangerous woman".

He had just finished his second cup of Mrs. McAllister's tea and was deep in thought about his meeting later in the morning, when there was a knock on the back door.

"Jesus Christ," he said involuntarily, "what now?"

He unlocked the door, slid back the bolt, opened the door and stared in awe at one of the most beautiful women he had ever seen.

"Hello, I am Carolyn Jardine, one of your neighbors. May I come in for a minute?"

"Of course. Please do."

Carolyn Jardine was tall, almost 5' 8", with short light brown hair. Her blue eyes sparkled and her generous mouth seemed to want to break into laughter. She put on a conspiratorial air and said, "I saw old nosey parker McAllister visit you and I thought it a good idea to let you see that not everyone is a geriatric on this snobbish street. Also, to be truthful, I was just as curious."

Her mouth did break into a lovely grin and her eyes danced with mischief.

"Anyway it's so damned boring with this war on. My husband's been gone for almost a year. He's not allowed to say where he is, or the censor cuts it out of his letters. It's so bloody stupid, you just have to go to the cinema and Movietone News shows you where the fighting is and sometimes even mentions which regiments are taking part in the action."

"No doubt old McAllister invited you to her house for tea. I am sure you would find it more interesting to visit me for a drink."

Once again she bathed him in her glorious smile.

"You just have to go out your back door, nip across Mrs. Bell's back garden and knock on my back door. I am usually home by six o'clock each evening. Here is my number if you want to check that I am home. Bring that with you," she said, nodding towards the whisky, "it's a better brand than I have. You will not disappoint me, will you?"

"Absolutely not, it's an excellent idea."

This time he was not lying. He watched Carolyn as she negotiated the low fence that separated his garden from that of Mrs. Bell. Her tightly drawn raincoat emphasized her swaying hips as she seemed to glide across the garden. He closed the door, locked and bolted it, and rested his back against it.

"That is one very, very dangerous woman," he breathed.

Within ten minutes he was in the car heading for the city. He parked on Sauchiehall Street and walked to an office building on Renfield Street. A skinny little porter sat behind a wobbly metal desk. His shiny dark blue uniform was about three sizes too large, probably that of a previous occupant of that desk.

"Good morning, I am looking for Mr. Johnston."

"Good mornin' Surr. Do you…Do you huv'…..Do you huv' an appointment?"

There was a look of intense concentration on the porter's face. He had obviously been practicing this phrase, and equally obviously, further practice was necessary.

"Yes I do, my name is Simpson."

After a studious review of the list on his desk, which anyone could see had all of three names on it, he said, "Right ye are, Surr, second floor, room 24."

He chose to run up the stairs, rather than take the lift. He was still breathing easily when he reached the second floor. He knocked twice on the door.

"Come in. "

He entered a large office, the only occupant being a big man wearing a pin-striped suit and sitting at a huge desk. His florid face was impassive as he said, "What can I do for you?" He had an incongruous little moustache which twitched while he spoke.

"My name is Simpson. I am expected."

The man stared intently at his visitor for ten seconds, pressed a button on his desk and said phlegmatically, "Room 47, take the stairs. Walk right in, do not knock. "

Again he ran to the fourth floor and entered Room 47. This time the room was small. Two men stood waiting for him dressed as doctors. A stethoscope lay on a desk. If they were doctors they were the most muscular ones Jack had ever seen. One motioned for him to raise his arms while the other frisked him thoroughly. Without saying a word the first one opened a door to another anteroom where two more men stood. They were both stocky, wore somewhat ill fitting suits, but of greater significance, they were Japanese. On a chair lay a pile of bandages. One of them held up his hand for the visitor to stop, while the other knocked on a door, poked his head round, said something then opened the door fully and waved the visitor in. At last he came face to face with the man he had spoken to the previous night. He was a handsome man, of slim build, with a smooth unblemished skin and he too was Japanese.

"Ohayoo Gozaimasu, Lord Hino."

"Good Morning to you, Campbell. How are you this morning? No ill effects from last night?"

Jack Campbell knew the perfect English with no trace of an accent was the result of Prep school, followed by Oxford and then the Naval School at Portsmouth. The British navy had played a major role in the development of the Japanese navy, including training many of their officers. In Lord Hino they had, inadvertently, helped train the head of Japanese Intelligence.

"Aren't you taking a terrible risk being here?" asked Jack. "If you are caught you will be shot, no questions asked. You may be able to disguise yourself but these two beauties out there could never be well enough disguised not to be recognized."

"Quite so. That is why we came in an ambulance and my two 'beauties' as you refer to my guards, had their faces bandaged. These men are the best trained and most trusted ones I have in my employ. They will obey any instruction I give them without question and without hesitation. As you correctly observed I do risk being shot, but not before I am questioned and probably tortured to reveal all I know. This is the reason why I must take the risk of their presence. Should something go wrong and we become trapped, I must never be captured alive. In such an eventuality, their instructions are clear; they must kill me. Of course they would then shoot themselves. I cannot trust such an action to anyone else."

"Care to join me in a cup of tea?"

At first, due to Lord Hino's matter of fact tone, Jack found it difficult to believe this, but as he studied the serious, yet somehow calm face, he realized he was telling the truth. The whole essence of this man's being was dedicated to his Country and his Emperor. His own life was of little consequence in this devoted service.

"Yes please," said Jack, in a hushed voice, totally in awe of the coolness of this remarkable man. He poured a cup from the elegant china teapot. Everything about Lord Hino could be described as elegant, from his perfectly tailored suit to the silver cigarette holder that he held delicately in his left hand. A student of English couture would have approved the right amount of cuff showing below his dark grey jacket sleeve. This highlighted the gold cufflinks that glittered on his Egyptian cotton shirt. Jack sat down, sipped his tea and gazed at Lord Hino.

"Please Campbell, stop this delay: Speak up man. Did you get it?"

Jack smiled; he enjoyed Lord Hino's discomfort, then he withdrew a package of documents from his inside jacket pocket. He passed these to Lord Hino who eagerly opened the package. A look of horror spread over his face as he stared uncomprehendingly at the written documents and the maps.

"What the hell have you done, Campbell?" he growled. "These plans all relate to Europe. How could you have made such a gross error?"

Jack smiled broadened as he said, "There is no error. These are documents I stole last night. Perhaps I had better explain."

Still looking very angry, Lord Hino said, "It had better be a damn good explanation."

"Last night, just as I planned, I was smuggled into the barracks by a group of lads from the Black Watch Regiment. I watched them drink quite a few pints of beer in the pub before I joined them. After a few more rounds it was almost closing time so I told them I had a two bottles of whisky with me and suggested we find a quiet place to drink them. They were only too pleased to oblige and suggested their barracks. It wasn't difficult to sneak in.

When the first bottle was consumed I gave the lads the second and snuck away. By this time a few were asleep and the rest were too drunk to notice."

"I raided four offices; three containing particulars about different parts of Europe and the fourth relating to Malaya. I took this European set and left the details from the other three offices strewn around as though they were of no interest. This way, British intelligence will now be changing their plans for this part of Europe. The information you so keenly desire regarding Malaya has been memorized and I can detail everything for you now."

"You crafty young bugger, I never ceased to marvel at your ingenuity. But I heard there was some trouble. Is this correct? Did you have to kill someone?"

"It was an unfortunate but necessary part of the plan."

"But surely you could have gotten out without this act?"

"That was possible but involved an element of risk that I deemed too high. There are many sentries and one could have been too observant. You told me this operation must be completely secret, therefore this degree of risk was unacceptable."

"And killing someone you just happened to bump into was acceptable and risk free?"

There was a slight edge to Lord Hino's voice.

"You asked me to plan this operation meticulously and I did. In prior visits to the pub, I heard the soldiers talk of their sergeant's final daily check of the barracks at eleven o'clock. I did not just bump into the sergeant, he was essential to my plan. You will recall I asked you to have a large bag left in the house you rented. This was to dispose of the uniform."

"If I had tried and been lucky enough to get out unseen, many of the soldiers in the barracks would have been questioned regarding a burglary. To a private in the army this would not affect him personally; therefore, he would not view it as a particularly serious matter and one of them would have owned up to smuggling me into the barracks and given a description of me. On the other hand, a murder will be viewed as very serious and could land anyone related to it in big trouble."

"I don't know what happens in the Japanese army, but in the British army a private learns, very quickly, that, number one, you never volunteer for anything, and number two, when the bullets start flying, you keep you head down and your mouth shut. No one will talk about my being smuggled into the barracks last night."

During this explanation Lord Hino had his eyes half closed in concentration. Now he opened them fully. Jack saw the gleam of appreciation in his eyes and not for the first time noticed how big Lord Hino's eyes were. There were certainly almond shaped but not pronouncedly slit.

"My congratulations, Campbell and please forgive my initial doubts. I seem to find difficulty in appreciating the depth of your intelligence. No, intelligence is not the correct word, your perspicacity. Now let's get down to your report."

Lord Hino drew detailed maps of Malaya from a drawer in the desk and for the next three hours Campbell carefully noted the information he had read the previous night. At the end of this debriefing Lord Hino sat back in his chair.

"Excellent, excellent," he breathed. "Now we can proceed with your training."

"Training? I thought I had completed my training program."

"This is a different type of training. To successfully complete your next mission, you must have a working knowledge of shipping and biology, marine biology, to be specific."

Now it was Lord Hino's turn to be amused at the perplexed look on Jack's face.

"Come, come, Campbell, I thought you would be pleased at the opportunity to visit Malaya."

"Malaya?"

"Yes Malaya. Please stop gawking or I will have to retract my previous comment on your intelligence."

Jack's perplexed look dissolved and was replaced by a smile of pure joy.

"Your next major assignment will be to validate the information you gathered last night. You will travel to Malaya in September. Your cover will be as a junior executive in a shipping company whose services have been seconded to the government to conduct a survey of harbor conditions in South East Asia. This will give you access to the harbors in Singapore, Malacca, Port Swettenham and Penang."

"Your other passion in life, in this role, is marine biology; this will give you a reason to visit the entire North East coast of Malaya which just happens to be one of the few breeding grounds for giant turtles. You will report to a Mr. John Gibson of the Red Funnel Line in Renfrew Street at 9 o'clock tomorrow morning. You will have one month to learn as much as a bright newcomer to shipping learns in two years. Don't be too alarmed, it is not a difficult subject."

"I have learned that knowledgeable middle level managers have a great fear of bright newcomers and dish out their knowledge in very small parcels. Many are afraid that their ten years experience will be discovered to be only one year's worth repeated ten times. You will work diligently, Campbell. It has taken me a great deal of trouble to arrange this training."

"Mr. Gibson is a very experienced person and I have had him informed that you are to be driven mercilessly. He was contacted through an intermediary, Sir Samuel Brown. Mr. Gibson has been instructed not to pry into your relationship with Sir Samuel. He has been told you are on a government assignment. Just in case he forgets and becomes inquisitive, you need only say you are under instructions not to discuss this subject. Your name will continue to be Jack Simpson."

Jack had found it difficult to sit still during this news. His excitement was so great. However the next piece of news caused him to leap to his feet.

"Prior to Malaya, you will spend your time in Japan."

"Japan," he exalted. "At last, at long last. Thank you, thank you Lord Hino. You have no idea how often I have dreamed of this opportunity."

Jack's eyes were aglow with delight as he paced around the room.

"Perhaps I do," said Lord Hino, pursing his lips; his eyes, again, half closed.

"Yes, yes, I believe I do. But try to control yourself, Campbell, we still have more to discuss."

"Ah, yes, marine biology training. Giant turtles seldom visit Scotland in winter, or even in summer," said Jack with a grin.

"If they did, they may have as much difficulty as I do in distinguishing any real difference in temperature between these two seasons in this country," replied Lord Hino.

"Your education on this subject will take place onboard the ship you take to Japan. You will study under Professor Mannheim. The ship sails from Lisbon in five weeks. I will make arrangements to have you escorted to Lisbon."

"A kraut," grunted Jack.

"No, not a kraut, a highly respected marine biologist and you will treat him with the respect he deserves. Is that quite clear?"

"Of course," replied Jack contritely.

"Now, let me hear you repeat you instructions," demanded Lord Hino.

Jack dutifully complied.

"You will be contacted in three weeks time with details of your travel plans to Lisbon. I hope you study well. I will return to Dublin tonight and will see you in Lisbon. We shall travel together to Japan."

With that Lord Hino extended his hand and said goodbye. Jack left the office with a joyful heart. A euphoric smile broke out on his face as he descended the stairs.

"Japan," he whispered, "Japan."

Chapter 3

Lord Hino watched Jack's lithe figure leave the office thinking how incongruous it was for Britain to lose such an enormous talent. Campbell was the jewel in his network and so vital to his plans that it was worth the dangers of this trip to hear firsthand how he had handled this difficult assignment. In matters of great importance he always believed in face to face meetings.

He called the Japanese guards instructing them that he did not want to be disturbed. Then he told the 'doctors' to buy some sandwiches for lunch; have everything in the offices cleaned and have the ambulance and 'patients' ready to leave at 4 o'clock. At this time of year it was dark in Scotland at that time.

He closed his eyes and concentrated on the report he had been given. The High Command in Japan would be pleased with the new information. One more piece of their plan was taking shape. Japan's goal was to become an empire as powerful as those of Britain and Germany. It had been relatively easy to take Korea and Manchuria then other parts of China. And when Germany had captured France, Japan took Indochina. The leaders of the Daibatsu or largest industrial companies were becoming even greedier and continuously urged the Military leadership to conquer more territory. While supporting the national plan of creating an empire, Lord Hino and a few other thoughtful men had two concerns.

Firstly, the growing threat of Japan in Manchuria, close to its border had caused Russia to finally react. Large scale clashes occurred in the summer of 1939. After almost three months of conflict Japan had planned and was preparing to launch a significant offensive. Tokyo was confident it would prove conclusive and persuade the Russians to withdraw. They had not reckoned with the aggression and brilliance of Stalin's greatest military strategist, Marshall Zukov. Daringly, he launched an all out preemptive attack smashing the Japanese Army. This made Japan seek an armistice in September. None of this was reported in Japan's press particularly as 20,000 Japanese soldiers had been killed in this campaign.

Secondly, the campaigns in China and Indochina had increased the antipathy of America toward Japan and resulted in embargoes on some essential materials to Japan. This had enraged the military leaders and worried the Daibatsu as about half of Japan's needs of essential items like oil, iron and steel were imported from the United States. The urgent need to find more reliable sources, combined with the aversion to fighting Russia impelled Tokyo to hasted plans to expand South rather than North.

Recognizing the strong negative reaction this would bring from Britain and possibly America, and being impressed by Hitler's ease in conquering France, Japan sought to strengthen its position by joining the Axis powers in September 1940.

Lord Hino had sought out his friend Admiral Yamamoto to discuss these things. It was Yamamoto's conviction that Japan should avoid war with America.

"As you know Hino, I have lived in America. I attended Harvard University. I know the industriousness and determination of the American people. We would be wise not to rouse them. Unfortunately several of my colleagues think America is only a paper tiger. Of course I will obey any command given to me, but in confidence, I am troubled that our present course will lead to conflict with this tiger which is not made of paper but is real and very dangerous."

It was this conversation that cemented his belief of the need for a backup plan. This plan was known to only five people including, of course, the Emperor. He had spent several hours carefully detailing this plan to His Majesty. It was critical not to imply any lack of faith in the might of Japan's Armed Forces; rather this was the normal practice of contingency planning. However he had pointed out to the Emperor that the creation of such a plan could be misconstrued, therefore it was best kept a closely guarded secret. To the five knowledgeable people this plan was referred to by the code name he had devised—Empire.

At the outset his plan was purely a contingency, indeed, he was impressed at the audacity of the military plan to take much of South East Asia. In particular, the incorporation of the lesson learned in Manchuria, being the advantage of a first strike. He agreed that Britain could be defeated in Asia as its primary focus was on Europe. The part of the plan which caused him the most unease was the talk of a preemptory strike against America. As Yamamoto had said America had vast pools of resources and a spirit of nationalism difficult to extinguish once aroused. The first strike had better be overwhelming.

Whatever the risks involved, Japan's rapidly increasing population demanded more goods and land. The future empire of Japan must have industrial materials and new food sources. They had confidence in their ability to obtain these easily from the surrounding Asian countries; tin and rubber from Malaya, oil from the Dutch East Indies and food from Thailand. These countries would offer no real resistance to Japanese rule. But the British army had to be thrown out of Malaya and Singapore. Singapore was the key to all shipping in the area and must be secured quickly.

Lord Hino smiled as he recalled his last visit to Singapore. How proud the British were of their prodigious guns and how confident they were of their ability to sink any possible invasion. The idiots! Why did they not study the words of one of their most famous poets, Samuel Taylor Coleridge who wrote, 'If men could learn from history, what lessons it might teach us!' It is inconceivable that the British Military leaders can have forgotten the lesson of Tsingtao. This German stronghold had many similarities to Singapore, yet Japan had taken it with ease. By avoiding a frontal attack on the heavily fortified German Base, General Kamio had laid siege to Tsingtao and landed troops further up the coast attacking the garrison from the rear. Kamio was even assisted by 1,500 British troops in this attack. Britain could not have forgotten this lesson; therefore, their tactics in Singapore demonstrated their arrogance in believing in their own invincibility.

Singapore's massive weapons were fixed, facing the sea and could not be used in any other direction. How could it be possible that no one had realized although the front door was so well guarded, the back door was wide open? The narrow straight between Malaya and Singapore would offer no protection.

To achieve this conquest, Malaya must be taken quickly. Any bogging down would be disastrous. So, the next piece of intelligence had to be an on the spot reconnaissance of the British defenses in Malaya. All information must be verified.

'The ideal job for Campbell,' he thought, 'but not yet.' First would come the training for his cover. He had no doubt in Campbell's ability to pick up sufficient knowledge in about a month. He also had confidence in his ability to improvise deftly should the need arise.

'But,' he thought, 'before Malaya there will be a visit to Japan. I had better refine the details for his stay.' This visit was not essential to the High Command's plan but it was to Hino's plan. His eyes opened, burning with passion, and his pulse quickened as his mind raced over the outline of his plan.

'Ah, yes, this will be the real victory for my Motherland and for my Emperor.'

A smile crossed his handsome face as he whispered, "And all due to this extraordinary Scotsman."

He had started his plan over two years ago and had other young men under instruction, but none of them was as perfect as Campbell.

Hino could still remember the night he had received a coded telephone call from one of his agents in Glasgow, requesting a meeting. He had left London two days later to meet with Nakayama Yasuo.

Nakayama was a young professor of Oriental Studies at Glasgow University. In addition he taught Judo classes to the students.

He affected the attributes of the classic 'absent minded professor'. His thick glasses, disheveled appearance, poor English, slight stutter and shuffling gait made him look the most inoffensive and meekest person imaginable. Nothing could be further from the truth. In fact, he graduated with honors from Tokyo University, Japan's most prestigious school of higher learning. He had to continually work hard at his role in Glasgow.

Glasgow University was well known as a center of engineering excellence. Its proximity to the large engineering and shipbuilding companies in the Clyde valley ensured the engineering faculty had an up to date knowledge of all that was going on, particularly during this time of war. As new projects were debated in the staff lounge, no one paid attention to Nakayama sitting in the corner, his nose in a book. His reports to Lord Hino were always thorough and highly prized.

"It is an honor to see you again my Lord. I apologize for my appearance, but I must be careful."

There was no trace of a stutter in Nakayama's speech. Hino knew of Nakayama's fastidiousness of dress in Japan and how much it pained him to dress so badly in his present role.

"Not at all, I am delighted to see you again. You must have learned of a very special project to call me for a personal meeting, rather than avail yourself of usual courier service. I can hardly wait to hear your news. Please tell me."

"Well," Nakayama hesitated. "I am ----"

Lord Hino had the highest regard for his top agents but he was a Lord and a busy one at that. He did not permit anyone to ever forget this. The one thing which angered him most was for someone to waste his time. His eyes hardened as he said, "Nakayama-kun, I have always admired your conciseness. Do you have news of a project or not."

When he addressed Nakayama he used kun and not san. This indicated someone of a much lower station in life.

"Not a project, a person, which is why I had to speak to you personally."

Lord Hino leaned back in his chair as he lit a cigarette. His eyes lost their appearance of hardness and became thoughtful. He recognized a palpable earnestness in Nakayama and realized this was difficult for him, but it must indeed be special to have called such a meeting.

"Take your time," said Hino.

Nakayama breathed deeply then began to tell his story.

"I have come across a man who is taking a doctorate degree. He previously studied mathematics, economics and then oriental studies. He can speak Japanese, not fluently, but quite well. He has an insatiable thirst for oriental knowledge, particularly about Japan. I sensed he was sincere in his admiration of our culture, but I had to be certain before contacting your Lordship. So, I listened carefully to the comments of other faculty members in order to piece together an accurate profile."

"His name is Jack Campbell; he is twenty three years old and was born in Glasgow. He comes from a poor background. He has a great dislike for British authorities. I hesitate to use the term hatred as it is so strong, however it may be more precise. This feeling springs from two sources."

"Firstly, his father died of injuries sustained during the last war with Germany. Apparently the details of his illness were never revealed by the authorities. Campbell believes some mistake was made and rather than make this public, they let him die. Later something bad happened to his mother, no one seems to know exactly what it was, except it involved the police. Unfortunately she died and again things were hushed up. He does not talk much about these things."

"And the second source?" asked Lord Hino.

"The second relates to the class system in Britain. He fervently wished to take Oriental Studies at Cambridge but was not accepted there. According to one member of the Glasgow faculty who studied at Cambridge, Campbell's academic qualifications were outstanding but his Glasgow accent and poor family went against him. This person said that Campbell was so upset at the rejection that he traveled again to Cambridge to plead his case. The reasons given were feeble. This same person speculates that Campbell was so incensed he broke into the university office and read the real reasons. 'Upbringing unsuitable. Not a gentleman. Bad accent.' Since that time Campbell has mastered a very cultured accent which he uses when it suits him."

"Hmm, you are correct; he is a very interesting person. Anything further?"

"Yes, he is very athletic and very strong. As you know I teach a little judo to some students."

"I believe as part of your cover, you pretend to be only somewhat knowledgeable in this art. Even though you are 'Go-Dan', fifth level black belt."

"That is correct, my Lord. Because of this Campbell beats me every time. In my opinion he could easily qualify for 'San-Dan', third level black belt."

Here Nakayama hesitated and Hino said, "What is it?"

"I have no concrete reason to say this but I must mention I believe Campbell sees through my act."

Lord Hino shot to his feet, his eyes blazing.

"How could this happen? Hold nothing back, Nakayama-kun, tell me everything. This could be of critical importance."

"As I said my Lord, I have nothing definite. This is difficult to explain; it is not just what he says, it's the way he looks at me. His eyes say more than his voice."

Now Hino was truly intrigued, "Go on, Nakayama-kun, go on."

"For example, my Lord, one time when were practicing judo, he stared into my eyes and said with a smile, 'Come on Nakayama-sensei, I *know* you can do much better'. Another time in class he was bombarding me with questions and at the end of the lesson, when everyone else had left he said in Japanese, 'Sensei, you really do know a lot. I could learn so much more from you if only you would share your real knowledge with me' and while he said this he had that smile on his face."

"We cannot afford to take a chance on this man. Before I decide his fate I will meet him. I have an acquaintance who is a good friend of the Head of the University. He was the one who first proposed your appointment. I will arrange a visit to the University with this acquaintance on the pretext of reviewing the current state of Oriental Studies in Britain. I will suggest a lunch with the class at the University. You will make sure this Campbell sits next to me."

A week later the visit and the lunch took place. He found Campbell to be reserved at the outset and it took all his skill to fully engage him in conversation. However, once Campbell warmed to him, he discovered a depth of understanding and a hunger to learn more of Japan that totally surprised him. He had not known what to expect of this meeting; therefore, he was amazed at the strong bond he felt towards Campbell. Hino was not a man to be easily impressed and his suspicious mind told him to look for a flaw in his findings. The only way to be sure was more time with Campbell, alone.

Although he was excited at the prospect of recruiting another agent he had to be careful even though time was short. The military leaders in Japan were becoming impatient for further conquests. He decided quick action was appropriate. He did this by suggesting Campbell may wish to consider furthering his studies at a University in Japan at some future date. When he saw an immediate positive response, he suggested a meeting later that day as he was traveling back to London that night.

And so the first private meeting took place.

During this meeting Lord Hino questioned Jack about his studies, his interests and his family background. On the last subject he found Campbell reticent to go into much detail.

"Please understand I cannot recommend you to such a noted university as Kyoto without satisfying myself of you suitability."

"I completely understand this necessity and will give you all the basic information you require."

There was a slight emphasis on 'basic'. It was readily apparent to Lord Hino that this young man was completely at ease and of greater importance was not one to be easily intimidated. Already his esteem for Campbell was increasing. He switched his questions to the more usual ones of what Jack would like to accomplish by studying in Japan and what use he would make of this experience. Almost seamlessly his questions turned to Jack's political views. The answers were so conventional and were delivered with such ease that Lord Hino instantly knew they were false. What disturbed him was he could not help feeling that Campbell knew that he recognized this.

After further general questioning he said, "Thank you for your time Mr. Campbell. I found our meeting most interesting. I will contact Kyoto University and let you know their response. Can you please give me a telephone number where you can be reached?"

Jack wrote down the university number, handed it to Hino and said, "I look forward to hearing the response from Tokyo and once again I do understand the need to question me carefully." As he said this he had a very slight smile on his lips.

Again Hino had the feeling that this young man was reading his mind. As he traveled back to London he tried to understand why he felt Campbell was one step ahead of him.

This had never happened before and he had dealt with some very high level people.

He recounted the conversation, remembering how impressed he was with Campbell's use of the English language. He chose his words with apparent ease but with great precision. One could not mistake his meaning.

Then it struck him. It was not just the manner in which he responded or his faint smile. When they parted Campbell had said he looked forward to the reply from 'Tokyo' not Kyoto University. Campbell had sent him a message that he understood what was happening.

Lord Hino was an expert in recruiting agents; however, he knew he had never met anyone quite like Campbell and he must be very careful. Could this possibly be a trap? He did not believe so; nevertheless, extreme caution must be exercised. He resolved this would require an extended interview to satisfy him of two things.

Firstly, he now believed Campbell was truly bitter about the deaths of his parents. But, was he bitter against the relevant authorities or did this bitterness transfer to the British way of life?

Secondly, would his obvious passion of things Japanese translate into an understanding of, and support of, Japan's political aspirations?

As the Flying Scotsman thundered through the night he smiled to himself at the appropriate name for this train. He wondered if his new Scottish acquaintance would also 'fly'. Somehow he sensed he already knew the answer and his excitement drove away sleep. His plan of action was taking shape in his mind. It was time for the gloves to come off. The next meeting with Campbell would be confrontational. He had to put him under stress. He must find a way to goad him into letting down his very effective guard and allowing his true feelings to be seen. The next meeting would be in London but he would wait a week to see if Campbell initiated contact.

Five days later he telephoned Nakayama asking if Campbell had mentioned anything about their meeting.

"No, my Lord. But he sometimes has that half smile on his face when he looks at me."

"This one is too clever to appear anxious. He wants to show me he can be patient and outwait me. Thank you Nakayama-kun, I shall contact him in a few days."

Lord Hino called the university asking that Campbell return his call. When he did Lord Hino said, "Kyoto University is interested in offering you a place; however, it will require the preparation of a special curriculum for you. Before going to this step they wish more information. Would it be possible to travel to London to meet me?"

"Of course Lord Hino. I could travel the day after tomorrow."

"That would be excellent. You can stay at my home and my driver will pick you up at the station. Just let me know which train you will be taking."

"I have already checked the timetable and can leave on the night train arriving at 8.15 in the morning."

"Very well, I will see you then."

As he hung up the telephone Lord Hino thought, 'You still have a few things to learn my young friend. You should have asked what questions the University had, to better prepare yourself for our meeting.'

When he arrived at the house, Jack was shown to a bedroom where he could unpack his few things and have a bath before joining Lord Hino for coffee.

"Ah it is good to see you again," said Lord Hino.

"It is an honor to see you again, Lord Hino," replied Jack.

"Please sit down and have some coffee. Did you manage to sleep on the train?"

"To be honest, not too well. The train was crowded and we had to stop several times. I believe there were several air raid warnings. That is why I arrived late. I hope I did not inconvenience you."

"Not at all. Would you like to rest before we start?"

"No thank you, I am eager to begin."

"As I mentioned on the telephone, Kyoto University is very interested in the possibility of you studying there and they are impressed by your credentials. However, as we say; if something appears too good to be true, it probably is. You appear too good to be true. The purpose of this interview is to find out the real Jack Campbell. Ah, I see you make no comment."

"It is better you ask the questions, then decide if I am truly suitable, rather than I make any protestations at this time. I believe you mean to be quite blunt, perhaps even severe, in your approach. There will be time for protests later."

"I told them you are wise beyond your years, Campbell-san, and you have again proved this."

Jack noted the form of address used by Lord Hino, referring to him as Campbell-san, and recognized this was an important step in their relationship.

"You are being offered this opportunity partly due to the influence of Dr. Yamato. He is Head of what can be loosely translated as the International Studies Department which prepares our brightest young people for overseas positions, both in government and business. Of more importance for you, he is from Nagasaki. I can see you are perplexed by this fact and are probably wondering how it could possibly reflect favorably on you. In Nagasaki, there is a revered landmark known as Glover House. Have you heard of this place?"

"No, I haven't," replied Jack.

"Thomas Blake Glover was born in Aberdeen, Scotland in 1838, and arrived in Nagasaki in 1859, following several years in Shanghai. Glover spent the rest of his life in Japan until his death in 1911. The importance of his birthplace is that in those days Aberdeen was one of the main shipbuilding centers in Great Britain.

It was Glover who brought an Aberdeen built slip-dock to Nagasaki. This was the beginning of the greatest shipyard in Japan, the Mitsubishi Yard. It was here that Scottish designed warships were built to defeat the navy of the Tokugawa Shogunate; greatly assisting in bringing the Emperor Meiji to the throne. He also supplied arms to the forces supporting the Emperor. For all this he was awarded the Order of the Rising Sun by Emperor Meiji. He further enhanced the Mitsubishi Company by opening coal mines and starting breweries. It is even rumored that one of his many exploits with Japanese ladies was the source of Puccini's opera, Madam Butterfly."

"For my part I thank Glover for his shipbuilding activities as we now have some of the best warships in the world. In Nagasaki, his home has become a national monument, almost a shrine. So that is why Dr. Yamato is eager to have a talented Scotsman in his university. In addition to teaching you, he wishes to learn some things from you. Don't be too flattered. He wishes to know how a country of only a few million barbaric people in the 15th century with over two hundred clans, could possibly have created someone as talented as Glover. How is this possible? After all the main attributes of Scots were cattle theft and senseless murder of each other."

He noticed Jack's involuntary flush at these words and thought, 'One arrow has struck its mark'.

"Perhaps our histories are not so different after all," said Jack.

"Nonsense Campbell, you have much to learn about Japan. There is no comparison between your uncivilized history and our cultural one."

"Dr. Yamato is also interested in learning how the Scots finally evolved form this ghastly background and finally made a few contributions to society's development, only to slide back out of prominence until today, where you are the lackeys of the English."

'Arrow number two,' thought Hino as Jack flinched at this comment.

"Come, come Campbell, there can be no denying this fact. The only people who refer to Great Britain are the Irish, Welsh and Scots. To the English it is only referred to as England. They talk of their English common law, their English Parliament and their English King. They only have one use for Scots and that is to send you barbarians into battle in the front line. They see no reason to dirty their lily white English hands when you are available. You have gone back to being a nation of stupid warriors. You play these abdominal instruments called bagpipes and off you charge. I tell you Campbell these screeching instruments eliminate all reason; they infest your brain and substitute stupidity for reason. The English have even made you think you are brave rather than idiotic."

And so it went on, through a light lunch, until seven in the evening.

"Let's break now. We shall meet for dinner in an hour."

The break gave both men the opportunity to ponder the day.

Hino was now almost convinced of Jack's suitability as an agent. To be one hundred percent certain he had to hear Jack freely state his willingness to betray Britain and serve Japan. While he had scored a few hits with his barbed arrows he had not been able to make Jack lose his temper. He greatly admired this characteristic. He knew from experience that most men would have done so.

This made him even more determined to recruit Jack and even more aware of the necessity to be careful. Very strong willed people could suddenly tire of the game he was playing and decide to quit the whole charade. He was under no illusions about fooling Jack with this story of enrolling in Kyoto University. Yet in keeping with his background training and knowledge as a master spy, ninety five percent of all he had told Jack was true.

Hino decided the dinner should be a more relaxed affair. There was time enough tomorrow to go on the attack, if necessary.

As they sat down at the dining table Lord Hino said, "I regret dinner will be quite mundane, given the rationing of food. We can still procure good beef on the black-market but many herbs and spices are difficult to acquire."

"It will be of no importance to me as the palate of the average barbaric Scot cannot distinguish excellent from atrocious cuisine. We usually throw food on the table and everyone grabs a chunk and gobbles it without really tasting it."

Lord Hino looked startled but then saw the half smile on Jack's face and realized Campbell was letting him see that his taunts had not succeeded in rattling him.

The atmosphere during dinner turned out to be convivial which pleased Lord Hino. Over a good brandy after dinner, Jack surprised Lord Hino by telling him more about his relatives. His poignant story touched Hino as he realized how much strife Jack had endured.

Once again Hino surmised that Campbell was not divulging everything. There were some things he did not want to share with anyone.

Suddenly Hino realized that Campbell was exhibiting all the earmarks of a fully trained spy. He was telling almost, but not quite the whole truth. What upset Hino was that despite all his truly expert knowledge he could not gauge if Campbell was telling sixty or ninety percent of the truth.

'This man is even more talented than I imagined,' thought Hino.

The next morning, following a light breakfast, they sat down to continue the interview.

"The true reason for all my probing questions and uncomplimentary comments yesterday was that I did not believe the remarks you made during our meeting in Glasgow. They were too glib. The type of answers one would hear from a well rehearsed candidate for political office."

"Pardon me for interrupting, Lord Hino. We could spend another day with you listing all the faults of the Scots; but I believe this would only waste time. I am certain you are a busy man, so I propose the following. There is a train at 11.30 this morning. Prior to that time I will try to give you a full picture of Jack Campbell. If at the end of this time you are still unconvinced that I am suitable, I suggest we go our separate ways. If I cannot convince you in three hours, then it is unlikely I could convince you in three weeks. Is this acceptable to you?"

"Perfectly," said Lord Hino, a little uneasily. Campbell was taking the initiative, which he admired, yet it left him with the feeling that he had just lost control of the situation. A feeling he was not used to and one he did not like.

"You were correct in your premise concerning my extreme dislike of British authoritarian figures. I believe I have the right to this opinion. But you are wrong in two of your points of view, and they just happen to be very important points."

"Firstly concerning Scots. It was not the will of the Scottish people to join England in the United Kingdom in 1603. It was the greed and political ambition of a few nobles. Oh yes the English were smart enough to put a Scottish King on the throne of the United Kingdom at the outset, but that was the only time London has really given any thought to Scotland. The everyday Scot is a proud person. Proud of his heritage and proud of his country. Yes, he is a good soldier and yes, he is abused by the British Army. However when he does hear the skirl of the pipes, he marches for Scotland."

"Your second error is one you share with Herr Hitler."

Lord Hino's reflex reaction to this comment pleased Jack. 'That's one back for all your shitty comments yesterday,' he thought.

"Oh yes, you both make the mistake of denigrating the British people and having a low regard for their resilience and determination. You think they will turn tail and run in the face of your reputedly strong armies. But you base this only on the people you have met who are from the so called 'upper classes'. Unfortunately the heirs of these greedy Scots Lords I mentioned earlier are now in this upper class. They send their children to Harrow and Eton; they even speak with an English upper class accent. The entire British upper classes are the ones whose only aim in life is to live the good life, the easy life, and only to socialize with each other. Their lack of vision, industry, creativity and backbone are the reasons why Britain is no longer the principle nation in the word. They squandered the heritage earned by prior generations. They have spent more time on learning to speak correctly than on learning to think. Most importantly they have forgotten the criticality of leadership. There are a few exceptions to this, one being Mr. Churchill."

"The average Britton, whether Scottish, Irish, Welsh or English will rise to the most difficult challenge if properly lead and Churchill will inspire and lead them, much to the discomfort of Hitler. But, in the end, I fear the elite will again find a way to maintain their class distinction. This is why I have lost respect for Great Britain."

There was a noticeable note of sarcasm in Jack's voice when he said 'Great'.

Lord Hino probed Jack on several other issues till close to ten o'clock. Then said, "Perhaps you should pack now. I will have my driver take you to the station. I will give a complete report to Kyoto University; however, I feel safe in telling you I believe any anxieties will be laid to rest. I should be in Glasgow in about a week and will be able to give you their answer."

When Jack left, Lord Hino sat down with another cup of coffee, reflecting on the morning's conversation. All doubts were now erased from his mind. He did not totally subscribe to Jack's point of view, feeling it was too personally emotional. Nevertheless the treatment of his father and mother which created this frame of mind made Jack a perfect candidate for his purposes.

A week later he met Jack in Glasgow and almost immediately and quite bluntly, made his proposal that he become an agent of Japan. When he did Jack replied with a smile, "What took you so long?"

"I am a cautious man," said Lord Hino still uneasy over his feeling that Campbell had been leading this negotiation more than he.

And so began Jack's training.

He was taught stealth skills. He spent hours learning codes. He thought he knew something about burglary, following his break in at Cambridge, but he quickly learned he was a neophyte. He was taught how to kill using a gun, knife and garrote. When it came time to study self defense, he believed he was ready because of his training in Judo. So, when he walked into a private tatami room in a Judo club, adjusting his uniform, he was surprised when the instructor turned around and bowed.

It was Nakayama.

"You once said you thought I could do better, Campbell, let's see if you were correct, shall we?"

It required a week of liniment rubs and hot baths before Jack's pains disappeared.

At the end of the training, the chief instructor was quizzed by Lord Hino.

"You are sure he is ready?"

"Yes, my Lord."

"Is he good?"

"The best we have ever trained, my Lord."

"That may not be good enough."

"Then let me tell you this, my Lord. I had not intended to mention it, but as you seem to have doubts, I will. One of my best instructors said, 'I hope the bosses are right about this man and he is truly on our side. If he is not I may consider surrendering now.'"

Lord Hino's eyes lit up and he burst out laughing.

"Excellent," he cried, clapping his hands.

Later after sending a coded message to Tokyo, he sat with a brandy and let his mind reflect on his good luck. He had decided Campbell would not only be a good agent but was the perfect candidate for his own special plan, Empire.

Chapter 4

None of Hino's recollections was on Jack's mind after being told of his trip to Japan and Malaya. He walked around in a daze for about an hour. There were so many possible new experiences forming in his mind that he completely lost track of time. When he finally focused on the time, he thought he better have a late lunch. In the upstairs area of the Horseshoe Bar they served one of the best steak and kidney pies in all of Glasgow. It was not a fancy place but it was clean. The food, although plain was freshly made, carefully cooked and delicious. His mind was still swirling with excitement and he found himself gobbling down his food. He forced himself to lay down his knife and fork, take several deep breaths and try to relax a little. He was startled out of his reverie when the waitress said, "Are ye finished son. Oh 'am sorry, I didnae mean to gie ye a fright."

"That's OK I wis thinkin' aboot somethin'. But 'am no' quite finished yit, missus, 'am haein' a wee rest," said Jack, using his thick Glasgow accent.

"Jest let me know if ye want puddin'. We've got some very nice apple pie and hot custard."

'Ah don't think so. This is an awfy big plateful an' so many tatties.'

"Aye well, suit yersel."

Jack ate more of his lunch, this time more slowly.

He decided to get more information on Malaya. He smiled at the thought of going 'home'. There was only one place to get the information he wanted. His 'home' was the Mitchell Library, the largest reference library in Europe. All during his studies he had spent untold hours at the Mitchell. The library had been financed by a bequest of almost 70,000 pounds from Stephen Mitchell, a wealthy tobacco manufacturer. He died in 1874 and the first library started in 1877 with 14,000 books. Within two years the number of books had doubled and in another five years doubled again. As it grew the library had to move. The present building was opened in 1911and was on North Street, not too far away. After paying his bill he walked to the library and for the umpteenth time admired its wonderful architectural structure topped by a beautiful copper sheathed dome. Two years ago an extension had started, Jack had no doubt it too would be fully utilized. He spent the next three and a half hours reading about the Malay Peninsula.

It was close to seven o'clock when he arrived back in Bearsden. He wanted to avoid Mrs. McAllister, so he parked his car in the next street and crept along Hillside Crescent. Luck was with him, he could see the outline of figures moving in her house, she had company. Taking no chances, he raced towards the door and made sure the thick curtains were drawn before switching on the light.

He quickly washed, shaved and changed clothes. He grabbed his whisky, switched off the lights and left by the back door. He remembered his instructions of this morning. He jumped over the fence passed through Mrs. Bell's garden and arrived at the back door of Carolyn Jardine. He then stopped to think, 'Is this a good idea?' He decided it most certainly was not, but muttered, "What the hell, all work and no play makes Jack a dull boy."

He knocked on the door. She was wearing a long black silk dressing gown.

"Oh, I am sorry I probably should have telephoned, perhaps I should come back another time," said Jack.

"No, no, please come in. I just finished my bath and I wasn't sure you would come. I did not hear your car so I decided not to dress. I hope I look OK." She had that mischievous smile and he new she was lying. Not only had she been indulging in Mrs. McAllister's game of peeking through the curtains, but she was dressed exactly as she planned.

"I am pleased to see you brought the whisky. Would you like water with yours?"

"Just a little, please."

"Do sit down; I'll be right back with the glasses and water. There are a few records on the sideboard. If you like music put one on."

Jack put on the top record in the pile, without looking at the label. As he suspected, it was a love song. He was now certain that the music and whisky were perfunctory interludes leading to the real reason she asked him over. He determined to let her make the running. It did not take long. After several sips of whisky, and when the record had finished, she got up, changed the record, held out her hand and said, "Do you dance Mr. Simpson?"

Before the three minute record had finished, they went from dancing to kissing to her leading him into the bedroom.

She was a tigress.

Jack enjoyed making love, but this was too desperate to be called love. This was animalistic. Close to the end and for reasons which escaped him, he wondered what Mrs. McAllister would say if she knew. He almost burst out laughing and had to choke back his mirth. Carolyn mistook this for an expression of ecstasy and whispered, "Its all right my darling, I thought it was wonderful too."

Later when he returned home, he had another whisky and sat, not thinking about Carolyn and sex but about Japan.

This had been his dream yet he had an uneasy feeling knowing he would not return to Glasgow for a long time. His roots were here and these thoughts brought back memories of his childhood.

Jack was born on 22ⁿᵈ August, 1916 in Partick, Glasgow. His father, Willie, was a day laborer and his mother, Jean, had worked in a grocer's shop. They had not been long married and were staying with Jean's mother, when war broke out and Willie was called to serve in the army. He was given five days notice to report to the Argyll and Sutherland Highlanders. In training camp his eyesight was deemed inadequate for a rifleman. This was a polite way of saying Willie was hopeless on the firing range. He was supplied a pair of glasses, previous owner unknown, and assigned to transportation duty. Having been a laborer he was strong, so loading and unloading a truck presented no problem. On completion of training, he was posted to a transit camp in southeast England, where soldiers from his regiment were billeted prior to being shipped to France.

In November he was informed of his posting to France. He was given a weeks leave starting December 1ˢᵗ and it was during this time Jean conceived. He did not see his son until March, 1917 on another leave. They had agreed to call the boy, Jack. Willie had strenuously averred his son would not be called James. As he explained to Jean, "If ye walk doon any street in Glasgae an' shout 'Hey Jimmy' mair than half the men will turn roon."

The war often seemed stalemated and time dragged on. Jack's first birthday was celebrated with his mother and granny, his only other relative. Granny was all of five feet tall; her hair was grey and pulled straight back and tied in a bun. Her face was remarkably free of wrinkles but her blue/grey eyes and slightly hooked nose over her thin lips let you know she was not someone to cross. She adored her grandson and had done her best to make the birthday party a special event. Jean thought it would have been perfect if only Willie had been there.

Everyone had heard the horrors of the trench warfare in the open fields of France. Naturally Jean worried for Willie's safety however her fear was somewhat tempered by the knowledge that he was not actually fighting. Two months later she received the terrifying news that Willie had been hospitalized. The details were sketchy. It appeared he was just feeling poorly. He assured her he had not been injured; however censorship prevented him from attempting to give further details. The main reasons being, firstly, the secret nature of this operation and secondly, the fact that it was such an abject failure and had taken so many British lives.

On April 22nd 1915, the Germans released deadly chlorine gas at Ypres. A yellowish green haze wafted on the breeze towards the 87th Territorial and 45th Algerian divisions.

Chemical Warfare was born.

The British immediately poured money into their previously neglected chemical industry. In 1916 plans for the development of gas weapons were made by the War Office and Ministry of Munitions.

By 1917 weapon production was in full swing. Chlorine gas was evilly efficient at killing hundreds of troops, but like all gases, it had the distinct danger of 'blow-back' should there be a change in wind direction. A British scientist developed a delivery system of a particularly virulent gas, which he claimed would eliminate this problem and most evil of all, would penetrate the gas masks used at that time. Like all theories it required test, and so the trial container was loaded onto a truck by Willie Campbell. The result was catastrophic. Not only did the delivery system fail to propel the gas forward at a rapid rate, it actually behaved like a boomerang.

The program was scrapped and all reference to the new gas was destroyed.

This killed many British troops and landed Willie in hospital.

It was another three months before Willie was transferred to a hospital in Scotland. He was sent to a soldiers' hospital on the south bank of the River Clyde at Erskine, six miles west of the Glasgow boundary. It was ten days before Jean was allowed to visit him. On the day of the visit she put on the best of her three dresses and carefully applied what make-up she had. Jean was a good looking young woman, four inches taller than her mother. Her dress, although somewhat ill fitting, did not hide her lovely figure. She, granny and little Jack got all bundled up to set out on the ten mile journey on a cold January day. Although only ten miles it involved traveling on a tramcar, a ferry and two buses; with the walking and waiting between these conveyances it took two hours.

They were greeted by a nurse and shown into a waiting room. After a few minutes a doctor arrived and before he could say anything Jean said, "Can I see ma husband now and why did it take ten days tae get permission tae come here?"

"Mrs. Campbell, there is still a war going on and we are overloaded with patients. In your husband's case, we have been running a series of tests which has taken quite some time. But to answer your first question, of course you can see your husband now. The nurse will show you the way and I will see you on your way out."

Jean saw the deep tiredness in his eyes and regretted her outburst.

"Thank you doctor," she whispered and turned to follow the nurse. Granny hung back saying, "Away ye go by yersel, Jean. Ah'll wait here wi' wee Jack. We'll come along in a wee while."

Jean followed the nurse down a long ward jammed with beds. Willie's bed had screens placed around it to give some privacy. When she saw Willie's gaunt figure propped up in bed with his greyish complexion and sunken eyes, she burst into tears. She knelt by his bed and fell into his arms sobbing uncontrollably. He stroked her brown hair, kissed her cheek and said, "There, there ma bonnie Jean. Ah know ah don't look sae great, but it will be awright now that ah'm wi' you."

They kissed and held each other tightly for a long time. There seemed to be no need for words at this time, they could come later.

At last she said "Yer son is here tae see ye," and as if by magic, Granny partied the screens and handed Jack to Jean. Willie waved an acknowledgement to Granny but he only had eyes for his son.

"This is yer daddy, Jack."

Jack clung to his mother being unsure of this stranger. Willie did not try to hold him seeing his uncertainty. He spoke to Jack softly for several minutes and then gently reached out and touched his hair. He continued talking to him until at last Jack held out his arms and went to him. As Willie cradled Jack in his arms, tears spurted out of his deep sockets. Granny watched this from the foot of the bed and tough as she was, could not stop the tears from running down her cheeks.

At the end of the visit they met with the same doctor.

"When will ma husband get well, doctor?"

"We still have a few tests to do before I can answer that question."

"Oh, ah see," said Jean.

Granny, ever outspoken, thrust herself towards the doctor, craned her neck to stare into his eyes and said, "Now dinae ye tell me ye dinae know, spit it oot, whit's wrong wi' him?"

The doctor shuffled uneasily under this attack. Scots normally accepted anything a doctor said in an unquestioning manner and he was taken aback by granny's aggressiveness. He looked at Jean with his tired eyes and said with a sigh, "Mrs. Campbell, let me be totally honest with you; we have never had a case like this, therefore it requires more time for observation and diagnosis. In my opinion, this time can just as easily be spent at home as here in hospital. Being home will certainly lift your husband's spirits and again being completely frank, we could use the bed."

Jean's face lit up at this, but because she had heard this type of news before, granny's eyes clouded over.

It was not until they were out of the hospital that Jean suddenly realized how impossible it would be for all four of them to live in granny's flat. When she mentioned this to her mother, granny said, "Ah'll talk to the council" and so she did. Perhaps it was more by luck than her redoubtable nature, that there was a recent vacancy at no. 16 Scott Street, a few hundred yards from her flat. The details of Willie's condition secured a privileged allocation for the Campbell family.

No. 16 Scott Street was as dreary and dismal and any other address in this neighborhood. The three-story stone tenement buildings were drab grey and monotonously similar but to Jean it was like a dream come true. Her first home and she was reunited with her husband. Little by little Willie told her of his war experiences. His job involved delivering munitions to the front. There he saw the devastation and heard from troops of the unspeakable horror of trench warfare. The only things he brought back from the war were two stone carvings. Jean was astonished when he told her of the source of these carvings.

"There wur hundreds o' Chinese laborers diggin' trenches. They worked really hard. One of them carved these, they are temple lions. Ah wis telt they guard holy places from evil, so I got them by tradin' my penknife fur them. Ah hope they guard you and wee Jack."

"How did ye manage tae talk tae the Chinese, Willie?"

"Some o' them spoke some English, but ah learned a few words. Ye know Jean, it's amazin' how pleased they wur when ah spoke ma few words. They wid laugh so much at ma pronunciation, but they wur nae laughing at me, they were laughing wi' me. Ah think that's why he traded me fur just ma knife. Ah thought lions wid look better on a mantelpiece than a set o' wally dugs."

'Wally dugs' or ceramic dogs were the most common ornaments in a Scottish home.

"Let me hear ye speak Chinese."

So Willie spoke a few phrases in a sing song accent, translating as he went.

"Oh Willie, that's wonderful!"

"Ah also learned a few words o' French. Wid ye like to hear them, Jean?"

Willie spoke his French with a surprisingly good accent. Jean listened in complete astonishment, and then threw her arms around him.

"Whit a talent ye hae fur languages, ma darlin'."

"Its no' sae difficult. Ye just huv tae try an' no' be too embarrassed tae practice. No' many o' oor soldiers tried an' when ah first saw the look o' happiness on a Frenchman's face when ah just said "good morning' in his language ah wis determined tae keep tryin'. But whit really motivated me wis a snotty remark by one o' the English officers o' another regiment. When he heard me speak some French he said, 'If you want to learn a foreign language, Scotty, Why not try English?"

"Anyway, ah'm glad ah learned a couple o' phrases. Ah wish ah could huv learnt more Chinese. These people were really nice an' as ah said, ah hope the lions bring ye good luck ma dear. Unfortunately they didnae seem tae bring me luck. It wis just three days after I got them that I got sick. We hud tae make a special delivery very early that day. It wis some type o' hush hush weapon. The officers were very nervous aboot it. I heard one say 'this will finish of Gerry and no mistake'.

The officer who received it telt us tae park a half mile back and wait fur further instructions. Well Jimmy, the driver, and me waited an' waited. After aboot an hour Jimmy began tae cough and a bit later so did I. Then a corporal ran up tae us, wearin' a gas mask an' telt us to put on ours.

By this time poor Jimmy wis in quite a state, so the corporal got some-one to drive us both back to base."

"The officer who hud been saying this would finish Gerry, wis runnin' aroon like a chicken wi' its heed cut off, yellin', 'Get these men into isolation in hospital'. So we wur taken to a special tent at the field hospital, where we stayed that night. Next day we wur taken in an ambulance tae a big hospital that looked like a castle. That's where ah wis kept fur three months. Poor Jimmy died after a fortnight."

"At the beginin' ah wis kept in a room by maself and everybody who came intae ma room wore a mask and white rubber gloves. They would take samples o' ma blood an' ma pee every day. Then after six weeks they put me in a room wi two other lads. They died just before ah wis sent tae Erskine. Ye know one o' the worst things o' bein' in that bloody hospital, Jean? The bastards took away everyone's uniform an' made ye wear a special one made of light blue material. Ah learned from an orderly, this wis to make ye instantly identifiable, in case ye tried tae run away. These lads hud risked their lives fur their country an' got wounded, an' the bastards couldnae trust them."

During his first three months at home, Willie would go out for short walks but then this became too much of an effort. He spent his days sitting in a chair or staying in bed. He listened to the radio for entertainment but his main entertainment was his son.

The war ended in November of that year and Europe struggled to find some semblance of normalcy. Willie's health had deteriorated all this time. The doctor from Erskine hospital visited each month. At the end of his December visit, Jean talked to him on the landing outside the flat.

"Willie's getting worse, doctor. Ah need tae know whit's goin' tae happen. We get a disabled soldier's pension, but its no' very much and naebody will tell us exactly whit happened in France."

The doctor hesitated then said, "If I knew I would tell you Mrs. Campbell, but I do not. I shouldn't say this but his hospital records from France were never given to us. They have been kept at Regiment head-quarters in Glasgow. I will write down the address for you."

Two days later she traveled to Regiment H.Q. with granny. The Sergeant at the desk was used to brushing off most inquiries; however, he met his match in granny. She was yelling so loudly he asked them to take a seat and he would get an officer to talk to them. They were shown into a meeting room where a Major joined them. He listened courteously then said, "I will look into this matter and get in touch with you soon. There may just be grounds to increase the pension."

"Increase the pension. Dae ye think that's why we're here?" cried granny. "We're no' leavin' this bloody place until we get some answers. An' don't ye dare try to tell me ye daenae huv all yer records here, this is the bloody headquarters fur God's sake! Now if you cannae gi'e us an answer, get off yer arse an' get someone who can."

The Major backed quickly out of the room. While they waited, a corporal brought tea and biscuits. Fifteen minutes later a Colonel entered the room, trailed by the Major.

"I regret keeping you waiting Ladies. I had to review our records. I am terribly sorry over Private Campbell's illness. I fully understand money is not your primary issue; nevertheless I am authorizing an increase in his pension to the maximum possible. Regarding the records of the incident in France, I regret to say we do not have these records. They have been retained at the Ministry of War in London. Apparently this mission was a secret one therefore all records are kept in Whitehall. I am really very sorry but that is all I can tell you."

Granny glared at the two officers, then turned to her clearly dispirited daughter and said, "Let's get out of here Jean. Ye know, it must be nice in the army. Ye can always pass the buck up the ladder."

When the Colonel returned to his office he telephoned London and reported on his meeting. His superior said, "You did the best you could, Charles. This fellow Campbell must be as strong as an ox. Everyone else is dead. It's a wonder he is still alive."

Willie died two months later. Jack was two and a half years old.

Chapter 5

Jack had been told these stories by his mother and by his granny. He would never forget them nor would he ever forgive the British Army for the treatment of a father he never really knew.

What often surprised him was how deeply etched in his memory were the sensory experiences of his childhood, all the sounds, sights and even the smells.

The entrance to No. 16 or 'close' as it was referred to in Partick, always had a distasteful smell. On days when one of the occupants had the job of cleaning the close it reeked of strong disinfectant. On Friday nights and Saturday mornings it had other unpleasant smells, those of urine and vomit. The pub was next door and as drunks staggered out at closing time on Friday night, the close at No. 16 was the first convenient location to perform these offensive necessities.

Jack always remembered one summer night returning home with his mother from a visit to his granny and being confronted with the terrifying sight of a drunk doing both things at the same time. The drunk feebly tried to clutch his mother saying, "What's your name hen?" and upon getting no reply plaintively complained, "whit's ye no talking to me fer?"

The Campbell flat was on the top floor. You entered into a very small hallway that housed the wooden coal storage bin. Turning to the right you entered the main area of this tiny dwelling. This one room was a combination of kitchen, dining, sitting and sleeping area.

On the right-hand wall stood the sideboard and a small table with a radio on top, the next wall housed the wash sink and window that faced the backside of the tenement. The third wall had the gas cooking range and the coal fireplace. Over the fireplace was a mantelpiece, on top of which sat the carvings his father had brought back from the war; two temple lions, a male and a female. Since he could remember Jack was fascinated by their beauty and used to examine them for long periods of time. There was a curtain over the fourth wall behind which was a recessed area containing a double bed. In the center of the room were a square dining table and four chairs. To the left of the entranceway was a small bedroom that had a single bed and a wardrobe. By far the most important aspect of this room was the window that overlooked Scott Road.

On summer nights, people would place a cushion on the hard brick windowsill and lean out of the window to talk to neighbors below, above, at the side and across the street. This was the main communication vehicle in Partick. Someone had just to say the all important words, 'Ye know whit I just heard?' and as if by telepathy, windows would fly up, necks would crane and ears strain to hear the latest gossip.

The only heat in the flat was supplied by the coal fire. Coal was delivered once a week by two men with a horse and cart. The cart was stacked with rough canvas bags, each one holding one hundredweight of coal. One man would deliver to all the residents in a close the other would do the same at the next close.

The one not delivering would place a bag at the edge of the cart and cut the string that held the top of the bag closed. The other would squat slightly so that the bag rested on his shoulders and back, grasp a corner of the opened end in each hand and grunt his way noisily up the stairs. The bag was tipped into the bin in the hallway, sending coal dust everywhere. No one complained because without coal one would freeze in these cold, stone buildings.

The flat did not have hot water, the faucet at the sink providing only cold water. Washing dishes involved boiling water in a kettle and pouring it into a basin in the sink. The same system was necessary to wash oneself. There was no bathroom therefore a bath for a small boy usually meant standing in the sink with a basinful of hot water on the draining board from which your mother washed you. While this was taking place, the youngster would be fervently praying none of his friends were out back and could see him. This potential embarrassment was not regularly present as baths were an infrequent occurrence. Obviously, adults could not stand in the sink, so their infrequent bathing was conducted in front of the fireplace by standing in a small zinc bathtub that normally hung on a nail above the coal bin. As all residents of tenements were in the same situation none of these aspects of life was considered a hardship.

The one aspect that always was distasteful was the communal toilet. This was located in the landing between the second and third floor and was used by all residents of the close. No matter how much disinfectant was sprayed around this area, unpleasant odors always seemed to be present.

It was not always possible to coordinate your body function needs with the availability of the communal toilet. For such emergencies a metal bucket was kept handy inside the flat and later the contents were ceremoniously flushed down the toilet.

Jack had no recriminations about his childhood circumstances. When your life centers in an area of less than one mile and everyone in that universe is in the same situation, one has no reason to be unhappy. In fact he was a happy child. Each day he played at the back of the tenement with his neighborhood friends. No one had toys to play with so games were invented. Some of them were a bit dangerous, like jumping from one washhouse to another.

These washhouses were built to service the needs of the people to wash their clothes. A family was assigned to a particular washhouse and was allowed to use it one day each two weeks. They were built of bricks. Inside was a rough concrete tub enclosed in a brick structure that had a firebox. The tub was filled with cold water and heated by lighting paper and wood, then adding coal. This could take quite a while to heat. There was a wooden cover for the tub to keep in the heat. The roof was about nine feet high and sloped to allow the ever-present rain to run off. The distance between roofs of two of the washhouses was only four feet, but to a young boy standing nine feet off the ground; it looked more like four yards.

The challenge was in two parts. Firstly to jump from one roof to another and secondly, not to be seen by your mother or a neighbor who was likely to report you to your mother.

The younger boys were allowed to leap from one roof and cling on to the parapet of the other roof then haul themselves up. The older boys had to clear the distance in one bound or face being called a sissy. If you were caught by your mother the punishment was instantaneous and severe ---- wallop!!! Or sometimes ----wallop wallop wallop. Usually this was followed by the dreaded words, "Just you wait till your father gets home."

This invariably resulted in a belting at bedtime.

Despite the dire consequences, Jack and his friends played this game frequently. There was no doubt that Jack was the leader of the pack. He was fearless as well as athletic and even older boys looked up to him. Being the leader did not always bring glory; there were occasions when a penalty had to be paid, whether deserved or not. It seemed to Jack that he was always being punished for something or other. There was one occasion when one of the younger boys misjudged the distance and his face hit the parapet, resulting in a bloody nose and a bruised face. When his wailing had stopped the lad actually felt quite proud as the older boys told him how brave he was and he would always be a respected member of the 'gang'. It was only when he went home and his mother shrieked, "What happened to you", that the wailer's pride deserted him and he said, "Jack Campbell made me do it." His mother then grabbed him by the arm, marched him down the stairs---clump, clump, clump; dragged him along Scott Road; up the stairs of No. 16 --- clump, clump, clump; and banged on Mrs. Campbell's door.

"Look whit your Jack did to ma poor wee boy."-----Wallop!!!

There was no court of appeal, no questions were asked, Jack was always convicted.

On another occasion, Jean went through a period of having to use a steel comb on Jack's head every night to get rid of head lice, or nits as they were referred to in Glasgow. By spying out the back window on the children at play she saw one boy who was constantly scratching his head. That evening she said to Jack, "I don't want you playing with Johnny Currie anymore."

"Why no'?"

"Because he's the one giving you these nits."

"But he's ma pal, Mammy."

"I don't care. I am fed up checking your heed every night. Now, do you hear me?"

"Aye mammy."

Next day the boys were playing tag when along came Johnny.

"Ah want tae play."

"Naw ye cannae," said Jack.

"Why no'?"

"'Cause ma mammy says yer heed is full o' nits."

Off went Johnny, crying to his mother.

"Whit's the matter wi' ye this time? Did ye fa' doon again?"

"Naw, Jack won't let me play."

"Why no'?"

"His mammy says my heed is full o' nits."

Without a seconds delay Mrs. Currie went racing down the stairs, along Scott Street, up the stairs of No. 16 and banged on Mrs. Campbell's door.

"Whit dae ye mean by sayin' ma boy has nits?" she screamed.

"Ah suppose your Mrs. high and mighty. Too good fer us other Glasgae folk, eh? Well let me tell ye this, ye'r nae better than anyone else."

The screaming was so loud that other people opened their doors in the close to see what was going on. Mrs. Currie stomped away and Jean went straight to the back window, opened it and yelled, "Jack Campbell, come up here this minute!"

When Jack arrived, Jean hissed at him, "Why did ye tell Johnny ah said he had nits?"

Wallop.

"But ye did, mammy."

"Don't ye be cheeky tae me. A'm yer mother."

Wallop.

"Ye had no right tae tell him ah said that. Look at all the embarrassment ye have caused me wi' the neighbors."

Wallop, wallop.

"Now get tae yer room an' stay there 'til ah tell ye tae come out."

Wallop, wallop.

In later years, Jack had reflected on this apparent anomaly of his childhood. How could he have been so happy and yet be on the receiving end of so many wallopings? He came to the conclusion that either he did not really receive as many as he thought, or a more likely explanation was that a wallop was just part of growing up in Glasgow. His parents had been raised this way as had all their friends and neighbors. It was the culture of the city.

Anyway his mother's wallop, or as she called it, a 'skelp' was never very painful. At least as long as you remembered to act appropriately. If you cried you were a sissy, you had to be appropriately contrite and try to remember not to argue or ask for a reason. Adults were always right; children had to be taught to obey without question. It was the Glasgow culture.

He was fifteen when his granny told him of Jean's misgivings on the Glasgow punishment system.

"She didnae like skelpin' ye, but ah told her it wis the only way young boys learned tae behave themsels an' tae respect their parents. She always thought ye were jist high spirited, but ah made her see it ma way. If it wis guid enough fer me, it wis guid enough fer everybody else."

At gang meetings, the boys would sometimes exchange their most effective attempts at contrition.

"Ye can never greet, but a wee sob now and then while ye say 'I'm awful sorry mammy,' works a treat," offered one lad.

"Ah know I'm a bad boy and I'm sorry for making you angry mammy, I'll be good, honest ah will," was another suggestion. This came from Tam MacTaggart, 'number eleven'. On a soccer team number eleven played on the left wing and although Tam was a good soccer player, his nickname was not related to sport. Tam suffered from a perpetual runny nose.

Like all the boys, his Monday to Saturday wardrobe was the same; underpants, undershirt, short trousers, dark blue long sleeved woolen sweater (no shirt), knee length wool socks and sturdy boots. No one had a handkerchief, so in poor Tam's case his sweater sleeves substituted.

In the excitement of playing games Tam would often forget to wipe his nose and two rivers of snot would form on his upper lip. Eventually someone would yell at him "Hey number eleven". Abashedly, Tam would then use one of his sleeves. This affliction was never maliciously used against Tam. He was a good natured boy and besides that he was a great soccer player.

The most outrageous suggestion to the gang came from wee Jimmy McCafferty.

"Ah don't greet either but ah bite ma lip to get tears in ma eyes, then ah look at ma mammy and say,' Miss Anderson, ma Sunday School teacher, says we huv tae be careful the devil disnae get into our hearts and if we're bad we should pray to God fur help. So ah'll just go and pray now."

"Your mammy isnae daft enough tae believe that," said Tommy MacPherson.

"She does so," retorted wee Jimmy.

"It must be because you're a catholic," opined Sammy White. "Ma mother would really batter me stupid if ah said that."

Poor wee Jimmy, he was always looked on as 'different' from that day forward.

One thing that all the gang agreed on was never to be defiant while you were being punished. Permanently etched on their memory was the horrible event that caused the Hogans to move from Scott Street.

Davie Hogan was jumping the washhouse roofs when his mother saw him. She came rushing out yelling at him, "Did I no' tell ye never to do that stupid thing again?"

"Aye ma."

"Then why did you do it?"

"Ah forgot."

"Then maybe you won't forget this."

Wallop.

Now Mrs. Hogan was a big woman and a wallop from her was truly a wallop. Davie's eyes welled up with tears. It was one thing to be chastised in your own home but quite another to have this done in front of your pals. In trying to be brave in front of the gang, Davie made his big mistake when he said, "That didnae hurt."

Wallop--- wallop.

Now there could be no holding back the tears of pain. Trying to make up for his crying Davie said, "That didnae hurt either."

Wallop, wallop, wallop, wallop.

The yells of pain brought Mrs.MacPherson running from one washhouse and Mrs. MacTaggart from another. Together they dragged an almost deranged Mrs. Hogan off Davie.

"You'll kill the laddie," said Mrs. MacPherson.

The two women managed to get Mrs. Hogan home where they were joined by other neighbors, some of them calming down Mrs. Hogan and some tending to a hysterical Davie.

Of course the shame of this incident made the Hogans move to another area. Jack overheard his mother whisper to a neighbor that Davie's jaw had been broken.

This was the topic of conversation for many weeks as the people of the neighborhood leaned out of their windows, elbows resting comfortably on cushions.

While attending university and studying the heritage of Scotland Jack came to the conclusion that due to their upbringing, most Scots were unable to question authority. Even when they were certain of their facts, they would always tend to shy away from confrontation with people in authority. This did not prevent them from complaining to their peers and so the character of the Scot was one of inner conflict between dislike of and inbred respect for, authority.

Chapter 6

Jack enjoyed school and was an excellent student. His ever questioning mind was encouraged by his mother who would direct him to an answer rather than give one.

"Why dinnae ye read yer schoolbook?" she would counsel. Another favorite was, "Let's go tae the library and find oot the answer."

Jack loved reading and the public library became a regular haunt. Of course when his pals complained about school, the dreaded homework, the exams (always unfair) and the horrible teachers; Jack would join in the chorus. You would be excoriated if you admitted liking school. One day when report cards were being taken home and were being compared, Tam asked Jack "How come yu'v got all A's. Dae ye cheat?"

"Ssh," said Jack, "dinnae shout sae loud, someone might hear ye."

Slow smiles of appreciation broke out on all the lads' faces. Their leader had discovered a way to cheat undetected.

"Boy oh boy, ye're really smart," said Sammy. "How dae ye dae it?"

"Ah cannae tell ye. If ma mammy ever heard aboot it she'd kill me fer sure," said Jack with a serious face.

The lads nodded sagely. It never entered one of their minds that hard work and interest would result in all A's. Jack could never tell them the truth. Working hard at school was beyond their comprehension.

It was granny who said, after proudly reviewing one of his report cards, "Ah see yer good at arithmetic, just like yer mammy. Ye should huv seen her in the grocery, she never used a paper an' pencil tae work oot anythin'. She did a' the addin', subtractin', multiplyin' an' dividin' in her heed."

Jack had not recognized this fact until granny mentioned it. Now he recollected the many times she would check his arithmetic homework while cooking at the stove. He would shout out the questions and his answers and she would immediately respond with a 'right' or 'better dae that again'.

Jack entered junior high school just before his twelfth birthday. He was in the highest form. Pupils from many elementary schools attended the one high school. Jack found very few of his prior schoolmates in his class. His new classmates were the cream of the district crop. This turned out to be a stimulating environment and Jack reveled in it. He had two new languages to learn, Latin and French. He had just finished his first year when his world disintegrated.

Jean died.

The cause and lead up to his mother's death were things not understandable to an almost thirteen year old boy in Scotland at that time.

His world involved his main pastime, soccer or as referred to in Glasgow, fitba'; school; getting into trouble; getting out of trouble; his mother and his granny. Girls were a nuisance, with one exception, Annie McBride.

His street soccer team would challenge other local street teams. One of the best of these was the Elgin Street team.

Now soccer was only played by boys, except for Annie McBride who captained the Elgin Street team. To say she was a tom-boy would be an injustice to Annie; she was as much a boy as any boy when it came to fitba'. She was a great soccer player who could kick the ball hard and was a ferocious tackler. She led her team to many victories and was roundly admired.

This admiration was certainly shared by Jack; however, it related purely to her soccer prowess and bore no romantic connotation. Romance was an undiscovered art to boys of Jack's age. Should a love scene appear on the screen of the local cinema it would be greeted by jeers of derision by Jack and his pals. And, should a friend of the family or a relative kiss Jack or any of his pals they would erase it with a wipe of their sleeve at the earliest possible moment.

Given this inability to be aware of anything romantic it was not surprising Jack had failed to recognize the signs of trouble evolving around his mother. The busy corner of Scott Street and Glasgow Road was a normal area for police to stand and observe their areas of responsibility. Jack had been unaware of the occasional whispered comments or low whistles of Police Constable Cameron directed at his mother. He thought it was the busy traffic at this corner which caused his mother to grab his arm and rush him along the street.

One day there was a knock on the door which Jack answered. He stared with consternation at Constable Cameron. His mother called, "Who is it Jack?"

"It's a polisman, mammy."

Jean rushed to the door but stopped short of the door when she saw who it was. Jack mistook her hesitancy for fear, an almost reflex reaction exhibited by Glasgow people towards the police.

"We are checkin' into shopliftin' charges Mrs. Campbell an' ah want tae ask yer son a few questions."

Without waiting to be asked, he walked past Jack into the main room. The front door was left open. Officiously, he took out his notebook and pencil.

"Now then ma lad, dae ye know anything about stealin' sweets from Woolworths?"

"No sur," said Jack.

"Are ye sure, ye better no' be lyin' tae me."

"Ah'm no lyin', ah didnae steal anythin'."

Jack's voice faltered towards the end of his denial, a sign recognized by his mother.

"Whi's been goin' on Jack," she demanded.

"Well one boy wis handin' oot sweeties last week an' ah ate one."

"Aha, so ye were acceptin' stolen goods. That's very serious."

"Ah don't know if they were stolen or not."

"Ye hud better go into the back bedroom an' shut the door while ah talk tae yer mother aboot this."

Jack did as he was told while Cameron put his notebook and pencil back in his breast pocket.

PC Cameron came closer to Jean and said, "This could mean ye will huv tae appear at the police station and maybe yer son will be put on probation."

Jean gasped involuntarily, "Oh no, not ma Jack."

Cameron came very close to Jean and said, "Maybe ah can help ye, ah suppose ah could be persuaded tae overlook this. That is if ye would *really* like me to do that fer ye."

"Oh yes please," said Jean.

"Of course ye would huv tae show yer appreciation fer this."

Cameron put one arm around Jean who backed away quickly. He advanced saying, "Ye better think aboot yer wee boy. Ah could make an awful lot o' trouble fer him. Ah might even be able tae show it wis all his idea an' he actually stole these sweeties."

"Ye cannae dae that."

"Ah sure as hell can and don't think fer one minute that ah won't. Everybody knows your Jack is the leader o' all the other lads. So just stand still ye might enjoy this after all ye huv been without a man fer a lang time."

Cameron again put one arm around Jean while his other hand fondled her breast. Jean struggled free. A few seconds later a voice called out, "Whit's goin' on here?" It was granny striding through the door with a thunderous look on her face.

"He said he is goin' tae charge Jack wi' shopliftin' from Woolworths an' he didnae dae it. He took a sweetie from one o' the other boys but he disnae know if it wis stolen or not."

"Ah'm just doin' ma job by makin' a few enquiries."

"Well dae yer job somewhere else an' get the hell oot o' here."

Granny's loud voice brought Jack running from the other room.

"Whit's wrong mammy? Huv ah done somethin' wrong?"

"No Jack everything's fine. The polisman is leavin' now."

Cameron strode out of the flat without looking back.

The next day granny went to the police station and heatedly reported the incident to the desk sergeant. She said she intended reporting this behavior to the town council and even to her Member of Parliament. The sergeant stood grim faced, listening to granny's tirade.

"And did you clearly witnessed this alleged assault?" asked the sergeant.

"Whit dae ye mean witnessed? Ma daughter told me aboot it."

"So you didnae actually see it yerself?"

"Listen ye big galoot, if that man sae much as looks at ma daughter again, ah'll bash him wi' a poker."

Granny brandished her fist with such ferocity that the sergeant backed away with alacrity. She then stomped out of the station muttering to herself.

Later that day the sergeant interviewed PC Cameron and asked for his side of the story. Cameron said, "That's a load o' bloody rubbish. Ah wis makin' inquiries because young Campbell is the leader o' that pack o' boys. Ah felt sorry fer that woman an' wis advisin' her to warn her son not to get involved wi' any o' the lad's who are shopliftin'. Ah am a happily married man wi' a wee daughter o' ma own an' ah offered tae speak tae her son if it would help. An' this is the thanks ah get fer it? Ye can be sure she will get nae mair help from me."

"Well ye just watch yer step Cameron."

PC Cameron left the station fuming.

About a week and a half later, on a Saturday, Jack led his street soccer team to a challenge match to be played in a park a mile from Scott Street. This was a significant event as the match would actually be played on grass rather than the usual games that were played on the street.

As the lads walked along Glasgow Road they were in high spirits, laughing and joking. Jack carried the ball and was in front with Tam Mac-Taggart striding purposefully towards the park.

The others followed a few of them stopping now and then to look in shop windows. The one shop that always caused a young boy to stop on a Saturday was Ross's Dairy and Bakery.

This was the day they baked potato scones and the aroma was divine. The last group of three had just torn themselves away from Ross's when a man stepped out of a doorway and asked in a slurred voice asked, "Are ye goin' tae play fitba'?"

"Aye," replied the lads in unison

"Where are ye playin'?"

"In the park," said Sammy.

"Aye well, guid luck tae ye."

The lads ran on to catch up with the others, while the man walked quickly the other way, towards Scott Street, staggering slightly as he went. No one took any notice of this as it was normal for men to drink to excess on a Saturday while the pubs were open between noon and three p.m. nevertheless P.C. Cameron, being off duty and therefore out of uniform, pulled his cloth cap down to avoid being recognized. He had been drinking for two hours and had just stepped out of the pub when he spied Jack passing the ball back and forwards with Tam. He quickly stepped into a doorway and turned his back until they had passed. Only when he was certain that they were well out of earshot did he stop the last three boys. It did not take long to reach Scott Street. He paused just before no.16 to be sure there was no one he knew before entering the close and climbing the stairs.

When Jean answered the door he pushed her back, stepped inside and closed the door. She tried to run into the main room hoping to reach the fireplace to pick up the poker as a weapon, but even though he was drunk, he was too quick for her. He grabbed her and swung her against the wall using his left arm across her shoulders and throat to both pin her to the wall and choke her to prevent her from crying out. She was helpless as he fumbled inside her blouse, finally losing patience and ripping it away. When he lifted one breast out or her brassiere and caressed it roughly he became even more desperate. He reached up her skirt and yanked at her knickers, finally managing to pull them part way down.

Now he was inflamed. The blood pulsed through his brain and he lost reason. His efforts to unbutton his fly with one hand were taking to long so he tried to use both hands. Jean took this opportunity to try to get to the fireplace.

"Oh no ye don't," he said thickly, slamming her against the wall. Her head rocked back violently on the brick surface and she went limp. Mistaking this for a sign of resignation Cameron finally unbuttoned his fly and said, "Ah'm glad ye'r seein' some sense."

He was astonished when she crumpled on the floor. His first thought was to force himself on her, however when he had almost removed her knickers without protest, he peered closely at her face.

Something in his brain clicked and he recognized trouble. Almost by remote control he buttoned his fly and left the flat closing the door quietly.

His brain was now functioning furiously as he descended the stairs. He knew what he had to do.

He raced along Glasgow Road to the pub where he had been drinking and stealthily entered. He edged to the bar and said in an exaggeratedly loud and slurred voice, "A man could die o' thirst in this pub. Gie me another pint fer God's sake."

He stayed until closing time and kicked up a fuss before being almost thrown out. He then went to a café where he ordered meat pies and beans complaining loudly that the pies were not hot enough and refused to pay. The proprietor sent his wife to get a policeman and when P.C. McLeod entered, he pretended to be asleep.

"Och it's you Cameron. Ah might huv known. Now pay the man and let's get ye hame."

McLeod got him home and said to his wife, "He's had a real skinful. Ah'll help ye get him tae bed."

Jack's team had won the game and the boys rejoiced all the way home by singing and clowning. Upon reaching Scott Street and saying their good byes they went their separate ways. Jack climbed the stairs and knocked on the door. Getting no answer he looked under the doormat---no key. So he went to the most likely place to find his mother, his granny's house. His granny was preparing her evening meal or tea as it was referred to in Scotland; dinner being the midday meal. Granny was always pleased to see him and said, "Oh it's you Jack, come away in."

"Is ma mammy here?" he asked before entering.

"No, ah huvnae seen her a' day. Just sit doon, ah am sure she'll be back soon. She must huv gone oot tae get somethin' fur yer tea."

"Naw, she told me she wis makin' scrambled eggs on toast. Anyway if she goes tae the shops she always leaves the key under the mat."

"Well let's take a wee walk along the street an' look in a few shops. Ah huv a key tae your hoose and if we dinnae find her ah'll wait wi' ye in yer hoose until she gets back."

"Thanks granny."

Granny took off her apron, put on her coat and they left together. Of the six shops Jean frequented only three were open at this time on a Saturday. Their search was fruitless so they walked to Jack's home with uneasy minds. While Jack's face reflected his concern; granny tried to appear calm and confident but her mother's heart was pounding with anxiety.

Granny was fumbling nervously with the key so Jack took it gently from her hand and opened the door. He raced ahead and granny could tell from his cry that there was a serious problem. She saw her daughter lying on her side on the floor with Jack kneeling beside her cradling her head. She gently pulled Jack to his feet hiding his face from the devastating scene.

"Just ye stand there a minute" she said as she got down on her knees with some difficulty. She turned Jean on her back and for the first time saw the exposed breast and the torn blouse. She covered Jean as best she could and put her ear to her chest. Involuntarily she said, "Thank God," then turning to Jack she said, "Ye'r mammy must huv had a tumble, but she's breathin' alright."

"Maybe the toilet wis busy an' she hud tae use the pail an' tripped over her knickers," said Jack.

Jean's left leg was partly under the table which is why granny had not noticed the pink knickers around the left ankle.

Although she wanted to wail with the agony she felt, somehow her protective instinct towards Jack overcame her own initial panic and her mind functioned clearly as she led Jack out the door into the landing and knocked loudly on the doors of both neighbors.

Quickly she told them there had been an accident and asked that one of them go to the police station for help, requesting a doctor and an ambulance be called. Mr. McPhee immediately ran to do so.

"Whit's happened?" asked Mrs. McPhee.

"Ma daughter has taken a tumble an' must hae banged her head. She's unconscious. If you'll excuse me Mrs. McPhee ah'll take the young laddie inside, he's awf'y upset."

Jack was shaking and crying with fright so she took him into the 'wee room', his bedroom, and held him tightly. It was not long before two policemen arrived, the same sergeant she had previously talked to, and a constable.

"An ambulance and a doctor are on their way," said Sergeant Thomson. "Can we come in?"

"In a minute," said granny. "Jack ma son, will ye go wi' the polisman tae yer room an' answer his questions? Ah'll take the sergeant into the main room an' answer his questions."

"Ah want tae stay wi' you, granny," said Jack fighting back his tears now that there were men present.

"Ah know, ah know, ma son, but it will nae take long an' it is better this way."

"If ye say so, granny."

As soon as Jack had closed his bedroom door, granny led Sergeant Thompson into the main room and whirled on him instantly.

"Just look at ma Jean," she hissed. "If ye don't put that bastard Cameron behind bars, ah swear tae God ah'll kill him masel'."

The sergeant was inured to nasty scenes, but this turned his stomach. He was a tall man and widely regarded as a fair man. His face, one considered good looking, was now a lined and generally stern one. It was now even grimmer as his eyes took in all the details. Methodically he took out his notebook and began writing.

"Are ye listenin' tae me," said granny, her voice cracking with emotion.

"Aye Mrs. Melville ah am. Now you listen tae me. The first thing we are goin' to do is get a doctor to examine Mrs. Campbell and then get her tae hospital for treatment. The next thing ah want you to do is look after that young lad. No young boy should ever see his mother this way. Ye will have tae watch him carefully; there can be very bad delayed reactions tae something like this. Ah am no doctor but ah have seen many cases of emotional breakdowns. It is obvious tae me that he is respectful of ye, so it is your job tae give him the support he will need."

Sergeant Thompson's voice softened and his eyes were sad when he next said, "Ah am afraid ah cannae give ye any advice on how ye can handle yer own sorrow. Ah have heard all the pat answers but in ma experience each person has tae find their own way. Now, what ah can assure ye is ah will do ma very best tae find out who did this. Ah will personally stay at the hospital and when Mrs. Campbell recovers ah will take down all the details. One last thing, Mrs. Melville, it does not matter a whit whether that person is a policeman or the Prime Minister, he is goin' to jail for this."

Granny could tell he was sincere. There were no histrionics with this man, just determination. She respected that and she was grateful for the advice on Jack. She did not have time to express this to Sergeant Thompson as the doctor arrived with two ambulance men, one carrying a stretcher. Following his examination the doctor supervised Jean being put on the stretcher and told granny she and Jack could drive with him to the hospital.

They spent the next three hours at the hospital before being persuaded to go home. A promise was made that as soon as Jean was awake they would call the local Partick police station and someone would let them know. Jack was allowed a brief visit to say goodnight to his still unconscious mother. Following this granny went in to visit her daughter. As Jack sat on the waiting room bench, Sergeant Thompson sat down beside him.

"How old are ye son?"

"Almost thirteen."

"Well now that you are almost grown up, ah have something important to say to ye. Your granny is a fine woman but she will need your support and help at this difficult time. Ah know you will miss having your mammy around for the next few days but you must look after your granny. Can ye do that?"

"Aye ah will, sir."

"Good lad. Here she comes now. How are ye getting home Mrs. Melville?"

"We will huv tae walk, ah didnae hae time tae go back tae ma hoose tae get ma purse."

"Here's a shilling, take the tram," he said. Then sensing granny's pride and probable stubbornness he added "It is only a loan. Ah expect you to pay me back tomorrow."

They went back to granny's house on the tram and granny was surprised that Jack took her arm to help her up the steps of the tram. When they arrived home they just had tea and toast, neither of them was hungry. Granny made the tea while Jack made the toast. This was a job he normally enjoyed, putting a thick slab of bread on a long fork and holding the bread close to the grating at the front of the coal fire; turning the bread over when the first side was done. When they finished, granny washed the dishes and Jack dried them.

Granny made sure the bed in the 'wee room' was ready and then kissed Jack on the forehead.

"Good night son."

"Good night, granny."

She closed the door but put her ear to it. She heard Jack's sobs and it almost broke her heart, however, she knew he would not want her to know he was crying again, so she stood at the door until he had cried himself to sleep. Then she went to bed and did the same thing.

The next day, Sunday, they were at the hospital at 9.00 o'clock. There had been no change in Jean's condition. Granny was surprised to find Sergeant Thompson in the waiting room reading a newspaper. She gave him his shilling and thanked him for his dedication. He gave Jack a few of the biscuits he had been eating as his breakfast and took granny aside.

"Ah had a check conducted on PC Cameron and he has a strong alibi. He was in his favorite pub from noon till three when he was almost thrown out because he was so drunk. Then he was in a café until four when he was collected by another constable because he was having an argument with the proprietor. He was taken straight home and put to bed."

"A full investigation is underway and I promise to keep you informed. Ah also have to tell you that my boss, the Inspector, has told me ah cannot remain at the hospital as ah said ah would."

"But yer here today."

"Today is my day off, so ah suppose ah can dae what ah like," he said with a tired smile.

"Ye mean ye huv been here a' night?"

"Aye, my wife was kind enough to bring me ma shaving stuff and a newspaper on her way to church. One other thing Mrs. Melville, whoever did this to your daughter did not molest her. The doctors have confirmed this."

"Thank God fer that."

Granny sat beside Jack and later a young doctor approached them to say that in cases like this patients could be in Jean's state for over a week and they should home. He felt sure Jean would recover in a few days.

He was wrong, Jean died the next day.

Jean was buried on Friday. Rain was drizzling, the kind of rain Glaswegians referred to as 'small rain', the type that soaked through to your underclothes. At the cemetery, Jack eschewed the offer of an umbrella and stood in his only suit, his shoes polished brightly, his hair plastered to his head totally bereft of all feeling. At the end of the service each mourner cast a handful of earth on the coffin in the traditional manner. When asked by his granny if he wanted to do the same, Jack took a flower from the wreath granny had bought and placed that on the coffin, saying, "Ah will not throw dirt on ma mammy."

Everyone had gone but Jack just stood there. Granny stood nearby under an umbrella. It was not possible to tell if he was crying because of the rain running down his face. He was. He had not realized the impact of the telling of the circumstances surrounding his father's death. They had left embers of bitterness in his heart. Now these embers began flaring. In a few years when he understood the complicity of the police in covering up his mother's death, these flares would turn into a raging fire of hatred for the authorities who permitted this to happen. The intense heat of the present flare dried his tears and he would never cry again as a boy. He turned around, walked to his granny, kissed her on the cheek, took her arm and said, "It's just you and me now granny but we'll show them, just ye wait an' see. We'll show them."

Granny Melville looked at him not really understanding what he meant but she saw the look in his eyes and could not help feeling a tremor of dread pass through her small frame. She sensed a terrible retribution lay in store for someone.

Three weeks after Jean was buried, granny went to the police station to find out what progress had been made. A different sergeant stood behind the reception counter.

"Where's Sergeant Thompson?"

"And who wants tae know?"

"Ah do, Mrs. Melville."

"Well, Mrs. Melville, he disnae work here anymair. He wis transferred last week. Can ah be of any help?"

"Ah want tae know whit the situation is regarding ma daughter's death."

"An' whit's her name?"

"Jean Campbell."

An immediate change came over the sergeant's face, one of extreme caution. He turned to a drawer and pulled out a folder which he pretended to study. Then turning back to granny said, "There are no further developments at this time. Ye don't need tae walk all the way doon here again. As soon as we hear anythin' we will contact ye."

A constable overheard this conversation on his way out the station to begin walking his beat. He waited outside and followed granny for a few hundred yards before stopping her.

"Excuse me Mrs. Melville," said PC McLeod, "ah heard whit the sergeant said. It's a shame aboot Sergeant Thompson; he's a really good polisman. Now whit ah am aboot tae say could get me booted off the police force so ye must keep it tae yersel missus. Can ye promise me that?"

"Aye, go on, tell me."

"Well, the Inspector and Sergeant Thompson got intae a big row over yer daughter's case. Sergeant Thompson kept diggin' intae Cameron's story and wisnae satisfied that it wis as watertight as he made oot. The Inspector yelled at the sergeant that his job wis tae protect his men, not tae try to hang them. It would be very bad fer the morale o' the police force tae prosecute one o' oor own. The Inspector said he was completely satisfied with Cameron's story and that was the end o' the matter. Then he had the sergeant transferred."

"Ah always knew it wis that bugger Cameron. Thank ye fer lettin' me know."

That night granny was going over in her mind how she could get revenge on Cameron. Then it dawned on her that if she did manage to bash him on the head with a poker she would undoubtedly be arrested and Jack would be put in some kind of home for orphan children.

She could not let that happen so she would have to forget any vengeful activity. Her first duty now was to raise and protect her grandson. Somehow justice would be served on Cameron. She did not know how this would come about, but she knew she must believe this to keep her sanity.

Jack moved in with his granny and it would be three years before she told him of PC McLeod's information. She had waited until he was sixteen, close to being a man. He was certainly no longer a boy. He had changed so much physically, but more so, mentally. His dedication to schoolwork was prodigious and she was intensely proud of his progress. She had heard him talk to classmates and knew he had an extensive vocabulary. Some of these conversations were beyond her understanding, but he never tried to impress her with these big words, he always spoke to her in plain Glaswegian. She loved him so much and her mind had been in turmoil trying to decide if she should tell him about Cameron but in the end he had the right to know. There could never be the close relationship they shared if she kept secrets of such importance. She still had deep regrets that she had not found some way to get back at him; perhaps it was this sense of guilt that finally persuaded her to seek Jack's approval of her inaction.

Jack knelt in front of her and held her tightly.

"Ah didnae know ma daddy and ah adored ma mammy and ah love you, granny. Ah could not have survived the last three years without ye. Ye have been ma harbor of safety and security and ah will always, always be grateful tae ye."

He had used this analogy because his grandfather had been a seaman and he thought it would be clearly understood by his granny. It was. Tears flowed down her cheeks as she clung to him.

It was in his third year of university when granny died of pneumonia.

Jack moved into a flat close to the university with two other students. A month later a policeman called Cameron apparently jumped to his death from his flat. In his pocket was a note addressed to a police inspector saying, 'I appreciate all you did by covering up the Campbell affair, but I cannot live with it any longer.'

An investigation followed and this inspector was ignominiously dismissed from the force, prosecuted, found guilty and jailed.

Sergeant McLeod often wondered about the wording of the note, he had never heard Cameron speak in such an educated manner. 'Still', he thought, 'justice has been done.'

In a mystical other world a grandmother's soul sighed with satisfaction.

Chapter 7

John Gibson had started in the Red Funnel Line as an office boy at the age of fifteen. His rise to manager of the Glasgow office at the age of twenty eight was considered meteoric. No one outside of the founding family had risen to such a position before the age of forty five. He was undoubtedly energetic and dedicated; however, he was aided by his appearance. Several years ago an important customer said to the then manager, "That Gibson is a wise old bird." He was twenty four years old, but looked forty with his balding head and stooped shoulders. He had always seemed older than his years but those who knew him well also knew of his quick wit and great joy in a good joke.

The shipping business was high risk during times of war and it took all of his experience, talent and even-temper to literally and figuratively, keep the business afloat. This was a time of great pressure being applied by a harried government to meet unrealistic deadlines. Long hours led to mistakes and frayed tempers and at such times his sense of humor was a saving grace for everyone in the office.

Given this situation, the strange request of Sir Samuel Brown to create a one month training program to a complete newcomer to shipping was a major distraction and a most unwelcome one, but he could not refuse a member of the Board of Directors. However his impishness could not resist taking his instructions to the limit. 'Work him mercilessly' he had been told, well he bloody well would. He was not malicious; this was not his nature, as proven by the time he spent with Jack on the first day explaining the fundamentals of the shipping business.

Later he had delivered to Jack's desk a huge pile of documents and files and told Jack to study them and prepare a report on his findings and suggestions. 'That will keep him busy for a week,' he said to himself with a smile.

Gibson was annoyed when two days later he found on his desk a six page report. 'This bugger has not taken time to study the information and believes the object of this exercise is to write a neat report that's only fit for toilet paper,' he thought. 'No one could have studied all that information thoroughly in two days'. His immediate reaction was to storm down to Jack's desk in the basement and tear a strip off his hide. Instead he began reading the first page. Thirty minutes later he sat back in his chair in total amazement, realized he had not touched the cup of tea brought by his secretary, ordered a fresh cup and sent for Jack.

"Have you not slept since I gave you this task?"

"Not much" admitted Jack somewhat ruefully. "To be perfectly honest I did not think I would enjoy this job, but I found it interesting and when I get interested I tend to become totally absorbed."

"But some of your comments and suggestions did not come from the files I gave you."

Jack looked a little uncomfortable, then said apologetically, "I'm sorry but when I do get interested in a subject I always look for at least two opinions before I make my own judgment. So I went to the Mitchell to look up other references. I hope this does not offend you."

"Not at all, not at all Simpson. I think your report is bloody marvelous. I am very impressed."

Thereafter Gibson gave Jack tasks of increasing complexity and as he believed he was working for the government, allowed him almost unrestricted access to classified material. He was in Gibson's office most days, reporting to him or asking questions or just leaving a report on his desk. The staff became used to seeing him go in and out of Gibson's office, even when Gibson was not present. This, combined with his willingness to work long hours finally gave him the opportunity to crack the code on Gibson's safe and read the secret material on ship movements in Asia. This would be a bonus for Lord Hino.

At the end of his stint he was excited over his imminent trip to Japan but that pang of nostalgia for Glasgow came back and he wondered yet again when he would next see her.

He had managed to resolve the problem of Mrs. McAllister by leaving her thermos on her doorstep around one a.m., along with a note of thanks. She had come out to see him the next day at seven o'clock, just as he was about to drive off.

"Thank you for returning my flask, Mr. Simpson. I really would like you to come over for a cup of tea one day, but as you don't get home until almost midnight and leave so early, I don't know when that will be. You don't get much sleep do you?"

Jack wanted to say, 'Obviously you don't either' but instead said, "In these difficult times we all must do our best."

"Good man, our country needs people like you," she said and waved goodbye.

Carolyn Jardine had left a note under his back door that same day saying, 'Where are you? I must see you soon!'

He visited her the next night and again three nights after that. She was not impressed by his patriotic duty and made it clear he better stop working such long hours and spend more time with her. He was relieved two weeks later when she told him her husband was coming home on leave and she would contact him the minute he left.

The day he was leaving Glasgow he left a note for Mrs. McAllister saying he would be away on a business trip for two or three weeks. He could think of no better way to broadcast his departure.

He followed the instructions he had been given and drove to Brown Street near George Square. As he turned into Brown Street a man walked into the street holding up his ungloved left hand while he guided out a driver of a parked car with his gloved right hand. He waved his thanks to Jack for stopping as he climbed into the car. This arranged event allowed Jack to park in a street full of parked cars. The driver behind Jack mouthed 'Lucky bugger' as he continued circling in frustration. Jack left the keys under the passenger seat and walked round the corner to Blair Street where the rear door of a car opened as he approached. He poked his head in the door and said, "Nice day."

The driver replied, "Aye, it's good tae see the sun shine."

Jack got in and the car drove off in the pouring rain.

The end of this first leg of his journey turned out to be a remote area on the coast of Ayrshire. He boarded a small motor launch and set off for Ireland where he landed at dusk, in County Antrim. Here he was met by a ramshackle looking small truck; however, when the driver turned on the ignition, the engine started with a powerful throb. The journey to the west coast of Ireland was extremely uncomfortable.

Although the engine was in excellent condition the shocks and springs were of the same vintage as the exterior. He reckoned he traveled further in a vertical direction, bouncing up and down, than in a horizontal one.

It was late when the bucking bronco as Jack had named the truck, finally arrived and he was immediately hustled into a small rowboat which he eyed with some concern; however they had only rowed for fifteen minutes before he was transferred to a fishing boat.

He had asked no questions of any of his escorts. He had been taught in his training not to do so. His trainer had emphasized that a most important aspect of any escort job was silence. Those who broke this rule regretted it. In about an hour Jack was just about to fall asleep when the engine stopped. He leapt to his feet but the skipper silently motioned it was ok and put his finger to his lips urging silence. In about ten minutes a rubber dingy appeared at the side of the boat and a German sailor motioned Jack to climb in. It was only a few minutes until he was boarding a submarine. The Captain greeted him saying, "Welcome on board. My crew has been told not to talk to you and you should not talk to them. Is that clear?"

"Perfectly."

"Good. You may use my cabin and if you desire anything you must ask me. We have put coffee and a light meal in my cabin for you."

"Thank you Captain that is most considerate of you," said Jack sincerely. He had suddenly realized how desperately tired he was and he was hungry. Before dropping off to sleep he realized the Captain did not keep the code of silence but also realized it would have been highly impractical to do so.

Next day, in a cold rain, he left the submarine and boarded a spacious motor launch. In an hour and a half he was disembarking at a beach close to Estoril, in Portugal.

Even in the drizzling rain he could see just how arid this area must be most of the year. He moved from the sandy beach and crunched his way through the shale to the road where a car was waiting. The driver was Japanese which did not surprise him. The driver did not speak to him as he was whisked to a house just outside Lisbon where he was met by Lord Hino.

"I do wish you would learn to be prompt, you are almost thirty minutes late," said Lord Hino in mock exasperation.

Jack opened his mouth to give a retort but decided against it when he saw the grin on Hino's face.

"Seriously, I am very pleased to see you again Campbell and I know the journey must have been arduous but security must take precedence over comfort. I am afraid you will get very little rest as we must leave on a similar but much less complicated journey to the ship."

Seeing the look of puzzlement on Jack's face he continued, "You didn't think we could just walk up the gangplank of this ship while she is at the dock, did you? Lisbon has more foreign prying eyes than any other city in the world. We must board the ship at sea and in the dark. She sails at dusk and will develop engine trouble an hour out of harbor, so we must leave soon. Don't roll your eyes like that; you will have lots of time to relax onboard. Oh, by the way, those two large suitcases are yours. We purchased some items of clothing for you. These should take care of your requirements on the ship, in Japan and in Malaya. Let's have a snack and then we must be off."

"Is the driver from your embassy in Lisbon?"

"Of course. He made all the arrangements. As I said, one must be particularly careful in this city of spies. Anything and everything is for sale at the right price and virtually everyone has his price."

"Just one more question, my Lord. Like your bodyguards in Glasgow, did each of my escorts have orders to dispose of me should we encounter trouble?"

"Come, come Campbell, do not get too swollen headed. Do you really believe you are that important?"

This lack of an answer told Jack his suspicions were correct. He also had a nagging feeling there was something else Lord Hino was keeping from him. Something important.

The snack turned out to be a quite substantial meal of baked cod (a Portuguese delicacy) with fresh vegetables and a wonderful salad. This was washed down with a very good white wine. Jack was beginning to feel quite mellow when with a start he looked at his watch and said, "You did say we had to leave soon didn't you?"

"My dear, untraveled, Campbell. You must learn that in Iberia 'soon' is a relative term; furthermore, the rushing of a good meal is regarded as being close to a criminal offence. Nevertheless you are right; we should be on our way."

Jack noticed the rain had stopped and the air was warmer as they walked towards the waiting car. The driver held open the door for Lord Hino and bowed very low as Hino settled himself in the back seat. Jack had to walk around the other side and open his own door. It was apparent the driver's only concern was this powerful nobleman. The car returned to the beach where Jack had landed; the same launch was there with its prow on the sand and a step was in place to assist in boarding.

As they alighted from the car Jack saw the same two men who had brought him ashore were standing in the launch.

A third man approached and said, "Good evening senores, let me help you with your luggage. It is a fine night for a sail; the sea is now very calm."

As he moved to the trunk of the car to get the luggage, the driver reached into his jacket for his gun, but Lord Hino quickly shook his head. He exerted all his willpower to hide his shock and anger at seeing a third man, one who broke the golden rule of escort service, silence. He looked at Jack and raised one eyebrow as a sign of concern and warning. Jack indicated he understood with a barely perceptible nod. Lord Hino muttered something to the driver and climbed into the launch. Jack followed as one of the men on board jumped onto the beach and with the unknown third man began pushing the boat to sea. As the boat bobbed in the water they clambered on board.

"Please be careful senores as there are fishing rods, buckets, cloths and other tackle at the back of the boat. It is not quite dark yet and we may have to pretend to fish should we meet up with another boat. One must be on guard these days, eh senores."

He moved beside the other two men at the wheel of the launch.

"Something's wrong. Why did you stop the driver from drawing his gun to find out what is going on?"

"It would have lead to shooting and I do not wish this man to die until I find out his plan and more important, does he know who we are. Also, has he told anyone else of our voyage? Obviously he is after money or else he could have ambushed us at the beach. We must let him make his move but be ready for quick action. I will stand at the front of the boat, you stay here."

They had sailed for half an hour when the third man said to the man at the wheel, "Stop the engine."

He pulled a gun from his belt and pointed it at Lord Hino.

"You at the back do not move or your boss will be shot. Now senor, why are you trying to escape from Portugal? You are certainly a criminal, most probably dealing in the black market. Maybe even dealing in currency, gold or guns, eh?"

Lord Hino's face had a look of complete surprise.

"How did you know," he gasped.

"I also am in this type of business. Of course I smuggle other things too. A smart man must take the opportunity of making money in situations like today."

He said something to the man standing next to the helmsman who then fumbled in a canvas bag finally producing a camera and took flash photographs of Lord Hino and Jack.

"Now senores I must have two things from you if you want to board that liner tonight. Of course you can refuse in which case you will both die. Firstly I am sure you are carrying a lot of money or even gold with you. I will take that. I really don't have to ask for it, I could just take it and kill you. But this would not be the action of a smart man. You obviously have many connections in Lisbon and I want to be your partner in whatever you are doing. You will give me the names of your associates."

"There is a reason for the photographs. If the information you give me turns out to be false or if you try to double-cross me then I will show your photographs around. Perhaps I did not mention that I make most of my money by selling information. I have contacts with many of the criminal organizations in Lisbon, as well as the embassies of Germany, Britain, France, Russia and America. I am sure one of them will want to know your whereabouts."

"All of them have contacts around the world and it would be a simply matter to send a telegram to have you detained or killed at your next port of call. You see I have thought of everything. I have done this type of thing before."

"You certainly have thought of everything. I can see we have no choice," said Lord Hino running his hand over his brow in, what seemed to the gunman, an obvious state of fear.

Jack took the signal and picked up a few cloths from the deck. The fluttering caught the eye of the gunman and he swung his attention to Jack. That was his first mistake. Like lightning Lord Hino's hand chopped down on his wrist causing him to drop the gun. He turned from Jack to pick up his gun. That was his second and final mistake. Jack wrapped one of the fishing lines round his neck, protecting his own hands with the cloths, and jerked the line tightly. The man died almost instantly. The helmsman tried to take advantage of the situation to escape by diving overboard. Before his feet left the side of the boat Lord Hino shot him twice. He fell dead into the boat and Jack heaved him overboard.

"You're a real Wyatt Earp with that gun," said Jack. "I did not even see where you kept it."

Lord Hino turned to the remaining man who was shaking with fright.

"Tell me why you informed this third man of our plans," he demanded.

"I did not tell him, senor, I swear."

Lord Hino raised his gun and pointed it straight at the man's head.

"It is the truth senor. Joao and I were waiting by the boat at the beach as we had been instructed by your driver, when Paolo came along the road on his motor cycle. Paolo is a cousin of Joao. He stopped and asked what we were doing. We told him to go away and mind his own business. Perhaps this was a mistake because he immediately became suspicious. He continued to demand an answer and finally Joao lost his temper and swore at Paolo and called him a cheap crook. As you saw Paolo is a big man. He grabbed Joao round the neck and put his gun in Joao's mouth. 'No one will miss an insignificant person like you. So perhaps I will just pull the trigger,' he said. Joao wet himself and Paolo laughed crazily. I was sure he was going to kill him. Joao told him we were to ferry two gentlemen out to a liner. Paolo said, 'There must be big money in this. No ordinary person could get a liner to stop at sea. These men must be big shots.' He let Joao go and told us what we were to do. He said that one false step from either of us and he would kill us both. In the panniers on the side of his motor cycle he had a lot of equipment including the camera. He also had another gun planted under the steering wheel and a knife hidden in the map drawer."

"I see he was ready for everything," said Lord Hino. "That is everything but us. Now can you steer us to the appointed rendezvous?"

"Of course, senor. And, senor, you can be sure I will not mention this to anyone."

It was not difficult to find the liner in the dark even though most of its lights were out. The launch approached the stern of the liner and stopped.

Jack saw a rope ladder was hanging from the stern deck and who should be climbing down but one of the bodyguards he met in Glasgow.

Lord Hino whispered something to him and he softly whistled. Instantly bodyguard number two appeared. One of the Japanese picked up some of the luggage and led the way up the ladder. Lord Hino followed and Jack went next carrying one of his suitcases. When they were on deck the Japanese guard led them to their cabins. Inside Jack's cabin was a bottle of scotch. Lord Hino joined him for a drink.

"As you saw tonight, Campbell, you must always be prepared for the unexpected. No one could have foreseen the unexpected coincidence of that man just happening to pass that particular beach at that particular time. Under the circumstances you handled yourself very well. It was as though you could read my thoughts."

"Your instructors taught me the importance of distraction. It works very well with non professionals like Paolo."

"True, but nevertheless you remained cool in a dangerous situation. I know we preach this, but it is not so easy to do in a real life situation. Cheers, here's to a hopefully uneventful voyage."

"What will happen to the man who sailed us here?"

"Unfortunately when someone betrays us, even though his life may be in danger, he cannot be forgiven. You must remember Campbell that one betrayal inevitably leads to another."

At that moment there was a single knock on the cabin door. Lord Hino motioned Jack to stay seated and he went to the door which he knocked three times. The reply from outside was two knocks. He opened the door. It was the guard who had stayed behind on the launch. He whispered something to Lord Hino who nodded his head, then closed the door.

"I suppose our friend went down with his ship?"

"Yes."

Chapter 8

A strong wind that would have kept most passengers inside buffeted Jack but he enjoyed the salty spray on his face. It was still early in the morning and he had not slept too well. He had never been on a sea voyage and was somewhat apprehensive. He hoped he would not be seasick however his main concern was being onboard for such a long time. He was sure he would be terribly bored. What was worse he had learned from Lord Hino the previous night that the ship would go round the Horn of Africa as the Mediterranean was considered too dangerous.

Although flying the flag of a neutral nation, the Portuguese Captain knew that mistakes could be made by still inexperienced officers on warships. Even more dangerous were the experienced Captains of warships. They had no qualms in using a harmless ship as a shield. A shield that would not be considered sacrosanct if the hiding ship was a prize target.

"Campbell, Campbell it is time for breakfast."

Jack turned to see the hunched up figure of Lord Hino clutching the edge of the deck door. He walked quite steadily towards Lord Hino who hissed in his ear, "You will kindly hold on to deck rails. Don't try to show how clever you are. One big wave and you can be swept overboard. I have not spent all this time and effort on your training to have you become food for the fish!"

"Very well your Lordship," said Jack somewhat ironically.

"Also, do not refer to my title during this voyage. No one must know of my position. Simply refer to me as Mr. Hino. I have already instructed my guards not to show any special deference to me. This will be extremely difficult for them, however I expect you to remember this at all times, even when we are alone in a cabin."

"Of course, Mr. Hino, might I suggest, in the spirit of keeping our cover intact, that you refer to me as Simpson and not Campbell."

Jack thought Hino would faint. He clung tightly to the door, his eyes tightly shut.

"Did I just call you Campbell?" he whispered.

"I am afraid you did. Perhaps you slept as badly as I did last night or maybe you are worried about something."

"It happens to be the true that I had a restless night, but it is no excuse. But I certainly have no concerns. How can I when I am in the company of the redoubtable Mr. Jack Simpson."

A smile had returned to his face as he said this and Jack could see he had recovered quickly.

"Now let me introduce you to Professor Dr. Mannheim. Like both of us he is early to rise and awaits us in the dining room."

"How much does this kraut, excuse me, German, know?"

"He believes I am in Japanese Naval Intelligence and that you have been recruited to spy on Malayan harbor readiness. I told him the plan is to pass you off as a marine biologist so that you may study the harbors. As I have taught you, the best cover stories are more than ninety percent true."

"Remember two things. Firstly, he is a very intelligent man and may well begin to suspect there is more to your mission than I have mentioned. Secondly, I have arranged for him to pursue research at the Yokohama Marine Biology Institute. Therefore, no matter what he may suspect, he will say nothing for fear of jeopardizing this opportunity. You must not refer to any of your training. Is all this clear?"

"Perfectly," said Jack again extremely impressed by the guile of Hino.

As they entered the dining room Jack noted the tables were set with starched white tablecloths and gleaming tableware. A Caucasian couple sitting at a corner table did not look up but a man sitting at a table at the opposite end of the room nodded to them. The man rose as they approached.

"Good morning Mr. Hino."

"Good morning Professor. Allow me to introduce Mr. Jack Simpson."

"It is a pleasure to meet you, Mr. Simpson."

"I am pleased to meet you Professor."

"I hope you do not object Mr. Hino, I ordered coffee."

"Thank you Professor."

"It should be here soon. I sent the first pot of coffee back to the kitchen."

The professor noticed Jack's quizzical look and said "Have you ever taken a long sea voyage Mr. Simpson?"

"This is the first one," replied Jack.

"I have taken many and learned one important thing. The service you receive can vary greatly. You can ensure good service by tipping almost every crew member you meet or, at the very outset, by being seen to be observant and requesting corrections be made if something is not up to a high standard. You should not be rude, but you must be assertive. There are various grades of almost every item of food and drink on board most ships. The passenger who demonstrates knowledge of this will receive the better quality ones. I say better as the best is always reserved for the Captain."

"In this case I considered the coffee to be of a low quality so I asked for a better one. We shall see if it works. The other thing I always do is inspect the cutlery. I found a spot on the underside of my knife so I sent that back also."

More out of curiosity than any fear of germs, Jack picked up his knife and was examining it when a voice behind him said, "Good morning senores, I am your waiter: my name is Joao."

Jack dropped the knife onto his plate with a loud clatter. The other couple looked over, startled by the noise.

"Forgive me senor," said the waiter.

"It's not your fault. I just didn't hear you come up behind me."

Lord Hino caught Jack's eye and nodded slightly indicating he understood how the mention of this name, so soon after last night, could have caused this reaction.

The waiter looked at the Professor and said, "I have brought a different coffee. I hope you will find it acceptable."

The professor tasted it and nodded his head.

"Much better, thank you Joao."

"May I take your orders senores?"

During breakfast Jack had the opportunity to study the Professor. He was taller than he and painfully thin. His receding hair was short somewhat curly, reddish with grey at the sides. He spoke with studied precision. His table manners were almost obsessive. Jack had never seen someone place each utensil back in exactly the same spot after every usage. He daubed each side of his small mouth with his napkin after each mouthful of food.

'Good Lord this is going to be even more boring than I imagined,' thought Jack.

As if reading his mind Lord Hino said, "I am certain Mr. Simpson will find your instruction very interesting, Professor Mannheim. It is a fascinating subject. I suggest you begin in, shall we say, thirty minutes. We took one of the larger cabins for the professor to give you both more room for Mr. Simpson's studies."

Jack felt Lord Hino was indulging his apparent joy at teasing him, although from his serious mien one could not tell. As they left the dining room several other passengers filed in, including Hino's two guards. Hino gave no sign of recognition and Jack almost choked in stifling a laugh as one of the guards stumbled into a table in an effort to curtail a bow. Obviously Lord Hino had been correct in surmising the difficulties to be faced by his guards in not displaying their customary deference to their Lord. Jack barely heard the second guard hiss to the offender, "Baka". Idiot would be a charitable translation.

At the appointed time Jack knocked on the cabin door of Professor Mannheim. Immediately the door opened.

"Please come in Mr. Simpson, everything is ready. I have placed your notebook and text book on the table. There is a selection of pens and pencils, both regular and colored. I believe we are ready to start."

'This joker is more like an elementary teacher than a professor,' thought Jack. 'I wonder if I have to raise my hand to go pee?'

Professor Mannheim was still wearing his tweed jacket and his tightly knotted tie seemed about to choke his scrawny neck. Jack had changed into an open neck sports shirt. The professor caught Jack's look at his tie, "Perhaps I am a bit too formal, I will take off my necktie."

"It will be a long voyage and we should be comfortable," said Jack.

"Quite so, I propose we dress informally from now on."

'One minor step forward,' thought Jack.

"Before we undertake the study of the magnificent giant turtles, I thought we could talk about the Malay Peninsula. I understand this will be your first visit. Is this correct?"

"Yes."

"Oh how I envy you. I have traveled there four times and was always impressed by the country's beauty. Of course you have read much about it, haven't you?"

"No, only a little. I did not have much notice of this journey."

"Then you will enjoy the experience all the more. I studied extensively before my first visit; however, I found all this effort only gave me a factually detailed, rather dry academic knowledge. Ach, I am not expressing myself very well. All my studies made pictures in my mind but they were all monochromatic. When I first saw the country, all these pictures came alive with radiant color. So my advice to you is to open up all your senses and let this country sweep into your soul. You will then truly appreciate its wonders."

"What is wrong, you have a strange look on your face. My English was poor?"

"No, no your English was excellent. It is just that I have never heard of experiencing something by opening all ones senses."

"When you arrive you will see that what I say is true. Your eyes will be dazzled with the colors of everything around you. The streets will fill your ears with vibrant sounds. You will taste the most delicious foods. Mr. Simpson, you are about to enter a wonderful dreamland."

"Professor Mannheim, I appreciate that in your country it is courteous to use the proper form of address when speaking to someone you do not know well. If you wish we can spend the weeks ahead referring to each other as Professor and Mister, but I would be more comfortable if you called me Jack."

"A very good idea, my name is Hans."

Despite this attempt at informality the Professor could not help standing up when he said this. He also bowed then held out his hand.

'Two steps forward and one step backwards,' thought Jack.

"I would like to propose the following structure for our discussions, Jack. We will start with information on the Malay Peninsula. I will share my findings with you, but you should feel free to stop me anytime to ask for clarification or further details. This way it will be a conversation and not a lecture. The next morning you may take time to write out any notes or thoughts you may have. In the afternoon we can review your notes to be certain we have communicated well. Is this agreeable to you?"

"I think it is a splendid plan, Hans."

The next two weeks passed surprisingly quickly to Jack. Hans seemed to be transformed when he talked of the Malay Peninsula. Jack had yet to see him smile broadly. The closest he came would have been described by Jack's granny as a gas pain, a tight lipped, somewhat lopsided, grin.

Nevertheless Jack calculated a five step improvement in their relationship; however, at mealtimes, he always acted in his original prim manner.

Lord Hino did not appear for all meals, in fact on one occasion, he was not seen for a two day stretch. He seemed preoccupied and Jack knew better than to ask the reason.

During his breaks, Jack noticed the officers always appeared vigilant, scanning the horizon at regular intervals. One day one of them left his binoculars on a deck table while lighting a cigarette and forgot to pick them up. Jack snatched them and went to his cabin where he too scanned the horizon. Somehow he was not surprised to see smoke coming from a warship, probably a destroyer he thought. He left his cabin and walked to the other side of the ship and scanned again with the same result. 'Aha we have an escort' thought Jack. He replaced the binoculars on the same table and returned to his cabin to work on his notes. That night he stayed awake looking through the porthole in his cabin and at precisely two o'clock he saw what he had suspected, a series of flashing lights. The destroyer had come closer under cover of darkness and was transmitting a message. He had no doubt who was receiving this message.

Two nights later when Jack was on the deck leaning on the rail he was approached by one of the Japanese passengers who spoke to him in Japanese. Jack shrugged his shoulders as a sign of incomprehension and quickly walked away to is cabin. He waited fifteen minutes, peeked out the door to check that no one was around then went to Lord Hino's cabin. He used the agreed system of knocks and entered the cabin after Hino had opened the door. Seeing the serious look on Jack's face Hino asked, "What is it?"

"We have a problem."

He told him what had happened.

Hino sat back in his chair and was silent for several minutes while he thought about this situation.

At last he said, "We need more information on this man. There is no logical reason why any Japanese would address a foreigner in Japanese. He would never expect the foreigner to understand him; therefore, he was testing you. Why would he test you? Most probably to determine your usefulness and relationship with another party. The most obvious party is me. The logical conclusion is that he is a spy for the British or the Americans. But to be absolutely certain we must find out his language capabilities. The only languages spoken on this ship are, Portuguese, German, Japanese and English. So let's find out".

"How will we do that?"

"I will take care of it" said Hino. "Meet me here tomorrow evening just before dinner. You look pensive, what is it?"

"I was wondering if this sudden interest in me is in any way connected to the messages you have been receiving."

"And what messages might these be?" asked Hino in a slightly menacing way.

"The Morse code message flashed from one of the two destroyers which are escorting this ship. If I could see the transmission of two nights ago, others could have noticed it too. And I assume there have been other messages since you have spent so much time in you cabin."

"You have learned your new craft very well; I will not ask you to explain how you discovered all this. Let me assure you the messages were so well coded that no one could have understood them. However, it is true someone could have seen the signals but they were important enough to take that risk. Good night, I will see you tomorrow."

The next day Jack did not see Lord Hino until their evening appointment.

"What did you discover?" asked Jack.

"The man's name is Tanaka and he speaks German and English. I have an understanding with the First Officer. He gave me his name and checked with the steward and waiter, both confirmed Tanaka speaks English to them and does not understand Portuguese."

"How did he find out he speaks German?"

"He did not, I did. I used one of the oldest tricks in this business. When Tanaka was sitting on deck I had Professor Manheim and the First Officer come up behind him quietly, then the professor said loudly, in German, to the First Officer, 'I tell you I left my camera on this chair, that Japanese man must have taken it, you know you can't trust these Orientals and how much they like good German cameras'. That caused Tanaka to jump up angrily and hotly deny the charge. Unwittingly he did this in German."

"Very clever. What do you plan on doing next?"

"Now we have no choice. Tanaka must disappear."

There were a few moments of silence and then staring at Jack, Lord Hino said, "You have that pensive look again. What are you thinking?"

"I have spent a good part of the afternoon mulling this over and I believe we are missing something. Firstly Tanaka's attempt to contact me in Japanese was clumsy and unprofessional. It seems to me it was a hastily devised scheme, not a well thought out one. Now the trapping of Tanaka into speaking German also demonstrates a lack of professionalism. This man has not been well trained."

"I can agree with what you have said so far, go on."

"The fact he speaks German may be related to my second point."

"Which is?"

"There is a couple who sit at a table close to ours in the dining room. The very first time we met Hans; they were the only other people in the dining room and were sitting at the opposite end of the room. I learned from Joao they claimed the wife was upset by sitting next to a porthole while eating and asked to be moved to their present location. I slightly moved our table so I could see them in the mirror on the far wall. They surreptitiously but constantly watch Hans. Something else I learned from Joao is they tried buttering him up by telling him how they enjoyed Portugal more than any of the other countries they visited in Europe. They claim to be Swiss so I did a little checking."

"How did you accomplish that?"

"As you know all passports are kept by the Captain until we dock. I simply broke into the Captain's safe and had a look at their passports. They have Swiss passports under the name of Schmidt but they are fictitious. They are brand new but dated as being issued five years ago and they have not been stamped by any country other than in Portugal on this trip. I believe they are German agents and they are after Hans."

"That does not make sense."

"Suppose Hans has no intention of returning to Germany?"

"That would be very serious. He is a world authority in his field and is enormously well respected not only as a dedicated and talented scientist but also as an honest and decent man. It would reflect very badly on the Third Reich if he were to defect. But, even if he did plan such an action, he would not broadcast it."

"I suggest you invite him back to your cabin for a nightcap after dinner."

"Alright, but this has to be handled very delicately. You should be present but let me do most of the talking."

After dinner they assembled in Lord Hino's cabin. Hans was nervous.

"Mr. Hino, I suspect you did not invite me here just for a brandy; therefore, if you have no objection can we get straight to your concern?"

Lord Hino raised an eyebrow at Jack as if to say,' I told you he was intelligent'.

'Certainly Professor, Mr. Simpson has noticed a couple who appear to be taking an unusual interest in you. We believe they may be Germans although they profess to be Swiss."

The professor was visibly shaken by this news. He closed his eyes tightly and grimaced.

"I think I will have that brandy now Mr. Hino."

Jack poured brandies for all of them and put one in the shaking hands of Hans.

"I would like to make one thing perfectly clear, Professor. Your country and mine are allies in this war; however, there are certain things we do not have in common. One is the persecution of a man simply because he devotes himself to art or science and not to war. I have offered you an opportunity to work at our research institute in Yokohama and I want you to know that offer stands, whatever your personal plans may be for the future."

He looked intently into the eyes of Hans to be sure he understood. Hans nodded in gratitude.

"Thank you, Mr. Hino."

"I do not want you to tell me your plans. I must not hear any word of this or I may be bound by my loyalty to my country to report what I have heard. Do you understand, Professor?"

"Yes."

"What I must know is, did you tell anyone of your plans?"

"No, no, no-one."

Then he paused.

"Professor?" said Lord Hino, sensing this was not completely true.

"Only my sister and she would never say anything. Believe me, we are very close, and it was actually she who suggested the idea. No one had any idea of my unhappiness but she felt it. She knew."

Jack and Lord Hino exchanged a meaningful glance. The professor may be intelligent but he was too naïve to know how vicious Hitler's regime could really be. One heard stories of other races, other people but never believed it could happen to your family. Not to a normal German family. But it could and it did.

Lord Hino covered up quickly by saying, "Then this is merely an unfortunate coincidence. This couple must have recognized you and are wondering what you are doing on this trip. No doubt they will report having seen you just to show how observant they are. That is their role, to travel and report anything unusual. You need not worry, Professor; you have proper authority to make this journey. One other thing Professor, do not make any contact with these people."

"May I ask why? I thought perhaps if I tell them of my approved study period, they would be satisfied."

Lord Hino sighed and said, "Unfortunately it would have quite the opposite effect. I have dealt with people like these. They are relatively unimportant and deep down in their hearts they know this. If they believe they have been very clever in identifying you and remaining undetected, their egos will be inflated and they will merely file their report with great pride. However, if they even suspect they have been uncovered they will be so afraid their superiors will learn of their incompetence that they will go to any lengths to atone for this by digging more deeply into your story, even inventing information to make themselves appear perceptive. No, Professor, you must stay away from them. As they would say in Mr. Simpson's country, 'let sleeping dogs lie'."

"Thank you for your advice, Mr. Hino, I will do as you say."

Then suddenly remembering something he said, "Oh what about the Japanese person you asked me to trick? Is he connected to this?"

"Not in the least way. No. His is a completely different situation; one totally related to me. But thank you again for your invaluable assistance. Now if you will excuse me gentlemen, I am a little tired."

They said their goodnights and as Jack walked with Hans he said, "I believe you can trust the word of Mr. Hino, Hans, you have no need to worry. I am sure everything will be fine."

Jack waited the usual fifteen minutes before returning to Lord Hino's cabin.

"What now?" he asked. "It was kind of you to be so considerate to Hans but you would not go out of your way to assist anyone if it would in any way jeopardize your plans. If merely eliminating Hans would resolve this problem then he would have an unfortunate accident. However I don't believe it would take care of this situation."

"You have become a cynical young man. Do you really believe I would throw the Professor overboard?"

"We both know you would, if it protected your plans."

"Perhaps you are right; however, it is a moot point as by associating ourselves with the Professor we have aroused the curiosity of these other people. They will continue to make a nuisance of themselves and submit a report which will be sent back to Germany. Reports have a habit of being intercepted. This is too great a risk and cannot be allowed to happen so we must work out a subtle plan."

He paused for a moment then said with a smile, "Who knows, perhaps it will even contribute to the furtherance of marine biology scientific knowledge by ensuring Professor Mannheim has a long and beneficial stay in Yokohama."

The smile told Jack he already had worked out a plan.

"OK, are you going to enlighten me?"

"Tanaka is not a problem. If he should get drunk one night and fall overboard there will be no great enquiry. The other two are more difficult. They will be expected in Japan and although they are not high level agents, their disappearance would create a hue and cry. Apparently the Professor has been under some suspicion; however, the fact he was allowed to leave means they had no reason to detain him. As he is so well known, they would not just throw him in jail without evidence, as they would with an ordinary citizen. We must assume that they are awaiting Schmidt's report when we dock in Japan."

"This is what we will do. In a few days we will dock at Luanda in Angola to refuel and reprovision. Just like Lisbon, this city is heavily populated with spies. Through my country's legation I will locate a suitable café where such people congregate. You will then telephone the British Consul from this café and in German accented English you will claim to be Schmidt and ask for asylum. You will offer as bait your knowledge of German Intelligence and particularly the codes they use. I will have someone there to verify your message was overheard and reported to the Germans. This will be done just before we sail. During this time one of my men will detain the Schmidts with their entire luggage in my cabin. Tanaka will be detained in his cabin by my other man. Once we are well out to sea, the Germans will join Tanaka. This will make it easier for my men to guard them."

"Don't you think the German authorities will radio the ship regarding the Schmidts?"

"Of course they will, that will make it even more believable. The Captain will check their cabin and discover their disappearance. The First Officer will then admit he had a problem with the provisioning and did not thoroughly check the reboarding of passengers. So the Captain will confirm they jumped ship."

"Why take the risk of keeping them alive till then, why not dispose of them now?"

"This area of Africa is open to patrols from both sides. It is a possibility, although a slight one, that the Germans might conduct a search around here; whereas in several days we will be off the coast of South Africa where there is a concentration of British in Cape Town. No German ship will venture there. I do not believe the bodies will surface as they will be heavily weighted, but why take a chance. It is just a precaution."

Once again Jack was in awe of this man's planning capability.

Everything went exactly according to Lord Hino's plan.

Chapter 9

In the next weeks Hans became even more deferential towards Lord Hino and even friendlier towards Jack. He seemed much less tense as though his secret being out had a cathartic effect on him.

Jack still met with him most days however their schedule was less rigid. One day while they were walking on the deck, Hans told Lord Hino, "Mr. Simpson has the potential of being a very good marine biologist."

"Perhaps so, Professor; or perhaps he has a rare talent to absorb new topics, particularly if they pique his interest."

"That may be true, Mr. Hino, but please forgive me if I continue to believe it is the irresistibility of my subject which makes him this way."

In fact the information on turtles proved to be extremely interesting to Jack and much to his surprise Hans' style of instruction was anything but pedantic. He recalled the first time the subject of turtles was discussed.

"Today Jack, it is your good fortune to learn something of Dermochelys Coriacea, the leatherback turtle. She is a magnificent animal. I say she, because as in much of the animal kingdom the female does all the work. Leatherbacks have existed for over sixty million years; therefore, they were living at the time of the dinosaurs. She is the longest living of all sea turtles and by far the largest. Leatherbacks can range from seven hundred to two thousand pounds in weight and can be eight feet in length. Unlike all other types of sea turtles the leatherback does not have a hard shell or carapace. Her carapace is formed by a series of plates and is slightly flexible and has a rubbery texture and can be up to four inches thick. Perhaps now you can imagine how magnificent this animal truly is."

"Oh we have a bigger sea animal than that it Scotland."

"Nonsense."

"Its true and she is a female also. We call her 'Nessie'."

Hans laughed loudly, "Have you ever seen you famous 'Loch Ness Monster, Jack?"

"Och no, she's a very shy wee lassie."

Hans continued laughing at Jack's accent then suddenly he stopped and looked troubled.

"What is it Hans? What is wrong?"

"We have become friends, have we not?"

"Yes Hans, we have."

"Much of my life has been devoted to the pursuit of scientific research. It has given me much satisfaction, yet it is a lonely activity. I have a number of associates and colleagues from all over the world; but, I have few friends. During this sea voyage I have had much time to consider this and it has made me sad to recognize that I may not see them for a long time. Yet in a quite short period of time I have come to think upon you as a very good friend and soon we too shall part. I have never had a good sense of humor, yet you make me laugh and when I do laugh I realize how much I will miss your company."

"You are traveling to a new adventure, Hans. To a country you have never seen before and I am sure you will make friends in Yokohama. Anyway I will be in Japan for a while and the first opportunity I have, I will visit you."

"That would be wonderful."

"Let's get back to the wonders of the giant leatherback turtle."

"Very well. Its shape is quite unique in that it is barrel shaped. Other turtles have a sharp angle formed between their hard carapace and their plastron or underbelly. As the leatherback does not have a hard shell, the plates of its carapace merge into its belly giving it this exclusive shape."

There were many other periods of instruction on these fascinating creatures. He learned that the females come ashore between June and September and it takes about one and a half hours for each of them to dig a nest, lay between sixty to one hundred eggs, cover them up and return to the sea. Meanwhile the males stay safely in the sea. It requires seven weeks for the eggs to hatch and then the two and a half inch young turtles must race for the relative safety of the sea.

"What do they eat to enable them to grow so big," asked Jack.

"Mainly jellyfish some other soft boded sea animals and plants".

Of particular interest to Jack was the beach location where the giant leatherbacks came ashore every year to lay their eggs. His mission on the upper East Coast was to thoroughly assess troop strength in relation to possible landing sites; therefore, his cover demanded a detailed knowledge of turtle habits to be totally plausible.

"The twelve mile stretch of beach where they nest is at Rantau Abang, about forty five miles south of Kuala Trengganu. My research leads me to believe they select this site for two reasons. One is its steeply sloping beach. A strong tide and this incline aid them to land their heavy bodies on the beach. Then they do not have to travel too far to dig their nests safely above the waterline."

"The second is a theory I am working on relating to the migratory habits of certain species of jellyfish. Some scientists believe it is a force of nature which causes them to return to the beach of their birth but in several tests this has been disproved. I believe it may be as uncomplicated as they follow their favorite food."

"After laying her eggs and covering the nest the leatherback leaves the nest unguarded. A small percentage of the eggs mature into adult turtles. On the beach they are attacked by birds and several predators await them in the sea. But by far the greatest predator is man. The local people dig up the nests for the eggs. They are considered a delicacy and believed to be an aphrodisiac."

"Aha, now I know why you are so interested in giant turtles, Hans. You dirty man."

"I do not eat the eggs you must not either Jack," responded Hans hotly. Then his face broke into his tight lipped smile and he said, "Perhaps one day I will not fall into your quick witted traps, Jack."

Their meetings continued in the same mixture of earnest study and good natured banter. Slowly, oh so slowly, Hans' sense of humor developed and occasionally he would ensnare Jack, on each such occasion his smile seemed to be a little less tight lipped.

"Are you prepared for the operation?" asked Lord Hino one evening as they enjoyed a whisky in his cabin.

"Yes I am, thanks to the outstanding tutoring by Hans."

"It sounds as though you have come to appreciate that 'kraut'," teased Hino.

"He is a fine man and I am concerned about him."

As if reading Jack's mind, Lord Hino said thoughtfully, "You are worried that his sister may have been forced to talk and German Intelligence may be waiting for him in Japan."

"Correct as usual. Can you signal your escort to have them find out?"

"I believe that could prove to be more harmful to the Professor. Such an enquiry requires great finesse. Unless I could talk directly to a trusted associate, I fear it could be clumsily handled and only alert my German friends. However when we arrive at Kobe, and if there is not a reception party awaiting the Professor, I will call a close friend in Tokyo to ascertain the status. Would that be suitable to you?"

"Thank you. I would appreciate that."

The days passed quicker that Jack had expected. Hans had a vast knowledge of subjects other than marine biology which greatly interested him, although he had to focus his attention primarily on his cover subject. Hans taught him much about other sea life including the green turtle which also frequented the east coast of the Malay Peninsula.

They experienced several days of stormy seas as they neared their destination. Jack weathered this period well and felt proud of himself; however, both Lord Hino and Hans were quite sick, particularly Lord Hino. It seemed to annoy Hino that Jack was not ill. Later Jack speculated this was probably the cause of an unpleasant dinner conversation.

The seas had calmed and everyone was looking forward to the imminent sighting of Japan. Dinner, on this particular evening, started jovially. Jack thought Hino was particularly jovial although his slightly red complexion told him Hino had been drinking in his cabin before dinner.

"Let's have a good bottle of wine to celebrate the completion of our voyage," said Hino. The 'good bottle' stretched to four good bottles.

It was Hans who inadvertently started the unpleasantness with a jocular request as the second bottle was being finished.

"Jack, please tell me the origin of the legend that all Scots are frugal. I believe it is also referred to as being stingy. Surely it isn't true. Is It?"

"Of course it is true," said Lord Hino. "They are the most tight fisted, mean spirited people on the face of this earth."

Jack had only seen signs of malice in Lord Hino on a very few occasions and felt this one was probably whisky induced. He decided to treat this comment with the studied composure he endeavored to display at Hino's less humorous jibes. However he also decided not to let an unremitting barrage of provocation go unanswered. So he chose his words carefully when he answered. "Thrift should be regarded as a virtue, not an undesirable quality and it should never, never be confused with a lack of generosity of the heart. Unfortunately Scotland is not an economically rich country and having a rich heritage does not feed a family. The average Scotsman struggles to meet the necessities of life but is always ready to help others in greater need if at all possible."

"The world would be a better place if people not only felt, but also exhibit respect for others in general; and in particular, displayed caring hearts for the needy. Instead many people seem to continually strive to hoard more and more possessions. Many more than they could possibly ever need for a comfortable life. The same could be said of nations. History teaches us that the greatest misery perpetuated on ordinary people has been by the avarice of strong nations in subjugating and enslaving weaker ones."

"Hah," barked Hino. "These are the rationalizations of a people devoid of pride. A people who have accepted their role as the serfs of the English. A people who make no contribution to the progress of mankind."

Hans tried to calm the situation by saying, "But surely you must agree Mr. Hino that Scotland has produced some great men. The impact on the world has been immense by literally hundreds of Scotsmen. Men such as Alexander Fleming and James Simpson in medicine; Robert Adams and Charles Rennie MacIntosh in architecture; Henry Raeburn and Allan Ramsey in art: David Hume and Adam Smith in philosophy; James Watt and Alexander Graham Bell in science; Walter Scott and Robert Burns in literature; and of course men like David Livingston and Andrew Carnegie."

"I thought you were supposed to instruct Simpson, it sounds like he has been brainwashing you, Professor," growled Hino.

Jack applauded Hans. "I could not have said it better."

"Furthermore Mr. Hino, with your naval background I would have thought you would have been well aware of two Scottish mariners of some note; William (Captain) Kidd, the famous Pirate and John Paul Younger who changed his last name to Jones and was so important in the creation of the American Navy."

Hino was clearly irritated by this history lesson.

"My dear Professor, a country cannot live on its past. It must have a vision for the future. To be fair this is not only the failing of Scotland but also of Britain. It is led by the so called noble class. A bunch of fat indolent men who sit in their clubs and long for the days of glory of their past empire, yet do nothing about building a future."

"At least we agree on that," said Jack.

"Yes the rich English are indolent and the Scots still do their bidding. They are incapable of lifting themselves out their own torpor. But despite the lecture on Scottish achievements given by the Professor, the fact remains your traditions are steeped in stupid clannish infighting and therefore when times are bad you lack the spiritual and cultural courage to fight your way out."

'Now you have gone too far' thought Jack. This unnecessary and unremitting barrage had to be answered.

"I dare say the Japanese are fortunate to have such a rich cultural heritage."

"Of course we are; we are a unique race" said Lord Hino rising to the bait.

Jack slammed the trap door shut when he said, "Scotland is not so fortunate as to be geographically placed next to the Korean peninsula. Otherwise it could have had the early migration of Koreans bringing their iron tools and Chinese culture to populate their land as they did in Japan. Once they took all they wished, they drove the early inhabitants, the Ainu, on to reservations in the furthest outpost in Hokkaido."

If Jack's comment was meant to elicit a hot response, it more than served its purpose; it got a volcanic one.

"That is the most monstrous lie I have ever heard," fumed Lord Hino. "There is absolutely no relationship between the Japanese and any other race. We are a pure race. To suggest a connection with Korea, of all places, is odious."

For once words failed him and his handsome face was distorted by his gaping mouth. He snapped it shut and lapsed into a sullen silence.

They had finished the third bottle. The fourth was drunk in a continued hush. Hans edgily glanced from one to the other but kept an anxious silence. When the last of the fourth bottle was consumed, they rose as if by some instinctive signal and went to their cabins. Hans and Jack exchanged goodnights, but Lord Hino did not speak.

The next morning Jack rose early and knocked on the door of Lord Hino's cabin. There was no answer. He went on deck and surveyed the calm sea. He almost jumped out of his skin when a voice said, "Good morning Mr. Simpson."

He whirled round to see the serious face of Lord Hino. He opened his mouth to say something, but before he could utter a sound Hino said, "Let's just agree that last night was an unfortunate aberration that we will do our best not to repeat. In terms of national slurs, shall we say the score is tied at one apiece and leave it at that? Shall we also agree there will be no rematch?"

"Agreed."

"No more racial insults?"

"Agreed."

Lord Hino bowed to seal the bargain. Jack returned the bow. His head was lower than Lord Hino's and he held this position until Lord Hino straightened.

"I was most impressed by what you said last night. Not about the origins of my country which were so blatantly wrong but regarding the manner in which people could improve the world."

Lord Hino paused for several seconds as he gazed at Jack.

"You are a strange dichotomy, Campbell. You have so much hate in your heart, yet you have the ability to eloquently communicate a philosophy of Man's ineptitude at attaining some semblance of equanimity."

They were silent for a while before Jack said, "You realize we broke our rule. You called me Campbell and we bowed to each other."

"I am aware of that; sometimes it is more important to repair a relationship than to be perfectly safe."

They both stared at the sea for a minute and then Lord Hino said, "Will you please inform the professor that all is now well. I fear we worried him more than each other last night."

"Poor Hans, he was troubled, wasn't he? I will set his mind at ease."

With that Jack left to talk to Hans. As he did, Lord Hino stared at his disappearing back and thought, 'I still find it difficult to believe how perfect Campbell is for my plan. His bloodline will be our salvation.'

Later that day they saw the island of Kyushu in the distance.

"Late tonight we dock at Kobe. Let us enjoy the last lunch of our voyage," said Lord Hino. They entered the dining room; Hans had to hold the door open for Jack who continued to stare at the coastline of Japan. At last he followed Hans to the table.

"With your permission Mr. Hino, I would like to propose a toast."

Lord Hino nodded his assent.

"To Professor Dr. Hans Mannheim, the best tutor anyone ever had. May he enjoy a happy sojourn in Japan."

They all drank to the toast proposed by Jack.

"You are too kind. It is I who am so deeply grateful to both of you. Firstly to you Mr. Hino for making this opportunity to conduct further research a possibility. It is a dream come true. A wonderful chance to begin a new life. Thank you, sir. Then to you Jack for teaching me to look beyond the world of academia and again realizing that life should have some time for joy. I promise to carry on spending time away from the solitude of my laboratory and seek the joy of seeing new places and meeting many new people. And of most importance, trying to do all this while remembering to keep a sense of humor."

"That is an excellent resolution Hans. It is totally in keeping with the sentiment of Goethe."

Lord Hino looked puzzled and asked Jack to explain.

"Please forgive my accent Hans while I try to quote your renowned poet."

"Es bildet ein Talent sich in der Stille
Sich ein Charakter in dem Strom der Welt."

"Can you translate that?" asked Lord Hino in a voice full of wonder.

"Genius develops in quiet places,
Character out in the full current of human life."

Jack was looking at Lord Hino while he said this. Then he looked at Hans who now stood with tears in his eyes, clapping his hands; and to his utter astonishment Jack saw that Hans' face seemed to have broken all its past bonds and was now wreathed in a most glorious smile which appeared to light up the room.

Chapter 10

It had been dark for some time when the ship docked. Lord Hino was first to disembark. He had asked Jack to stay with the Professor while he reconnoitered the situation. Jack was every bit as eager as Hans to be on deck; however, Hino had specifically requested that Hans remain in his cabin and thoroughly check that Jack had all of his notes and answer any last minute questions that Jack may have.

After twenty minutes of this it was obvious that Hans was no longer accepting this story as the cause of the delay.

"What is the problem, Jack?" he asked worriedly. "Where has Mr. Hino gone? Is he not going to say goodbye? Please tell me if my stay is in jeopardy."

"Everything will be all right, Hans. As you have observed Mr. Hino is a very careful man and is checking all the details of my arrival. It has nothing to do with you. As a precaution he has asked me to stay out of sight until he returns."

Jack was very convincing. Hans was immediately apologetic.

"Oh please forgive me Jack for being so selfishly worried and completely forgetting how difficult your situation must be. You see I suspected that Mr. Hino is a very powerful man in Japan as my position could only have been approved at the very highest level. My suspicion was confirmed by the way he was greeted when he left the ship. All the people on the dock were bowing so low, I could see them from my cabin window."

'This spy business must be rubbing off on you' thought Jack.

"Because of this, I assumed Mr. Hino would have arranged everything for you," continued Hans.

"In this line of work even powerful men have enemies. As this operation is very important to him, I am sure he is merely being especially careful."

Jack knew the more he talked the weaker his story would sound but luckily for him Lord Hino returned.

"Your luggage has been taken ashore Mr. Simpson. Everything is in order."

Jack caught the almost imperceptible nod of his head and knew Hans was safe.

"We shall say our goodbyes now Professor and wish you well in Yokohama. The ship will depart in an hour. I have cleared your documents with the authorities here; therefore you will have no need to clear customs in Yokohama. Professor Hayashi will be waiting for you."

They said their goodbyes with promises to keep in touch. As Jack descended the gangway to step foot on Japan for the first time, he felt an odd mixture of exhilaration and melancholy. As they entered the waiting car Jack was somewhat surprised at the feeling of loss he had experienced when he said goodbye to Hans. Hino had been right, he had come to not only appreciate this 'kraut' but also to value his friendship. Lord Hino sensed this and was quiet for a while.

"You never asked why we were staying in Kobe, Campbell."

"No my Lord, I knew you would tell me when you deemed the time to be appropriate."

Hino smiled in the darkness of the car.

"How insightful of you. Well there are two reasons. The first is this happens to be the current location of Professor Nishikawa whom you will meet tomorrow. This will be most instructive to you. The second is that I will have the great pleasure of meeting my niece who lives here."

"I believe you know my home is in Tokyo therefore we will stay in a delightful, small ryokan here in Kobe. As you know a ryokan is a Japanese inn. You now will have the opportunity of sampling the culture you have read so much about."

The car stopped in a dimly lit street where they entered the stone courtyard of the inn. It seemed to Jack the entire staff lay prostrate at the entrance. Lord Hino stepped out of his shoes and marched imperiously straight in. Jack fumbled with his laces and hurried after him. Like a flock of birds the maids arose and came twittering after them.

"This is your room, Campbell. We shall have a civilized bath, then a light snack before retiring. Put on your yukata, the maid will show you to the bath."

He gave the orders to the maids and they all bowed and set about their tasks. One maid bowed to Jack as she slid open the door to his room. Jack stood inside the door and stared in admiration at the Japanese room. It was sparsely yet elegantly furnished. It had a tatami mat floor with only a low table on it. At one end was an alcove with a beautiful flower arrangement above which hung a long hand painted scroll with golden tassels. He told the maid in Japanese how beautiful it was. She bowed in acknowledgement of the compliment then helped him off with his jacket. She then motioned for him to remove his shirt. She giggled at his hairy chest and held up the yukata or Japanese robe for him to put his arms through. Then with his back to her he took off his remaining clothes. When he had tied the belt round his yukata, the maid led him to the bath. Outside she handed him a cotton washcloth and opened the door.

Inside, the bathing area was filled with steam. A voice from the mist said, "Hang your yukata on a peg to your left and select a stool and a bucket. Do you know the procedure, Campbell?"

"From what I remember reading, you squat on the stool at the side of the bath, use the bucket to scoop water from the bath, lather up with soap then rinse off again using the bucket. Only when you are completely clean can you enter the bath to soak in the hot water."

"Excellent Campbell. Oh by the way, I asked that the bath be cleared of all other guests. I don't want you scaring the ladies."

That's when Jack remembered that bathing in Japan was a communal experience.

"Why are you just standing there? What is the problem?"

"In my reading it failed to mention the stool was only six inches high. This will take a little getting used to."

"Ha! Ha! Ha! Now isn't this more civilized than your ridiculous and unhealthy system where you lie in your own effluvia?"

Jack had to admit it was. When he had completed washing himself and was ready to enter the bath, Lord Hino warned him to be careful of the water temperature. Jack thought he could handle it. He was wrong. He immersed one leg in the scalding water then quickly withdrew it. Gradually he tried until he finally managed to sit in the bath with the water up to his neck. Once he became accustomed to the hot water Jack found soaking in this bath the most relaxing experience of his life. It was not too long before he became drowsy and almost asleep. Lord Hino noticed this and said, "I think that is quite enough time for your first Japanese bath."

Reluctantly Jack climbed out of the bath and stood looking around.

"Now what is your problem, Campbell?"

"I thought there would be a towel but I don't see one."

"You left it on your stool."

"No, that is my washcloth."

"It is also your towel."

"You must be joking."

"I am afraid not. Just keep wringing it out. With your present body heat, you will be surprised how effective it is."

And he was surprised. It was not perfect to Jack's mind but it was adequate.

He followed Lord Hino to his room where food had been set on the low table. Jack ate little and Hino could see he was sleepy.

"Let's call it a night," he said and walked along the corridor with Jack to his room.

The table had been moved to one side and a mattress or futon was spread on the floor. Jack slipped under the cover and said goodnight.

"Sleep well, tomorrow you attend school."

With that Lord Hino closed the sliding paper door. Jack was surprised how comfortable the futon was. He wondered what lay in store at this particular 'school' .He resolved not to be surprised with whatever it was and to 'out-Japanese' the Japanese by showing no emotion. His mind refused to allow him to think more and he drifted off to sleep.

In the morning he ate breakfast with Lord Hino in his room. Breakfast consisted of a small piece of fried fish, some pickles and rice. All of it served cold. Only the green tea was hot.

"We Japanese sometimes have sake with breakfast; however, I do not believe you are yet sufficiently Japanese to merit this privilege," said Lord Hino with a chuckle.

"Today you will meet the foremost authority on the mythological origin of Japan. He will conduct a special class for you and will explain how this belief has assisted in the shaping of the culture of Japan. I trust you will pay close attention at this special school."

School was an unprepossessing series of wooded buildings. They were met at the entrance by two young girls in blue uniforms, white blouses, black shoes and thick white ankle socks over their stockings. They bowed low, not raising their heads while saying their polite greetings. With their feet together, Jack noticed the slightly pigeon-toed slightly bow legged stance of many Japanese women. Far from being offensive it was somehow quite charming he thought. The rest of the welcoming group consisted of a phalanx of guards who were anything but charming. If they were meant to scare visitors, they succeeded. Unusually tall for Japanese, taut muscles showed through their uniforms, but the major impact came from their ferocious facial features. Their heels clicked in unison and they too bowed very low.

Two of these gruesome guards accompanied Lord Hino and Jack down several corridors. The highly polished floors creaked as they strode along. Lord Hino stopped outside a glass and wood door. 'Just like a bloody school,' thought Jack.

Lord Hino entered without knocking.

"Good morning, Nishikawa-sensei."

"Good morning, my Lord."

"This is Campbell, the one I referred to on the telephone."

"Ah, I am pleased to meet you," said Nishikawa in English.

"How do you do. I am very pleased to meet you Nishikawa-sensei," said Jack in Japanese.

"Do not get your hopes up too high, his Japanese is not perfect. You must speak English to avoid misunderstandings."

"His accent is very good."

"One of Campbell's many talents is to mimic well. I hope he will pay close attention, thereby learning much from your great knowledge."

When Lord Hino left, Nishikawa eyed Jack closely.

"So you want to learn all there is to know about Japan in six hours?" Nishikawa's demeanor had undergone a complete change. His servile manner had completely disappeared, being replaced by a swaggering posture. His lips curled as he spoke. His English was technically correct but his pronunciation was poor. 'He has studied well but has not lived abroad,' thought Jack.

Nishikawa Hiro was the first-born son of a military officer but a birth defect left him with one leg shorter than the other. This caused him to hobble in an ungainly manner. The shame this brought not only to himself but also to his family, particularly his father, had been almost too much to bear.

It was only at Tokyo University, where he so excelled, that his father, at last, managed to speak to him. His career as a Professor of Political Science at that same hallowed university distinguished him to such an extent that Cabinet Ministers, even the Prime Minister, sought his counsel. Only when his father was on his deathbed did he admit to Hiro that it had been his strong desire to sell him as a young boy to a farming family that had no children of their own. His mother threatening to commit suicide had stopped this. His perpetual fear of a friend of the family knowing of this and letting it slip still haunted him and had given him an insecurity psychosis of enormous proportions.

His superior intellect allowed him to hide his problem; however, he was a bitter man and he took delight in ridiculing students and almost anyone who disagreed with his point of view. He particularly disliked foreigners.

"Tell me why I should waste my time on you."

'The obvious answer is, you stupid arse, because you have been told to do so by Lord Hino,' thought Jack. Sanity prevailed; Jack looked at the floor and said, "I am deeply sorry to cause you so much trouble Sensei. I do not deserve this honor. All I can say is the Land of Amaterasu, The Sun Goddess, is intensely interesting to me. I am conscious of my lack of knowledge of the Japanese people and their unique culture and consider it a great honor to have the rare privilege to listen to the greatest authority on this matter."

Jack thought, 'I better stop here or I will throw up.'

Nishikawa had been buttered up by the best in his time, nevertheless he was impressed by the quick wittedness of Jack and he thought, 'At least he shows respect by not looking me in the eye like most foreigners'.

"You are probably worthless but out of respect for my Lord Hino I will try to get a little knowledge into that thick head of yours."

"Thank you Sensei."

Nishikawa moved to the other side of his desk and sat down. From his low seat, Jack could just see his head. It reminded him of a fairground coconut stand, in fact with his tufts of hair sticking up; Nishikawa's head looked like a coconut. Jack wished he had a hard ball; he would dearly love to knock his supercilious head off his 5' 3" frame.

These feelings were soon forgotten, and for the next six hours Jack was mesmerized by the skill with which Nishikawa gave his view of glory of Japan's history and its future role in the world.

He started where Jack had left off with the myth of Amaterasu as reported in Nihon Shoku, the Records of Japan, written in 720 AD. Amaterasu Omikami the supreme deity of the Shinto religion sent her grandson, Niniginomikoto, to lead the Gods on the Descent to Earth. One account claims he hurled his sword to earth where it landed on top of a volcano, now called Takachiho, in Kyushu, the southernmost island of Japan. His great grandson, Jimmu, became the first Emperor of Japan in 660 BC.

Campbell already knew much of this, however, the interesting part came next being the explanation of the importance of Shintoism to the basic culture of Japan. Shinto was the first religion in Japan, probably starting 500 to 800 BC and unlike most other religions does not have a founder. The essence of Shinto is usually misunderstood when translated as The Way of the Gods. It is The Way of the Kami. Kami can be classified into three main types. Ancestral deities, such as Amaterasu; deification of a power of nature, such as wind, rain, trees or mountains; or, dead leaders, such as emperors or great heroes. There are perhaps 100,000 Shinto shrines in Japan, each one dedicated to a particular kami. Shintoism stresses purity which is why one must ritually wash one's mouth and hands before approaching a shrine. This purity denotes respect for the Emperor, Japan, ancestors and family. Perhaps this is why the Japanese consider themselves a pure race and tend to be intolerant of foreign encroachment.

The other main religion observed in Japan, Buddhism, was imported from China in the sixth and seventh century.

"Unlike your Western nations where religions compete with one another, here in Japan we happily embrace both Shintoism and Buddhism. Some of us even have a third religion, Christianity. This was introduced to Japan by the Portuguese Jesuit St Francis Xavier in 1549."

"By 1600 much of Japan was Christian and then the Tokugawa Shogunate banned it and persecuted Christians. Today, maybe ten percent of Japanese are Christians."

When the lesson was over, Jack expressed his appreciation to Nishikawa and this time he meant it. Jack's earnest and insightful questions during the lesson had impressed Nishikawa. He said to Jack, "I too enjoyed this meeting. I will report to Lord Hino you have been an attentive and intelligent pupil."

Late in the afternoon Jack sat with Lord Hino in his room drinking tea. He sensed a difference in Hino's mood but said nothing. He suspected something had gone wrong in the war. He waited. Hino stared into space almost in a trance. Finally he spoke in a low intense manner.

"I fear history will judge us badly following this war. Nishikawa-sensei will no doubt have told that Japan has been a collection of fiefdoms for most of its history. The feudal Lord had absolute power over his people.

Some of these Lords would kill with as little thought as swatting a fly and for the same reasoning, that they had been annoyed. Due to this, the common person has been repressed for too long. War can be an excuse to vent one's anger and I am afraid we have already seen this in China."

"To a foreigner, there is an apparent strong desire for perfection in the Japanese. They see our tea ceremony; our ikebana flower arrangement; our fastidiousness for cleanliness, both in our homes and our personal hygiene; our gentle geisha; even our origami paper folding. If a keen observer were to peer under this veneer he would discover a coarseness created by centuries of repression that can erupt with lightning speed and when we look at its consequences, we are sick with remorse."

"Unfortunately there is a very dark side to our national character which war always seems to expose. Perhaps this is true of many nations; however, it still shocks us when we are confronted by it."

Campbell now knew Hino was struggling with a dilemma. This lecture was his way of resolving some issue in his mind. Hino continued, "Every race of historical importance has a complex character; it is easy to see the surface but dangerously wrong to predict actions based on such a superficial analysis. But war, Campbell, lays bare some of the facets of national character for the insightful observer. Oftentimes we would prefer that these observations were never made, we do not want to study ourselves too closely in the mirror of war."

After thirty seconds of silence Lord Hino seemed to shake himself out of his reverie.

"Enough of this moral sermonizing. I heard you were a good pupil. It takes a lot to impress Nishikawa-sensei, so I have a reward for you." Smiling broadly, he continued, "I have arranged dinner for you. Unfortunately I must attend a meeting but you will dine with my niece at her house. It is not too far from here. My own car has arrived from Tokyo therefore I can drop you off."

Hino's car turned out to be a Rolls Royce. Jack had noticed many British cars on the trips to and from school. He commented on this to Lord Hino.

"Some of these cars are manufactured in Japan under license agreements. Since we Japanese drive on the left side of the road like the British it is easier to transfer technology which needs no modification than to import technology from say Germany. One should never do anything complicated when there is a simple solution."

It was a short drive to Nishinomiya on the outskirts of Kobe. The house was surrounded by a wooden fence six feet high. As if by magic the door slid open and two servants bowed from a kneeling position, their heads touching the polished wood floor. Lord Hino slipped off his shoes without untying the laces. This was a skill Jack had yet to master, so he sat on a cushion on the step and untied his shoes. The maids quickly placed them on a rack at the side of the entrance. Hino marched through the open shoji doors into the main room.

"Ah, Michiko, good evening. This is my friend Jack Campbell. Campbell, may I introduce my niece, Kojima Michiko."

She was kneeling on the tatami, her head bowed in respect. Beside her a low lacquered table was set for dinner. When she looked up, Jack's breathing stopped. He was looking at the most beautiful sight he had ever witnessed.

"Good evening my Lord," she said in Japanese, then stood up in one flowing motion and extended her hand to Jack.

"I am pleased to meet you Campbell-san, my uncle has told me much about you," she said in English.

Michiko was taller than the average Japanese woman, perhaps 5' 4" Jack estimated. She wore a cream colored silk kimono with a floral pattern in subdued blues and yellows. As she stood waves of light flowed rhythmically through her thick black hair.

"It is my honor to meet you Kojima-san," said Jack in Japanese.

"Now that you two have been introduced, I must go. I should be back in about two hours."

The shoji door closed silently behind Lord Hino.

"Please sit, Campbell-san."

"Thank you, Kojima-san. After you."

"No. You must learn that in Japan it is always the man who sits first. It is our custom. And as you say, 'When in Rome do as the Romans do.' I have never been in Rome, but I can assure you that in this country we are rigid in following our customs."

Jack sat on the tatami. No sooner had Michiko sat when the door opened and the maids brought in three appetizer dishes, a bottle of beer and two small bottles of sake. Michiko was describing the appetizers as she placed one of each on Jack's plate. His silence caused her to look at him. He just sat, immobile, staring intently into her almond shaped eyes. He was mesmerized by these beautiful deep pools full of luster. She put down the serving hashi, said something while lowering her head. Drawing himself out of his trance, he realized she had been talking to him.

"I, I, I'm sorry," he stuttered. "I did not hear what you said."

She was silent for a moment then said in a low voice, "You were looking at me so fixedly; I asked you if there was something wrong with my appearance. I know we are different from western women. Perhaps we Japanese women displease you."

"Oh no, no, no."

Now it was his turn to lower his head, gulping for air. He struggled to breathe. Finally, with his head still lowered, he said, "Please forgive me for staring. It was most rude of me. I cannot apologize enough. My only excuse is that I have never seen anyone of such beauty in my entire life."

He glanced up. She still had her head lowered.

"In Japan, It is not customary to say such things to a lady whom you have just met."

"Once again I can only apologize. Such behavior is not customary or acceptable in my country, either. Since I have caused you so much anguish, I had better leave."

He stood and turned towards the door.

"My uncle wished us to have dinner. We should honor his wish. Please sit."

"Perhaps we can start over," said Jack sitting.

"My name is Campbell and I am very pleased to meet you Kojima-san."

"My name is Kojima Michiko and I welcome you to my humble home."

She said this with a slight smile and Jack's heart soared.

Again she explained the appetizers and then asked, "Would you prefer beer or sake, or maybe a whisky from your country?"

"Thank you, I would prefer sake."

Michiko poured the sake noting his good manners as he held his sake cup in both hands.

"May I offer you sake?" asked Jack.

"Thank you."

When he had poured he raised his cup, saying, "Campai."

"Campai," she responded.

Jack sipped his sake noticing Michiko raised her cup to her lips moistening them, but did not drink.

"Don't you like sake?" he asked.

"I do not drink alcohol."

She saw the look of puzzlement on his face.

"In my country it is not usual for a man to pour sake for a lady, except perhaps in a geisha house, but almost never otherwise. You did me the honor of offering to pour me a cup. It would have been impolite to refuse."

"I have studied much about Japan but I see I have much still to learn."

Michiko said "Wasn't it Alexander Pope who wrote 'A little learning is a dang'rous thing'?"

Jack tried to hide his astonishment at this quotation.

"You are very well read, Kojma-san."

"Thank you, my uncle provided excellent tutors for me."

The next two hours flew past. Jack learned she was not only intelligent and well read but she also has a sense of humor. She asked him if most Scots were heavy drinkers. He had to admit many were, but not all; why did she ask?

I have read many poems written by your famous poet, Robert Burns. I did not understand all of the Scottish language. One I liked very much concerned a man who seemed to drink a great deal which upset his wile. It was called Tam o' Shanter. I especially liked the lines describing his wife waiting angrily for him as he was again late and no doubt drunk. Do you know these lines?"

Jack quoted them.

"Whare sits our sulky sullen dame,
Gathering her brows like gathering storm,
Nursing her wrath to keep it warm."

"Yes, yes," cried Michiko, clapping her hands.

They were laughing over this when Lord Hino appeared.

"Did you enjoy dinner, Campbell?"

"Oh yes, it was wonderful, an epicurean delight."

"Ah so. May I ask what type of fish you ate?"

"You may indeed, my first taste of fugu."

Jack had read of this poisonous blowfish, native to the Pacific Ocean and considered a delicacy in Japan. When under threat this fish will inflate its body and project spikes which contain a particularly nasty poison, tetrodotoxin, reputed to be more than one thousand times deadlier than cyanide. The poison is stored in the liver and it is said there is enough poison in one fish to kill thirty people. The meat of the fish is usually served as sashimi. Jack had read unofficial reports that hundreds of people die each year in Japan due to fugu chefs being insufficiently skilled or careless.

"I am honored to have enjoyed the one delicacy the Emperor is not allowed to eat."

"You see how much he has read about our country Michiko?"

"He says he has much more to learn, my Lord."

"Ah, it is only a wise man that recognizes how little he knows. Now we must go."

"May I use the toilet before we leave?" asked Jack.

"Of course" said Michiko, clapping her hands to summon a maid, "she will show you the way."

When Jack had left, Lord Hino turned to Michiko and said, "Well, my niece, what do you think?"

"He appears to be a nice man."

"Can you do it? This is essential to the future of our beloved country and next to our Emperor you are the person I love most. I would not have asked you to do this if I did not absolutely believe you are the most talented person for this task. Will you do it?"

"You know I could never refuse anything you wish my Lord."

Hino's voice softened as he said, "I know, my dear Michiko, but you must do this willingly or it will be of no avail. Please remember Campbell must suspect nothing. He is not to be underestimated. He has the uncanny ability to almost read people's thoughts."

"I will do my very best." Michiko daubed her moist eyes.

"Ah, here is Campbell, I will say goodnight Michiko."

"I thank you for a truly delightful evening, Kojima-san, and hope to have the pleasure of seeing you soon," said Jack.

'You will, Campbell, my niece has agreed to guide you around Kobe, the day after tomorrow."

At the entrance Jack had to sit on the step to put on his shoes while Lord Hino just stepped into his. They said their goodbyes and as they went to the car Jack felt as though he was walking on air.

Chapter 11

The next day was spent going over the plans for Malaya. To Jack the day dragged on and on and on. That night he found it very difficult to sleep. He arose at six in the morning and had bathed, dressed and eaten breakfast by seven thirty. Michiko was to arrive at nine so he spent the next one and a half hours pacing around the small garden.

At precisely nine, Michiko arrived in a chauffeur driven car. She was wearing a pale yellow dress and Jack thought his heart would burst. He had to gulp for air before he could say, "Good morning Kojima-san. That is a beautiful dress. How are you today?" 'That sounded all wrong,' he thought.

"I am well, thank you, Campbell-san. My uncle kindly provided a car for our tour of Kobe. Shall we begin?"

Her tone was almost business like, even a little chilly. She had not responded to his compliment. Jack was crestfallen. Since he left her house, all he could do was think of her and look forward to this moment. He had not been sure what to expect when they met again; but it was not this formal greeting. Perhaps he had upset her more than she had acknowledged the night before last.

"Before we begin, Kojima-san, I would like to apologize again if I in any way offended you the other night."

"There is no need to apologize Campbell-san. You were not to know our customs. Let us not mention it again. Now shall we begin?"

"Of course, Kojima-san."

The driver held open the door for Michiko, bowing low as he did so. Jack opened the door on the other side of the car and climbed in next to Michiko. She said something to the driver who replied, "Hai, wakari-mashita" meaning, 'yes I understand'.

"I have asked the driver to start our tour at the docks. I understand it was already dark when you arrived and due to the black out regulation you could not see all the dockside area. I trust that is acceptable to you?"

"Of course, Kojima-san."

He sat in a dejected silence, wondering how things could have changed so much.

Michiko had not slept well for two nights, wrestling with the weight of the dilemma into which her uncle had placed her. She understood the request her uncle had made last year could be vital to the future of her beloved Japan. At the time she had reluctantly agreed, again for the sake of Japan and the Emperor. She had an obligation to the Emperor as she, too, was of Royal Blood. She came from a different branch of the Royal family than the Emperor nevertheless, she could never refuse anything His Majesty asked. Yet His Majesty had not instructed her to do this terrible thing, he requested she consider it. She felt she could still back out. Last year when she had agreed, it all seemed so theoretical. Now it was real.

At four in the morning, Michiko had made her decision. She would conduct this silly tour of Kobe, then she would tell her uncle he would have to get someone else, she would not do it. But she was nervous, so the sooner she faced her uncle the better.

She came out of her reverie and recognized how quiet Jack had been. She felt a pang of guilt. None of this was his fault yet she had treated him as though he was to blame for her sleepless nights and internal turmoil. She turned to him and said, "Perhaps you are wondering why we are going to the docks."

"What?" he answered in a startled manner. He had been lost in his own unhappy reverie.

"I beg your pardon, Kojima-san. What did you say?"

She readily noticed the difference in his face from the happy one he wore when he first greeted her this morning and again felt a pang of guilt.

"I said you may wonder why we are going to the docks."

"It does seem a bit unusual."

"Kobe is the most cosmopolitan city in Japan, even more so than To-kyo. This is because it has historically been the port most open to foreign shipping. You can still see the offices of many of these foreign companies around the dock area. As it is a relatively small city, the foreign population became a much larger percentage of the total population than anywhere else in Japan. So Japanese people in Kobe became used to the different customs of foreigners and because of this, they became more tolerant towards them. All of this makes Kobe a special Japanese city hence I thought we should start at the docks; because, that is where Kobe really started."

"Thank you Kojima-san, that sounds like an excellent plan."

Jack's voice was flat but courteous. Michiko noticed this and thought, 'I was not wrong about this man; he is a decent person at heart.'

The tour of the docks did exactly what Michiko had described; it vividly demonstrated the historic international aspect of Kobe. Despite his great disappointment, Jack was fascinated by the description Michiko gave of early Kobe and asked many questions. When over, Michiko suggested they climb the nearby Mount Rokko.

"You can see all of Kobe from there. Kobe is a very narrow city wedged between the Rokko mountain range and the sea. Would you like to do this?"

"Yes please," said Jack in a more animated voice.

She noticed this too and felt – what? – a warmth within her, 'it's only gratitude that he is responding positively to my instruction,' she told herself.

The car took them along a winding road part-way up the mountain.

"We can walk from here. We may not get all the way up but we should get close to the top."

As they left the car to begin their climb, she wrote a note to her uncle telling him it was important that they meet tonight. She told the driver to deliver the note to her uncle and to return in three hours.

There was a well defined path indicating many people climbed this mountain on a regular basis. To Jack it was hardly a mountain, probably somewhere between two and three thousand feet high. Not that Scotland had very high mountains, Ben Nevis the highest was only four thousand four hundred feet, nothing compared to the Himalayas or the Rockies.

"Rokko-san is very special to us even though it is tiny compared to Mt. Everest."

Jack's footing slipped and he finished up sitting on the path.

"Campbell-san, did you hurt yourself?"

Jack laughed. "Not in the least. I was so startled by your comment that I tripped."

She looked at him quizzically.

"Believe it or not, but I also was thinking of the Himalayas. It was as though you read my mind."

He got up and dusted himself off.

"I am not usually so clumsy. I beg your pardon if I worried you. I seem to be either saying the wrong thing or doing the wrong thing when I am with you."

She laughed with him and helped remove some of the dust from his back.

"As I said Rokko-san is not very tall, only nine hundred and thirty meters. Not nearly as high as Fuji-sama that is three thousand eight hundred meters. And not nearly as high as the Himalayas."

They continued the climb stopping occasionally to admire the view.

"What is the name of that other mountain?"

"That is mount Maya. As you can see it is smaller than Rokko-san. Both can be seen from anywhere in Kobe and also from Osaka."

After another half hour Michiko said, "If you do not mind I would like to rest for a while Campbell-san."

"Of course, lets sit over there it has some shade."

He took off his jacket and spread it on the ground for Michiko.

"This may keep your dress from getting dirty."

"Thank you."

They sat looking at the city, not talking, for quite some time. Finally she said, "Please tell me about Scotland Campbell-san."

He told her of the beauty of the highlands and the lochs; of the rugged west coast and the pastoral peacefulness of the border country. She could tell by the tone of his voice even more so than the words how passionately he felt for his country.

They sat admiring the view. It came as a greater shock to him than her when suddenly he said, "My parents are dead."

It came as a shock to her when she heard herself say, "As are mine."

"I am sorry," he said.

"They died six years ago within four months of each other."

"My father died from injuries in World War I. I was only two years old. My mother died when I was thirteen. I still miss her."

Without warning tears began to stream down his face and then he started to sob quietly. He had never grieved as much as he did now. Michiko put her arms around him, tears sliding down her own face. He put his arms around her and they sat there for a long time rocking back and forth. At last he pulled out a handkerchief and handed it to her. She daubed her cheeks and eyes and handed it back to him to dry his tears.

"I don't know what made me so emotional. It has never happened before. I hope I did not offend you Kojima-san."

"No one ever fully recovers from the death of a beloved parent and the smallest thing can bring back unhappy memories. I have been told it is even more painful for a parent to lose a child. I believe it is inevitable to grieve from time to time and I feel honored you could do so with me, Campbell-san."

They continued to sit and look at the view of the city, saying nothing but thinking a lot.

She had that warm feeling again and rationalized it as merely a feeling of sympathy for a grieving fellow human being; someone whose grief had brought back her own. Yet why did this foreigner she hardly knew, have the capacity to bring out these emotions in her when no one else had been able to do so? She had no answer for that question. He felt a strange calmness and at first thought it was the cathartic effect of grieving yet his instinct told him it was more than that. Each time he had met Michiko his emotions jangled as though by electric shock. But now he realized the peacefulness he had never felt as an adult was caused by her.

As a boy he had loved his mother and his granny. He had never loved as an adult. Perhaps this dichotomous condition of being jolted by passion yet being able to feel gloriously serene was adult love. To someone as insular as he, it was a thrilling yet frightened thought. Nonetheless he believed Michiko was someone he could share his innermost thoughts with and feel secure in doing so. The more he pondered this, the less sure he was of this new sensation; even his considerable intellect could not aid him in this situation.

Almost as though he had no control over it, his hand stretched out palm upwards. He did not dare speak. Michiko hesitated for a few seconds then, not looking at him directly, placed her hand in his.

Several more seconds passed before she looked at him.

"Thank you for being so understanding Kojima-san, I feel much better now."

"You are welcome Campbell-san. I also feel better."

She withdrew her hand gently and said, "I am a very inconsiderate hostess. You must be hungry. May I suggest we have lunch?"

"That would be great."

"Have you ever had sukiyaki?"

"I have read about it but never eaten it."

"I know a good restaurant. Our Kobe beef is quite famous in Japan. Did you know that the cows are massaged with sake and are occasionally given beer to drink?"

Jack laughed, "You are joking with me, aren't you?"

"No it is true. It is said to relax the cows thereby making the beef tenderer."

"This will be the first time I have eaten drunken cow."

They laughed and she said, "I am sure you will enjoy it. Shall we go?"

They walked back down the hill to where the driver was waiting. Michiko gave him instructions and he took them to a quiet street on the outskirts of the city.

As they entered the restaurant Jack said, "Oh oh, shoes off again."

"Yes this is a traditional Japanese restaurant and we will eat in a tatami room."

One of the young girls who greeted them scurried off upon seeing Michiko and returned with the owner who touched her head to the floor in a most respectful greeting. Jack had wondered before about the unusual amount of respect shown by others towards Michiko, but was too enthralled by the prospect of spending more time with her to ask questions.

They were led into a private room already set up for dining. In the middle of the room was a hibachi in which charcoal glowed brightly. They sat down on opposite sides of the hibachi and almost immediately a kimono clad lady appeared and after greeting them, sat at the end of the hibachi.

She asked them what they would like to drink; Michiko ordered an orange soda and Jack a beer. When the drinks had been served the cook put a large piece of fat in the pan on top of the hibachi.

She melted just enough to coat the pan then placed very thin slices of beef in the pan. While they were cooking she cracked an egg into each of the two serving bowls and whisked them vigorously. The cooked beef was put into the raw egg and handed to Jack first. He had never tasted such succulent beef and said so to the cook. After that came various vegetables including bamboo shoots, followed by more beef. The cook kept up a steady stream of banter during all this time to the amusement of both Michiko and Jack. He surreptitiously glanced at Michiko from time to time and the few times she caught him doing so she held his glance for a several seconds before looking down.

In Japanese fashion they refilled each other's glass with their respective drinks. Jack offered beer to the cook. She made a fuss of such a kind offer, but there could be no doubt she was happy to accept. She took Jack's glass and dunked it several times in a bowl of water. When she finished her beer, she did the same then wiped the rim on a clean napkin before returning the glass to Jack. Michiko explained in English, "In your country I believe it is customary to offer someone a drink in a different glass; however, in Japan if the server is offered a drink it is always from your glass."

Jack offered the cook several glasses of beer. Each time there was a display of a little reluctance quickly followed by eager acceptance.

"Many of the ladies who work in restaurants like this one are very strong drinkers. Some guests made the mistake of challenging them to a drinking contest and always lose. Most Japanese men are not strong drinkers."

"I had better be careful then," he said in mock seriousness.

Once again they were laughing. It seemed the entire time had been spent in an amusing and easy flowing style.

When rice was served it signaled the end of the main course. For dessert they were served juicy musk melon and coffee.

Jack looked at his watch and could not believe they had been in the restaurant for an hour and forty five minutes. He said, "Perhaps I have taken up too much of your time Kojima-san; however, I have had a wonderful tour of your lovely city. Thank you very much."

"I have enjoyed it too Campbell-san. I am sure I will see you again. My uncle will inform me when he wishes us to meet again. Now I will take you back to your hotel as I have an appointment later today."

Jack was tempted to hold out his hand again in the car but thought better of it. He believed the iciness of this morning had completely thawed and did not want to risk jeopardizing the current situation. They chatted animatedly all the way to the hotel. He said goodbye in the car and stood waving until the car was out of sight.

He sighed deeply in satisfaction as he walked towards the entrance. As soon as he was spotted the flock of welcoming maids began flapping and twittering.

As Michiko entered her house a maid mentioned her uncle was waiting in the garden. She had not expected to see him until later. She hurried to the garden where Lord Hino was pacing up and down with a cup of green tea in his hand.

"Good afternoon uncle, I am sorry to keep you waiting, I thought our meeting was tonight."

"Good afternoon Michiko. It was, but I could not contain my curiosity as to the reason you requested such an urgent meeting."

"It is no longer urgent, uncle. I have changed my mind."

Hino stopped pacing. Blood seemed to drain from his face leaving it pale. He steadied himself as he carefully chose his next words. He could have a fierce temper and this had been known to make men quake in their shoes. Women would dissolve in tears. But he knew his niece; she had more steel in her spine than most men he knew. If he let his temper get the better of him it would only increase her stubbornness. His carefully thought out plan, Empire, was in danger of being thwarted.

'But Michiko, last year you gave this very serious and careful consideration before accepting."

"That is correct uncle and I will continue to do so."

"To do what?" Now some exasperation was creeping into his voice.

"Why, to give it serious consideration of course uncle."

Lord Hino felt weak at the knees. He was completely lost.

"My dear niece, please sit down and stop pacing. Just now you said you had changed you mind. This means you are no longer willing to help your Emperor and your country."

"Not so uncle. That was before I changed my mind."

Hino sat down with a thump and Michiko stared at him with concern.

"What is wrong uncle? Are you unwell?"

"I am completely confused my niece."

"Let me explain. I did not sleep last night trying to decide what to do. Early this morning I decided not to proceed with my role in Empire and to tell you to get someone else. Now I have changed my mind and am willing to give it serious consideration. I am not yet certain I can go ahead but I do not feel nearly as negative as I did this morning. Is that clear to you uncle?"

"I think so."

Hino laid the teacup on the garden table and said, "May I have a whisky Michiko?"

"Of course uncle."

She ran to the house calling on the maid to bring whisky. When he had two large gulps of whisky he turned to her again.

"Michiko, this is one of the most important things in out Country's future, yet you are almost dancing around lightheartedly. This is most unlike you. Please tell me you understand the importance of Empire."

She stared into his eyes and said gravely, "I do uncle, believe me I do."

"Thank you Michiko," he said, worriedly gulping down more whisky.

"Did you enjoy your tour with Campbell?'

"Yes uncle."

"That is all you have to say just 'Yes uncle'?"

"Well he is not what I expected from your description."

"In what way?"

"When you described him you used words like, intelligent, strong, resourceful, confident and determined. He most probable has those qualities; however, he is also caring, honest, respectful and has a deep rooted sense of loyalty."

"No, no my niece. There you are wrong. If he were loyal he would not be working for us."

Michiko poured him another whisky. He nodded his thanks.

"Forgive me uncle but I do not believe I am wrong. For you loyalty is all about your country. It is given unconditionally because that is the way you were raised. For him loyalty is to his family and his friends."

"From what you have told me the authorities of his country treated his family abominably, therefore to him they do not deserve loyalty. I believe he feels loyalty should not be given without thought; it should be earned like respect."

Lord Hino listened with his eyes closed.

"You are wise beyond your years my niece. You have the ability to analyze situations and particularly people, quicker than anyone I have ever known. This is not the first time I have witnessed this skill. Yet I find it hard to accept your analysis of Campbell given the short time you have been with him. If you are correct he is much more talented then even I have recognized and therefore much more valuable. Are you agreeable to continuing to see him?"

"Yes uncle. I would welcome that opportunity."

He looked up quickly but Michiko was staring at him guilelessly.

"Do you know my niece; I am beginning to recognize you have been manipulating me for a long, long time. All these years I have thought you were a very obedient child. Instead you have been making me do exactly what you wanted but somehow making me believe it was all my idea."

"How can you say such a thing, uncle?"

She pouted then burst out laughing and threw her arms around his neck.

"Perhaps we are too much alike my dear uncle."

"Perhaps."

"How long will you stay in Kobe uncle?"

"Probably two or three weeks, then Campbell and I must go to Tokyo. I think it would be good if the three of us had dinner tomorrow night. Then you should continue to show him around. Perhaps you could spend some time in Nara and Kyoto."

"As you know uncle, I love Kyoto. You have taken me there so many times. I am sure Campbell-san would find it most interesting."

"Of that I have no doubt. But I do not want his interest to be restricted to Kyoto; I need him to be interested in you."

Chapter 12

Four days later they were on their way to Kyoto; Jack, Michiko and her two maids. Lord Hino decided to stay in Kobe citing some important meetings. He took Jack to the train station where they were to meet Michiko. He bought the tickets, two first class ones for Jack and Michiko and two third class ones for the maids, and handed them to Jack along with a wad of money.

"This is for incidental expenses. The hotel will send the bill to me."

"Thank you. That is most generous," said Jack eyeing the large sum of money.

"You must take good care of my niece, Campbell, and to do so can be expensive. I know this from experience."

They were standing at the platform when Michiko arrived. Perhaps arrived doesn't adequately describe the scene; made her entrance is probably more accurate. She was wearing a light blue kimono and was followed by her two maids, each carrying two handbags. Bringing up the rear were four aki-bo, or red caps as the porters were called, struggling with eight large suitcases. Following their greetings, Jack looked at his one case and said to Michiko, "I thought we were only going for a week."

"We are," said Michiko, "that is why I only brought six suitcases, the other two belong to my maids."

Jack looked at Lord Hino who arched his eyebrows in an amused look.

It took some time to get everyone aboard the train. First it was the luggage which took a little organizing, then the maids who changed carriages three times before being satisfied and finally Michiko and Jack.

As the train chugged out of the station they waved goodbye to Lord Hino. Michiko and Jack sat opposite each other by the windows. They were the only passengers in their compartment. Jack, ever fascinated by this new country, stared out of the window at the passing scenery. The small wooden houses with their brightly colored tiled roofs were built close together. Some of them were two storied but most had only one level. Virtually every one had one or two futons hanging over a pole or a balustrade to air. Other poles sported washing hanging out to dry.

"You really like Japan don't you Campbell-san?"

"Yes, I do. Almost everything is so different from Britain, yet, somehow, I feel comfortable here."

The ticket collector noisily announced his arrival. He took off his hat and bowed before inspecting, then clipping their tickets. When he left Jack looked over at Michiko as she picked a handkerchief out of her purse. As she looked up and caught his gaze he moved next to her.

"The last few days have been a wonderful time for me."

"I have enjoyed it too, Campbell-san."

"May I hold your hand Kojima-san?"

"That would not be proper, Campbell-san."

He was very disappointed and his face clearly showed this. When he looked at her she was smiling broadly.

"To hold hands would only be appropriate if we knew each other well. And if we did, you would not call me Kojima-san, you would call me Michiko. And I would not call you Campbell-san, I would call you Jack."

He assumed a very serious look and said, "May I hold your hand Michiko?"

She stopped smiling and also put on a serious face when replying, "Yes Jack."

They both burst out laughing and sat holding hands until the train stopped in Osaka. A man opened the carriage door, as he entered Jack quickly resumed his original seat. Michiko grinned behind her hand in a conspiratorial fashion almost all the way to Kyoto.

They took three taxis from the Railway station to the hotel. One for Michiko and Jack; one for the maids; and the third for the overflow of luggage which did not fit in the other two. The taxis were immaculate. The drivers had been cleaning the outside with feather dusters as they arrived. On the inside the seats and floors looked as though they had just been vacuumed and each headrest had a white linen cover. Each driver wore a dark suit, freshly pressed white shirt and a dark tie. All wore hats and white gloves. It seemed the Japanese dedication to cleanliness was not limited to personal hygiene, but extended to everything, even their taxis.

The hotel was again a Japanese style one, a ryokan, and was on top of a hill. The road leading up to it was cobble stoned and had rail lines for a tram service which happily clanged its way up and down. Jack's room was on the third floor of the hotel. Michiko and her maids had adjoining rooms on the second floor. His room was more spacious than the one in Kobe and the water painting in the alcove, more beautiful. He counted the number of Tatami mats and found it was two mats larger than Kobe. He had learned that the Japanese measured the size of a room or even a house by the number of tatami mats. All mats were made to a standard size, 1.9 x 0.9 meters and the common measurement of a room was in tsubo. Two tatami mats equaled one tsubo. It suddenly struck him how rapidly he was adapting to Japan if the first thing he did upon entering a hotel room was count the number of tsubo or admire the long painting which always hung in the tokonoma or alcove.

The shoji door slid open and one of Michiko's maids asked if he would like to join her mistress for tea. He stepped into the slippers which were outside his door and followed the maid as she glided down the hallway to the stairs. Michiko was seated at the low table in her room while the second maid was pouring tea.

"Would you care for green tea Campbell-san?"

He noted the return to formality in front of the maids.

"That would be very refreshing; thank you Kojima-san."

"After tea we should have lunch before we start our tour. My uncle has arranged with the hotel to supply a large car for all four of us therefore travel will be very convenient. You probably know that Kyoto is right-fully famous for its Kaiseki, its traditional Japanese food; however, there is a very special restaurant here which specializes in a very simple food, noodles. I would like you to try this food first. Would that be all right?"

"Yes it sounds delicious, Kojima-san."

"While we are enjoying our tea, tell me what you have learned of Kyoto so I do not bore you on our tours by informing you of things you already know."

Jack sipped his tea to give himself time to organize the memories of his studies.

"Kyoto was the capital of Japan from 794 to 1868. The Emperor Kammu moved the capital from Nara to Nagaoka, just outside Kyoto, in 784, then to Kyoto ten years later. As he greatly admired the culture of China he called the city, Heiankyo meaning 'Peace Capital'. It ceased being the capital when the court of Emperor Meiji moved to Edo, now Tokyo, in 1868."

"Very good Campbell-san. What else have you read?"

"Kyoto is different from every other Japanese city in its layout. It was planned based on the well organized Chinese city of Ch'ang-an, today called Sian, the capital of the Tang Dynasty. The Imperial Palace was built in the center and all the streets were constructed on a grid therefore streets intersect at right angles. This makes it simple to find your way."

"I have read that Kyoto has over two hundred Shinto shrines and over one thousand Buddhist temples. Unfortunately the city was almost totally destroyed in the 1400's and 1500's by two warring armies that used it as a battlefield. The reconstruction of its beauty is credited mainly to Toyotomi Hideyoshi in the late sixteenth century. Even though Tokyo is today's capital many people regard Kyoto as the 'Spiritual Home' of the Japanese."

He stopped talking and Michiko stared at him for several seconds then said softly, in a voice full of admiration, "I believe you must be the guide Campbell-san and I will be the student."

"No Kojima-san, reading can never be a substitute for seeing something with your own eyes and having it explained to you by someone who truly understands and deeply cares for the subject. Kyoto will come to life for me under your instruction."

And so it proved to be.

The days were filled with one wonder after another; the majesty of the Imperial Palace; the grandeur of the Temple of the Golden Pavilion; the magnificence of the Heian Shrine; and so many more splendors. But among all of these the most spiritual experience came on the last day when they visited the Ryoanji Temple, the Temple of the Peaceful Dragon.

Inside this temple lies a very famous rock garden. It has fifteen rocks in five groups laid out in a meticulously groomed and raked bed of white sand.

When he asked one of the priests the significance of the garden's layout, he was told the interpretation of the garden is best left up to each individual. Some people saw it as islands in a vast ocean; others as a view from on high looking down on mountain peaks bursting through the clouds. Jack was literally entranced. They had arrived at the end of the day when all other visitors had left and Jack sat for over half an hour without moving, just staring at the garden. As they were about to close the Temple,

Michiko sent the maids to bring the driver to the gates and she knelt beside him.

"Jack I am afraid we have to leave."

He did not seem to hear her so she gently shook his arm and repeated her message. He turned his head and stared into her eyes. Their faces were close together. Very tenderly she placed his head between her hands and kissed him. They did not move for almost a minute and then he stood and helped her to her feet. Still holding her hands he said, "Michiko I adore you. I never believed such complete and utter happiness was possible; however, now I know it is; but for me it is only possible if I am with you."

She looked down and when she raised her head she had tears in her eyes. Before she could say anything one of the maids appeared to announce the car was waiting. She daubed her eyes and they walked to the car in silence.

That evening all four of them had dinner served in Michiko's room. Although the conversation was light, the maids exchanged knowing glances at the way their mistress was looking at the foreigner. At the end of dinner he longed to kiss her again but knew this could not happen in front of the maids, so he bowed politely and returned to his room.

Next day, on the train, they again had a carriage to themselves. This allowed them to hold hands the whole way to Kobe and to kiss several times.

As the train drew into the station Jack saw Lord Hino waiting on the platform to meet them and this gave him an uneasy feeling.

"I hope you both had an interesting time. He stressed 'interesting' and when Michiko nodded her head he beamed and said, "You and I must leave for Tokyo tomorrow, Campbell."

Jack's response was automatic, "So soon?"

"Yes, I will explain it to you tonight over dinner. Just the two of us," he added with some emphasis.

Seeing the disappointment on both their faces he said, "If it would not inconvenience you too much my dear niece, perhaps you could join us in Tokyo next week."

Her eyes lit up.

"Oh yes, it would be a pleasure to visit you."

She was looking at Jack when she said this.

That evening Jack had dinner in Lord Hino's room. One of his guards sat at the end of the hallway and another outside his door. He mentioned the guards as he entered Hino's room.

"Do not alarm yourself Campbell, there is no danger. They are merely a precaution to keep unwelcome people away including overly curious maids. Please sit, help yourself to a whisky or we can order sake."

"Whisky will be fine, thank you."

"The reason for our visit to Tokyo is that the final touches are being made to our plans to take Singapore. As you well know your next mission is to verify much of the information you acquired in Glasgow. We have many agents in Malaya and Singapore but frankly speaking I am a little nervous of some of the information we are getting."

"Why is that?"

"The most important part of Military Intelligence is getting sufficient information to form a reliable base on which a military operation can be formulated and successfully executed. Ah, I see you look at me as though any child would understand this. The problem is always the same—timing! Invariably there are delays prior to the intended start of a major operation. The military is not quite ready; the weather is not suitable; or the politicians decide to have one more attempt at negotiation. Inevitably during these delays conditions change. And when the leaders finally say they are ready, Military Intelligence must restudy the prior hypotheses to verify their present validity. And what happens next? Of course the present situation differs from the past and the plan must be adapted. This causes intense frustration in political and military circles and so the cycle starts again and when the new plan is ready—another delay."

"My reason for belaboring this point can be better understood when I tell you a plan to attack Malaya, spearheaded by landing troops in South East Thailand and North East Malaya, was formulated four years ago.

Unfortunately the British General in charge of Singapore and Malaya at that time was a particularly good one. He had brought out a new head of Intelligence who was also very talented."

"One of their Japanese speaking agents trapped one of my most senior agents and extracted details of our plan from him. We later learned that London thought it was a bogus plan as, in their 'expert' opinion; no one could land on the east coast during monsoon season. Actually we specifically selected this time of year, as due to the poor visibility, it offered us maximum protection from a possible counter attack by air or shelling from the sea. To convince London of their error in judgment, this British

General conducted exercises proving that it could be done. Obviously we postponed our attack."

"Then to our utter amazement both these men were returned to Britain. They had been extraordinarily competent in discovering many of our top agents thereby leaving us with a very weak network. Their successors spent a great deal of time attempting to disprove their theories and stopped much of the work against our remaining agents. They claimed that Asians could not be that clever and that no British person would ever divulge secrets. We could hardly believe we were so lucky."

"But having a cautious disposition, I cannot be certain that some of the information we have received may come from a source which has been compromised. That is why it is vital to have a completely untainted, unknown resource travel around to verify that our latest information is accurate. Time is short as the northeast monsoon starts in November."

"Surely you have a few unimpeachable sources in Malaya."

"I believe we do. Actually one such agent happens to be an English Captain who has been in Malaya since the end of last year. I recruited him two years ago when he was on vacation in Japan. He is based near Penang and I hope you have the opportunity to meet him."

He paused, looking fixedly at Jack, "So much depends on your mission Campbell. That is why some members or the High Command want to meet you. To be assured you are as competent as I have claimed."

"Ah so," said Jack nodding his head with mock wisdom.

"Please leave the expressions of inscrutability to Asians, Campbell. They do not become a Scot."

"Of course, my Lord. I will be the epitome of decorum."

Even Lord Hino had to laugh at this.

Chapter 13

Next day, on the journey to Tokyo, Jack was quiet. Lord Hino was not sure if he was mulling over last night's conversation or was thinking of Michiko. Deciding it was the latter he chose not to interrupt and became occupied with his own thoughts for the next few hours.

"We are lucky the weather is fine. You will have a clear view of Fuji-sama in about ten minutes."

It was an awe inspiring sight. This large volcano with a few remaining traces of snow at the peak was perfectly symmetrical and stood all alone, majestically, with nothing to spoil the view. Jack stared at it until it disappeared into the distance.

"The train will stop here at Hakone. It will not be long until we arrive in Tokyo."

When they arrived at Tokyo Station the two guards who had been on the train were joined by two others waiting on the platform. They formed a close escort around Lord Hino and marched in step with him towards the exit. Jack was forced to march along behind, carrying his own suitcases.

Lord Hino's car had left Kobe the previous day and was waiting for them. Behind it was a second car. Lord Hino and Jack sat in the back of his car and one of the guards sat with the driver. The other three followed in the second car.

They had just pulled out of the busy traffic surrounding the station when Lord Hino pointed out the Imperial Palace. It was surrounded by a high wall made from enormous stones and had a wide moat. Swans swam gracefully across the water.

It seemed somehow incongruous that such a scene of serenity could exist in the capital of a nation bent on such aggression.

"My home is in Setagaya-ku, which is in the North West area of Tokyo. It is a quiet neighborhood and there are many parks. It used to take about forty minutes to get there, nowadays it takes much longer. So I also have an apartment in the Palace Hotel, just over there; however we will stay at my home until we have details of our schedule. These will be delivered tonight."

Lord Hino's home was set in magnificent woodland. A lake lay on one side of the property and the driveway followed it for half a mile. A lovely gazebo sat on an island which was close to the shore and connected by an arched red wooden bridge. As they turned between two rows of big pine trees Jack saw the house. It had large wooden pillars and a thick thatched roof which swooped in graceful curves.

"Do you recognize the styling of my home?"

"It reminds me of some of the shrines I saw in Kyoto."

"Excellent Campbell. It was built over a hundred years ago by one of the builders from Kyoto. I hope you will be comfortable here."

Jack was comfortable but unhappy. Already it seemed an eternity since he last saw Michiko and the news that night was not encouraging. The earliest the 'important' meeting could take place was in four days.

"Why did we have to rush up here if the meeting cannot be held for four days?"

"Unfortunately several of the officers who will attend the meeting were called away urgently. You must have patience Campbell."

The days dragged by. Jack was restricted to Lord Hino's home.

"There is much for me to do and I will spend my nights at my apartment. I must ask you to stay within the grounds as it could be dangerous for you to wander around on your own. I know you could easily find a way to elude the guards, but please do not do so."

"OK I promise not to leave the grounds."

The afternoon before the meeting Lord Hino returned.

"Let's sit down Campbell. I want to explain the process in which you will be involved. Tomorrow you will meet with a committee of fifteen young officers drawn from the Army, Navy and my intelligence group."

"Will you be there?"

"No, I will not be with you as it is inappropriate for someone of my seniority to be involved at this stage. They are very bright young men and their task is to go over all details of our attack plan. In doing so they will come up with the most important items which are not currently validated. These items will become your mission. Your opinion will be sought on the best methods of acquiring the necessary information and every aspect will be debated. Included in this debate will be details of our key agents to whom you can turn if you need to and contact passwords will be developed."

"Can I really participate in a meaningful way toward military strategy?"

"Perhaps not; however it is our way of building consensus to have everyone involved in the total plan. You must remember one important thing. You must not speak Japanese during this meeting."

"You are concerned that I may be too proud to say I do not understand something, or misinterpret something."

"Yes that is possible. However it is more probable that you may not recognize the importance of a particular piece of technical jargon; and furthermore, your language ability may give these men a false sense of comfort and they may slip into idiomatic or military slang that even the interpreter will not understand, and that could cause you to miss something important."

"There is no room for error. Do I make myself clear on this Campbell?"

"Perfectly clear."

"One of the negative aspects of using an interpreter for everything is the meeting is apt to take three times as long. That can't be helped."

"What happens after the meeting?"

"The committee will prepare a written report for its superiors. This group will conduct a review with the committee to ensure nothing had been overlooked."

"And then?"

"The war cabinet will be apprised of the modified report and will be asked for approval to proceed."

"Isn't all this just a little bit bureaucratic?"

"That is an opinion you will not repeat to anyone!"

"OK, OK. Perhaps being cooped up for so long has made me a little impatient."

"Or perhaps you are wondering when Kojima-san will arrive?"

"Perhaps."

"She will be here at the end of the first meeting. I cannot risk you becoming distracted; you need to focus all your attention on that meeting.

Now let's have a drink and some dinner. We have an early start tomorrow."

"Although I will not attend your meeting, I will escort you there and make the necessary introductions."

The car which arrived in the morning was not Lord Hino's. Strangely it was an American car, a very large Cadillac which had the double identity protection of darkened windows with curtains. The curtains were drawn so Jack had no idea which direction they were taking.

"Do not be concerned Campbell, we do not have too long to travel in this situation. As it is early we should be at our destination in about thirty minutes. For the next few nights you will stay at the Palace Hotel. Someone will escort you there and back again in the morning. Your suitcase will be in your room tonight."

"Did you say nights?"

"Yes. This meeting could last several days."

When they arrived Jack saw they were at the back of a large brick building.

"This is the Ministry of Post and Telephones, an unassuming building which serves our purpose well. We shall be on the third level."

Jack thought it an unusual choice of words to refer to the third floor as the third level. When he stepped into the elevator he discovered it was an accurate description. It was the third level down!

They entered a conference room which had a table capable of seating thirty people. Maps were hung on every wall. The committee was already assembled; most of them were drinking coffee. Lord Hino introduced Jack and motioned for him to sit near the center of the table next to the interpreter. When he left the meeting began.

In front of Jack was a folder which contained an agenda, copies of several maps, a notepad and several pencils. The interpreter explained to him that the usual custom of being served tea or coffee by a young girl would not be observed during this meeting for security reasons. Everyone should help themselves from the flasks placed on a large sideboard. Almost immediately Jack was impressed by the professionalism and the self discipline of the participants. As one person made a comment others would defer responding until the interpreter signaled he had concluded his translation.

He discovered he had more to say than he thought. At first he was listened to politely however by the end of the first day he was being treated like any other member of the group. Although the meeting was conducted professionally it did get very heated from time to time and Jack found himself being caught up in the verbal skirmishes.

Lord Hino was correct. The meeting would last a few days.

In fact it lasted five days.

It concluded at five in the afternoon of the fifth day. The chairman barked a command to an attendant and trays of sake were brought in. Jack noticed that in lieu of the normal delicate sake cups, small glasses were used. A toast was proposed to the Emperor followed by three resounding rounds of 'Banzai'. The chairman then approached Jack and refilled his glass. Jack picked up a sake bottle and refilled the chairman's glass. All the others filled their glasses and the chairman proposed a toast to the success of Jack's mission. There was a huge roar of approval.

When he left the building Jack was surprised to see Lord Hino waiting for him.

"Hello Campbell, to reward you for your arduous endeavors I thought we should have dinner in a very good restaurant."

"Thank you my Lord. I had thought of just collapsing in bed; however, having a relaxing dinner will be much better."

"I have had several reports on your participation in the proceedings of the committee. I am not surprised that you impressed most of the members."

"I do not believe Saito was impressed."

"I am afraid that, intelligent though he may be, his xenophobia will never allow him to recognize your talents."

They drove in the Cadillac to the restaurant. After exchanging their shoes for slippers they followed the maid along the traditional wooden hallway. She slid open the door saying, "Doozo ohairi kudasai", 'please enter'. Jack stood back to let Lord Hino enter first, but he turned away saying, "Please go on ahead Campbell, I will visit the toilet."

Jack stepped out of his slippers and walked into the tatami room and the door slid shut behind him. This being so unusual he almost didn't see the other person in the room.

"Michiko."

"Oh Jack."

She was in his arms and he held her tightly, kissing her hair. He held her at arms length to look at her afraid she was only a dream. They kissed for a long time. He suddenly realized Lord Hino could return at any moment and he stepped back quickly looking at the door. She laughed.

"You need not worry, Jack, my uncle has already left. He planned this surprise for you. He thought we might enjoy dinner together."

"Well I'll be damned! Oh pardon my language Michiko. I never would have believed he would do such a thing."

"My uncle does surprising things. Just when you think you know him well, he shows another aspect of his character that completely astounds you."

"Perhaps it is his unpredictability that makes him so good at his job."

"Let's not talk about my uncle."

She came into his arms again and kissed him passionately.

"I have missed you so much, Jack."

"Not nearly as much as I have missed you, my darling Michiko."

He glanced at the door again knowing that it was the custom for maids to open a door first before asking permission to enter. She sensed his unease.

"It is all right, we have a buzzer over there and I left instructions not to be disturbed until we call. You look so tired Jack, let's order now."

They arrived back at Lord Hino's home at nine thirty. He was still working in his study but came out to greet them when he heard the car.

"How was dinner?"

"It was quite good uncle. Some chefs in Tokyo must have been taking lessons from our Kobe chefs."

"You see what I have to put up with Campbell."

"Thank you so very much for your considerate arrangements my Lord."

Jack bowed very low and stayed in that position for quite some time.

"Come, come, Campbell that is enough. You deserved a decent dinner after your hard work and I think my niece probably enjoyed the evening. By the way, I have been informed that the committee's report will be reviewed in four days. This will allow my niece three days to show you around Tokyo. I suggest you get a good night's sleep and please feel free to stay in bed as late as you like tomorrow morning."

It was just after ten o'clock when Jack got into bed and it was ten when he finally wakened next morning. He came downstairs thirty minutes later and saw Michiko in the sitting room. He was about to embrace her when he noticed one of her maids standing nearby.

"Good morning Kojima-san. Please excuse me for being so late."

"Good morning Campbell-san. I am pleased you slept well. You must have been very tired. Would you like some breakfast?"

"Just coffee and toast please."

She asked her maid to have the cook prepare this for Jack. When the maid left he quickly ran to Michiko and kissed her. He just had time to sit when the maid returned.

"My uncle has arranged a car and a driver for us; however he insists that in addition to my maid, one of his guards accompanies us. Nevertheless I am sure we will have an enjoyable time."

And they did. During the next three days they toured much of Tokyo. There were only a few opportunities to be alone and even then for no more then ten minutes at any one time. Jack had never been happier.

The day of the next meeting arrived and as they were driving in the Cadillac Lord Hino explained the process.

"There will be six senior officers including me. There will be sharp questioning of the committee and it may become uncomfortable for some members of the committee. Once again you will not speak Japanese. The interpreter will find it more difficult to keep up with the proceedings as no one will wait for his translation to be complete. He will have to whisper the translation to you to avoid interrupting the meeting. Even if you fully understand what was said allow the interpreter to do his job.

When you are questioned speak in a forthright manner, do not be obsequious with this group."

The meeting lasted until nine at night. There had indeed been some sharp questioning however the committee members acquitted themselves well. Jack had only been asked four questions, the most difficult one coming from Lord Hino. On the way home he remarked on this.

"Did you expect me to show you leniency, Campbell?"

Then he understood. Hino had to appear unbiased in front of the other members. Or, maybe he was truly unbiased. Jack realized you could never tell with this master spy.

"The meeting with the War Cabinet will take place in three days. I thought you might like to visit Yokohama to see Professor Mannheim."

"That would be wonderful!"

"Near Yokohama is the town of Kamakura where there is one of the largest statues of Buddha in the world. You might enjoy a side trip there. I am sure my niece would be fascinated to meet the Professor. Remind me to brief Michiko on the cover stories we used with the professor. You will continue to be Simpson and you must not use my title."

"Don't you think Hans will have learned of your real identity by now?"

"Possibly but even if he has we must not acknowledge this."

Michiko, her maid and Jack caught an early morning train. As they would only be away for one night, Jack carried a light bag with a fresh shirt, socks, underwear and his shaving kit. Michiko and her maid had two large suitcases. Jack would have bet there was not much of that space for the maid. It was not far to Yokohama and they traveled on a local train which made several stops. As there was only one class of carriage, all three were together so there was no chance to hold hands.

He had just helped Michiko alight from the carriage when a boom-ing voice yelled, "Jack, Jack." The maid hid behind Michiko as this tall, thin apparition came racing down the platform, long arms waving like a windmill.

"Hans, it is so good to see you. Allow me to introduce the niece of Mr. Hino, Miss Kojima Michiko."

Hans took her hand held it close to but not touching his lips.

"It is a pleasure to meet you."

The maid peeked out from behind Michiko long enough to bow her greeting. Hans escorted them to the institute and gave them a tour. He was obviously enjoying his research as his voice was full of enthusiasm as he explained his work.

"Do you know that Jack is now very knowledgeable on marine biol-ogy, Miss Kojima?"

"No I did not know that."

"Yes, yes. He has a natural affinity for the subject. He could be quite expert if he allow me to continue the lessons we had on the ship."

While Hans was bubbling on, Jack stood behind Michiko and when he caught Hans' eye, he carefully shook his head. Hans understood the signal and changed the subject.

Later they had lunch then toured Yokohama before driving to Ka-makura that evening. Hans was still bubbling with excitement at seeing his friend.

"We are staying at a Japanese inn. I have not yet been to Kamakura so I am really looking forward to this visit. This is such a pleasant surprise to see you again Jack."

They had a rollicking good time at dinner that night. There seemed to be no end to the funny stories Hans was recounting of his time in Yoko-hama. Jack was delighted that his friend was so happy.

The tour of Kamakura was enjoyed by everyone and when it came time to board the train back to Tokyo, Michiko could see the sadness in the eyes of both Hans and Jack. They promised to keep in touch and Hans stood for a long time after the train had left, staring after it.

The carriage was crowded so Michiko did not say anything, but she could see Jack was deep in thought. When they were in the car, Jack trembled and she asked, "What is it Campbell-san?"

"I have this feeling I will not see Hans again."

"Of course you will."

"I hope so. The world needs more people like Hans. People who want to make this a better place for mankind."

"He is a fine man. You should be pleased to have him as a good friend."

"I am not only pleased, I am honored" he said softly as he stared out the window of the car. She looked at him and knew she truly loved him.

Lord Hino was waiting for them and after inquiring into their trip, he told Jack the meeting would take place at five pm the next day. It would be at a new venue and they would leave at three o'clock. As the meeting would take several hours they would stay at the hotel.

The same black Cadillac dropped them off at ten minutes past four. The new venue turned out to be the Imperial Palace.

"At this meeting you will not sit at the main table. There will be an outer ring of chairs and you will sit there along with the aides of the main participants. Most probably you will not say anything. You are here to be seen not heard. In addition to the War Cabinet, there will be the group of six and the chairman of your committee. As you have no real part in this meeting, there will not be an interpreter."

"May I ask why the meeting is being held here?"

"Whatever the Cabinet decides must be communicated to the Emperor right away. His Majesty has the power to overrule any decision. This is seldom invoked but consultation is required before the signing of the document authorizing a major act of war. It is probable I will have to remain after the meeting; therefore, I have arranged to have you taken to the hotel where I will see you tomorrow morning at eight o'clock."

"I understand."

The Prime Minister opened the meeting at precisely five o'clock. He was an elegantly dressed man with a courtly demeanor. Sitting on his right was a smaller bespectacled man with a shaven head and a small moustache. The Minister of War did not engage in any pre-meeting greetings, he just sat there and glared at everyone. Jack could follow much of the discussion. It was obvious that war against the Western Allies was inevitable. The debate as to the most appropriate strategy raged on for a long time. Finally it was agreed that to provide Japan with the raw materials it so desperately needed it was mandatory to first take Malaya and then the Dutch East Indies. Critical to the success of this task was the taking of the fortress, Singapore. Such a bold move would inevitably bring America into the war; therefore a simultaneous strike on the American Pacific Fleet was essential.

The War Minister cleared his throat noisily. There was silence before he spoke.

"This entire venture depends on accurate information of the enemy's strength and determination in Malaya and Singapore. Am I to understand that our esteemed Intelligence Service will rely on a foreigner to verify this absolutely critical task?"

"That is correct," replied Lord Hino.

The War Minister addressed the Prime Minister.

"Your Excellency, are you in accord with such a brash plan?"

"I am, if I have the assurance of Lord Hino that this man is the best possible solution; what do you say Lord Hino?"

"Our planning would not be so far advanced if it were not for the information obtained by this man in Glasgow. Furthermore he has passed all of our training tests and is well equipped to carry out this mission."

"Does that satisfy you War Minister?"

"Unfortunately it does not, Your Excellency. So he has completed one mission. We are talking about the future of our nation and we are going to leave it up to a foreigner."

His lips curled into a sneer as he said this.

"What does he understand of the spirit of our forefathers, the essence of our codes of life? I understand he is well read but books do not teach culture."

Lord Hino was about to reply but the Prime Minister held up his hand.

"I am also interested in hearing a reply to the questions raised by the War Minister. I think we should hear from this young foreigner."

Lord Hino stood up and said in English.

"Please come forward Campbell."

The War Minister snickered, "He even has to speak English to him."

Lord Hino continued in an unruffled manner.

"Please do as the Prime Minister requests. Answer the questions. In Japanese!"

Jack bowed to the Prime Minister.

"Your Excellency, My Lords, Honored Members of the Imperial War Cabinet, please forgive my crude effort to communicate in your delicate language."

Jaws dropped all round the table.

"I do have a great passion for your country and its culture. However the War Minister speaks the truth when he says the spirit of Japan cannot be learned from a book. I did not fully realize this until I visited Kyoto recently. By spending a great deal of time in the Temples and Shrines of that magnificent city, I now have some understanding of the spirit of Japan. Yet I cannot point to a specific time when this happened, it seemed to seep into my bones the longer I was there."

There were nods of understanding around the table.

"Now that I have visited Kobe, Tokyo, Yokohama and Kamakura, I have witnessed that this spirit lives, not only in Kyoto, but in every Japanese person. Japan is one nation and one people because its every day activities are ruled by one culture. It is my fervent desire to learn more of the spirit of Japan and if in the meantime I can be of service it would be a treasured honor."

Now there were cries of appreciation from around the table. A few even applauded. The Prime Minister held up his hand for quiet.

"Tell me Campbell-san, what most impressed you about Kyoto?"

"My whole inner being was calmed when I beheld the beauty of the Rock Garden at Ryoanji."

This time the cries from around the table were louder and there was more applause.

"Campbell-san, you have answered the questions to my complete satisfaction. Thank you. Now it is time to vote on whether or not we wish this young man to undertake the important mission in Malaya and Singapore. All in favor?"

There were loud assertions from the room.

"War Minister, I did not clearly hear your vote."

"I agree."

The meeting went on for another two hours. From time to time Jack noticed the members stealing a glance at him. When the meeting ended Lord Hino took Jack aside.

"I thought you laid it on a little thickly, Campbell, but it worked beautifully. Congratulations."

"To be honest My Lord I was caught completely unaware by your request. Words just came to me. Perhaps the 'treasured honor' was a little colorful."

Lord Hino smiled. "Goodnight, I will see you tomorrow."

Chapter 14

The next morning Jack was just leaving his room when he noticed the piece of paper on the floor. It was a note from Lord Hino saying he had been called to an urgent meeting. Jack should have breakfast and if he had not returned by nine o'clock then Jack should go to his house. His driver would be waiting at the front entrance of the hotel.

At nine o'clock Jack walked out of the Palace Hotel. The Rolls Royce was waiting for him. The driver said he would take him to Lord Hino's home. As they were entering the driveway another car pulled in behind them. It turned out to be Lord Hino.

"Ah Campbell, I have very good news. We have received the go ahead. Your days of leisure are over it is time to go to work. Next stop Malaya."

"I am sure you have arranged a convoluted strategy to get me into Malaya. I just can't be dropped off on a beach, can I?"

"Ah Campbell, so intelligent, yet still a neophyte in the art of Intelligence. One must only use convoluted strategies when the risks to a network or a prized agent are high. It is always better to keep things as simple as possible, and then even a Scotsman can remember what is expected of him."

He burst out laughing at his own joke.

Jack remained unruffled saying, "We did have an agreement to cease further national slurs."

"Forgive me Campbell."

"OK, tell me the plan."

"It is simplicity itself; over a month ago a young Scot named Jack Simpson boarded a Red Funnel liner in Glasgow bound for Port Swettenham. As you already know Port Swettenham is a main port for Kuala

Lumpur. Shortly after departing Glasgow poor Mr. Simpson became ill has been confined to his cabin; therefore the other passengers have not had the pleasure of his company. His steward has taken all his meals to him and is the only person to have seen him. When the ship is at anchor outside the harbor awaiting its turn to dock, you will take his place, disembark and assume the role created for you when you started your training program under John Gibson."

"And the ailing Mr. Simpson?"

"All has been arranged, you need not concern yourself about such details," said Lord Hino in a serious voice.

"Ah so," said Jack. There were several seconds of silence before he said, "I suppose another claustrophobic journey in a submarine is imminent?"

"Yes."

"Ah well, what could be more stimulating than the gray walls of an iron coffin?"

"This mission is too critical for such flippancy," snapped Lord Hino; then immediately regretting his outburst he said, "forgive me Campbell." He paused then continued, "That's the second time I have asked your forgiveness today. This is truly one of the most important tasks we need done and I am probably a bit too tense. I know you will do well."

"That's OK, I understand."

But he did not understand. Obviously he appreciated the criticality of this mission but he had witnessed Hino remain icy calm in other difficult situations. Something else had caused this uncontrolled outburst.

There was an even more momentous matter praying on Hino's mind. He had sensed this previously but he was no closer to discovering what it was.

"I have something for you Campbell. Actually to be exact I have two things for you."

He motioned to his guard who had been in the car with him. He brought a suitcase into the sitting room.

"Another suitcase, I now have quite a collection, only this one is not new, it is a little worn."

"Exactly, that's why it will not attract too much attention. Let me show you a few things."

He opened the case which appeared normal. It had a dark gray lining throughout which was riveted to the frame.

"Now Campbell, hold down the upper left rivet and press the lower right rivet twice."

Jack did this and heard a faint click and the bottom of the case came out to reveal two pistols and ammunition strapped inside the false bottom.

"Now try the inside lid of the case."

Once again it revealed another two pistols.

"Each side has a similar compartment. At the moment they are empty. Now the second present for you."

He gave Jack a leather toiletry bag, also suitable worn.

"Is this my cyanide pill?" laughed Jack.

"Yes it is."

Jack stopped laughing.

"There are many other things, let me show you. Here are your anti-malaria pills, do not neglect to take them. Also a bottle labeled mouth wash, which contains a recently developed lotion which wards off mosquitoes.

This bottle labeled eau de cologne contains a fast acting sleeping potion. The other two boxes should go in the secret side pockets of your suitcase. The blue box contains poison pills. These are not quick acting; they are intended to be used on an enemy. The yellow one has your cyanide pill."

"I can't just walk around carrying a cyanide pill."

"We have tried putting it in a cigarette or in a packet of chewing gum, but all these tricks are well known. If you are going on a particularly dangerous job, it is better to just have it in the cuff of your trousers or in the waistband of your trousers. Slit the cuff or waistband with a razor and insert the pill. I do not think you will have need of it on this mission."

"Well I seem to have everything; oh, what about a camera?"

"No camera, Campbell. Your cover story is well backed up in UK and will sound very plausible to the local authorities. However someone taking a series of photographs around harbors could cause a more attentive person to ask questions. The lower your profile on this mission the better it will be."

Once again the depth of thinking by this man impressed Jack.

"When do I leave?"

"In two hours."

"So I just have time to wash, pack and say goodbye to Michiko."

"The first two, yes. The last, alas, no. My niece left for Kobe early this morning."

"Without saying goodbye?" said Jack incredulously.

"That was my instruction to her. You have become quite fond of my niece haven't you?"

"She is one of the most wonderful people I have ever met."

"Only one of the most wonderful, not the most wonderful?"

My mother was also a wonderful person and my grandmother was very special to me."

"Ah I see. Well if is any consolation to you I believe she likes you. However I had an important task for her; also sorrowful goodbyes are to be avoided in this business. They can cause one to lose focus on the job at hand. It is much better to remember the happy occasions rather than a sad one."

"I would still rather have said goodbye."

"Believe me Campbell it is better this way. Now you must hurry as you have an aeroplane waiting for you."

"What is my destination?"

"You will not travel directly to Malaya; first we have to tone you up after all your lazing around in Japan."

"Oh really," said Jack.

Hino noticed Jack's laconic expression and smiled to himself. It was becoming quite difficult to surprise Campbell these days. But it was Hino who was completely surprised by Jack's next comment.

"Am I in for some jungle training?"

Even Hino's normal equanimity could not control his spluttering reply.

"Who told you that?" he demanded.

"It seemed a reasonable deduction and it is very like you to spring this sort of thing on me at the last minute."

"Your deduction is correct," said Hino more than a little huffily.

"You will fly to the south of Kyushu and then be taken by boat to a little populated island. This island does have thick jungle. You will undergo one weeks training. This will give you the chance to acclimatize somewhat to the conditions you will experience in Malaya. One week is not nearly enough time for a realistic acclimatization; however, I was loathe to shorten your time with my niece. You earned the break and you seemed to be truly happy."

Jack had learned to be a bit suspicious of Hino's words. So he looked deep into Hino's eyes and judged he was being sincere.

"Thank you very much. I really do appreciate your thoughtfulness."

Now it was time for Hino to study Jack's face carefully and he also came to the same conclusion. Campbell was being sincere. This greatly pleased him as he thought to himself, 'This part of Empire is working out well'.

When Jack arrived on the island he was met by three men. One of them greeted him in broken English. He was shown to a very primitive hut which was to be his home for the week. From the comments they made about him they obviously did not know he spoke Japanese. He decided it would be to his advantage if they continued to think that.

The training was conducted exactly as Jack expected. Demanding, thorough, intense and exhausting. He was sure the trainers took an almost sadistic delight in pushing him to the limit of his endurance. No doubt under the instruction of his dear friend Lord Hino. What he did not know was the trainers were becoming just as exhausted as he was. They had expected this 'gaijin' or foreigner to beg them to slow the grueling pace. When he didn't, they had no choice but to keep going themselves. They could not lose face in front of a "gaijin'. Therefore, it was with great relief they bade Jack farewell. In doing so, the three trainers bowed in unison. To Jack this was a surprising gesture of respect. Jack bowed even lower which accorded even greater respect to the trainers. When he straightened he could see the look of appreciation in their eyes.

A small craft took him back to Kyushu, to the port of Kagoshima. The sea was rough but Jack hardly noticed as his weary eyes closed and he slept the entire way. The boat did not dock at the harbor but stopped just outside the entrance. He was ferried by a rowing boat to the waiting 'iron coffin'.

Chapter 15

The journey to Malaya was remarkably uneventful. He was transferred, at night, to a powerful motor boat from the submarine. This took him just north of Malacca, then to a small fishing boat which, almost casually, took him alongside the Red Funnel ship. A rope was lowered; he quickly climbed up, was met by the faithful steward and spirited to his cabin. A few minutes later the steward appeared with his case. It all seemed so easy.

Next morning he disembarked with everyone else and had no trouble in meeting the representative of the Red Funnel line, a Mr. Knight whose pale features disappeared into the clothes he wore. He was resplendent in a short sleeve white shirt, baggy white shorts, white knee length socks, white shoes and was holding a sign with Mr. Simpson printed in large letters on it.

Jack waved as he approached this apparition, who said in a loud jovial voice, "Mr. Simpson is it? Welcome to Malaya. I am George Knight from our KL office. Our car is just over there. I have already taken care of the formalities. No need to stand in line. You certainly want to be as anonymous as possible since you are on government hush hush business. Eh?"

"If my business was hush hush you seem to have announced it to the whole dock," said Jack in a low voice.

"Oh I say I'm most dreadfully sorry. Not used to this sort of thing you know."

Now he was hissing.

"Let's just speak in a normal tone of voice, shall we?" said Jack.

"Oh righto, jolly good."

Jack groaned inwardly as they got in the car.

"The Managing Director, Mr. Williams, has put you up at one of our houses in KL. It's a very nice house and I am sure you will be comfortable there. We will drive there first to let you unpack and freshen up, then we will have lunch with the MD. It will take about an hour and a half from PS to KL."

He noticed the puzzled look on Jack's face.

"Oh, I probably should explain that everyone uses acronyms for names out here. You will get used to it in no time at all. PS stands for Port Swettenham and, of course, KL stands for Kuala Lumpur."

"What is your job Mr. Knight?"

"Please call me George. Well to be honest my uncle got me a position with the company. He is an ex-MD in London. As it turned out I am not terribly well suited for this type of work. No use at figures, you see. So, as they can't send me home, I have become the special assistant to the MD. I make arrangements for meetings with Government Officials, take care of visiting VIP's and handle the press. Things like that. As a result I have a vast knowledge of not very important facts," he said with a self deprecating smile.

"For example this port was named after Frank Swettenham, a very important man in the development of this area."

Not long after leaving the port area, the road became quite narrow as it snaked its way through a large rubber estate. Jack stared with interest at the perfectly straight rows of trees which stretched for miles.

"It must take a great deal of effort to keep the ground clear of undergrowth between all those trees."

"Oh indeed," said George, "this is truly a tropical country and the jungle would take over very quickly. Things grow almost overnight here. Are you interested in rubber and rubber growing?"

"I know absolutely nothing about it," replied Jack.

"Ah, that does surprise me," said George.

"Why?" asked Jack.

"Well you being a Scotsman, I thought you might remember that the great chemist, Charles Macintosh, established a factory in Glasgow in 1923 to manufacture waterproof cloth, from which was made rainproof garments."

"Of course," said Jack.

"If you like I can give you my quick review of rubber."

"I would like that," said Jack.

"Oh good. That will save me a lot of trouble."

When Jack looked quizzically at him George explained, "Most times when I escort guests from PS to KL, they ask me questions about this part of the world. However the MD likes to impress guests with his knowledge of this area's history. On more than one occasion a guest has interrupted him saying, 'George already told me all about that'. As you might imagine, that eventually caused me problems. So I have learned to stay away from history."

Jack had the feeling that George probably knew much more about local history than Mr. Williams.

"As you probably know rubber trees grew wild in South America. This continued to be the main source of world supply until 1876 when the British explorer, Sir Henry Wickham, smuggled 70,000 seeds out of Brazil. As the government of Brazil prohibited the export of seeds, one could better describe his action as stealing. These seeds were successfully planted in the greenhouses of the Royal Botanical Gardens at Kew in England. From this beginning, plantations were started in Ceylon and later here at the turn of the century.

The British brought Tamil Indians from Ceylon and the south of India to tap the trees. That is the main reason for almost ten percent of the population being Indian."

"Interestingly enough, many of the plantation managers and supervisors are Scots."

"Why is that?" asked Jack.

"Well, I believe it is due to their hard-headed, no-nonsense approach to getting things done. You see rubber tapping is more of an art than a science and one must be constantly vigilant to see the trees are well treated. Tapping begins before dawn. The tapper cuts a downward spiral into the bark, extending about half way round the tree. The sap of the tree then runs into a cup tied below the cut. Two days later the tapper will return to the same tree and complete a similar cut just below the previous one. This is continued until the entire side of the tree is tapped. The other side is then tapped and then the tree is left to regenerate its sap and grow a new bark. If the cut is too shallow there is not enough sap and if it is too deep the tree can be severely damaged. The sap which is called latex is collected at the end of the shift and diluted with water then treated with acid which makes the rubber particles stick together. It is then passed between rollers ending up as sheets of rubber. These are then transferred to the smoke house to be dried. The thin sheets are then ready for shipment."

"George you have missed your calling, you ought to be a lecturer."

George actually blushed and said, "Anyone can learn this. As I said my stock-in-trade is knowledge of a large amount of not terribly important facts. Anyway, just to finish the story; rubber is now the main export with tin the next most important. Maybe over a drink one evening, I can tell you the story of tin."

"You're on George."

Jack watched the countryside gradually change as they left the rubber estates and passed through several small villages. The car suddenly swerved violently throwing Jack on his back. There was a thump and the car sped on.

"Sorry sir," said the driver, "I tried to miss it but it came into the road too quickly."

"What was it Hamid?" asked George.

"A goat, sir, sorry."

"Slow down a bit Hamid. I have already warned you twice about driving too fast."

"Shouldn't we have stopped George? Is it not customary to pay the owner if you kill his goat?"

"Sometimes we do. If there is only one person around we usually stop and give some money. If there is a crowd you must never stop."

"Why?"

"Out here people can quickly become very angry and dangerous. One urges on another and before you know it there is violence."

"Surely that can't be the case if you are offering to pay for the animal?"

"The problem is several people will claim to be the owner, which leads to a fracas then you are in trouble."

Jack shook his head in an uncomprehending and doubtful manner.

"Believe me Mr. Simpson; you must be careful when traveling through a kampong. Oh, a kampong is a Malay village."

Jack thought about this attitude towards the local people as they drove on.

"Ah we are getting close to KL now Mr. Simpson."

"I am not a very formal person, George, so please call me Jack."

As they came into the city Jack noticed the large ditches along both sides of the road and asked what they were.

"Monsoon drains. You have never seen such heavy rain in your life. In some areas the drains are three feet wide and four feet deep and they can be overflowing within half an hour. Often it is impossible to drive as the windshield wipers just cannot keep the windshield clear. Then you just have to pull over and wait till it eases."

"Ah, we are now in the Ampang area which is probably the most desirable residential area. This is where you will be staying."

The car slowed and turned into a long gravel driveway on Ampang Road.

"Here we are, No. 25," said George.

Jack gazed in admiration at the large black and white Tudor bungalow. It was built on a platform about three feet above ground level. Jack guessed this was to protect against the monsoon rain. On one side of the entrance was a veranda running all the way to the corner of the house. There were green slatted shades to protect against the strong sun. Dotted along the veranda were heavily cushioned rattan chairs, footstools and sofas. Directly behind the veranda were the sitting room and dining room. In these rooms the furniture was made of teak and the upholstery was covered in silk. Along the front and side were floor rails for the folding wood and glass doors which were pulled open. Several overhead fans whirred in an attempt to cool the house. Jack had never seen anything as luxurious in his life.

As he and George reached the top step of the entranceway, Jack heard a whishing noise and two figures came hurrying to greet them, their slippers appearing to glide over the highly polished floor.

"Mr. Simpson, may I introduce Ah Kang, the number one cook on Ampang Road and his wife Ah Eng."

Both Chinese bowed to Jack and Ah Kang said, "Please to meet you Mistah Slimson. My wife no speak vely good English, but understand vely good if you speak slowly. She do all cleaning and washing and ironing. Anything you want to eat for dinnah, you tell me in morning and I cook. After dinnah you tell me what you want for next day breakfast and I cook. You leave clothes in basket in bathroom, my wife take care of evelything. That alright Mistah Slimson?"

Jack stretched out his hand to Ah Kang who stared at it before taking it with some trepidation.

"I am pleased to meet you Ah Kang and everything you mentioned is perfect. Thank you."

He then faced Eh Eng bowed slightly and said, "It is a pleasure to meet you Ah Eng."

They both bowed again and swished away.

"I will show you the bedroom; Hamid has already put your suitcase there."

As they entered the bedroom George whispered, "I say old chap, it's not expected that you shake hands, I mean they are servants."

"No George, they are human beings, who happen to earn a living by doing this type of work."

"Have it your own way old man, but you will find out that things are different out here. For example when I told you Ah Kang is the number one cook in this rather prestigious road, I did not mean he is just the best cook, he rules all the servants on this road. No one can accept a position here unless he approves, not even in one of the diplomatic bungalows. Every servant who works on this road pays a part of their wages to Ah Kang."

This did surprise Jack.

"Anyway you go ahead and unpack and have a bath. I will call for you in an hour if that's ok."

"That's fine, I'll see you then."

George had been gone for only five minutes when there was a knock on the bedroom door.

"Come in," said Jack.

It was Ah Kang carrying a tray with tea.

"I bling you tea Mistah Slimson. It's alright?"

"Thank you very much Ah Kang. It's just what I need."

Ah Kang beamed. Jack poured a cup of strong tea and sipped it appreciatively.

"Just the way I like it, Ah Kang."

Ah Kang beamed again and turned to leave but he hesitated at the door and then as though summoning courage turned to face Jack.

"My wife say you a vely nice man Mistah Slimson. You do her much honor by speaking so nice to her. Thank you so vely much. You want anything you just ask me."

Impulsively Jack reached out his hand, this time Ah Kang grasped it firmly.

"Please tell Ah Eng that it is both of you who honor me by helping me during my stay. I appreciate that very much."

The bedroom was as elegant as the rest of the bungalow. Again all the furniture was teak. There was a large desk in one corner, a dressing table and two armchairs, but the dominating feature was the huge four poster bed. It stood high off the floor and on each side was a two step footstool, presumably for ladies or more elderly gentlemen. Suspended from the ceiling and surrounding the bed was a mosquito net. Even the bathroom was large with the washbasins and bath made of marble.

'If this is just a guest house I wonder what the Managing Director's house must be like,' thought Jack.

He began unpacking, hanging his clothes in the built-in wardrobes. He then bathed and changed clothes. He enjoyed walking around the large garden and was admiring the orchids when George arrived. He was right on time and greeted Jack cheerily. He had changed into a starched long sleeved white shirt, a necktie and freshly pressed trousers.

"Do I need a jacket?" asked Jack.

"Better not, old boy. The MDs of some companies insist on one wearing a jacket when in their presence. In those companies everyone has a jacket hanging in the office in case you are called by the MD. This may only happen a few times a year, but heaven help you if you do not have your jacket. Our MD is of the other school. He wears a jacket and no one else should be as well dressed as he."

"Hold on while I get my jacket," teased Jack.

George was about to say something when he noticed the grin on Jack's face.

"Thank you for your understanding Jack. Anyway, what do you think of our guest bungalow?"

"It's more like a small palace" said Jack. "I was wondering what the homes of the senior executives must be like."

"Most of them are equivalent to No. 25, except, of course, the MD's home. That one is like a small palace with a staff to match. Let's see, including his syce, oh that's what we call a driver, his wife's syce, the gardeners, or keboons as we call them, the amahs for the children, the cook, the head boy, and the maids, he has twelve servants. You will no doubt see his home. It is furnished with the most exquisite antiques and full of Persian carpets. His wife decorated it beautifully. You see each time we have a new MD, the house is completely refurnished."

"But that must cost a fortune," said Jack. "What do they do with the old furniture?"

George gave Jack a look of amusement.

"Normally the MD of a major business has spent most of his career in Asia. His tenure as MD may only last five years before he is transferred back to the Head Office in London or retired. During those five years his wife is busy collecting antiques, carpets and other trinkets. All of this is shipped home to England and the company pays for everything. Living out here does not cost the MD a single penny. All expenses are paid by the company."

George laughed at the astonishment on Jack's face.

"Another way to look at it is, each year a fresh batch of recruits is sent to KL and to other Asian cities on a six year tour of duty. They live in bachelors' quarters owned by the company and are forbidden to marry during this first tour. Half of them are deemed unsuitable and sent home before their tour is completed and half of the remainder are sent home at the end of their tours for the same reason. Those who are asked to stay on become junior Managers and of those half will be gone within ten years. So the chance of a raw recruit becoming MD after say thirty years is probably one in five hundred. As I mentioned to you earlier, there is no doubt I would have been sent home long ago but for my uncle."

"So you see a Managing Director feels he has earned his tangible rewards. What is even more important, old boy, is that his wife feels this even more keenly. One must always be wary of Mrs. MD. Many a career of a really bright junior has been ended because his wife said something which upset Mrs. MD. These women can be dragons."

"What a life," said Jack, "why would anyone want to go through this purgatory?"

"The money old boy, pure greed, aided by ambition and for many, particularly the wives, social position. There is a good chance of a Knighthood at the end."

"Is that worth it?" asked Jack, but he already knew the answer. Social position was the most important thing in the world to this type of person. 'The British disease which must be eradicated if the country was to have a chance of success in the future,' he thought.

"Oh by the way, Jack, before we get into the car; I thought over what you said about the servants and came to the conclusion you were absolutely correct. I must have sounded like a pompous ass. Perhaps I have been out here too long."

"Maybe it's the company you keep" said Jack.

"Talking of company we had better get cracking. It is not good form to keep the MD waiting."

Chapter 16

As the car pulled away from No. 25 Ampang Road, George said, "We are having lunch at the 'Dog'."

"We are going to the dogs?" asked Jack incredulously.

"No. Not the dogs old chap, the 'Dog'. The proper name is the Selangor Club. Exactly how it came to be called the 'Dog' is a bit unclear. The popular belief is, many years ago a lady used to arrive at the club every day in her carriage and tie up her Dalmatian to the hitching rail. The locals then referred to the club as the 'Spotted Dog'. This was contracted to the 'Dog' over time. It's a wonderful club for socializing and for sports. On the padang in front of the club we play rugby, soccer, cricket and hockey. Oh, there's that look on your face again. What did I say that you did not understand?"

"What is a padang?"

"It's a playing field, or it can just mean an open space. You'll see when we arrive. It should only take about another fifteen minutes."

Jack was entranced by the kaleidoscope of color he saw as they drove. The vegetation was so lush and the flowering trees cast blossoms all around. But it was the dress of the people which most caught his attention. The Malay ladies wore their tight fitting sarongs and tops. The Indian ladies wore their saris and Chinese ladies in cheongsams. The Chinese men all seemed to wear shorts and a short sleeve shirt hanging outside their shorts. The Malay men wore a sarong and a similar garment was worn by Indian men. The vivid colors of the clothes added to the spectacle.

The roads were crowded with bicycles, motor cycles, trishaws, buses and cars. Many of the bicycles had two passengers as did the motor cycles which sometimes even had three.

Each method of transport seemed incapable of traveling in a straight line. They constantly wove in and out, yet no one appeared upset, everyone traveled in cheerful chaos.

Jack kept the car window next to him open. This way he could not only hear the cacophony of noise but experience the smells emanating from the shops they passed. 'Hans was right,' he thought, 'your senses are truly brought to life by this country.'

As the car turned towards the Selangor Club, Jack let out a "Wow".

"Stop the car Hamid," ordered George, "you can get a good view from here Jack."

The club was a long low building with a red tile roof and a Tudor exterior. In front of it was the manicured 'padang'. It was big enough for two soccer fields, a cricket ground and two tennis courts. Impressive though the club was, what took Jack's breath away was the building across the street from the padang. It was a two story Moorish style structure with sweeping arches and wide verandas. At one end was a circular tower, twice as tall as the main building, atop which was a gleaming copper cupola. The portico in the center was topped by the dominant feature of the entire building, a square tower, one hundred and thirty five feet tall. It too had a lacquered dome on top. Just below the dome was a four faced clock. The outside of building was two tone; beige and white. In the bright sunlight it glistened like a jewel.

"That's the Government building. It was completed just before the turn of the century. It has an interesting history. The state architect, Mr. Norman, planned to design it in a classical Renaissance style. When the state engineer, C.E.Spooner, heard of this he ruled it out, saying the design should be in keeping with that of a Muslim country. The Moorish style architecture has been used on several other buildings in KL. You must see our railway station; it's like something out of the Arabian Nights."

"OK Hamid, drive on."

They entered the club and were greeted by a Chinese waiter dressed entirely in white.

"Hello Woon, we are lunching with Mr. Williams."

They sat at a table next to the veranda and Jack noticed the large number of waiters in the dining room. They had been seated for several minutes when George said, "Sorry Jack for not offering you a drink but I have to wait for the MD to order first. Ah, here he comes now."

The man approaching the table was about 5'8" tall, slim built and wearing a light weight tan suit with the obligatory white shirt. He wore his school tie, Cambridge, and his shoes were burnished brown. His brown eyes and sandy hair offset his sallow complexion.

His most striking feature was his nose which was too large for his small head and was accentuated by his small neatly trimmed moustache.

George sprang to his feet.

"MD may I introduce Mr. Jack Simpson."

Almost without stopping he offered a limp handshake, said, "Ah yes, Simpson" in an off-hand manner, sat down and called out, "Boy!"

The waiter who was standing right behind Williams came to his side.

"Gin and Tonic."

George turned to Jack. "Would you care for a drink?"

"Yes please, limeade."

"Same for me," said George.

"I am pleased to meet you Mr. Williams."

Jack somewhat emphasized 'pleased' to contrast the discourteous greeting of Williams, but this subtlety was lost on Williams. However the mention of his name seemed to temporarily befuddle him. It was as though he had no idea whom Jack was addressing. Jack reckoned this was because he always expected to be deferentially called MD.

"I am grateful for the excellent accommodation you provided."

"What? Oh quite."

By this time Williams was engrossed in the menu. He ordered as soon as his drink arrived. George and Jack followed suit.

"This your first time in these parts?"

"Yes, it is, and I am looking forward to seeing as much as I can of the Malayan Peninsula."

"Ah, you said Malayan Peninsula. Good man. Most people make the mistake of calling it Malaya. Shows some education on your part. Which university did you attend, Cambridge or Oxford?"

"Neither, I attended Glasgow."

"Glasgow? Well then you probably don't know much about this area. There are three entities on this peninsula, the Straits Settlements, the Federated Malay States and the Unfederated Malay States."

"You are quite correct that my knowledge is very limited. I know nothing much more than the first entity you mentioned is comprised of Penang, Malacca and Singapore. The Federated Malay States are Selangor, Negri Sembilan, Perak and Pahang. The Unfederated States are, Johore, Perlis, Kedah, Kelantan and Trengganu."

George had to bite his tongue to stop from shouting 'Bravo'. Instead he looked at Jack with intense admiration.

Williams squinted his eyes as though seeing Jack for the first time before saying, "Yes, quite. Well if it suits you, I can tell you a bit more about the history of some of this area. But first tell me, how are things in London these days?"

"I believe the people are showing great resiliency in the face of the air raids."

"No, no," interrupted Williams. "I know all about that sort of thing. I mean the fashion. What are men wearing these days? One can have a suit made out here but they are way behind the times in fashion."

While he was saying this the soup arrived and Williams began eating his right away.

Jack could hardly believe his ears. This conceited ass was only concerned over the number of buttons he should have on his next suit while thousands of people were dying in the bombing of Britain.

"I am not up to date on the latest styles in clothes. The only fashion trend I am aware of is the tendency for more men to wear a moustache. Probably due to the respect accorded the brave pilots of the RAF."

George looked at Jack and wondered, 'What are you up to now Simpson? I have only just met you but I bet you are not the type to be flattering someone like the MD. What's your game you sly old fox?'

Williams stopped eating for a second, fingered his small moustache lovingly and said, "Utter nonsense to have one of those vulgar large moustaches. A chap should be neatly turned out."

"These days it seems that people in Britain tend to associate a small moustache with Mr. Hitler," said Jack with a look of innocence on his face.

George thought he would die.

He tried desperately not to guffaw out loud. Choking back his laughter resulted in him coughing a mouthful of soup into his raised napkin. He was gagging for breath and tears were running down his cheeks.

"For God's sake Knight, what is wrong with you?"

"I beg your pardon MD; I choked on the vegetables in the soup. Please excuse me."

With that he stood up and jogged to the toilet. He barely got there before he burst into the most uncontrollable laughter. It took him a few minutes to regain some semblance of control. He splashed water on his face and returned to the table, walking with as much aplomb as he could muster. He did not dare look at Jack for fear of having another fit of laughter.

"I must say it's a poor show when a chap can't behave decently at the table. Look you have slopped soup on your shirt."

"I am most dreadfully sorry MD. If you will forgive me, I shall go home and change."

"Yes you had better. Come back in an hour or so. That will allow time to brief Simpson on KL."

George left the table with a huge smile on his face. As he left the club he thought, 'I was right; you are a cunning one Simpson. Definitely someone to watch.'

Williams had stared at George's back as he left.

"Complete waste of money, that one. He will never amount to anything."

Jack kept his head down over his food. He had had his fun; there was no need to skewer Williams again.

"You must understand Simpson there are many chaps like Knight out here. Come out for a few years and learn nothing. Spend their time drinking and carousing. Now take me, I have spent considerable time researching the history of this place. Helps one keep a handle on things."

Jack thought, 'I know I should keep my mouth shut but this blowhard is too much to take.' So he said, "That's very impressive. I am sure it must be invaluable when dealing with the local people. They must really appreciate a man of your stature understanding their cultures."

"Understand their cultures? Deal with the locals? What a lot of rot! You haven't been listening Simpson. I do not talk to the local staff. That's the job of the junior managers. No, you have completely missed the point. This country was built by the English. They would still be living in mud shacks if it were not for us. These people have no culture."

'I seem to have heard this tune before,' thought Jack.

"Now take KL for example. In the mid 1800's a group of about ninety Chinese prospectors came up the Klang River in search of tin. They camped at the meeting point of the Klang and Gombak rivers. They named that place Kuala Lumpur which simply means Muddy Estuary. Within a month about seventy were dead from malaria. However they did find tin deposits just to the east in the Malay village of Ampang and others flocked to this area despite the risk from mosquitoes. Most of them were immigrants from China escaping a life of punishing poverty. To them the lure of riches was worth the risk. It did not take long for secret societies to begin operations. In addition to taking a percentage of immigrants' wages, they controlled the opium dens, the brothels and the gambling halls."

"The two controlling societies, the Hai San and the Ghee Hin fought continuously and soon KL became a rowdy, violent, dangerous town. This worried the Sultan of Selangor, Abdul Samad who then used a technique employed previously in other areas of the peninsula. He appointed one Yap Ah Loy as 'Kapitan China', the Chinese Headman of Kuala Lumpur. Yap was a tough Hakka and pledged the support of his society, the Hai San to the Sultan."

"About this time the ruler of Klang, Raja Mahdi, decided to stop paying his dues to the Sultan. The Ghee Hin sided with the Raja and civil was broke out in Selangor. Now Raja Mahdi was a highly respected warrior and was much more popular with the people than the Sultan. It seemed inevitable that he would prevail; however the Sultan called on the English Colonial Government in Singapore which sent its troops to his aid. This sent a resounding message throughout the peninsula; being that even a weak, disliked ruler can prevail with England on his side. We have run things ever since."

Williams continued exalting the role of the English in creating this country until George reappeared in a clean shirt and tie.

"Well I must get back to the office. If you need anything just ask Knight. We will make hotel arrangements at the ports you are visiting. Perhaps you can take care of that in between dribbling food all over yourself Knight."

"Of course MD."

"I don't suppose I will see you again, Simpson so I will say goodbye. Knight, be in my office at five o'clock."

With that he turned and left.

"He is a charming man," said Jack sardonically.

George who was obviously upset by William's command did not pick up on Jack's sarcasm.

"Oh, do you really like him?"

Then he saw the grin on Jack's face.

"I say Jack that was awfully naughty of you to compare him to Hitler. I thought you might be having some sport but I did not see that one coming. I almost peed my pants."

"Mr. Williams did not see any irony in my remark. He seems to be oblivious to most things except himself, a complete narcissist."

"Steady on old chap you never know who may hear you," said George looking around worriedly.

"If my remarks get you in trouble I am sorry George."

"Not your remarks old chap, my reaction to them."

"What will happen to you?"

"Oh, probably the usual. A jolly good reaming out. You see, I shouldn't say this but the MD is a bit of a coward. What he will do is gather a few of the directors, the ones who never disagree with him, tell them of my outlandish behavior and ask them what they think. One by one they will try to outdo each other in condemning me. At five he will have the same directors in his office and they will berate me mercilessly. One wouldn't mind a telling off from him personally; however, he must always have others to support him."

"May I ask you a question George?"

"Of course."

"Why do you put up with it?"

"I really like it out here Jack. When you see more of this country you will see what an absolutely wonderful place it is. There is one other reason. My uncle has never said anything to me directly but I suspect he and perhaps others in London know the MD's personality. I think he would be disappointed in me if I gave in to this bullying."

"Ah, I see. May I ask you another question?"

"Of course Jack."

"How long did it take you to rehearse Williams in the history of KL?"

George looked shocked at this question and then a conspiratorial smile broke out on his face.

"You really are an astute person Jack. It took almost six months."

"Let's not dwell any longer on Mr. High and Mighty Williams. What shall we do next George?"

"I have a couple of suggestions."

"No George, I do not want suggestions. I want you to decide. You are in charge."

"Oh, I say, well if you say so old man. I will show you a few more of the sights in KL. Along the way we will stop at one of the ubiquitous coffee shops for a cup of local strong black coffee, called kopi-o. You will drop me off at the office at a quarter to five so that I can reserve the bungalow at Klang before my meeting with the MD. The car will take you back to No.25 where you will have a restful evening and I will pick you up at nine tomorrow morning. We will travel to Klang which is the town at Port Swettenham, where you will spend two days on your review and then we will return to KL."

"That is an excellent plan, George."

George smiled rather shyly.

"Thank you for forcing me to make a decision, Jack. You know, it felt rather good."

Upon his return to the bungalow Jack was greeted by Ah Kang.

"Good afternoon, Mistah Slimson. You like to have tea?"

"Yes please Ah Kang that would be very nice."

Ah Kang beamed and rushed away. Jack sat on one of the comfortable sofas on the veranda. In a short time his tea arrived. Ah Kang poured a cup and hovered nearby awaiting Jack's reaction. When Jack tasted it and smiled his approval, he too smiled.

"Once again this is excellent tea. Thank you very much."

"You go out for dinnah tonight, Mistah Slimson?"

"No Ah Kang, I will stay in tonight. Would it be possible to have a sandwich?"

Ah Kang looked shocked.

"No, no. I cook for you. What you like, lamb chops, roast beef, maybe roast chicken?"

"You are most kind but those dishes would be too filling. I am not so hungry. Would it be possible to cook a local dish?"

Ah Kang's eyes lit up.

"I make something for you. What time you want to eat?"

"Would 7.30 be all right?"

"No ploblem, Mistah Slimson."

Ah Kang slid away towards the kitchen and Jack could hear him explain everything to Ah Eng.

At exactly 7.30, Jack sat at the highly polished dining table laid with silver and china and imagined he must be in the finest restaurant in the world. When Ah Kang laid a mountain of fried rice in front of him, he knew he was indeed in the best restaurant in the world. Somehow the term 'fried rice' could never explain the sumptuousness of the dish that lay there tantalizing his senses. This dish included wonderful fresh vegetables, but featured soy cooked strips of pork and a huge amount of the most succulent shrimp all toped with crispy fried onions and garnished with glistening slivers of green onions, slices of scrambled egg and small dried fish called ikan bilis. Side dishes of sliced chili included red chilies in vinegar and really hot green chilies. Jack sat and stared at this meal for almost a full minute before he could say, "Ah Kang, I have never seen anything so appetizing in my entire life."

"I will serve you Mistah Slimson. Maybe you like a beer?"

"That would be wonderful."

After eating the first plateful Jack could not resist having a second plateful and had to force himself to stop at that. His mouth still tingled from the multitude of flavors it had experienced. With some effort he rose from the table. As if by magic Ah Kang appeared.

"Anything else Mistah Slimson?"

'I am not so slim now' thought Jack. "No thank you Ah Kang, I am going for a walk and then to bed."

He stood in front of Ah Kang, looked into his eyes, bowed and said, "I have never had such a delicious meal. Thank you."

Ah Kang bowed in return and out of the corner of his eye Jack saw Ah Eng in the kitchen doorway and she was bowing too.

"I could not stay here too long Ah Kang or I would swell up like a balloon. He stuck out his belly and held out his arms to show how fat he would be. Ah Eng burst into a raucous giggle in the kitchen. As he walked down the driveway to Ampang Road, he could still hear her uproarious cackling laughter.

Chapter 17

Next morning George arrived promptly at nine o'clock. Before he could utter a greeting Jack said, "Well, what happened?"

"Just as I thought, the MD and three others were waiting for me. They took turns of telling me I must learn to represent the Company in a better manner or I should consider another career. Luckily the MD's secretary came in after only ten minutes to say he had a telephone call. He had just started to remind her in a loud voice that he was not to be disturbed when she said it was his wife. He took the call in the office and we could hear her strident voice reminding him of a dinner party they were giving that night and telling him to get home now. That ended our meeting."

"I was rather hoping you would have lost some of that well bred decorum you have and punched one or two of them in the nose."

George was about to answer when he noticed Jack's mischievous grin. He laughed and said, "You know Simpson you are the type of fellow who could easily get a chap into hot water."

Hamid loaded their bags in the car while Jack said goodbye to Ah Kang and Ah Eng, promising to see them in a few days. Once they pulled away Jack told George of the delicious dinner he had the previous night.

"Oh do be quiet Jack. You are making me hungry just listening to you. There are a few very good crab restaurants in Klang. If you enjoy spicy food we can have chili crab tonight."

"Great, but I will have to either skip lunch or have something really light."

"Not to worry old boy we can have a bowl of mee goreng. You had fried rice last night; today you can have mee goreng, fried noodles."

They drove in silence for a while; Jack soaking up the sights once again.

"I can see you are really smitten by KL."

"It is so completely different from any past experience. It is utterly fascinating."

"How far did the MD get in his lesson on the history of KL?"

"Down to the civil war in Selangor, then he began to ramble a bit."

"After the civil war KL was a terrible mess. Many of the Chinese workers wanted to leave; however, that indomitable man Yap Ah Loy quelled much of the clan warfare and persuaded the tin mines to reopen. Luckily in 1878 the price of tin doubled and real prosperity began. Two years later the British Resident moved the State Capital from Klang to KL."

"Perhaps you may remember I mentioned when we first met that the port at Klang was named after a Frank Swettenham. He was the architect of the FMS, the Federated Malay States and became its Resident General. His energetic planning of KL was the driving force in changing a shanty town into the bricks and mortar capital of the FMS in 1889. He later became the Governor of the Straits Settlements. I believe he retired in 1904. He is still alive, living in London. He even had his portrait painted by Sergeant, the American painter. I saw it once. Even in oils he made me shake in my shoes."

"I recall Williams seemed to greatly admire him."

"He was reputedly a single minded somewhat irascible bugger. Maybe he had to be to accomplish all he did. I don't know. It always seemed to me that you should be able to lead without fear."

"I am sure it can be done George, but only by the most talented of people. Some people believe the end justifies the means. Who knows? Maybe they are correct. The only thing certain is that they believe they are correct. However the scales of justice have a way of balancing out in the end; oftentimes to the chagrin of those who were once so certain they and they alone were right."

George pondered this for a few moments before saying, "You know Mr. Jack Simpson; you are probably the smartest person I have ever met. You could probably accomplish anything you set your mind to. But if you did I would not want to be someone blocking your path. I think you would get the job done no matter what the consequences."

"I am not sure if that is a compliment or not."

"To be honest neither am I. I do know one thing; I would consider it a great privilege to be called your friend."

"I feel the same about you George. Let's shake hands to friendship."
They shook hands.

"This is becoming a little melodramatic, George. Tell me more about this wonderful country."

George talked for most of the rest of the way to Klang; however Jack was only half listening. George's insightful comments had made him begin focusing on his mission and the consequences of his actions.

"Well here we are. I suggest we go to the bungalow first and drop off our bags."

"Fine with me," said Jack.

"I will introduce you to the harbormaster and then leave you to get on with your work. I am sure someone will arrange a light lunch of mee goreng for you. I have plenty of work at our office here, so I will see you tonight."

The next two days were very busy for Jack. In addition to his cover assignment he was picking up a lot of other useful information. They left Klang mid afternoon and returned to KL. That evening George took Jack to the 'Dog' for dinner.

"Let's have a drink in the Long Bar before dinner."

This was indeed a long bar, Jack reckoned it was over thirty five feet long. There were about ten tables between the bar and the veranda. The walls were decorated with photographs of past and present sports teams and there were several trophies on the shelves.

"This bar is for men only and the habitual patrons brook no exception," said George.

"It sounds like a few places I know in Glasgow."

They were just about to order a drink when a waiter rushed in and whispered something to George.

"Damnation," he said vehemently.

"What is it," asked Jack.

"I have been summoned to the MD's home. I believe I know the subject and it will only take a few minutes to brief him. I will tell the boy to serve you and put it on my chit. I'm sorry. I'll be back shortly."

"Don't worry I'll be fine."

George dashed off and Jack was about to order a drink when a Scottish voice said, "I heard you mention Glasgow. May I offer you a drink?"

"That is very kind of you."

"We Scots always take care of one another. My name is John McKay."

John McKay was about the same height as Jack. His fair hair was curly and short. He would have been described in Scotland as 'raw boned' meaning he was big shouldered and rangy. His hazel eyes shone under his bushy eyebrows and his generous mouth had a quiet smile. Jack estimated he was five or six years older than he. McKay held out a large hand in greeting.

Jack shook the proffered hand.

"Jack Simpson. I am pleased to meet you."

"What would you like Mr. Simpson?"

Before Jack could answer a voice from one of the tables called out loudly, "Three more stengahs, Loon. Make it quick, chop chop."

One of the barmen began pouring the three whiskies.

Jack replied to Mr. McKay, "I would like a whisky and water, please."

McKay turned to another barman who was standing in front of them and said something which Jack did not understand, but he heard the word stengah. The barman bowed slightly to McKay and quickly made two whisky and waters. Jack noticed it was a much superior brand to that which the other barman had used and the amount of whisky was significantly more generous.

"Thank you," Jack said to the barman.

Then he thanked McKay before offering the traditional Scottish toast, "Slaandjivaa."

Jack sipped his drink appreciatively.

"This is very good; I guess a stengah is a whisky and water."

"Yes, it is the Malay word for half and is commonly used for a half of whisky with water. You must be new out here. When did you arrive?"

"Only a few days ago."

"And what are your first impressions of this country?"

Jack stared into his drink for several moments before answering.

"A friend told me I had to appreciate this country by opening up all my senses and let it sweep into my soul. I didn't really understand what he meant."

He transferred his gaze to McKay.

"I believe I am beginning to understand now. There is more energy, gracefulness and happiness here than I could ever have believed possible."

He stopped self consciously before saying, "Excuse me I am talking as though I know something of this country. That is presumptuous of a four day visitor."

"Aye it may be, but it seems tae me you have learned more in four days than most people learn in four years. You will do well out here."

"Unfortunately I am only here for a few weeks. But I plan to return one day."

"If it is not too impertinent to ask, what line of work are you in?"

Jack smiled and McKay asked, "Did I say something funny?"

"Oh no Mr. McKay, You see my granny raised me from I was thirteen and she always used the word impertinent. Usually when she rebuked me for forgetting my manners by speaking out of turn, it brought back lovely memories, that's all. I am in the shipping business."

"I am a rubber planter myself."

"I was told there are many Scots out here working on rubber estates. Is this so?"

"Aye we have our fair share, and in tin mining too."

"I was also told the Scots were good at managing rubber estates because of; let me think of the exact phrase, ah yes, 'their hard headed no nonsense approach'. Is that also true?"

"You wouldn't have been told this by an upper class Englishman, by any chance?"

"As a matter of fact, yes."

"Aye I thought so. You see it is hard work on a plantation. And it is true that there are times when you have to exert discipline, but most of our employees have been with us for some time and they are very good workers. Success as an estate manager does not come from being merely hard headed; it is the ability to manage people of very different cultures. The first thing a new expatriate must learn is language. Malay is a necessity of life and must be learned quickly. To be frank it is not a difficult language to learn. Next a pay increase is awarded if you learn Tamil. Most of the tappers on our estate use Tamil. This is a much more difficult task. If you succeed you find this ability to communicate with your people helps you better understand their way of life and their culture. The respect you gain pays off in many aspects of your work."

"What dialect of Chinese were you speaking when you ordered the drinks?"

"Cantonese. It is the most prevalent dialect in KL. I am by no means proficient, but I know enough to greet people and order a meal or a drink."

"It seemed to work well. You received a splendid brand and amount."

"That just proves the point. If you are courteous to people they respond in kind. If you are like that loudmouth over there you get minimal service. I hate to say it but this rudeness out here is not limited to the English, there are several Scots who are just as bad."

The barman delivered two more drinks without being asked. Jack thanked him and McKay said a few words in Cantonese. The barman smiled before he replied and then moved away to serve someone else.

"Thank you, Mr. McKay. I feel guilty at not being able to buy you a drink."

"Think nothing of it and please call me John. If it is all right with you I will call you Jack."

Jack nodded his assent. "Please do."

"By the way I am not treating you on this round; Ah Song gave us these drinks. Of course he does not have to pay for them: probably it is being made up by giving less than the full amount to these charming gentlemen behind us. You see Ah Song knew as soon as you entered the bar that you were not a member. He thought you very polite when you thanked him for his service before you thanked me. As a token of his appreciation he gave us these drinks."

"I hope I did not offend you John by thanking the barman first."

"Not at all. I saw it was an instinctive action and was pleased to see someone be polite."

"How do I say 'thank you' in Cantonese, John?"

McKay told him and he practiced it twice. The next time Ah Song passed he held up his glass and said, "Mg Goi". Ah Song's dark eyes darted around the bar and as no one was paying attention to him, he bowed deeply, his slightly balding head gleaming under the lights of the bar.

"I am sure my accent was terrible."

"That doesn't matter; in six years out here I have never once had anyone mock my attempts to speak their language. The fact that one is trying is the most important thing."

Jack was enjoying his conversation with McKay when George returned. He introduced George to McKay.

"Ah a fellow countryman I see," said George. He was as surprised as Jack when McKay denied this.

"You see he is from the west coast and I am from Dundee on the east coast."

"I thought we Glaswegians only had trouble with Edinburghers," said Jack jokingly.

"You Glaswegians have no idea what real trouble is until you meet a Dundonian."

They both burst into laughter.

"Would you care to join Jack and me for dinner, Mr. McKay?"

"That would be a great pleasure. Thank you very much."

Despite their dispirit backgrounds, the evening was a huge success with much good humor. At the end of the evening McKay and George exchanged business cards. McKay also gave one to Jack.

"If your travels take you down Seremban way drop by and visit me. I know this is the usual farewell comment, but I really mean it. I would truly enjoy showing you around a rubber plantation and Seremban is not too far from KL."

"If I can finish my other business in time I will certainly do so."

George chimed in, "You will pass through Seremban on your way South in a few weeks."

"Then I shall certainly take up your kind offer, John. I will contact you in two weeks if that is OK."

"I will look forward to that."

They shook hands and said their goodbyes. As if by telepathy, Hamid drove up as Jack and George emerged from the club.

"Doesn't your driver ever get time off?"

"Actually quite a lot. I only use him when we have guests or if I am attending a Company dinner. I prefer to drive myself."

As they pulled into the driveway on No.25 Ampang Road Jack asked George how things had gone with Williams.

"He wanted to know a minor detail on a contract. As I was able to quote all the relevant information I believe I am now out of the dog house. Shall I pick you up at eight thirty tomorrow?"

"That would be fine. There is quite a bit of final information I need from you and I need details of my trip to the East Coast."

"Everything has been organized. I will brief you tomorrow. I had a wonderful time with you two Scots. Goodnight Jack."

In the morning Jack sat down to a superb breakfast of ripe papaya with fresh lime, followed by two perfectly poached eggs on toast. He had just finished his third cup of coffee when he heard the car arrive.

"Good morning Jack," called out George cheerily.

"Good morning George, you are very chipper this morning."

"The MD is off to Singapore today; therefore, apart from the inevitable telephone call or two I can devote myself to helping you."

The day passed quickly. Jack had now gathered quite a store of information on military shipments and their destinations in and around Kuala Lumpur. Most of this was committed to memory but some specific figures were written on separate pages in code. As he had been taught, these pages were kept in different files and in random order.

George had given him a detailed itinerary covering his visits to the East Coast followed by Penang on the North West Coast, then to Malacca stopping briefly on the way in KL and Seremban and finally Singapore.

There was sufficient flexibility in the schedule should one place take a little longer than anticipated. Jack studied this itinerary before saying, "George your talents are wasted here. This is perfect; you seem to have planned for any eventuality."

"As you can see you fly to Kuantan tomorrow. I wrote on your itinerary that you will be met by a good friend of mine Captain William Mc-Cartney. Bill is a first class chap; I think you will like him. He has arranged your lodgings in Kuantan and a meeting with Colonel Jackson the commander of the garrison. Bill is also arranging your visit to Trengganu."

The flight to Kuantan was a bumpy one. Jack was a bit concerned by the effect of some of the turbulence; however the Australian pilot, who kept an almost constant commentary during the flight, assured the passengers that this was normal at this time of year. It was particularly bad as they flew over the Pahang Mountains which were covered in jungle. He breezily told them of his treks into this area and if anyone should venture there they should not worry too much about the tigers.

"They probable won't bother you if you don't bother them. You will be in much more danger from the mosquitoes. They are big enough to carry you off."

Jack got his greatest fright as they hit one patch of turbulence and the pilot, who had obviously forgotten to switch off the intercom system, yelled out, "Oh shite!" A few nerve-wracking moments later he announced, "Sorry about that ladies and gents, please pardon my French. No worries, I just spilt me bloody coffee all over myself."

Jack had enjoyed the scenery but was happy to land. Prior to their approach they had to circle due to the military aircraft activity. As they landed he counted ten Hudsons of a Royal Australian Air Force squadron and nine Vildebeestes and eight Blenheim Bombers of the Royal Air Force.

A burly six foot army officer was waiting holding a sheet of paper with Jack's name written on it. Jack identified himself and received a very firm handshake.

"Pleased to meet you. Sorry about this piece of paper but George insisted I do this. Said he didn't want any cock ups when meeting his good friend. As if the British Army ever had a cock up," he said with a broad smile.

Jack liked him instantly.

"You are booked in at the rest house. The Colonel doesn't like civilians staying on post. You will probably be more comfortable there anyway. Have you stayed at a rest house?"

"No, is it some type of hotel?"

"In a way, yes. They were initially established to house government officers traveling on business. Now they accept non government guests. They are not luxurious but they are clean and much better than the local Chinese hotels."

"How long have you been here?'

"Almost a year now. This is an Indian Battalion and a few of us have been seconded to train the troops."

"The jungle must be a difficult place for training."

"Luckily we don't do much of that. Our principal job is to protect the airport. Oh before I forget, Colonel Jackson would like you to join him in the mess for dinner at seven thirty."

"That's very kind of him. Shall I see you there?"

"Yes, yes, I shall be there; however as luck would have it I have an early start in the morning therefore will not be able to stay for the fun."

"What fun?"

"The old man likes to get to bed early so he usually leaves around nine thirty. His wife is more of a live wire and she stays up to midnight some evenings. She likes to dance so the gramophone is hauled out. Just to be sure everything goes well and nothing gets out of hand, the Colonel's number two, Major Dunbar, stays to chaperone Mrs. Jackson."

"Does she need a chaperone?"

"If the old man has been unusually stuffy and they have had words, she is likely to have quite a few more drinks. That's when the trouble starts."

"Surely no officer would take advantage of that."

"Not while Dunbar is there. But she is the one who seems to lose control. That's when the Major escorts her home. However there will be two of three other ladies there tonight so all should be peaceful. Tell you what, I will wait for you while you freshen up a little and we can have a drink before we go."

"Sounds good to me, am I dressed all right?"

"You are fine. I have arranged a car for your use while you are here; it is at the rest house. After our drink you follow me to the camp then as I have to leave early you can drive yourself home. I have a pass to get you in and out of the camp. It is in my bag."

Jack went to his room and began washing his face. He heard a slight noise at his door and was immediately on alert. He ran to the door and quickly swung it open but no one was there. As he was closing the door he noticed a piece of paper on the floor.

He recognized it was in code. He carefully checked outside the door again before locking the door and decoding the message. It contained the time and location of tonight's meeting. More correctly it was tomorrow morning's meeting. It was at two thirty a.m. in the jungle. 'At least at that time it will not be difficult to get away unseen,' he thought.

Dinner was a stifling affair, full of silly platitudes and even more inane toasts to the invincibility of the British Army. When Colonel Jackson stood and proposed a toast to 'King and Country' the mess resounded with a chorus of 'Here, here.' Jack noticed two of the ladies did not join in the chorus. One was Mrs. Jackson and the other was a dark haired lady with dark eyes that flashed in the lights of the mess. Twice Jack had caught her staring at him but he had no interest. His heart already belonged to someone else. However his interest in her picked up after he overheard two officers talk of special precautions to be taken that night and extra guards to be posted around town.

This was an unexpected complication that made him uneasy and his mind began developing alternate plans. He had no idea what part she could play in any new plan but he had learned never to overlook any possible diversionary opportunity and an innocent accomplice was always a high priority in any subterfuge. He had to learn more of what had prompted the increased alert. Surely it was not connected to his visit. After dinner he deftly guided an unsuspecting Bill to a spot close to the same two officers, who were still discussing their assignments for that night.

"Remember Charles, have sentries posted at every hotel in town."

Now the gears of his brain were whirring as he finalized a plan to get out of the rest house without raising an alarm. This girl could be very useful after all, if she was a willing and unsuspecting participant.

Bill had overheard the conversation of the two officers and hissed, "Shut up you idiots. Are you trying to broadcast your duties to everyone?"

"Oh, sorry Captain."

"Stupid young pups."

"Pardon Bill what did you say?" said Jack innocently.

"Oh nothing Jack, just Army business. By the way what did you think of dinner?"

"It seems you have a well motivated group," said Jack diplomatically.

"Well motivated but green as grass. We would do better to make our budding officer corps read Sun Tsu and learn never to underestimate an enemy. Most of these lads think the Army is a club and not a deadly business."

"Sorry Bill but I had my mind on other business. Who is that attractive girl with the dark hair?"

He had formulated the outline of a plan in his head.

"She teaches English at the Chinese Girls High School. Her name is Jessica Taylor. I don't suppose you would like to meet her, would you?"

"Yes please."

"Well I have only time to introduce you then I must be off. I hope to see you again Jack."

The music had started. Bill just managed to take hold of Jessica's arm before one of the young officers asked her to dance.

"Jessica, may I introduce Jack Simpson, another civilian."

He made a face of mock contempt.

"Unfortunately I have to go and I am afraid this wild Scotsman may start doing a Highland Reel or whatever they do in the frozen north. Would you do me a huge favor and teach him to dance respectably."

As they danced she said, "It seems to me you need no lessons in dancing."

"They say one can only dance as well as one's partner."

"Oh a smooth talker too. What do you do that gives you all these skills Mr. Jack Simpson?"

"Nothing glamorous I am afraid. I am in the shipping business."

"I see. I also noticed you did not eat much dinner. Was the food not to you liking or was it the company?"

"Oh no, I had a late lunch," he lied. "Since you noticed so much I really have to apologize to you."

"Apologize, Why?"

"You probably caught me staring at you all during dinner."

"Actually I thought you were trying to ignore me."

Jack appeared to be flustered and deliberately misstepped causing them to have to stop dancing for an instant. As they started again she said, "I am sorry. I am too outspoken sometimes. It probably comes from being a schoolteacher."

They danced closer and closer together as time passed. When at just after eleven, the Colonel's wife decided to have an early night, the music stopped.

"Well Jack, this turned out to be a lovely evening. I should be getting home now."

"Can I drop you at your house?"

"I have my own car."

"Jessica, would you think it rude if I offered you a nightcap? I happen to have a quite good brandy at the rest house."

"I was hoping you would ask. I will follow you in my car."

He kept his arm around her as they walked to the door. He wanted others to notice their budding intimacy. He noticed the soldier on duty outside the rest house as he pulled up. To be sure he got his attention he waited for Jessica to stop then opened the car door for her and when she got out gave her a long kiss. She did not object.

"That was nice, Jack."

When they entered his room they kissed again and again and again. When his hand touched her breast she moaned and held him tighter.

"I must use your loo. I will be right back, my darling."

Jack quickly open his case and got the sleeping drops out of the leather bag. He put a few drops in a glass and was adding brandy when she returned.

"I don't think I need a drink," she said.

"Let's just have one to toast our meeting."

She kissed him first then drank the brandy quickly, returning immediately to his arms. He slid one hand inside her dress and touched her breast again.

"Perhaps we would be more comfortable on the bed," she said.

She began unbuttoning her dress as Jack undressed and switched off the light. They were caressing each other and her moans were becoming more urgent. He was not sure how long the drug would take to put her to sleep. He did not have long to wait. As he was running his hands over her body her moans started to become quieter and her breathing deepened. Soon she was sound asleep.

Jack went to his case and took out a slim flashlight and the three pistols from the false bottom.

He strapped the pistols to his body then tied a knife to the inside of his leg. He put several packets of cigarettes in a pouch which he tied round his waist. Then he dressed. Every item of clothing was black including his rubber soled shoes. Next he picked up the most important item, his compass. He had memorized the coordinates of the meeting place and the directions but he knew he could easily get lost without his compass.

It was twelve fifteen when he slipped out the back window and stealthily made his way towards the jungle. He thought that once in the jungle he would be relatively safe but he was wrong. His training saved him. He had been taught to travel in a zigzag pattern stopping every five to ten minutes to listen to the sounds of the jungle. He had been warned to be on alert if animal noises stopped and at all costs stay clear of any wide paths.

He had been traveling for half an hour when he heard it. What he heard was silence. The noise of the jungle had stopped. He crawled under a bush and waited. It was five minutes before he heard the sound of people coming. They were certainly not well trained in silent patrolling. Seven Indian soldiers passed within fifteen yards of him. They were following a pathway and grumbling quietly to one another about their duty. They had decided they had traveled far enough into the jungle and it was time to return.

Jack waited another five minutes before resuming his journey. He arrived at the meeting place an hour ahead of the appointed time. This was according to his plan. He reconnoitered the area thoroughly before taking up a position of advantage.

He had not fully realized how grateful he would be to the Japanese scientist who had developed the odorless mosquito repellent he had rubbed on.

The Australian pilot had only exaggerated a little when he said they could carry you off. They were big and active.

Chapter 18

A gentle breeze rustled the trees in the jungle as five figures dressed completely in black crept along in single file. The leader of the group held up his hand and waited until they had all caught up with him. He was tall for a Chinese, about five feet ten inches, and like the others had a heavy wool sweater tied around his waist. Most people think of the Malayan jungle as a perpetual steam bath; however, in the mountains of Pahang, it is a cold place at night. Even during the day the dense cover of the jungle allows no sunlight to penetrate and, although humid, it is not hot. They had traveled a long way that day, first a circuitous route from their camp near Mount Tapis to the river near Sungei Lembing, then a canoe ride to a spot four miles from where they now were. These last four miles had been particularly hard on the men, as they had to hack their way through the jungle.

"No more using parangs," he hissed. "Only three miles to go."

Surprisingly he spoke Malay, although only one member of the group was Malay, the other four all being Chinese. Virtually every person born in Malaya spoke Malay, whether they were Malay, Chinese or Indian. Two of the Chinese spoke Hokkien and Teow Chiew, the other two spoke Cantonese and Hakka; therefore, the only language all four Chinese had in common was Malay. The leader was also fluent in English and one other Chinese spoke halting English.

The leader, Ah Tong, repeated his order, "No more using parangs, they make too much noise and there may be patrols."

The parang is a broad bladed, curved knife about eighteen inches long. It is used by farmers to clear undergrowth, and is necessary when traveling through the jungle. In the right hands it is also a formidable weapon. All of them slung their parangs through their belts except Tan, one of the

Chinese, who carried his at the ready. His blackened teeth seemed to be in a permanent grin because of the scar that ran from his left ear to the corner of his mouth. This was the result of a fight with a drunken English tin miner when he was only twelve. He had been walking past the three Englishmen who were sitting outside a small restaurant drinking beer. In his drunkenness one of them had knocked his change off the marble table. Tan stopped to pick up the money and was placing it on the table when one of them grabbed his arm and yelled, "You little bastard, trying to steal my money, eh?"

He punched Tan in the face. Trying to break his hold, Tan punched back and was almost free when one of the others grabbed a sharp knife from the table and flailed wildly at Tan. The first swing missed, the second did not.

Reflecting on this incident several years later, Tan thought he could maybe, just maybe, have forgiven a dunked man who was not able to control his reactions; but he could never, never forgive the three men for laughing uproariously at the skinny little kid who staggered away with blood pouring down his face. This was to be the last knife fight he lost. Although he was still slim and his grinning face appeared amiable, he was exceptionally proficient with his parang, as eleven men had already discovered.

Even Ah Tong was careful around Tan.

It was 2.00 am when they finally arrived at the appointed area. Without a word being spoken, they spread out in a circle. A maneuver they had practiced and used many times. Now, one of the most difficult parts of any operation, waiting. Even for the most experienced guerilla, this was always a nerve-wracking time. Ah Tong knew the statistics of such an agonizing venture. More than 90% of the time nothing untoward happened. Yet recently, six of his men had been killed in ambushes. No matter how hard he concentrated on this problem, he could not figure out how the British suddenly became so smart.

To be sure they had some seasoned troops and they were now using Gurka troops. These soldiers were to be avoided at all costs, as their skill with their kukris almost equaled that of Tan with his parang. He had heard of a religious rite of the Gurkas where one had the honor to be selected to sacrifice a bullock. He did this by beheading the beast with only one blow from his kukri. Just thinking about it caused Ah Tong to tremble.

He was awakened from his thoughts by a voice saying, "You can come out now boys."

All the others were as shocked as Ah Tong. Somehow Jack had slipped through their cordon. This had never happened before, never. They quickly refocused their attention, four of them staying hidden, but now ready to fight, only Ah Tong moved forward.

"Put down your gun and put your hands on your head," commanded Ah Tong.

Jack unbuckled his gun and laid it on the ground.

"Before I put up my hands, let's get the formalities out of the way. How is the jungle moonlight?"

"It grows brighter every night," said Ah Tong.

Jack put his hands on his head as Ah Tong approached.

"By the way, you will find two more pistols inside my shirt. They are for you, I'm sorry to say I could not get too much ammo'. I also brought some cigarettes, I suppose you can get some from your sources in the towns, but I brought these anyway."

Ah Tong approached warily and searched Jack. He grunted as he found the knife strapped to Jack's inner leg.

"Don't you trust anyone?"

"No, you live longer that way."

"Smart man," said Ah Tong as he signaled the others to come out. As they approached, Jack tossed a pack of cigarettes to each man, giving the rest to Ah Tong.

"Now tell me, how did you get through our ring?"

"Well, I knew you would probably arrive early. As a precaution I also arrived early and have been here for about an hour. I climbed that tree about thirty minutes ago to wait for you."

Ah Tong repeated this explanation in Malay for the benefit of his men. Jaffar, the Malay, stared with respect at Campbell, while Tan said to Ah Tong, "We should keep this Englishman he could become one of us. He is clever."

Ah Tong turned to Jack and said, "I am the only one good in English, Leung speaks a little only. We usually speak to each other in Malay. I will translate what Tan just said."

When he finished Jack grimaced.

This immediately caused the others to grasp their weapons and glare at Jack.

"Why do you make such a face," demanded Ah Tong. "You think you are too good to be a communist?"

"Although I am not a communist, I don't mind being called one. However, I will never be happy to be called an Englishman, I am a Scotsman."

A smile broke out on Ah Tong's face and again he translated for his men. Although all of them did not fully understand this distinction, the fact that Ah Tong was smiling eased the tension. Ah Tong made a hand signal and his men disappeared in the jungle to take up sentry positions, but close enough to still hear Ah Tong's voice.

"Your translation of my last remark seemed a little long," said Jack.

"Well, I had to explain that Scotsmen wear skirts."

"Not skirts, kilts."

"I know, I know, and they are good fighters. Are you a good fighter?"

"Only when I have to," replied Jack.

"I think Tan was correct, you are smart, Scotsman. I did not mean any disrespect just now. Even though you knew the password, I must be careful. I have lost too many men recently. As a precaution I designated this meeting place only yesterday. The original meeting place was closer to town. I decided that was too risky."

"So you tried to bait me by talking of skirts, to study my response, hoping I might give you a clue as to my true identity.'

"Oh, I know your identity, Mr. Simpson. You match the description my contacts gave me."

Just for a moment Jack was startled, however he recovered quickly.

"I think you are a clever man. I am sorry about your men. Perhaps---," Jack's voice trailed off and his eyes were thoughtful.

"What is it, what are you thinking," demanded Ah Tong.

"Oh, it was nothing, just a feeling of unease. Probably the jungle makes me uneasy. I am not used to the sounds and the smells."

"It takes time but a man can get used to the 'ulu'."

Ah Tong used the Malay word for jungle.

"But, you must never believe you know everything about the ulu. That's when you become careless and then you are in danger. There is always danger in the ulu. Enough of this talk; I must give you the information you want, then we must return."

For the next fifteen minutes Ah Tong gave Jack highly detailed information of troop positions and strengths, even quoting the names of the regiments. However, the most important part was his assessment of their capabilities. Ah Tong colored his comments with specific instances gathered by his spies and those of other groups operating in different areas.

"This is terrific," said Jack. "Thank you very much."

"It is our duty to do this for my country."

It was then Jack realized Ah Tong had been convinced Japan would grant his country independence after defeating the British.

'How cunning,' thought Jack.

"One other thing Ah Tong, the soldiers were expecting something to happen tonight. They put extra guards on all the hotels and I passed a patrol closer to the town. They did not see me and they were not very professional, but they were looking for something. I believe they knew of someone arriving today for a meeting but not who was meeting."

"My orders were to tell no one who you were. My men did not know your identity until tonight. This is bad news. We had better go. Be careful when you return to town."

Ah Tong called to his men and after saying their goodbyes, they left.

Jack thought about the information he had received and how difficult in must be to be a member of such a group. As he considered this the troubling feeling came back.

'What is it?' he thought. 'Something is not right, but what?'

He began pacing in a large circle trying to focus his thoughts and then he saw it. Something glinted in the night. He picked it up to examine it closely and saw it was a small piece of silver cigarette paper.

"Wonderful! You gave out some cigarettes and now you found a piece of cigarette paper. You're a genius, Jack, a real Sherlock Holmes."

His voice dripped with sarcasm as he whispered these words.

"Wait a minute, think Jack, damn you, think."

Then it struck him. No one smoked. It would have been too dangerous. So why tear off a small piece of the wrapping paper?

He again walked in increasing circles around the spot where he found the paper until he found another piece. When he found the third piece, he had the direction. Each piece was about five yards apart. He found two more pieces, then nothing.

"What the hell? What happened?" he grunted.

He returned to where the sixth piece should have been and searched the ground. Nothing. It was then he realized the spot where the paper should have been was occupied by a tree. He climbed up to the second branch before he found it. Wedged it a crevice was a cigarette packet. He unfolded it and his blood chilled. Only one word was written----- SIMPSON.

Now the fog lifted from his brain and he understood what had troubled him. He jumped to the ground and began running as quickly as he could in the direction Ah Tong had gone.

It was slippery in some parts and he made as much noise as he could by crashing through some plants. It was not too long before a voice said, "I warned you to be careful in the jungle, Scotsman. You are not only putting yourself in danger, but all of us too with all this noise."

"I wanted to be sure you heard me, I was not sure which direction you had taken."

"We could have heard you a mile away. What is so important that you would do such a crazy thing?"

"I must speak to you alone, come with me."

Ah Tong followed Jack warily, his hand on his parang.

"I can now repay you for your information; I know why you have lost so many men. Back at the meeting place I told you I felt uneasy. Now I know why. While we were talking with your men around us I noticed the eyes of one of your men watching us closely. It wasn't until you had gone that I realized he understood all we were saying. He understood English perfectly, yet you told me none of your men spoke English well. Then I found these pieces of silver cigarette paper used as markers. They lead to a tree where I found this."

Jack showed him the red cigarette packet.

"Then I remembered that all but two of the cigarette packs were Players. The other two were Craven A, which come in a red pack. One of the Craven A was given to you, the other to the man whose eyes betrayed him, the Malay. My name is written on the red Craven A pack you have in your hand."

Ah Tong's black eyes burned like coals. He took several deep breaths to regain his composure before saying, "To-night you have become my friend for ever but you had better go now and go quietly."

"What will you do with him?" asked Jack.

"First I will do a strange thing. I will save his life by preventing my comrades from killing him. Then I will have Tan make him tell us everything. Jaffar must have been very well trained by the British. It will not be easy to make him talk, but Tan can be very persuasive."

Involuntarily Ah Tong shivered. Then he shook Jack's hand, looked deep into his eyes, nodded and turned away.

As Jack walked back along the path he had created, he heard a muffled cry. In his mind he visualized the crooked grin on Tan's face and he too shivered.

Chapter 19

As he approached the edge of the jungle, Jack stopped behind a large fan palm tree. He stood motionless for two minutes then lobbed a stone into the bushes about thirty yards away. Nothing stirred, so he stealthily crept along a narrow path just inside the tree line until he was about one hundred yards from the rest house. Now for the difficult part, he must sprint to the back of the rest house. His training had taught him that indecision was anathema in any mission. The only thing worse was haste. Again he waited two minutes, scanning the surrounding terrain and then raced to the rest house. He waited one minute to be sure everything was clear then climbed through the window back into his room.

Jessica was still breathing deeply. He stripped off his damp sweaty, clothes spreading them out on the two chairs. He hoped they would dry by morning. Naked, he slipped under the mosquito net, lay down next to Jessica and within a few minutes was asleep.

He was awakened at eight o'clock by Jessica shaking him gently. She was fully clothed.

"Hey, I have to leave now. I had hoped you would waken earlier so you could give me a proper sendoff."

She grinned at him while saying this and then added hesitantly, "Was it ok for you?"

"Are you kidding?"

"What do you mean?" she asked anxiously. "I think I must have had too much to drink, because I am a little hazy about last night. Tell me, was it good?"

"It was truly an unforgettable night," he said truthfully, although not referring to the time he spent with her. She thought he was and her face took on a smile of satisfaction.

"Don't you remember how many times we did it? No wonder I slept so long. It may take me a week to recover."

Now she was beaming.

"Oh I do wish I could stay, but I have to go home, bathe, change clothes and be at school by nine. I will see you tonight shan't I?"

"You can count on it," he lied.

She ran out of the room and Jack got out of bed. Bathing at the rest house was certainly a new experience. A door led from his room to an enclosed outdoor area with a three feet high water jar. He expected to see Ali Baba jump out of it at any minute. Resting on top of the jar was a large ladle. Of course the water was cold and he had to ladle water all over himself and then wash with soap, finishing off by using the ladle again to rinse off the soap. On a ledge was a very small mirror to use for shaving, again with cold water. Having grown up in Partick, he was used to washing in cold water but the al fresco bit was a new experience.

He dressed, laid out his clothes of last night to be laundered and went for a leisurely breakfast. His meeting with the Colonel was not until eleven o'clock.

He arrived at the camp fifteen minutes before his appointment and was met by Major Dunbar.

"Good morning Simpson."

"Good morning Major."

"Come into my office."

Jack followed the Major into the small office and Dunbar closed the door.

"How is the rest house?"

"It's fine."

"You didn't mind bathing in cold water?"

"The bathing was no problem. Shaving was more of a challenge."

"Ah, we obviously forgot to put you wise to the proper procedure. What did you have to drink for breakfast?"

Jack looked puzzled as he replied, "Tea."

"That was the correct choice. You see what you have to do is ask for a cup of coffee to be delivered to your room just as you get out of bed. The coffee is bloody awful, very weak, and you use the coffee to shave."

"Anyway Simpson I have some bad news for you. Colonel Jackson cannot see you today. Confidentially something went wrong with an operation last night. The intelligence boys had promised the old man some juicy information and it didn't happen. We have had to send out patrols to gather whatever intel we can. At the present moment he is quite unhappy and is personally coordinating activities to find out exactly what went wrong. He asked me to take care of you as Captain McCartney was sent on an important mission to Kota Bharu. As I understand it you would like a look at the docks here in Kuantan and then you are going off on a personal jaunt to Trengganu to see the turtles."

"Yes I believe I will just catch the end of the season and while I'm on the East Coast I would like to see Kota Bharu. It is not too far from Trengganu and the beaches are beautiful I am told, particularly one called The Beach of Passionate Love, said Jack with a twinkle in his eye."

"Talking of love, I understand you did some studying last night."

Jack feigned astonishment at his actions being discovered. Obviously his plan to be noticed going into the rest house with Jessica had succeeded. He would not be surprised if someone had observed her leaving this morning.

"She is a very nice lady," he said abashedly.

"Don't worry; we will not broadcast it around. I have already told the soldier not to put it in is report and to forget all about it."

"Now here is what I propose. I will take you to the docks and introduce you to the harbor master. I should tell you there is not much to see. Then you can continue to use the car you presently have and drive to Kuala Trengganu this afternoon. I will have someone make a reservation at the rest house for two nights. Also we will make a reservation at the rest house in Kota Bharu for two nights. There are a few hotels along the coast but I think you will find the service much better in the rest houses. I will alert McCartney and he can catch up with you in Kota Bharu."

"As your next stop after that is Penang there is little point in driving all the way back here, we can make a flight reservation from Kota Bharu straight to Penang. Just leave the car at the rest house and I will arrange for someone to pick it up."

"That is most kind of you, given how busy you must be."

Jack had the feeling that Dunbar would be very pleased to see him go. He probably disliked being a guide to a civilian. When they arrived at the docks Jack understood what Dunbar had meant by there not being much to see.

The heavily silted mouth of the river Kuantan permitted only shallow draft boats to unload at the docks. Due to this, large ships had to anchor offshore and be unloaded by lighter.

To play the part, Jack asked several questions of the harbor master who referred some of the questions to his assistant, an intelligent young Chinese. Jack took notes in a studious manner. When he had finished he turned to the Major and said, "As you indicated, I can see there is not much activity."

"We never use this facility; it is much easier to bring our supplies by rail."

"Major Dunbar, I am very grateful for all your assistance. I regret not having the pleasure of seeing the Colonel again please give him my best wishes. I will go back to the rest house, pack up and be on my way."

They shook hands then the Major jumped into his jeep and his driver sped off. Jack had a long last look at the river mouth thinking, 'The important aspect of Kuantan is the airport, not the seaway.' The harbor master had gone but his assistant walked Jack to his car.

"I am sorry you did not see our port at its best, unfortunately we are not so busy today; you should have come tomorrow."

"Why tomorrow?"

"We will have a large shipment from the mines."

"Oh I am sorry I will miss that. I am sure the mines are running at capacity these days."

Jack kept his voice calm and unrevealing but his heartbeat had risen. He had no idea what this young man was talking about.

"Oh yes, that is true and as you probably know the mines at Sungei Lembing are the largest lode tin mines in the world."

"It must take a great amount of preparation to schedule all the lighters to handle such a huge shipment."

The young Chinese smiled indulgently, "Of course, that's why we ship much of the tin by road to Jerantut, which is in the center of the peninsula and on the main railway line south. There is an excellent road from here to Jerantut."

Now Jack's heart was racing, this was new and vital information. Kuantan had suddenly taken on a great deal more importance. Still feigning only a slight interest he said, "It would have been nice to see your port at its best; however, I have all the information I need. Goodbye."

The young Chinese seemed disappointed that his information had not raised any apparent interest in Jack. He did not even write anything further in his notebook. He waved goodbye and trudged back to the office.

Jack drove slowly away paying much more attention to the area around the dock. Now he saw them. Several well camouflaged gun emplacements. He decided it would be dangerous to investigate too thoroughly. To do so would mean deviating from the road to the rest house and could cause questions. He had learned enough and there was no point in running any further risk. 'So Major Dunbar you were being very cagey, not wanting me to poke around the docks too much' he thought. 'Well I was lucky today. Let's hope my luck holds out.'

He arrived at the rest house and went straight to his room where he encoded the new information and filed away the papers. Then he packed his suitcase, paid his bill and drove to the school. At the school office he left a note for Jessica saying he had been called away and hoped to be back soon. This was not a total lie; he did want to return to this interesting and beautiful place.

He had a choice of two roads to Kuala Trengganu. He could take the quicker inland road which had bridges over the various rivers or the coast road.

He had been advised to take the inland road as a few of the coastal ferries were not always reliable. For Jack there was no choice, he had to take the coastal road. The first ferry was a little scary. It seemed to Jack to be an outsize rowboat. It was drawn across the river by a rope which turned on a pulley driven by a seriously underpowered diesel engine. Luckily the river was not at all wide but Jack stood outside the car ready to leap overboard at any minute. Sensing his discomfort the elderly boatman gave him a toothless smile and waved his pipe as though warding off evil spirits.

After that experience the other ferries, except one, seemed not too bad. Some of them even had their own engine to power them across. The one really bad scare was again on a small ferry and again an elderly pipe smoking boatman. Jack thought he could have been the twin brother of the first ferry boatman. This man was different in that he had teeth; all of them were very yellow, but they were teeth. As the ferry was pulling away from the bank he began yelling at the engine operator who stopped the ferry and made it return to shore. He then had a heated discussion with a skinny young man and would not move until this man and his bicycle were offloaded. Jack thought, 'My God that man and his bicycle can't weigh much more than ten stone. If that is all the margin of error we have this could be trouble.'

As they left the bank it became clear that this river was flowing quickly. The boatman was in conversation with a passenger and was waving his pipe when it slipped from his hand and fell into the river.

Just then the diesel engine began to sputter so the boatman jumped up and began hauling on the rope. Jack went forward and assisted by also pulling on the rope. For a few seconds they were stationary and just as Jack thought the river would win this battle the engine picked up its beat and gradually the ferry made its way to the other bank.

When Jack pulled away he saw the boatman start walking toward the row of shops just down the road. When the waiting passengers called out to him, he yelled back and from his hand signals Jack understood he was going to buy another pipe. There would be no more sailings until the spirits could be repelled.

As he drove along the coast he saw clusters of turbaned fishermen sitting under the shade of coconut trees mending their nets. He waved to each group and without fail he got waves and smiles in response. He thought these must be among the nicest people in the world.

Jack was beginning to get hungry and stopped at a picturesque little village called Paka. He thought it probably hadn't changed in the last fifty years. He ordered the local fish and was not disappointed. It was fried and served with fresh vegetables cooked in a wok and, of course, a bowl of rice.

His next stop was Rantau Abang, the twelve mile stretch of golden beach where the giant leatherbacks laid their eggs each year. One local man told him the season was virtually over but if he came back that night he may be lucky. He walked along the beach and could now understand the point Hans had made regarding the eminent suitability of this beach for large turtles. The slope was very steep which aided the turtles in crashing their enormous bodies on the water's edge.

He took off his shoes and socks and tried to wade in the water up to his knees. His legs were swept from under him and he struggled to get back on shore. He was soaked through and thoroughly shaken by the speed at which he had been swept to sea. He made a mental note to discuss with Lord Hino the vital importance of beaching the landing craft at the time of invasion. Fully packed soldiers would stand no chance with this strong undertow if they had to wade any distance.

He stood on the shore, in the late afternoon, trying to dry himself. At last he had to leave and make his still soggy way to Kuala Trengganu. The receptionist at the rest house stared in amazement at him when he checked in. He decided not to explain but merely asked for a wake up call at one o'clock in the morning.

It was close to two thirty when he arrived back at Rantau Abang. There was a crowd gathered on the beach and they were lucky. About twenty giant leatherbacks fought their way up the beach and laid their eggs. In addition there were several green and hawksbill turtles laying eggs on the beach.

Hans had stimulated Jack's interest in this event on an intellectual level; however, seeing these magnificent animals created an emotional bond. A few had pieces of their fins missing signifying predator attacks, probably sharks, which only increased Jack's admiration for these turtles. He watched until four o'clock before starting the drive back to the rest house. The next night he returned but no leatherbacks appeared. There were several other turtles but it was not quite the same without the behemoths of the sea. He would never forget this experience and it gave him one more reason to promise himself a return to the East Coast area.

Next morning he set off for Kota Bharu at nine thirty. This seemed early to Jack since he had gone to bed at four that morning. As he drove away his mind began going over the checklist of things he had to do. The most important was a survey of defenses on the coast near Kota Bharu. He felt pretty sure the beaches would be watched or even guarded, but he had to find a way to spend time there. He also wanted to check the beaches south of Kota Bharu and he had already thought of a way to do this.

As he got closer to Kota Bharu he stopped at a few beaches to study the situation. There were no guards in sight at the first three, however when he got to the fourth he was halted by a patrol and an Indian soldier asked what he was doing. He then used his previously thought out plan. He pulled out the marine biology textbook given to him by Hans and pointed to the section on giant turtles. The Indians laughed and told him they came ashore south of Kuala Trengganu. He looked crestfallen and asked he leader if he was sure. When he was told yes he asked if he could walk on the beach for a few minutes. They gave him permission and he scouted the next stretch of beach but saw no gun emplacements. He waved goodbye to the patrol and drove on to the rest house in Kota Bharu. It was late afternoon when he arrived and he had just had his al fresco bath when he was informed that a guest had called for him.

"Well Jack, did you manage to see your turtles?" asked Bill McCartney extending his hand.

"Yes I did, I was very lucky as this is the end of the season. I had thought there may be other nesting places closer to here and was almost arrested by a patrol."

Bill smile faded.

"You must be careful Jack. Some of these chaps are a little nervous and might rough you up. If you want to wander around the beaches I had better get you a pass."

"Well I did have my heart set on seeing the Beach of Passionate Love."

"Let me make a telephone call before we have a drink and then dinner. I will have a pass waiting for you at the reception by tomorrow morning."

"Thanks that would be great."

He returned shortly, "All arranged. The pass will cover you for tomorrow and will be here by nine o'clock in the morning. Now let's have that drink."

They sat in the bar and had ordered their drinks before Bill asked, "What type of patrol did you bump into?"

"It was a bunch of Indians chaps. Actually they were very nice. Once they realized I was clearly mistaken they let me admire the beach and then take off."

"Did they ask for identification or a pass?"

"No."

"Too damned lax," muttered Bill as the drinks arrived. "Anyway, cheers and welcome to New City."

"New City?"

"Yes that's what Kota Bharu means."

"Bill, what did you mean when you referred to laxity?"

"Well you could have been someone spying on the coastline."

Jack kept a light tone in his voice as he said, "You mean they should have dragged me off to jail as a spy?"

"Jack there are a lot of planters in this country who claim they are Dutch and I have no doubt that a few of them are in fact, Germans. You could have been one of them. Security has to become better around here. I am giving away no secret when I say that almost seventy percent of the troops here come from India. It is also no secret that back in India there have been several big demonstrations organized by the Indian Independence League. Agents of this organization continually try to sow seeds of discontent among our troops. So far they have not been successful; however, it does make it more difficult to keep discipline. Every time an Indian soldier is severely reprimanded there are a few grumbles about British imperialism. Most of these lads come from rural areas and need considerable training. This is the Army not a debating society and as such orders must be followed without question if lives are to be saved."

Bill stared moodily into his glass before swallowing the remaining whisky in one gulp.

"Oh what the hell, let's have one more before dinner."

When the drinks were served Jack said in a low voice, "Bill, I don't want to add to your woes but you are absolutely right, your chaps should have arrested me. You see I am a spy."

Bill choked on his drink.

"I am a fully subscribed member of the Scottish Independence League."

Bill broke into laughter and said, "Jack, I am very pleased to have met you. I need to laugh more often and you are just the fellow to make me do so. Although I must admit that I sense there is more going on in that head of yours than I fully understand. Drink up, let's have dinner. I know of a very good restaurant near here."

Dinner was an enjoyable time for both of them. The conversation was light and the food was excellent. Bill told Jack he had to leave early nest morning to return to Kuantan.

"As I said earlier Jack, it has been a pleasure to meet you and I hope we meet again someday. You know, I could believe you are a spy for some Scottish independence group. I am very careful about security and you have not asked me one question that would raise an alarm bell to sound; yet I have been on the verge of telling you too much on several occasions."

Jack knew that Bill was the type of person one would be lucky to have for a friend yet he was glad he would not see him the next day.

Bill McCartney was entirely too perceptive for comfort.

Chapter 20

Jack arose at 7.30 the next morning and felt the already high temperature and the high degree of humidity in the air. The 'Ali Baba' water jar with its cool contents provided some relief from the heat but not from the humidity. His shirt was still sticking to his back as he walked along to the dining room. Following breakfast he inquired at the reception desk and was pleased his pass was already there. Back in his room, he gathered his swimming trunks, two towels and a spare shirt and set out to explore the Beach of Passionate Love.

Driving along the road he passed many artisans and decided to buy something for Michiko. There were several types of shops but two of them were the most renowned in this part of the country. One type made and sold a dazzling woven silk cloth with gold and silver threads, called songket. He was told this material was used to make clothes for special occasions, particularly weddings. The other indigenous specialty was delicately hand made silver filigree products. He thought the songket cloth was beautiful but probably most appropriate in its homeland, therefore he decided to select something in silver.

The silversmiths worked right at the edge of the road and he finally picked a beautiful necklace from a man called Abdullah. He knew he was expected to bargain and did so in a half-hearted manner. Abdullah gave him a reasonable discount but when Jack saw his two lovely young daughters peeking round the side of the shop he gave most of the discount to them. Their eyes opened wide at this gift and Abdullah put his hand over his heart in a sign of gratitude.

The beach turned out to be about six miles from the town and as he drew near, he was stopped at two checkpoints. On each occasion he was asked by an armed, serious faced guard to provide identification as well as his pass. Two other guards held their rifles at the ready until he was cleared. Obviously Bill had wasted no time in tightening security.

When he reached the beach he parked the car at the side of the road and admired the pristine beauty of this idyllic spot. Coconut trees were dotted along the roadside and swayed rhythmically to the beat of the trade winds. These winds whipped the waters of the South China Sea creating a fine mist all along the beachfront. He walked slowly across the grassy verge and stood in the shade of the casuarinas on the beach. A few children were playing on the beach. One of them was flying a locally made kite. It was in the shape of a bird and was colored red and bright yellow. It dipped and soared in a realistic manner under the expert control of this child who looked no more than nine years old.

Looking up and down the beach front he spotted two patrols, each about two hundred yards on either side of where he stood. Casually he returned to the car and changed into his swimming trunks in the back seat. He left his clothes in the car; not bothering to lock the doors and strolled, with one of the towels over his shoulder, back to the casuarinas where he spread his towel under these lovely shade trees and walked to the water's edge.

The beach was steeply sloped so he had to dive into the waves and strongly swim for a few hundred yards before he could get away from the undertow. The leader of one of the patrols came down the beach to watch him for about five minutes before returning to his men.

Jack floated on his back and carefully scanned the beach; he could count seven pill boxes and memorized their locations. He knew he could not stay in the strong sunlight for too long but he had to make a show of enjoying his swim to demonstrate this was the purpose of his visit. He swam for another twenty minutes before again resting on his back.

After a few minutes one of the soldiers from the second patrol decided to take a keener interest in him and started walking down the beach as he turned towards the shore.

'Now for the tricky part,' he thought. Getting in was difficult enough but getting out would be more difficult. He waited for a large wave and swam as fast as he could just behind its crest. He was smashed onto the beach but managed to avoid being dragged back out to sea. A bit bruised and scraped he walked a little unsteadily to his towel to lie down. The member of the patrol who had been observing him approached and asked if he had a pass. He told him it was in the car and he would get it in a few minutes when he had caught his breath. The soldier backed off about twenty yards and waited.

After a few minutes Jack got up, smiled at the soldier and walked to the car where he handed over his pass. The soldier looked at it, asked Jack to stay by the car and took the pass to the patrol leader. Jack turned his attention to the young boy flying the kite, applauding the various moves. Out of the corner of his eye he could see the patrol leader beckoning him to come over but he pretended not to see him.

The patrol leader was not going to lose face by walking over to Jack so he finally gave the pass back to the soldier and barked an order. The private had to walk two hundred yards back to Jack before handing over the pass without speaking.

Jack thanked him with a smile which caused his pock marked face to scowl before he trudged back to the patrol.

'Bill would not be pleased with this effort at security,' thought Jack. 'They asked for my pass but not for identification. Sloppy work! One more demonstration of poor discipline.'

He watched the kite for some time before drying himself and changing into his clothes. He did not want to appear in a hurry to leave so soon after being asked for his pass. He shouted a goodbye to the kite flier and he and all the other children replied cheerfully. He did not look at the patrols as he drove away slowly, but he sensed their watchful eyes.

To the west of him was the mouth of the River Kelantan with a series of small islands in the muddy estuary. This had no interest for him so he headed east. To do so he had to backtrack and drive past the airport. Here the security was much tighter. Not only was he asked for his pass and identification but his car was searched. He said he was looking for a safer place to swim and his wet swimming trunks and towel backed up his story. He was allowed to pass and in fifteen minutes arrived at the place he had been instructed to most carefully survey, Pantai Dasar Sabak.

Nearby was a small Malay kampong and the beach was adorned by a fleet of perahus, Malay fishing boats. These boats were particular to the East Coast and were brightly painted in horizontal stripes. On the prow of each perahu was a carved figure many of which resembled the mythological figures of the popular village shadow plays. Others were in the shape of a 'garuda' a demon birdman of Hindu origin, yet others had dragons with realistic scales and fiery red eyes. Fishermen were either painting their boats or mending their nets and they all returned his greeting.

He changed into his still wet trunks and walked along the beach. The kampong was at the mouth of a narrow river, an offshoot of the river Kelantan, whose banks were covered in lush nipa bushes. He noted these bushes spread from the river to cover a lot of the coast to the east. 'A perfect hiding place for an advance landing group to conceal itself at night,' he noted. He counted another four pill boxes in this area and again memorized their location. The sea was not as difficult to deal with here and he enjoyed his swim. From the sea he had a better view of the guards near the pillboxes and could see that they were not in large numbers. Again they were all sitting, sheltering from the sun.

The undertow was not as treacherous as the previous beach and he constantly tested his footing on his way back to the beach. Sitting on the sand ostensibly admiring the fishing boats he scrutinized every detail of the potential landing area and came to the conclusion it was definitely acceptable. Everything would depend on the tide conditions but he reckoned that even with a strong tide this was the best location. The fact that generations of fishermen had chosen this beach to pull their boats out of the water cemented his opinion. He had now seen enough and decided it was time to return to the rest house and encode his notes.

On the way he stopped at a small restaurant and ate a deliciously flavorful Malay chicken curry made with coconut milk. He thought this was a very late lunch but when he ordered a second beer and desert, he decided it was an early dinner. He would not eat again tonight but would go to bed around nine o'clock, as he had a very early flight next morning.

The flight to Penang, on the opposite coast, left at six o'clock. Once again it was a bit bumpy as they had to first fly south and therefore once again cross the mountains.

The pilot apologized for the turbulence and informed them that if they could have flown in a straight line to Penang they would have avoided the higher mountains. However as Kota Bharu is less than twenty miles from the border with Thailand such a flight path would have taken them into Thai air space. Jack was now regretting he had eaten so much curry. He tried to put the queasiness he was feeling out of his mind by concentrating on his mission and focusing his attention on the terrain below. It did not work, and he was very happy when the pilot announced they would land in fifteen minutes.

There was a representative of The Red Funnel Line waiting for him at the airport. This puzzled him as he had not told George of his change in plans. The young man introduced himself as Andy Jamieson.

"How did you know I would be on this flight?"

"George Knight called me yesterday. Of course we already knew of your visit but frankly we were expecting you to arrive tomorrow from Kuantan. A Captain McCartney told George of the change in plans."

'Thank goodness for the efficiency of Bill,' thought Jack.

"I hope I have not created too much havoc."

"Not at all. I merely added one night onto your hotel reservation; if you wish to change that just let me know. Perhaps the best thing is to take you there now and along the way we can discuss the program we have prepared for you."

"That will be fine. Where is the hotel?"

"In Georgetown; on the island itself. I know your main interest is the port facilities in Butterworth on the mainland; however, that is only a short ferry ride and the hotels are better in Georgetown. As you probably know, the State of Penang is part of The Straits Settlements and is made up of the island of Penang and a strip of land on the mainland, called Province Wellesley."

"Are you about to give me a 'George Knight' history lesson?"

Jamieson looked embarrassed and said, "Sorry, of course I won't if that's what you prefer. And you are right; it was George's idea that each office should know something of the history of its surroundings."

"And do you think that is a good idea?"

"Actually I do. I think he is correct to ask us to study local history in order to better understand the traditions of the place where we earn our living. And some of our visitors enjoy it."

Jamieson spoke avidly not defensively and Jack liked that.

"As a matter of fact, I agree with you. So please go ahead and give me the sixpenny lesson."

Jamieson grinned at Jack.

"I can see George made a good impression on you. I hope I don't let him down by disappointing you. Well here goes, I will give you the condensed version since you only asked for sixpence worth."

"Penang was formally introduced to history by an employee of The East India Company, Mr. Francis Light. As you no doubt know the income produced by this company was so important to Great Britain that it almost became a branch of the Foreign Office. Its trade with India was of national importance and the company was looking for ways to augment this by increasing trade with China. Francis Light believed the EIC, the East India Company, needed a Far Eastern port to facilitate this trade."

181

"He bargained with the Sultan of Kedah whose territory was being raided by the Siamese and the Burmese. He promised British protection in exchange for Pulau Pinang. By the way this name translates into Betel Nut Island. This was agreed in 1786 along with an annual rental of thirty thousand dollars. But Light was a crafty negotiator and the ships which were sent to Penang were not used to protect Kedah until the rent was reduced to six thousand dollars. Several years later a further condition was added, that of a piece of the mainland, Province Wellesley."

"Therefore Penang was the first British settlement in the Malay Peninsula and was followed by Singapore in 1819 and Malacca in 1824. These three places became the Straits Settlements and gave Britain control of the quickest route from Europe to China."

"I am impressed by your knowledge Mr. Jamieson and I shall so report to George."

Jamieson blushed at the compliment but recovered quickly and said, "Since you are so interested I will give you an extra pennyworth for free. When Light gained Penang in 1786, it was virtually uninhabited and covered in thick jungle. He had great difficulty in persuading Sepoys to clear the jungle in order to build Georgetown. Folk lore has it he filled a cannon with gold pieces and fired it into the jungle and that motivated the clearance for this town."

"Penang is mainly populated by Chinese. As in many areas once the British created law and order, the Chinese were the first to capitalize on the commercial possibilities. You can see many very large homes built for the Chinese towkays along a street referred to as millionaires' row."

When they arrived at the hotel and Jack had checked in, he said, "I think it may save trouble if we start tomorrow as originally scheduled. Today, I can just wander around and get acquainted with Georgetown."

"That would be great as we have a ship arriving this afternoon. Would you care to have dinner tonight?"

"Yes thank you, where shall we meet?"

"I will call for you at seven, if that's OK."

"Perfect. Oh by the way, is there a post office nearby?"

"Just down this road to your right, about two hundred yards. But I can mail something for you at the office."

"Thanks but I haven't yet written the letter. I'll see you at seven."

Jack went to his room and unpacked. He took his notebook from the false side of his case and memorized a telephone number, then went down to the restaurant for a cup of coffee. As he left the hotel he carefully checked the faces nearby. It was unlikely he was being observed but he chose to be vigilant anyway. When he arrived at the post office he again paused at the door and scrutinized passers-by. Satisfied he entered and went straight to a pay phone booth. It had been drilled into him never to trust using a hotel telephone; there are too many inquisitive ears. He dialed the memorized number and left a coded message with the answering receptionist at Alor Star airbase. This done he went on a tour of Georgetown and later enjoyed a sumptuous Chinese meal with Jamieson.

Next morning as he was leaving the hotel he was given an envelope that had been left at the front desk for him. He did not need to use the code book as the message was short and simple to decipher. He had a meeting that night.

Jack was becoming quite proficient at doing his cover job and spent the day asking insightful questions of the various officials at the port. There was nothing remarkable about the port and he noted it was not as strongly fortified as he thought it would be. Once again everything was committed to memory. Jamieson picked him up at the end of the day to drive him back to the hotel and was visibly disappointed when Jack turned down his offer of dinner.

"I really must catch up on my report to the Ministry. I will have a quick bite in the hotel restaurant. There is one thing you could do for me."

"Certainly, what is it?" asked Jamieson eagerly.

"I did get through quite a lot today and will not require another two full days to complete my report. So instead of flying to KL, I wondered if you could supply me with a car and I will drive there."

"Let me see if I can find a driver and I will let you know tomorrow."

"Oh, I would prefer to drive myself. If I could borrow one of the company cars, I would leave it with George in KL."

"That's no problem; however, it is a long drive and with security checks, it will take more than one day."

"I looked at a map and believe if I leave after lunch the day after tomorrow, I can comfortably reach Ipoh by nightfall. And if I leave there early next morning I should be in KL by early evening."

"That's true but you would be better leaving no later than noon as there is a lot of security at Taiping which is just over half way to Ipoh. I will arrange a hotel for you in Ipoh and inform George of your plans."

"Thank you very much. I'll see you tomorrow."

It was exactly seven o'clock that night when there were three sharp raps on Jack's door, followed by a pause, then two more. He opened the door and said to the young army Captain who stood there, "You must have the wrong room."

"Or perhaps the wrong hotel," was the reply. The Captain walked into Jack's room.

"Nice to meet you Jack," he said.

"A pleasure to meet you Patrick," replied Jack. "Would you care for a scotch?"

"Yes please."

"Soda or water?"

"Soda, please."

"How dangerous was it for you to come here tonight?"

"Dangerous? Not in the least. Security is a joke here. When I arrived here in October of last year with my Punjab Battalion, the Commanding Officer took a dislike to me and ordered that I be posted as far away as possible. So what happens? The first available posting is to a three month training course in Singapore. Off they ship me to this course. And what do you think is the subject of this course? Air intelligence Liaison! After training they send me back here but now as a grade GSO3 which gives me access to secret air force information."

"Now I am at the main airbase at Alor Star which is north of here, close to the Thai border, and I have information on all troop and air force dispositions in the north of Malaya. I have sent most of this on to Tokyo through couriers. In case any of my messages did not get through, I will give you an update of everything and you can take it back with you. If you don't mind we should start as I should be back on base by midnight."

Jack poured another round of drinks and they started the debriefing. When they finished Jack could hardly believe the detailed information he had been given.

"Even though you are cleared for secret work some of this information must be of a much higher classification than secret."

"You are quite correct. I got some of it from the Station Commander's safe. Actually they knew someone had seen the contents and I believe they might suspect me, because I have been asking so many questions."

"Perhaps a little caution might be wise, Patrick."

"There is no need to worry, Jack. Old Churchill has repeatedly told the House of Commons that the Japanese will never attack this area and these Commanders continually parrot the party line until they probably even believe it to be the truth. Anyway I had best be off. It was a pleasure meeting you. Take care of yourself."

When he closed the door, Jack whistled a sigh of wonder at the information he had received; yet he could not help feeling some concern at Patrick's total disregard of being discovered. He thought, 'There is a fine line between being confident and being cavalier; I hope you have not crossed that line Patrick.'

He carefully stowed his precious notes in the false bottom of his suitcase and went to bed.

Chapter 21

The next day and a half went quickly; Jack even had time to visit the famous Snake Temple. He was astonished to see so many poisonous snakes slithering with complete freedom around the temple. A priest told him the heavy smoke from the burning incense sticks kept them lethargic during the day and that they were well fed at night with eggs. Even with this assurance he was nervous of these green and yellow striped pit vipers. He regretted not having time to visit the north shores where the most beautiful beaches were situated. 'Maybe next time,' he thought as he took the ferry from Georgetown to Butterworth.

The drive to Ipoh did take longer than he expected. Jamieson had been right, there were many security checks. This did not bother Jack; in fact it was exactly what he wanted. It gave him the opportunity to note the various regiments at these locations. He also used simple techniques which he had devised to measure their competence. He passed three check points by merely saying his ID was locked in his suitcase which was in the boot. At others where this failed he claimed not to have proof of owner-ship of the car. Out of all the stops he only encountered two where a thorough check was completed.

He found the hotel in Ipoh where Jamieson had made the reservation and ordered a light meal in his room. He had learned of the superb Chinese cuisine in this town which was the main tin mining area of the peninsula, but he had to encode all the information he had gleaned today.

One of the most relevant pieces of information was the superb condition of the roads. At least the British had done one thing correctly. He reflected on this and decided it was too harsh a judgment. The bridges were also very well constructed; maybe even too well. Should a retreating army not be sufficiently expert in demolition, there was a good chance many of the bridges would survive.

He kept to his plan and left early next morning. Jamieson had told him that George had arranged for him to stay at No. 25 Ampang Road. He found he was eager to reach KL and was surprised at how much he was looking forward to seeing George again. He had thought of him several times since landing in Penang and had decided he wanted to have a serious conversation with him concerning his future. For the present though he had better concentrate on making accurate observations along the road.

It was almost 7.30 when he pulled into the gravel driveway of the bungalow on Ampang Road. Before the car came to a stop two figures came rushing down the steps. Both Ah Kang and Ah Eng were beaming from ear to ear.

"Mistah Slimson, Mistah Slimson, so vely good see you again," said Ah Kang, while Ah Eng bobbed up and down in an excited greeting. She said something to Ah Kang who translated, "Ah Eng say you look vely tired. She has prepared bath for you, then after I serve you dinnah. That allight Mistah Slimpson?"

"Wonderful," said Jack extending his hand in greeting.

He then turned and bowed to Ah Eng.

"I am very pleased to see you again Ah Eng; but how did you know when I would arrive and when to run a bath?"

Ah Kang translated and she giggled as she replied.

"She say she keep emptying bath and refilling every fifteen minutes since six o'clock."

"Thank you very much Ah Eng you are very kind."

Jack took his suitcase out of the car and Ah Kang relieved him of it over his protests and carried it to the bedroom. There waiting for him was a steaming pot of strong tea. Jack shook his head in wonderment and put his hand on Ah Kang's shoulder.

"Thank you so much Ah Kang."

Ah Kang bowed and left, a smile still of his face.

Somehow Jack knew what would be served for dinner. Nevertheless when the fried rice appeared he was once again in awe of its enticing aroma. A glass of cold beer was also put on the table and like before he had seconds of both.

"That was absolutely delicious Ah Kang."

"You like some dessert, Mistah Slimson?"

"No thank you. I could not eat another thing."

"How about cup of coffee?" asked Ah Kang.

"You can read my mind, yes please. Oh Ah Kang, did Mr. Knight leave any message for me?"

"Yes, he come here five o'clock."

Ah Kang's face broke into a smile, "Ah Eng told him you be vely tired and he must come back tomollow. He say he come at nine o'clock."

Jack also grinned. Apparently George knew better than to argue with Ah Eng.

Next morning feeling totally refreshed, Jack met George as his car pulled up.

"Hello Jack. It is very good to see you again."

"It is good to see you, George. How are you?"

"Very well indeed and how about you old chap?"

"I am well thank you, George. Let's have a cup of coffee before we go."

"Jolly good idea and we can discuss what you would like to do."

They sat on the beautiful silk covered furniture on the veranda and Ah Kang brought them a fresh pot of coffee. Before Jack could say anything George said, "Thank you very much Ah Kang."

Ah Kang looked startled at hearing this from George. Jack gave Ah Kang a knowing smile and he left with a puzzled smile of his own.

"Oh, before I forget, the MD would like to see you at eleven o'clock."

"Oh really, what about?"

"I am not sure but he has asked me on several occasions about your assignment and I know he has asked Andy Jamieson what you have been doing. I believe he has also made enquiries of our Singapore office to see if they have any more details."

"It sounds like he is peeved at not being kept fully informed," said Jack.

"The MD guards his territory very jealously Jack and does not like anyone coming into his back garden without his express approval. I know he was upset at the telegram he received from London instructing him to show you every courtesy but giving no specific details. This may be compounded by the realization you were tweaking his nose when you had lunch. If so, his spiteful nature will not allow him rest until he knows more about you and just how powerful your connections in London are. He simply cannot abide anything less than total fealty."

"Let's not concern ourselves about this matter George. I will learn all about it at eleven. Now, about the next two days, here is what I would like to accomplish."

As they talked Jack's mind was racing over the alternatives open to him to handle a nosey Williams. His cover story would stand a certain amount of scrutiny but it would not be wise to allow a constant pecking by this wet hen.

His attention was brought back to George when he heard the name McKay mentioned.

"Sorry George I missed that."

"I was saying I had a call from John McKay asking about your itinerary. I told him you would be leaving here around the end of the week and he asked me to reiterate his invitation to you to spend a few days with him."

"I would like that. How would I get there?"

"You can keep the car you have and drive to Seremban, it is quite close to KL. Then following your visit, drive on to Malacca and drop it off at our office. When you have completed your review of Malacca, they will provide transportation to Singapore."

"OK that seems to cover everything, George. We should probably head into the office."

As they were driving, George said, "The MD has instructed me to take care of a minor matter at our office in PS today. Therefore, I am afraid I must leave you to your own devices at lunchtime but we can have dinner tonight if that suits you."

"That would suit me very well."

At one minute before eleven Jack presented himself at the desk of Williams' secretary, Miss Anderson. He had carefully thought out his approach to Williams and knew it had better succeed. The contingency, should it fail, was severe.

"Just one moment; I will see if the MD is available."

She knocked quietly on the door and entered after being summoned in. She reopened the door and beckoned Jack to enter.

Williams did not rise from his desk nor did he offer his limp handshake.

"Ah Simpson, come in. Have a seat. Would you care for tea of coffee?"

"Tea, please."

"Make that two, Miss Anderson."

"Well now Simpson, have my people been taking good care of you?"

"Yes Mr. Williams, everyone has been most cooperative and generous in spending time with me. I cannot tell you how much I appreciate you making all these arrangements."

'Careful,' he thought as Miss Anderson brought in the tea, 'if you get any oilier you will slip to the floor'.

"Excellent, excellent. I am glad to be of assistance."

He paused as he sipped his tea.

"When will your report be completed?"

"In a few weeks, before I leave Singapore."

"Excellent, excellent, and as a matter of courtesy, send me a copy, there's a good chap. Tell me Simpson how did you get to know our people in London?"

The order to 'send me a copy' had been slipped into the sentence, with emphasis. No request; simply do it!

"Actually I have not met any of your company's people in London. I did have the opportunity to meet people in your Glasgow office. They were most helpful."

"So you do not know any of our Directors?"

"No I am afraid not."

"Then this assignment must be a low level one, in which case there is no need to wait for your report. Tell me exactly what you have been doing and all your findings so far."

Williams' voice had changed from the pleasant one at the outset to a slightly menacing one.

The cat had trapped the mouse.

He was slightly taken aback when Jack smiled cordially and said, "Why of course Mr. Williams. Not a problem. But first I must inform a few people connected with the assignment. This is in accord with my instructions. May I ask your secretary to send a telegram?"

"Of course," he replied triumphantly.

The cat was now playing with its catch.

He pressed the intercom and said, "Miss Anderson, please come in here and bring your notepad."

When Miss Anderson was seated he said, "Simpson must send a telegram. OK Simpson, go ahead."

The cat was now drooling.

"Thank you for your assistance, Miss Anderson, there will be a letter and a telegram. The letter is to the office of His Excellency the Governor, and reads, 'Please be kind enough to transmit the following telegram to Whitehall by the most secure method.'

The cat stopped drooling and had a puzzled look on its face.

"The telegram reads, 'To the Minister of Transportation in the War Office. Sir, In accordance with your strict instruction to keep all information most secret surrounding the assignment your gave me, I must hereby inform you I have been requested by the Managing Director of The Red Funnel Line in Kuala Lumpur to break your order and give him a full and complete account of my report. Since your own orders in this matter came from the Prime Minister I thought it wise---"

The cat was suffering cardiac arrest.

"Stop, stop. Miss Anderson, give me these notes! And forget everything that was said. Do you understand?"

"Yes sir," she said in a shaking voice.

He ripped up the pages as Miss Anderson closed the door.

"You should have told me about this Simpson."

"My orders were explicit. In such an eventuality, I was not to enter into a debate about the matter but to immediately send a telegram."

"Oh my God."

His sallow face seemed to have turned yellow.

"I am also under instruction that if anyone seems to be showing an undue interest in this assignment, I am to report his name to the Minister."

His face was now deathly white.

"Oh my God, oh my God."

"Mr. Simpson, Jack, I was only asking in case there were things you had discovered where we could improve our operations. I was not prying. Please believe me. You must believe me."

"I will take your sincere plea into consideration prior to my final report being concluded in Singapore. However, I am bound to inform you that if I hear you have made one further enquiry I will have no choice but to report it immediately. I regret this Mr. Williams; however my orders were most explicit. I also regret to inform you of another part of my orders which was to tell anyone showing undue attention to my assignment that the penalty would be most harsh."

"Oh my God."

The cat was now on its back with its paws in the air.

"As I said earlier you and your people have been most kind and I will take this into consideration before reaching any decision. I had better get along now. Good day Mr. Williams."

As Jack left the office, Williams was slumped in his chair, his body twitching. He heard him ask Miss Anderson, in a weak voice, for another cup of strong tea.

Jack finished the things he had been working on and decided to take a walk and look for a place to have lunch. After lunch he spent the next few hours enjoying the atmosphere of Kuala Lumpur. He finished up at the railway station to admire the architecture. George had been right; it did look like something out of the Arabian Nights. He spent quite some time looking around the station, then hailed a taxi and headed for Ampang Road. As he neared the bungalow he glanced at his watch and was surprised to see it was just after five o'clock.

When the taxi pulled into the driveway he was amazed to see George's car at the front door. George was pacing up and down the veranda and ran down the steps as the taxi pulled up.

"Where have you been?" asked George in a worried voice.

"I did a little more sightseeing. Weren't you supposed to be in PS all day?"

Ah Kang was hovering in the background with a concerned look on his face.

"Is something wrong, Ah Kang?" asked Jack.

"Mistah Knight vely upset. He walk on velanda last half hour."

He gestured with his arm indicating the path George had apparently been pacing.

"Maybe you like tea Mistah Slimson?"

"That would be most welcome. Thank you Ah Kang."

Ah Kang hurried to the kitchen where Ah Eng was standing in the doorway. Jack could hear them chattering excitedly.

"Now George, what the hell is going on?"

"I was having lunch in a small noodle shop near the office in PS when a messenger from the office came running in to tell me that I had to call the MD right away. When I called he was upset that I was not in the office in KL, saying he had people looking for me everywhere. I reminded him that he had sent me to PS. He seemed very confused on the telephone and was somewhat incoherent. I had trouble understanding what he was saying. I finally gathered he wanted me to drop what I was doing and race back to KL to be certain you had all the information you required.

Furthermore I was not to be concerned about expense; I was to be sure to entertain you in the best possible manner. Well, when I returned to the office you had gone, so I came here. When you were not here I did not know what to do. I knew I could not call the MD to say I had no idea where you were. He sounded quite hysterical earlier, so I just waited here. What did you do to the MD to cause this trauma?"

Ah Kang arrived with the tea before Jack could reply.

"Thank you Ah Kang," they chorused. Jack continued, "Everything is OK Ah Kang, it was simply a misunderstanding."

Ah Kang's previously taut face of worry relaxed and creases reappeared as he smiled once again even if it was still a slightly dubious smile.

"One more thing Ah Kang, could you make dinner tonight for Mr. Knight and me?"

Now the uncertainty left his face and he said, "I got one vely nice duck, you like Mistah Slimson?"

"That sounds wonderful, thank you Ah Kang."

When Ah Kang left, George said, "I was told to take you to the best restaurant in town, Jack."

"And you are George; there is no better chef than Ah Kang. Now regarding my meeting with Williams, as you noted he was upset at not being fully informed of my assignment. Like you, he knew it was Government authorized but he wanted all the details. When I told him the name of the sponsor and that my instructions were to discuss it with no one, he backed off with alacrity."

"That's all?" asked George seeming unconvinced.

"Look George, I cannot divulge any more information to you. Let me just say the person I named put the fear of God into Williams. You have been under the thumb of this ogre Williams for too long. You have already recognized he is a coward but perhaps you do not know just how much of a coward he really is."

"There is one other matter I would like to discuss with you George and it is related to Williams. He seems to have convinced you that your future is bleak. I have watched and listened to you and in my opinion nothing could be further from the truth. It will be true if you stay here working for him. I know you love this country but you must leave."

"I don't believe I could bring myself to leave Jack."

"Look here George you have identified your weakness in financial matters, but that can be corrected. Go back to London and attend a college specializing in this subject. I know you can do it; but you have to want to do it."

George sat pensively sipping his tea. He glanced at Jack but said nothing.

"Tell you what, George, let's freshen up for dinner. You can use one of the other bathrooms. We can talk about this later, if you wish."

Dinner was divine. Jack could think of no other way to describe it. George was quiet throughout dinner. Jack wasn't sure if the reason for this was the earlier conversation or the fact that his mouth seemed to be permanently full of duck. After dinner they sat on the veranda and enjoyed coffee. They chatted for quite a while but George did not raise the previous subject.

"Well, I think I will call it a night, old chap. What time would you like me to pick you up in the morning?"

"George," said Jack hesitantly.

"Yes Jack?"

"Why don't you come with me to Seremban, tomorrow? I am sure John would not mind."

"Actually he did invite me too, when he telephoned the other day."

"Well there you are. We could drive down together and your driver could collect you in a few days and bring you back to KL while I drive on to Malacca. What do you say, George?"

"Jolly good, let's do it. I think it will be fun and I really liked John McKay. I will call him first thing tomorrow morning and make all the arrangements. What about the office?"

"Oh I don't believe I need go to the office. Let's see what best suits John's schedule but if we could leave here mid afternoon, I think that would be ideal."

"Right-o Jack. I shall call you in the morning. Good night."

"Good night George."

Jack was pleased that George was much chirpier. He continued sitting on the comfortable sofa enjoying the stillness of the evening. Crashingly, this was broken by an almost animalistic cry from the kitchen. Jack raced to the kitchen where there were two other Chinese ladies as well as Ah Kang and Ah Eng. It was one of the other ladies who was wailing in anguish and Ah Eng, with tears streaming down her face, was holding her in comfort. Ah Kang motioned Jack back into the dining room where he joined him.

"Solly for disturb you Mistah Slimson, I ask them go home soon. That lady cousin of Ah Eng. She just get bad news. Her mother, father live in China and she hear they killed by Japanese soldiers. They old people, I don't know why Japanese kill old people."

"I am so sorry. Please give my sympathies to her and to Ah Eng. Please let them stay as long as they would like."

Jack returned to the veranda and poured himself another whisky. This poor woman's grief crystallized something that had been growing in his mind since he arrived in Malaya. The attack he was helping finalize would happen soon. What would become of Ah Kang; Ah Eng; George; John McKay; the lovely people of the East Coast and the rest of the country. He also had concern for Bill McCartney whom he had come to admire and like but he was a soldier and a soldier had to do his duty.

Everything about his role as an agent had been conducted with a clinical dispassion. That was until he arrived in Malaya. Now he had a nagging unease over his part in the impending invasion. 'Get a grip of yourself Campbell. Such maudlin thoughts are only worthy of an old woman.' But he could not stop thinking of that old woman in China. Like Ah Kang he wondered why she had to die. Then his mind went to another old woman; one who had lived in Partick and had raised him since he was thirteen.

Would she be proud of him now?

Chapter 22

It was a dark eyed ogre that stared back at Jack in the mirror next morning. His night had been one of nightmares full of terrifying images of soldiers performing unspeakable acts on civilians. What horrified him most was many of these despicable soldiers wore kilts and he was one of them.

At breakfast he offered his condolences directly to Ah Eng. She looked haggard but greatly appreciated Jack's words which as always were translated by Ah Kang.

Ah Eng may have been haggard but she was not unobservant. When Ah Kang returned to the kitchen after delivering Jack's breakfast she immediately asked him what as wrong with Jack. He had noticed it too but could shed no light on the matter. Not one to be deterred when she wanted an answer, she crept into Jack's bedroom while he was eating and saw the rumpled, sweat stained bed sheets. Now she knew the reason for his appearance but not the cause of the problem.

It was around ten when George telephoned. Everything was arranged with John and he would meet them just outside Seremban and guide them to the estate. George said he would call for Jack at two o'clock.

This gave Jack plenty time to pack his bags and then drive into town to collect the presents he had ordered. When he returned he asked his two dear Chinese friends to sit with him on the veranda. At first they would not sit. It was not proper for a servant to sit with a master. He asked them it they would do so as his friends and as a special favor to him.

They did so but they sat like birds on a branch, always looking around for danger and continually fluttering their wings, ready to take flight at a second's notice. They talked for a long time and gradually the wings stilled and the looking around ceased.

Jack told them of Scotland and his life there and they told him of their early life in China. All three of them drank Chinese tea. When Ah Kang asked to be excused to begin preparation of lunch, Jack urged him to stay saying that he only wanted a sandwich. Ah Kang was disappointed he could not cook fried rice; however, he surmised from Jack's appearance that he was not well and consoled himself that a heavy meal would not be appropriate since he was going on a car journey.

He finished his snack at one thirty and asked his friends to join him in the living room. He had wanted to give them money but he knew they would never accept, so he had bought presents. He made a little speech about how much he would always treasure their friendship and wanted to give each of them a gift as a token of everlasting friendship. They both shook their heads emphatically that no gift was necessary. He was prepared for this and had made up a story to tell them. He said in his country a gift given before leaving a friend acted as a charm to one day draw them back together again. He had been right in thinking that such a supernatural tale would be irresistible to the Chinese. So they nodded their heads in acquiescence.

He presented Ah Eng with a beautiful pair of jade earrings. When she opened the box and saw them she dropped the box. Jack caught it before it hit the floor. He again placed the box in her trembling hands.

She looked at Jack then at Ah Kang, her mouth moving but no sound coming out and then she buried her head in Ah Kang's chest and sobbed. When she calmed she stared again in disbelief at her gift and raising her tearstained face to Jack said, "Tank you". Jack then gave Ah Kang his gift; it was a gold Omega watch. When he saw it his thin frame began shaking and his knees started to buckle. He leaned on Ah Eng and Jack quickly put an arm around him.

"No, no Mistah Slimson, too much, cannot accept. Take back to shop get your money back."

Jack smiled at him, "The shop will not accept it back. Look at the back of the watch."

When he did he saw it was engraved, 'To Ah Kang, from Jack.' Now tears flowed down Ah Kang's face. He translated for Ah Eng and they stood together crying. Jack put his arms around them and was hugged tightly by both of them. They were standing that way when they heard George's car arrive. Gifts were quickly put in pockets away from other eyes as they all walked to the front entrance.

Hamid put George's case in Jack's car and left while Jack said his final goodbyes. George offered to drive to Seremban since he had done so several times. This suited Jack and they pulled away he craned his neck to see the two waving figures as long as he could.

"I say old chap, you look a bit off color. Are you all right?"

"I had some trouble sleeping last night. But I'm fine."

Jack had decided he had better concentrate on his job and the prior night's qualms had been pushed further back in his mind. As George had offered to drive, it gave him the opportunity to pay more attention to the type of things he had been noting on the way down from Penang. The drive was peaceful to Jack and George seemed to be his old self again.

Near Seremban they passed a large army camp of Gurkha troops. Jack took note of the Battalion designation.

"The Gurkhas are jolly good soldiers," said George.

"Yes I heard them praised when I traveled on the East Coast," replied Jack.

As they were approaching the crossing where they were to meet John McKay, Jack looked at his watch and saw they were a half hour early. However, they had just pulled up when John arrived.

"Hello there," shouted John from his car as he braked to a stop. He leapt out and walked quickly towards them with his hand extended.

"It's a pleasure tae see you both."

"It's very nice to see you John," said Jack.

George responded, "It was kind of you to invite me Mr. McKay."

"Now look here laddie, do you want tae be here or not?" demanded McKay of George.

"Of course I do," replied George with a bewildered look.

"Then remember this. My name is John. Next time you use Mr. McKay, you will be walking back tae KL."

George saw the huge grin on John's face and said, "Very well John, I shall remember."

"Now if you will follow me, we will head to my bungalow."

The bungalow was cleverly designed in an L-shape. One leg of the ell had three bedrooms and the other had a large living room, a dinning room and the kitchen. Behind was a servant's house which was connected to the bungalow by a covered walkway. The design allowed a maximum of daylight to each room which engendered a feeling of spaciousness. The furnishings were quietly tasteful and the entire place was spotless.

Both Jack and George were impressed by John's home and it was George who commented on the elegance of the design.

"When was it built?" he asked.

"It was finished five years ago."

"Was the architect from KL?"

"There was no architect George, I designed it."

"Wow, had you designed a house prior to this?"

"No, but I find if you desire something strongly enough and work at it hard enough, its surprising how effective you become in achieving your goal."

Jack noticed a pensive look come over George's face.

"Anyway let's have a cup of tea on the veranda," said John.

The next two days were filled with so many new discoveries for Jack that time evaporated as quickly as the morning dew on the evenly cut grass of the estate. George had toured a rubber plantation before and had been the one who had first explained the process to Jack. Even though he had this rudimentary knowledge, Jack discovered the combination of John's unerring ability to explain the most intricate chemical or technical detail in layman's terms and the opportunity to actually see everything for himself gave him a deeply satisfying, thorough understanding. Even George was gaining insights he had never before fully understood, again because of John's exceptional elucidation.

On their last evening they had a delicious curry dinner. It was quite spicy and Jack had to keep drinking cold water in addition to his beer.

"Is it too spicy for your palate, Jack?" enquired John.

"Almost," admitted Jack, "but the flavor is wonderful."

"I asked my cook to make it mild. This is mild for Madras."

They moved to the veranda and coffee was served along with brandy.

"May I again thank you John," said George, "this has been a delight as well as and education."

"You are welcome to drop by at any time George."

"If I may say, I was particularly impressed by the attitude of your people. Not only do they work well but they seem so content."

"Thank you George. They are very good people."

"I wanted to ask you something John, haven't you had any trouble with the Indian Independence League?" asked Jack.

John smiled. "We had a call from their representatives. Would you like to her about it?"

"Indeed I would," said Jack.

"I would find it interesting too; as there was a terrible fight in PS in May, partly related to the Tamil estate workers going on strike. We were informed the IIL created the fight between the Tamils and the estate managers."

"Yes we know about that. It was definitely instigated by the IIL. They used one of their organizations called the Central Indian Association, which is rumored to be funded by Japan, to start this conflict. The fighting was so intense, the police could not control it and they called on the Army. Our gallant Army truly bollixed things up by sending in troops from the Indian Army instead of the British Army. Then you had Indian fighting Indian.I am sure that created even more ill will towards Britain in the hearts of many Indians."

"Let me get back to our encounter. It happened in July. A member of the IIL crept into our village one night in an attempt to stir up discontent and ask our people to go on strike. To his utter amazement he was held captive by our people and one of our foremen came to me asking that I call the police to arrest this man. I decided against this and suggested to the foreman that the IIL representative be invited to come to the village to address all our people and answer any questions they may have."

"You did what?" sputtered George.

"I know it sounds a wee bit daft. Even my foreman thought I might be drunk. But I persuaded him it would be all right and on the night of the meeting I would take all my managers to Seremban for dinner."

"Surely that was risky, they could have sabotaged your equipment or damaged your trees," opined Jack.

"I considered that but was convinced my people would never permit such things to happen."

"But why did you request such a meeting take place."

It was George's turn to indicate his continued incredulity.

"One thing you must understand is that the Indian mind is one of the most curious in the world. In the Scotland I grew up in, they would be glibly and mistakenly labeled 'nosey-parkers'. They do poke their noses into almost everything and absolutely delight in gossiping over things. This is because of their insatiable need to know microscopic details on almost anything."

"Once you understand this, you will come to realize that things shut off, or partially hidden from them will eventually ferment into a huge secret so potentially cataclysmic that they will invent a multitude of possible reasons for being kept in the dark. These reasons will be constantly debated until some leader of the group persuades the others that one of these reasons is the gospel truth. So if we turned away the IIL you can bet your last penny someone would come up with the idea it was because we were afraid they would learn some evil we were harboring. I am still confident that over ninety percent would not think ill of us; nevertheless, it seemed to be smarter to let the IIL have its say."

George was nodding his head as he said softly, "You were giving them enough rope to hang themselves."

"You hit the nail on the head, George, well done."

"What happened?" asked Jack.

Apparently four IIL representatives came along and after telling our people how they were being exploited by the lazy, greedy, unscrupulous white men; they said their plan was to take the estate away from us thereby making every Indian very rich. The question and answer period went something like this."

"Who will run the estate?"

"The IIL."

"Our present company has offices all over the world which they use to get orders for our rubber. Who will get orders in the IIL?"

"We don't need to. We can sell it to Chinese traders here and they will sell it overseas."

"But the Chinese do not like us Indians and they are smart. They will beat our prices down and down until they make most of the profit."

"Don't worry about such details, everything will be all right."

"What will happen to the Company run hospital?"

"We will take care of you. Don't worry about it."

"You said the IIL would run the estate. Does anyone in the IIL have experience running a rubber plantation?"

"Well, no. But if these lazy white men can do it, it must be easy. Don't worry about it."

"Will we get paid the same wages?"

"You don't need these pitiful wages you will all be rich from the huge profits we will make. In fact you will be so rich when you go back to India you can live like a Maharaja."

"Who said anything about going back to India?"

"All Indians will return to the Motherland. We will not need this foreign land anymore."

John paused, "Probably that was the last straw, the bit about shipping everyone back to India. These people left India because of the extreme difficulties they were experiencing. This land is like a paradise to them. At any rate the crowd had had enough. Almost as one they arose and pounced on the four representatives, tied them up and this time took matters in their own hands, and called the police. When we arrived back on the estate it was all over."

"Brilliant," said George.

"You are training to be a businessman, are you not, George?"

George looked uncomfortable, "I have always hoped to have a position with some authority."

"I have taken much time in an attempt to analyze what it takes to lead a company. I have come to the conclusion it can be done in many different ways. On one end of the spectrum you can be dictatorial and bully and threaten your employees."

Jack noticed George stiffen at these words.

"Och aye, you can rule by fear and it has to be said it can work very well for a while. The problem is that you will never get the maximum use of your people's brainpower. They will give no more than they have to under such a regime. And you will not train a competent successor."

"The way I now believe works best is to keep people informed of the major issues. For example we tell our people if there is to be a significant capital investment, or an expansion, or if we win a large order. We continually post the latest world prices of rubber on our bulletin boards. This constant sharing of key information creates trust, George. I know they trust me because of this. However, by leaving the estate when this meeting was held; they know I trust them. Because we award a bonus in a good year and because they have earned good bonuses every year; they respect my abilities as a manager. So, George, the two things you need to create in your organization are respect and trust."

George had been listening intently. He sat quietly for a while then said, "Thank you John. You are the first person to teach me something about management. I appreciate that enormously. I shall not forget this lesson."

The tenor of George's voice gave Jack chills. There was as awkward silence before John said, "How about one final brandy?"

The next morning's goodbyes were more difficult and more emotionally charged than Jack anticipated. He had come to admire John in the short time he had known him and felt cheated by not being able to spend much more time with his new friend. However, it was seeing the look on George's face as he said goodbye that really hurt because he felt the way George looked. Jack had never taken the time to realize how lonely his adult life had been, until now. It was as though he had been trudging through a desert almost dying of thirst and had been given a glass of water which after only two sips was snatched away. To have known the joy of friendship only to lose it seemed crueler than if he had never known friendship.

These thoughts kept revolving in his head on the drive to Malacca. Then they began intermingling with the qualms of his last night in KL. The qualms he thought he had buried; but like troubled spirits they refused to stay interred and were now floating hauntingly around in his mind. He found himself trembling and was having trouble concentrating on the road so he stopped in a village and had a cup of coffee. The owner stared at him and asked if he felt unwell. He said he was all right, but it was only after the owner brought the coffee and was still staring at him that he noticed the dark stains of sweat all over his shirt. He left his coffee unfinished, changed his shirt and started towards Malacca.

He willed himself to concentrate on his driving and rather than by close observation, he mechanically noted the conditions of the roads and bridges and the details of the units at the checkpoints.

It was early evening when he checked into his hotel. He had a light dinner and went to bed to wrestle with the bed sheets in a fitful sleep.

During his two days in Malacca, he merely went through his cover routine and noted the points of importance for Lord Hino. He displayed little interest in this historic town, only half listening to the eager information given by the manager of the company office. He vaguely remembered being told that Malacca was founded by a prince from Sumatra who selected it for its sheltered harbor. The fact that it lay at the crossroads of the monsoons was instrumental in it becoming one of the largest trading posts in Asia. This allowed traders from Arabia and India to sail down on the trade winds, bringing spices, scented woods and textiles. These goods were traded for porcelain, silks and metal ware brought by Chinese sailing on the monsoon winds.

As the port flourished, its wealth attracted the European colonial powers. It was captured by the Portuguese in 1511; then by the Dutch in 1641 and finally by the British in1824. Jack did admire the terracotta red Dutch buildings in the town square, but did not visit the remains of the Portuguese fort, A Famosa, on St Paul's Hill overlooking the harbor.

Normally he would have been intensely interested in all of this; instead he struggled to stay focused on his work during the day and struggled with his demons at night.

At the conclusion of his assignment, he was driven from Malacca to Johore Bharu, the town directly across the narrow channel from Singapore. There he transferred to another car which took him over the causeway bridge into Singapore. The Malay driver smiled shyly at him and said, "Welcome to Singapore". Something clicked into place in his brain as he recognized this was the last stop before returning to Japan.

No! Not to Japan. He was returning to Michiko! He visualized her beautiful smiling face and many of the clouds which had blackened his mind dissipated. Unconsciously a broad smile crossed his face and the driver seeing this in his rearview mirror took it as a sign of his pleasure at being in Singapore and his shy smile broke into a wide beam.

Chapter 23

Jack had been engaged in one of his favorite pastimes of looking at the enchanting scenery of life in Asia. The road from the causeway took them through several small villages full of open fronted shops on streets thronged with people. He was awakened from his reverie by the driver saying, "My name is Mansoor, is this your first time in Singapore, sir?"

"Yes, it is Mansoor. I have heard it is a very beautiful island. It also seems very busy. There are a lot of people on the streets."

"Oh yes sir. This is the main road from the causeway to the city and many people live along this road."

"What is its name?"

"It is called Bukit Timah Road. Bukit Timah is the highest hill in Singapore and is just over there to your left. The name is Malay and means Tin Hill. It is a funny name is it not?"

"It does sound a little funny in English but I think it sounds much better in Malay. Are we going straight to the International Hotel?"

"Oh sorry sir, I should have told you earlier; your hotel has been changed. You are now staying at the Raffles Hotel."

"Is that near here?"

"No sir," laughed the driver. "It is on the other side of the island, the south side, by the sea. It is the best hotel in Singapore. The Managing Director ordered the change. I believe he left a letter at the hotel to explain everything."

Jack went back to being absorbed by the sights until they arrived at the hotel. It was an impressive building and in keeping with its grandeur was the very tall Sikh doorman who opened the car door for him. He was over six feet tall and his turban added to his imposing stature.

"Good afternoon sir. Welcome to the Raffles Hotel. I hope you enjoy your stay with us."

"I am certain I will. Thank you."

Jack thanked Mansoor who said he had been assigned to drive Jack while he was in Singapore and would park at the hotel.

"Just ask the doorman to call me when you wish to go out."

The clerk at the reception desk greeted Jack and said, "There are two messages for you, sir."

He handed Jack two envelopes, both bearing the Red Funnel Line logo. He decided to wait until he was in his room before opening them. When the door to his room was opened by the bellman, Jack let out a whistle. It was the most opulent room he had ever seen and had a wonderful view of the sea. He said to the bellman, "Will you please wait until I make a telephone call?"

"Is there something wrong, sir? Do you not like the room?"

"The room is magnificent but it must have been given to me in error."

He dialed the front desk.

"I think there has been a mistake in my room assignment."

"No sir. This is the room specifically reserved for you by your company."

"I am terribly sorry and embarrassed, but I am sure I could not afford this room."

"Your company, the Red Funnel Line, asked that all charges be sent to them. I trust you will find everything in order sir. Should you require anything further please do not hesitate to ring me."

He smiled self-consciously at the bellman.

"It seems it is my room after all. Just leave the suitcase on the bed; it will be easier to unpack. Thank you."

When he sat on the sofa, he noticed the basket of fruit with a note from the hotel manager welcoming him to Raffles. That reminded him of the letters he was given at reception. In all the excitement of seeing his room he had temporarily forgotten them. He opened the first one which was from the Managing Director, Donald Chapman. Mr. Chapman apologized at not being able to meet him as his father had died and he had to return to England. He wrote that his second in command, Neil Stuart, would take care of Jack in his absence.

He also noted he had been requested by the London Office to book Jack on the Red Funnel Liner leaving for England in two weeks. Accordingly, Neil would give him his ticket.

The other letter was from Neil Stuart, welcoming him to Singapore and inviting him to dinner that evening. He would call for him at six o'clock and they could have a drink before dinner.

'Well,' thought Jack, "two weeks to complete everything. I don't have too much time'. With the briefing he had received in Japan regarding the docks, he knew it would take at least four days to complete his cover assignment The problem would be getting a first hand look at the military defenses.

He knew the docks were not too far from his hotel, but the naval base was not close to the docks, in fact it was on the opposite side of the island. It was near the causeway on the north coast. Mentally he began ticking off his other tasks. Somehow he had to get a better understanding of the 'Big Guns'; their exact location and any improvements that may have been made since Lord Hino last saw them. Then there were the airfields. There was some doubt as to how many were fully commissioned and their primary missions. And, of course, which army units are on the island, their strength and location.

'It is quite a list,' he thought.

His contemplation was interrupted by a knocking on the door. It was a waiter with tea. He thanked the waiter and said, "Your timing is perfect. This is the British answer to all problems; a cup of tea."

The waiter smiled uncomprehendingly.

He savored the tea while he unpacked. It was good, as one would expect from a first class hotel; but it was not as good as the tea served by Ah Kang.

Jack went down to the lobby just before six. He hoped Mr. Neil Stuart would turn out to be as friendly and useful as his other contacts; however, when he saw the burly blond headed man come striding through the entrance he knew he would be disappointed. He had recognized the tie as that of Oxford University but it was the swagger which told him this was not the type of person to whom he would relate well. He walked towards Stuart, "Mr. Neil Stuart?"

"Yes, yes. You must be Simpson. Nice to meet you."

The accent was much more English than Scottish which confirmed his fears about this man.

"Let's head for the bar and have a beer. What do you say?"

"Good idea, thank you."

When they had ordered, Stuart said, "Presume you got the notes. The MD was sorry to have missed you, but under the circumstances, I am sure you understand."

"Of course. Had his father been ill for some time?"

"No. It was very unexpected. A massive heart attack. The MD left yesterday. He asked me to fill in for him, so anything you need just ask me."

"Well, first, I must thank you for the hotel arrangements."

"Ah yes. Quite an interesting situation. I understand you were booked at the International. The MD got a call from old Williams in KL asking that you be well looked after. Most unusual. You see our offices run quite independent of one another, in fact, there is a bit of rivalry. My MD is of the old school, worked his way up from the bottom and did not have the benefit of a decent education like Williams or me. Nevertheless he is very successful and is highly regarded back in London. Williams has never been able to produce anything like the results of Singapore and it must really irk him. Given this situation, you must either have very powerful friends in London, or you must have done something extraordinary to impress Williams to cause him to deign to ask a favor of our MD. So what's your secret, Simpson?"

Jack looked around, then leaned forward and whispered, "I am the illegitimate son of the Prime Minister."

Stuart was about to take a drink of his beer but upon hearing this, his mouth gaped open and he dribbled beer down his chin.

"The devil you say," he hissed. Then seeing the look on Jack's face he burst out laughing. "You bugger. You really had me going for a second. I should have known better. I heard you were from Glasgow and should have expected this sense of humor."

"Sorry, I could not resist the temptation. To be honest, I have no idea why Mr. Williams would take such an interest," he lied.

"I understand your assignment is for a Government Department and we must not be inquisitive."

"It is really quite mundane, but I have been given strict operational instructions and therefore must be guided by them at all times."

"As it happens I will not be in a position to spend much time with you. The MD's sudden departure means I must spend more time in the office, but as I said earlier, feel free to call me if you need assistance. Of course I will accompany you tomorrow to the Keppel Docks to introduce you to the Harbor Master. Then you can come and go as you please. A driver has been assigned to you to get around. Oh one other item; I will have your ticket for your passage back to England, in a few days. Now how about some dinner. The restaurant here is very good."

"That sounds fine. Perhaps I should tell the driver to go home."

"I'll have the doorman do that. I'll ask him to be here at eight thirty tomorrow morning and take you to Keppel Harbor where I shall meet you."

During dinner Jack learned that Stuart's family owned lots of land in the Scottish border area just outside Selkirk. He had been sent to board at Harrow at an early age and then attended Oxford.

He seemed to regard his present job as something of a penance as he did not do too well in his final exams at Oxford. Apparently his father was so vexed at this he refused to financially support Neil in London and from the conversation Neil liked to spend a great deal of money.

"A few more years out here and then the old boy will have forgiven everything and I can get back to the city. You see I am the only son and soon he will be after me to marry and have a son to keep the family name going."

"Don't you find the work interesting?" asked Jack.

"Oh it's no too bad. Actually the old MD has our office running like a Swiss watch, so it doesn't require any particular brilliance. However the social life is wonderful. Lots of sports, lots of girls and lots of parties. Talking of sports, do you play rugger?"

To most people the game is called rugby; however, Jack recalled a few of the fellows at university calling it rugger.

"I am afraid not. I played football."

"That's a pity, I play for the Cricket Club and we have a game on Saturday. We are looking for players as so many of the chaps have either joined the forces or have gone home. Tell you what Simpson, why don't you come along to the game. We are playing the chaps from the Navy. It should be a cracking good game. Afterwards we always have a drink in the bar then go out somewhere to eat."

Jack had immediately recognized the potential of gleaning information from bar talk with lads from the Navy.

"I would enjoy that, thank you. But, explain to me why a cricket club has a rugby team."

"Well it is one of the oldest clubs in this part of the world. Although cricket was played on the padang in the 1830's the Cricket Club was founded in 1852. Since then it has added several sports and is the premier sports club in Singapore. Today, in addition to cricket, it offers rugger, football, tennis, hockey, lawn bowls, darts and billiards. Although it is an all round sports club, it has kept its original name."

"What time does the game begin?"

"Come along about half past four and I will get you a beer. The game will start at five."

The next two days, Thursday and Friday, were very busy ones for Jack, as he was determined to finish his cover assignment as quickly as possible. He knew he would need all of the remaining available time to gather information on Singapore's defenses. By just listening to the conversations in the harbor he had learned that engineering work had indeed been carried out on the 'big guns' to give them a much wider angle of fire. The two Artillery Fire Commands were on Mount Faber, just behind the city center, and Changi, on the North East Coast.

On Saturday morning he wandered around the city then began walking up toward Mount Faber. He was stopped and asked where he was going. He said he had heard of a famous cemetery which had the grave of Iskandar Shah, the last king of Temasek which was the name of the kingdom before it became Singapore. The soldiers held a meeting which resulted in one of them calling their unit HQ. After a moment the sergeant got confirmation that the grave did exist.

He asked for identification papers and said he could only allow Jack to proceed if accompanied by one of his troops. Jack readily agreed and proceeded with his guard into the cemetery. Jack found the cemetery very interesting.

The soldier was obviously bored with the whole thing but he perked up when Jack motioned towards the guns and said, "These are really big guns. Were you specially selected to guard them?"

"Well we did get training for this assignment. We guard these and the ones at Changi, which are even bigger," he replied with some pride.

"This must be a great responsibility."

"They are the protectors of Singapore. No enemy will get near us with these guns firing on them."

Jack continued to butter up the soldier.

"Can you actually fire them?"

"We have been trained on them in case of an emergency, but it is the job of the artillery boys."

"Wow, what a thrill it must be to fire one of them. I know it is not possible but I would love to stand next to them just to get a better view."

"You're right. If you tried to get near them we have orders to shoot. Tell you what, since you are so interested, have a quick peek through my field glasses. Crouch down behind that headstone and for Pete's sake don't let the sergeant see you."

"They are gigantic. Even the shells stacked next to them are huge. What do the letters painted on the side of the shells stand for, APC and HE?"

"Armor Piercing shell and High Explosive; most of our shells are APC and the big boys at Changi only use APC."

"I had better not take up any more of your time. Thank you very much."

Jack went back to his hotel room and spent the next several hours encoding a detailed report. He understood the importance of a minority of shells being HE. APC's were essential to sink ships but caused much less damage if aimed at ground forces. Due to their high angle of descent they would burrow twenty feet or more into the ground before exploding. It was the instant fragmentation of HE upon contact which did real damage to ground forces. Therefore, even though some of the guns had been altered to allow them to swivel toward Johore, they had the wrong shells to counter any such land attack.

After secreting his report in his suitcase he ordered a sandwich and took another shower before leaving for the Cricket Club. He was met at the door by Stuart who was already kitted out for the game.

"Ah there you are Simpson. Come along, I would like you to meet Charlie Ward, Captain of the football team. I told him you play and he needs a man for a game next week."

He had mentally decided he did not have time for a football match; however, when it turned out that the game was against the Air force and would be played at Seletar Air Base, he changed his mind.

"That's excellent," said Charlie. "We will all meet here at the club next Thursday at three thirty and drive to Seletar. I have some kit downstairs in the dressing room; let's make sure we have a spare pair of boots in your size."

They did find the correct size boots. Charlie said he would bring everything along with him on Thursday.

The rugby match was more entertaining than Jack had imagined. The Cricket Club team gave a good account of itself in the first half but the superior fitness of the Navy team took its toll in the second half and they won by six points. As was usual in rugby the ferocity of the game was later replaced by camaraderie in the bar. The treatment for split lips, bloody noses, a few missing teeth and other cuts and bruises was not any externally applied unguent, but internally consumed large quantities of beer.

At the bar, Jack was introduced to many of the players from both sides but his attention was focused on the Navy team. It did not take long to identify the more senior men and he stood next to one. After about three beers the Captain of the Cricket Club team announced, "All right chaps, one more round, then down to the showers. After that we will go out for something to eat and of course, more beer!" This was acclaimed with a universal roar. Jack had been careful to keep his beer intake to only two pints including the final round. The sports conversation with his neighbor had petered out when he was asked, "What do you do out here?"

"I am only here on a visit. I am doing some harbor studies."

"You have something in common with Lieutenant Commander Wright; he is in charge of ship movement in and out of the base."

He waved his arm to the man five places down the bar. "Frank, come meet Jack."

They only had time for a few pleasantries before both teams began trudging toward the showers.

"I'll see you at dinner," said Frank.

Jack sat next to Frank at dinner in the Chinese restaurant. Each round table sat ten people. When the waiter asked for drink orders Jack offered to buy the first round. Everyone wanted beer but Jack said he would have a whisky and offered one to Frank which was readily accepted. After the third course and the second round of drinks, Frank said, "So what are you reviewing, the efficient loading and unloading?"

"Yes and the effective positioning of ships waiting in the roads as well as the timing of engine start ups and the use of pilots to get ships out of the lanes; all of this to cut down on idle time."

"Well I wish you would tell whatever branch of government you report to that somebody made a stupid decision when they put our base in its present location. Do you know our ships have to navigate twenty miles of narrow channel to get to base? What's worse if we have a need to pass in the channel it's likely as not to result in one ship hitting a sand bank. It's a bloody nightmare. They say it's impossible for an enemy to penetrate the jungle of the mainland. I hope there are bloody well right, as if anyone did, our ships are sitting bloody ducks. Oh forget it, let's have another round."

Then he leant close to Jack and whispered, "Look Jack, as you seem to know so much about efficiency, is there any chance you could have a quick look at the base and give me some advice. Of course it would have to be completely unofficial and you could not put it in your report."

"I could spare some time on Friday."

"That would be great. I will make arrangements and contact you. Which hotel are you staying at?"

"Raffles."

"I'll leave a message for you on Tuesday."

When Jack got back to the hotel that night he jotted down all he had heard and next day when he was completely sober he encoded another vital report. 'Who would have believed sports could turn out to be so useful' he thought. 'Rugby has given me the Navy information and hopefully football will give me the Air force information.' That left the Army and, as yet, he had no idea how he would get that information.

He managed to finish most of his cover work by Wednesday morning. It was during lunch that he heard two friends greet each other.

"Hello there Jim, I haven't seen you in ages."

"Hello George. How have you been?"

He had a pang of guilt when he heard the name, George. He had not thought of calling George in KL. His days had been full and the nights were filled with thoughts of Michiko. How he longed to see her. He hurried back to the harbor and asked the telephone operator if she would call George at the Red Funnel Line in KL.

"I am sorry sir but they say Mr. Knight is not in the office."

"Thank you I will try tomorrow."

He was wrapping up the final details of his assignment the next morning and tried George again but got the same response.

Jack played a good game that afternoon and scored two goals in his team's 3-2 victory. Their hosts supplied dinner in the mess and it was in the bar after dinner that he got the information he needed from Flight Lieutenant Thompson. There were four fully operational air fields; Seletar and Changi to the north; Kallang to the south and Tengah in the west. Thompson was quite jealous of the missions of Tengah and Kallang as it allowed them to fly more interesting surveillance of the offshore islands; whereas the role of Changi and Seletar was mainly to protect the naval base.

He went back to his hotel well satisfied with the night's information. 'But,' he thought, 'where oh where am I to get the Army information?' Time was running out.

Furthermore he had not been contacted on his route back to Japan; and that really worried him. It was only the belief that he and Michiko would be reunited that kept away the demonic nightmares of Malaya.

Chapter 24

Jack was surprised at how sore his legs were when he awakened next morning; then he reflected it had been two years since his last game of football. He decided to relax his muscles in a hot bath before ordering breakfast in the room. He was in no hurry as his appointment with Frank Wright was not until eleven o'clock and Mansoor was picking him up at ten. Just after his breakfast arrived the telephone rang.

"Good morning Simpson, Neil Stuart here. I am terribly sorry that I have not had time to entertain you properly, but I am sure you understand. Unfortunately I am tied up with an official dinner tonight and I have an engagement tomorrow night. I have a few friends coming to the house on Sunday for curry tiffin. Would you care to come along?"

"That is kind of you, yes I would enjoy that."

Jack hoped he sounded convincing. Actually he would much prefer not to be with people like Stuart but he had better keep up the pretense of being the grateful guest.

"Oh good. Ask Mansoor to bring you to the house about one.
Well, must be off, Goodbye."

"Goodbye."

He told Mansoor of Sunday's arrangements while driving to the base.

"Mr. Stuart has a very good Indian cook. She makes very good curry. Many people like to go to his house on a Sunday for curry. I will call for you at half past twelve."

"Thank you Mansoor, I am sorry to upset you week-end."

"No problem sir," beamed Mansoor, "I get overtime pay for Sundays."

215

As they approached the base, Jack began to get a little worried. There was no doubt he had learned much from John Gibson in Glasgow; easily enough to complete his assignment, but what if Frank Wright was a true professional in logistics, he would be found out to be less than an expert.

He need not have been concerned; Lieutenant Commander Wright was a sailor who had been pressed into this job. A job he knew little about and one he did not care for. He wanted to be on board a ship. Jack's agreement to assist had been a way of identifying the types and numbers of ships stationed at the base. Therefore he had to draw a fine line between helping the British Navy and doing his job for Lord Hino. He could not be too useful to Wright; however, he had to offer some advice. At the conclusion he thought he had been a bit skimpy in the useful advice area but Frank Wright's effusive thanks made him wonder if he had gone too far. If Wright was happy, he was delighted. He had learned much more than he had expected.

He arrived back at the hotel at five o'clock and told Mansoor to go home as he would get something to eat at the hotel. He thought it a bit early to have a drink then said to himself, 'What the hell have a gin and tonic, that's not a drink it's only a refreshment.'

He was sitting at the bar when he heard a distinctly Australian voice say, "It's no bloody good you wearing your diplomatic hat Sam, we need better barracks for my lads. You have to get tough with these pomeys."

"Keep you voice down Bill, I told you I would do my best."

Jack used his training to unobtrusively locate the couple who were in a booth by the window. He said to the barman in a slightly louder than normal voice, "My name is Wright and I am waiting for a friend. I will be sitting over there by the window. When she arrives send her over please."

He moved to the booth next to the Australians.

The strident voice had started again.

"Sam you are our bloody High Commissioner, so get off your arse and get me better quarters for our boys."

"Now listen to me Bill. I will put down your abusive language to a few too many drinks. I told you I will talk to the British High Commissioner. In the meantime you should make your case in a reasoned argument to the C-IN-C."

"I apologize Sam. But the Brits have their troops in huts. Even the Indians are in huts and our lads are in tents."

To add weight to his argument, he reeled off the identities of the brigades and divisions both in Singapore and in Johore. Jack could not believe his luck as he scribbled down as much information as possible on his napkin. He then left the bar and went to the front desk to collect his room key.

As he was collecting his key he was given an envelope.

"This was left for you, sir. The gentleman did not leave a name."

"Thank you."

He opened the envelope as soon as he had locked the door to his room. It was in code. His heart began beating faster as he got out his code book. It did not take long to decode the message. He was to be at a restaurant called Yeow Lee, in Chinatown, at seven o'clock where a table under the name of Jackson had been reserved. The address was given and the note also specified what he should order. He decided this was a technique to make identification easier.

He burned the message then began writing a report on the conversation he heard. When he had encoded this report he burned his notes then showered and dressed.

He considered taking his gun but decided instead to strap his knife to the inside of his lower leg. He did not hand in his key instead kept it in his pocket. As he had been trained, he walked for ten minutes to get away from the hotel before hailing a taxi. He asked to be taken to the Thian Hock Keng Temple or Temple of Heavenly Happiness, the most famous Hokkien Temple in Singapore. He waited until the taxi had gone before turning away from the temple and asking directions to the street where the restaurant was located.

When he entered Yeow Lee he was shown to his reserved table. It was against the wall and although the restaurant was very busy the tables on either side of his were not occupied but had a reserved sign on them. The coded message had instructed him to order sharks fin soup, chicken in a paper bag, steamed prawns and rice. When he placed his order the waiter smiled.

"You know our specialties, sir."

He had just about finished his soup which was delicious, when the chair of the table at his back scraped along the floor as someone sat down. He heard the occupant order in Chinese. He saw the waiter deliver soup to the table behind him and shortly thereafter reappeared with his chicken. This dish was bite size pieces of chicken each wrapped in parchment so that the juices stayed in the paper bag during cooking. Once again the food was delicious but he had to open the paper bag carefully as the chicken was very hot and he burned his fingers on his first attempt. The person behind him was now slurping his soup noisily.

He was on his third piece of chicken when a voice behind him whispered, "Do not turn round, I think I have been followed. The man standing in the shadows by the door."

Jack opened another bag with deliberate clumsiness and let out a yell as the juice burned his fingers and spilled on his trousers. He stood as the waiter rushed up with a cloth. He was muttering to himself as he wiped his trousers. He had previously noticed the fat owner who sat by the door in a singlet and shorts, checking all the bills by clicking away on his abacus. Now the owner said something in Chinese to another waiter who laughed. The man standing in the doorway did not laugh but as he moved a little to get a better view he came into the light and Jack saw he was Caucasian.

As he sat down the waiter delivered his prawns and a bowl of rice. As soon as the waiter left the voice whispered, "When you enter your cabin on the ship you will find a black shirt and a pair of black trousers under your bed. Strap all your important documents to your body, put on the black clothes and wear soft shoes. Once out of the harbor area the ship will stop to let the pilot off on the starboard side. Leave your suitcase in your cabin and climb down the rope you will find on the port side near the stern. Be quick. The waiting boat will take you from there. Give me ten minutes after I leave here before you leave. Goodbye."

The chair creaked and he was gone. Jack saw the figure in the doorway stare at him then turn to follow the messenger.

Jack had been taught always to follow the instructions of a local agent as he understood the customs of the area. However every fiber of his body was bristling with signals of danger. He got up, threw some notes on the table and hurried out of the restaurant. The perplexed waiter gathered up the notes and gave them to the fat owner who just shrugged and said, "These foreigners always order too much food."

Jack hugged the buildings as his eyes searched for either one of the two men. At last he saw someone who looked like the messenger get into a taxi. As he had only seen the back of the messenger he could not be sure. The tension combined with the tropical heat made him sweat profusely. Then he saw the Caucasian stand out on the roadway to look after the taxi. After a few seconds the Caucasian ran to an open sided public telephone booth and began putting coins into it. Jack raced along in the shadows and took up a position in the darkness of a closed shop doorway nearby. He heard the Caucasian clearly as he excitedly spoke into the phone.

"That is two days I have followed Kwong and nothing has happened to convince me he is involved. No sir, not a thing. No sir, he has not gone anywhere near any of our other suspects. He just had a very quick dinner and I heard him tell the taxi driver to take him to his home. He sat at a table next to a foreigner but as far as I could see there was no conversation. No sir, there were definitely no messages passed, I could see their hands at all times. Yes sir I am certain. But sir I have no idea who that foreigner was. I only caught a quick look at him. Yes sir. I will go back to the restaurant and see if he is still there. Yes sir, I will question the owner and check taxi companies to find out where he was picked up. Yes sir, I understand I must do this as I am the only one to have seen this foreigner Yes sir. I do appreciate how important any information could be. Yes sir, yes sir. I will go right back there now. Goodnight sir."

Jack now knew that his instincts had been correct and this was a very dangerous situation which required an immediate and permanent solution. The street was crowded as it was every night in Chinatown. As the Caucasian moved away from the telephone, Jack moved quickly towards him, waving his left hand in a greeting. The other man stopped with a look of complete surprise on his face which became much more surprised as Jack slid the knife into his heart. Without stopping he caught the man under his armpit and propelled him into the darken doorway where he had been standing. He let the body slump to the ground and walked casually away. Chinese had become used to seeing foreigners fall down after drinking too much and it took ten minutes before someone discovered that the man was dead.

Jack walked all the way back to the hotel. He waited until the doorman was helping an old couple into a taxi before slipping into the hotel. Having his key in his pocket, he went straight to his room and locked the door. A quick examination of his clothes revealed only a minor amount of blood on his shirt sleeve. He washed it off and had another shower.

Next morning he did not need the sweat soaked sheets to tell him he had a bad night. The nightmares had returned and with a vengeance. He quickly got out of bed and went straight to the shower. As the water cascaded down on his head he analyzed why his sleep had been so disturbed. Obviously it was related to the killing. He knew his training had conditioned him to act decisively and he was certain he had no option; he had done the right thing. Yet as he thought about it he realized he had not committed this act merely to protect himself as a spy. His primary thought had been that if he were to be caught he would never see Michiko again and that he could not allow that to happen.

Most probably the man he killed worked for British Military Intelligence and they would be actively looking for the killer. He was not concerned about Mr. Kwong, they may question him but once they checked with the taxi driver they would know he was in the clear. No, they would be looking for a foreigner, about whom they had no information, not even a partial description. He remembered that the man had not mentioned which restaurant Mr. Kwong had been in. This would make it more difficult. It would take time to get a description. Today was Saturday and he would leave on Tuesday. He felt safe.

He spent the day strolling around Singapore then sitting by the hotel pool and had a quiet dinner in the hotel. The next day Mansoor was at the hotel on time and drove him to Stuart's home. The house was in Victoria Park on a rise above Bukit Timah Road. As they drove through the gates, Jack saw it was a large house on considerable grounds. A big brown dog came bounding happily towards him, followed by a striding Stuart.

"It's OK Simpson, she is very friendly. Just don't try coming through the gates at night, she becomes a different animal. Come in and meet some people. Oh, by the way, congratulations!"

"Congratulations?"

"Yes, I understand you were the star of our football team."

"I enjoyed the game and the Cricket Club boys played well."

After tiffin, which was delicious and obviously appreciated by all the guests, Stuart motioned to Jack to join him.

"Just a bit of work old chap. Did you get every thing you required?"

"Yes, everyone was most cooperative."

"Good. Oh I had a call from old Williams in KL. He asked how you were and if we were taking good care of you. It's not like him to be so solicitous, you really must have impressed him. Anyway he was mainly asking if we had a good junior available as his assistant quit."

"George?"

"Yes, apparently Knight suddenly resigned and boarded a ship for England on Friday. Not that Williams had much time for Knight, it's more the inconvenience of his abrupt leaving."

"Did he say why George left?"

"I got the impression that Williams did not believe the given reason. It seems that Knight said he was planning to return to university. Williams thinks that the job was just too much for him."

Jack smiled to himself and thought, 'Good for you George. Good for you.' He said to Stuart, "As my work is over and I return on Tuesday I would like to have something special. Do you happen to have champagne?"

"Yes I do. I will get you a glass."

"Thank you, I feel like celebrating."

Jack had two glasses of champagne before leaving at four o'clock. On the way to the hotel Mansoor said, "Did you enjoy the curry, sir?"

"You were correct Mansoor, it was excellent."

"I thought so, you seem very happy sir."

"I am Mansoor. I am very happy."

He would soon be on his way to Michiko. The combination of visualizing her lovely face and the incredible news about George had again blown away the black clouds from his mind. He did not know how long they would stay away, but for the moment he was indeed happy.

Chapter 25

The journey to Japan had seemed interminable. Getting off the ship near Singapore had worked perfectly. He climbed down the rope into a waiting sampan where the boatman indicated he should stay under the canopy. He was rowed for an hour then waited on the bobbing sampan for another fifteen minutes before transferring to a motor launch. This took him to a small island where he was hidden in a shack for two days. Then the motor launch took him out to sea, traveling most of the night until he was met by a submarine. The submarine made several stops, both under-water and at night on the surface, before Kyushu was reached.

He landed in Kagoshima and was immediately taken to a small airstrip where he boarded a small plane and was flown to Fukuoka in northern Kyushu where he landed late at night. At the airport he was able to bathe and was given food. He was provided with a cot and slept soundly until he was awakened at six thirty in the morning. Again he had the luxury of bathing and shaving before a simple breakfast. He was given clean clothes which were of a large size in Japan but which were a very tight fit for him. At seven thirty he took off in a military plane and flew to a military base just outside of Tokyo.

As he came down the steps from the plane he was disappointed that Michiko was not there; however, he was not surprised to see the slim elegant man who awaited him.

"Good afternoon Lord Hino."

"Good afternoon Campbell, I am very pleased to see you again."

As they walked towards a guarded building Lord Hino said, "We must go to Tokyo almost immediately. A special meeting has been arranged to hear your report. I trust you are not too tired as this meeting could last several hours."

They passed through an outer door into the guarded building and Lord Hino opened the door to an office.

"I said almost immediately; however, my life was threatened if I did not allow you twenty minutes here."

He smiled as the door swung open and Jack's heart missed a beat. Inside stood Michiko. The door closed behind him and he stood speechless for an instant and gazed at her radiant beauty. She raced towards him with tears of joy running down her cheeks. Her arms wrapped around him and her fingers dug into his back.

"Jack, my darling Jack, are you all right? You look so tired. Have you been hurt?"

"No. I am all right now. Now that I am holding you."

He kissed her gently.

It seemed to Jack that only a few minutes had passed before there was a knock on the door. Lord Hino entered the room.

"It is time to go Campbell."

"I regret to tell you I cannot go with you," said Jack.

Both Lord Hino and Michiko looked bewildered.

"At least not until one thing is settled."

"What is that?" snapped Lord Hino.

Jack turned to Michiko who was still clinging to him, "Michiko will you marry me?"

Tears sprang from her eyes and she kissed him.

"Yes Jack I will marry you."

He then faced her uncle, "My Lord Hino, do I have you approval to marry your niece."

"I doubt that I have a choice. My niece is behaving in a most un-Japanese manner."

Then, with a broad smile he kissed Michiko on the cheek and then bowed to Jack.

"Mr. Jack Campbell, you have my approval."

Jack returned the bow.

"Congratulations my niece. I am sure you will tell me when the wedding will take place. I believe we will be very late and probably will have to stay in the hotel tonight. We will see you tomorrow morning by which time you will no doubt have worked out all the details. A driver will take you to my house."

Jack kissed Michiko once more.

"I love you so much."

"I love you too, Jack."

"Campbell, my niece was thoughtful enough to have me bring along a change of clothing for you. I do believe you need it. Please change quickly we must hurry."

The meeting started at three o'clock and was held in the same room of the Ministry of Post and Telephones. Attending, was the group which attended the meeting in the Palace plus an outer ring of subordinates, many of them from the original committee. The Prime Minister sat at the head of the table with a microphone in front of him. Another microphone was set up at the opposite end of the long table and Jack was led to this spot. Lord Hino sat next to him.

The Prime Minister opened the meeting in Japanese.

"The purpose of this meeting is to review the findings of Campbell-san and make any modifications necessary to our plans based on these findings. The War Cabinet will then set the date for the implementation of our plans and consult with His Majesty asking his approval. With this as our purpose we must be very thorough and detailed in our discussions. I have requested that this meeting be tape recorded for an accurate record. We all know that Campbell-san has an excellent grasp of our language; however, there is not the slightest room for any error in our deliberations. Therefore, I have asked that we use an interpreter. I have also asked Lord Hino if he would be kind enough to verify the interpretation as a further measure of security and he has graciously agreed."

He bowed to Lord Hino who returned the bow.

Continuing in Japanese he said, "Welcome back Campbell-san. We are all most anxious to hear your report. I understand your return trip was quite arduous and took more than two weeks. I hope you have had time to rest. When did you arrive in Tokyo?"

Without waiting for the interpreter Jack replied in Japanese, "This afternoon."

The Prime Minister looked perplexed and said to the interpreter, "He misunderstood my question, ask him in English."

Lord Hino intervened, "No Prime Minister, he understood perfectly. He got off the plane at a base just outside Tokyo one and a half hours ago."

A murmuring broke out round the table.

"Do you think it wise to proceed with this meeting if he has had no rest, Lord Hino?" asked the Prime Minister.

"Perhaps he is better able than I to respond to your question. What is your answer, Campbell?"

Jack stood with a sheaf of papers in his hand and addressed the Prime Minister.

"Your Excellency, I am prepared to proceed. I believe time is of the essence and having gathered this group of very busy people it would be disrespectful on my part to ask for a postponement. Further, I took careful notes on every area I traveled. All these reports were encoded; however, on the submarine I had time to decode all of them. Should I be the least bit doubtful on any point I will refer to my reports. I believe we can proceed."

At this, the Minister for War looked at Jack and gave a somewhat reluctant grunt of respect.

"Very well, thank you Campbell-san. Gentlemen this is how we shall conduct this meeting. We will take one location at a time and thoroughly review it before going to the next one. Is that clearly understood?"

They responded in the affirmative and the meeting began. It lasted seven hours. The Prime Minister then asked if anyone had anything further to say. Jack raised his hand.

"Just one other point, Your Excellency. I took the opportunity to drive from Penang to Ipoh; to Kuala Lumpur; to Malacca and finally to Singapore. And although it was not requested, I do have information on the conditions of the roads and bridges and the identities of the troops manning the checkpoints along the way. All of this information is contained in my reports."

"Well done," said one of the generals, "that will be most useful."

This was discussed for another thirty minutes then the meeting was ended. The Prime Minister walked to the other end of the table and extended his hand to Jack.

"On behalf of all of us, I would like to offer our sincere gratitude for the work you have done."

"Thank you, Your Excellency."

There was a cough from the other end of the table and the Minister of War stood. The room became very silent.

"May I be allowed a comment, Your Excellency?"

"Of course."

"At our last meeting I made a remark concerning the entrustment of this critical task to a foreigner. I wish to state that seldom have I witnessed such a comprehensive intelligence report. As an army man I can categorically state that it will be of the greatest use to our forces. I would like to offer my apologies to Campbell-san. He did a magnificent job."

He bowed to Jack who returned the bow. The room exploded in a roar of approval. When the applause stopped the Minister continued, "Also I owe an apology to Lord Hino for questioning his judgment in this matter. I should have known better. His Lordship has always served our country in an exemplary manner."

He bowed to Lord Hino who acknowledged his apology. Once again there was a round of applause. Everyone was standing but no one was leaving. Lord Hino whispered to Jack, "I think they are waiting for you to exit, Campbell."

As Jack walked to the door, they formed two lines, one on each side of his path and applauded and bowed as he left.

As they stood outside the building waiting for the car, Jack turned to Lord Hino and said, "May I make a request?"

"Let me guess Campbell; you would like to proceed to my home rather than stay at the hotel."

"Yes."

"I think that is an excellent idea. Let me add my congratulations to those of everyone else. I expected good work from you; however, you exceeded my expectations, your report was truly exceptional."

"Thank you My Lord."

Jack was pleased with the unusually fulsome praise from Lord Hino; but he felt he should have been delighted, not just pleased. Something wasn't quite right. He then thought of Michiko and suddenly everything felt right.

The next morning he arose early. He had not slept well. He put this down to the thoughts of marriage. While he bathed he wondered if his proposal had come too soon, after all Michiko and he had known each other for only a short time. He knew his love for Michiko was real and would be lasting. He knew this was not only due to her beauty but also because of the wonderful sense of serenity he felt when he was with her. He finished bathing, quickly dressed and almost ran down stairs. To his surprise Michiko was already up and was drinking tea with Lord Hino. When she saw him she ran towards him and kissed him.

"Good morning my darling Jack, did you sleep well?"

"Fine, thank you."

He had not lied by saying yes. Fine was a relative term.

"I am surprised to see both of you up so early."

"You can say 'good morning' to me Campbell," said Lord Hino.

"I beg your pardon, good morning My Lord."

"It would be a better morning if my impatient niece had not wakened me at five thirty and insisted I get bathed and dressed immediately," he said grumpily. "Did I not tell you she would have everything planned by this morning?"

"But uncle, I knew you would wish to approve my suggestions before I discussed them with Jack. Was that not correct?"

"Yes of course you are correct," he said much more gently as he struggled unsuccessfully to keep a smile from his face.

"Perhaps you had better tell Campbell of your proposals while I have coffee brought to him."

"All right, please sit down Jack."

"Is this news so terrifying that I have to sit down and have coffee?" he joked.

Lord Hino let out a loud laugh as he rang for his servant.

"I hope not," she said somewhat hesitantly. "I do hope you do not think me too forceful for making proposals to my uncle without consulting you. Perhaps I made a mistake and you will not approve, my darling. Please tell me if you wish to change the entire plan."

He held both her hands and looked into her eyes before saying, "My darling Michiko, I have complete trust in your judgment on our wedding. Furthermore I wish this to be the happiest day of your life as it will most definitely be mine. My only hope is that it will be a traditional Japanese wedding."

"How did you know? Oh my darling Jack."

She threw her arms around him and kissed him.

"Are you certain you do not object?"

"I think it is a splendid idea, provided someone tells me what I am supposed to do. My studies did not extend to getting married."

Lord Hino said, "You do very little, the Shinto ceremony is short and requires very little participation. I will explain it all to you."

Jack's coffee arrived; he took a few appreciative sips before saying, "What else do you have to tell me Michiko? How about the date and the place?"

Lord Hino laughed, "Already he can read your mind my niece."

Michiko smiled, "I would very much like to be married at the shrine in Hibiya. The Hibiya Daijingu is an important historical shrine and is very beautiful."

Jack nodded, "Is it not where Emperor Meiji was married?"

Michiko had just picked up her teacup and now she almost dropped it. Tea spilled on the floor.

"How did you know that?"

"My dear niece, I try very hard not to be astonished at the extent Campbell's knowledge; however, this does surprise me. You are right Campbell. The Emperor married Empress Haruko in 1900. It is said that this wedding popularized Shinto weddings."

A servant mopped up the tea before Michiko continued.

"If it is acceptable to you Jack, I would like the wedding to take place on 8th November."

"That sounds perfect. Where shall we live?"

"I thought my house in Kobe would be suitable."

"Excellent and may I suggest we spend a few days in Kyoto just after the wedding?"

"Oh yes Jack that would be lovely."

"Good, let's have breakfast, then I had better start making arrangements," said Lord Hino.

Chapter 26

Jack awakened from a deep sleep to the sound of the alarm clock. At first he did not know where he was, he did not recognize his surroundings. Then he remembered. He was at the Palace Hotel and today was Saturday 8th November.

A week ago during a discussion on the wedding, he had told Michiko and Lord Hino of the Scottish superstition that the groom must not see the bride on their wedding day before they meet at the church, as it brought bad luck. He should have known better than to mention this. The oriental mind is obsessed by superstition no matter how well educated it may be. Immediately Michiko had said he must not stay at her uncle's house on the night before the wedding. He was surprised at how strongly Lord Hino had supported Michiko on this.

So thanks to his big mouth here he was stretching in front of a hotel window admiring the view. The sun had risen and was gradually creeping up a cloudless blue sky. There were very few cloudless days in Scotland. In fact there were not many days when it did not rain. On one of these lucky days when the sky was clear in Glasgow you would hear the following greeting on the street, 'Aye it's a guid day fer it.' The 'it' was never specified and could have referred to a football match, a horse race or just taking the dog for a walk. But today the 'it' was his wedding day and the weather was peerless. He said out loud, "Aye it's a fantastic day fer it."

He had a leisurely breakfast and read the English language newspaper. It was full of dire forecasts of what would happen if America did not lift its embargo on essential goods. War was crawling its way inexorably closer. For today at least he would put such thoughts out of his mind.

He went back to his room and began preparing for the ceremony. He bathed and began dressing in his black kimono with the tasseled white sash. He had just about finished when there was a knock on the door. He opened it and greeted Lord Hino.

"I never thought I would say this of any foreigner but you look very elegant, Campbell, and quite dashing. Now you remember the procedure?"

"At this moment I do, I only hope I don't forget during the ceremony. I am feeling a bit nervous. I honestly did not believe I would, but I am. I can't tell you how honored I feel to be marrying your wonderful niece."

A strange cloudiness came over the eyes of Lord Hino and he looked almost sad.

"What's wrong My Lord? Do you have doubts about Michiko marrying a foreigner?"

"Not at all Campbell, I know many of my countrymen would not agree with this union, but I wholeheartedly do. For a moment I was thinking of your future life here in Japan, you know it will be difficult. I fear that you may not be comfortable in Kobe when the war starts. I must look for a more rural place where you both can enjoy life. I do not believe Michiko realizes this possibility and frankly I am glad. She should enjoy this day and not be concerned over these things yet."

He stressed the word yet.

Jack turned away and pretended to make adjustments to his wedding kimono. He did not want his concern to be recognized by this astute man. He had a feeling that Lord Hino had not spoken the truth and it was a very strong feeling. Something else had caused that almost mournful look Jack had seen on his face

. Once again he felt that Lord Hino was keeping something from him, something very important. He composed himself and turned around.

"When do we have to leave?"

"In about ten minutes. Campbell there is something I want to say but find it very difficult to find the right words."

'Could this be the mystery?' Jack wondered. But it proved not to be.

"Michiko is not my daughter although my feelings for her could not be stronger if she were. She has enjoyed an excellent education and is a well poised young woman. However, Japanese young women of her class are not knowledgeable about certain aspects of life."

Jack held up his hand for Hino to stop.

"Let me see if I can help you with the words, My Lord. I will promise you I will always treat your niece with the utmost respect and gentleness in every part of our life together."

Impulsively Lord Hino put out his hand then while shaking hands he put an arm round Jack.

"Thank you Campbell-san," he whispered.

Now Jack was really worried. A Lord calling him 'san' was in itself unique but an arm around his shoulder was uncharacteristic of any Japanese. There was something dreadful troubling Lord Hino. He knew it would do no good asking so he resolved to be even more observant in the future.

"Well are you ready? As I have never been married I can give you no last minute words of wisdom. Let's go."

The drive to the shrine took only ten minutes. They waited for Michiko in the courtyard as they would enter the shrine together. He had been warned by Michiko that he may not recognize her in her wedding attire but when she arrived he almost did not.

The white silk kimono was beautiful and obviously covered a number of other layers that a stranger seeing her for the first time could never tell if she was slim or obese. Her face was caked in white powder and garish bright red lips had been painted over this austere mask. He had been warned that she could not smile at him for fear of cracking this mask.

A huge headdress shadowed much of her face. It protruded about six inches from her forehead. Lord Hino had told him that in Japanese folklore this outsize hat was to hide the bride's horns from an unsuspecting and naïve bridegroom. He had added, 'Only when the wedding ceremony is over and it is removed does the innocent man see the horns of a woman and by that time it is too late.'

It was a small group that entered the shrine. Awaiting them was a priest wearing a purple robe and a tall woven hat tied under his chin. He first performed a purification service of all present then took a multi folded paper from inside his robe, opened it out and began chanting. After a few minutes he carefully refolded the paper, slipped it inside the breast of his robe and clapped his hands several times. Then he reproduced the paper and began a further series of chants. This was followed by the 'San-san-kudo' ceremony meaning 'Three-three-nine'. The bride and groom, in turn, held a special nuptial sake cup in both hands and turned it three times, paused then three more times, another pause and then a final three times before drinking from the cup.

The brief ceremony culminated in both the bride and the groom placing small branches on the altar as an offering to the Kami. These branches symbolized twigs from the 'Sakaki' or sacred tree.

A photographer took shots of every conceivable combination of people including the priest; then it was off to Lord Hino's house for the reception. Lord Hino rode in the second car with a few friends. He did not talk much, his mind was on the private conversation he had with Michiko two weeks ago.

She had come to him hesitantly and said, "I need your assistance uncle. As I have no mother I have no one to explain to me what I am supposed to do on our wedding night."

She was blushing as she went on, "Of course I have heard my married friends talk of this but I have had no education on this matter. Can you help me?"

The usually urbane aristocrat was reduced to a parody of a stammering bumpkin. He finally caught his breath, thought for a minute and then said, "I know the mama-san of a geisha house of the highest quality. I will ask her to discuss this with you."

"Thank you uncle," she said as she hurried away in embarrassment.

It was he who was embarrassed to ask her on the day after her meeting with the mama-san, "Was the meeting useful?"

"Oh yes uncle. Thank you far arranging it. Mama-san was very patient and helpful."

He did not know what to say in response, so he scurried off.

He was brought back to the present by a question from one of his friends.

"My Lord, is it true that this young foreigner received a commendation from the Prime Minister?"

"Yes but I cannot discuss it as it is a matter of the highest security."

"Ah so."

Each of the other passengers repeated this phrase twice and nodded their heads in unison. He had to exert great control not to laugh out loud as he was reminded of one of Campbell's astute observations.

"In Scotland when we are completely baffled by something someone says, we tend to say in an agitated manner, 'I have no bloody idea what the hell you are talking about.' Whereas, in Japan, you adopt a thoughtful demeanor, nod your head and say, 'Ah so'.

He was saved from further comment as the car turned into his driveway.

The reception proved to be another learning experience for Jack. Almost immediately Michiko excused herself and reappeared in a western bridal gown; this time without the powdered face. She looked stunning. During the course of the reception she changed clothes another two times. Jack had no idea what he was supposed to do; finally Michiko said he only had to change just prior to their departure for the train to Kyoto.

Even with the tutoring of the mama-san, Michiko was very nervous of their first night together, however their lovemaking was tender. As the days passed she was shocked at how much she looked forward to making love. She also enjoyed their daily visits to the temples and shrines of Kyoto and she sensed the deepening spiritual awakening within Jack during these visits. Everything was perfect and they could not have been more in love and so it was with some regret that they left Kyoto and traveled to Kobe.

The next two weeks were full of new discoveries for Jack. He puzzled Michiko by his interest in food shopping with the maids.

"I want to see ordinary people and try to understand how they live their lives," he explained. What he discovered surprised him greatly.

Not surprisingly, the young children were intensely curious about him and the older people were more suspicious. What did shock him was that although the adults bowed to him and appeared polite, before they knew he understood Japanese, their comments were seldom complimentary. He was most definitely a foreigner and therefore one not to be accorded the politeness normally given to Japanese. What first made him aware of this was the reaction of the maid to comments made in one of the first shops they visited and her quick intervention by telling the shopkeepers that Jack understood Japanese.

When he asked the different shopkeepers if they ever sold imported food like beef, rice, vegetables or fruit; he got a horrified look and was told foreign foods were not good enough for Japanese, their quality was inferior. When he asked if they had ever tasted foreign foods, they again looked horrified and said, "No!"

He was beginning to understand the chauvinistic and insular nature of Japan.

The other extraordinary discovery was the bifurcation in the nature of most people. One aspect of Japanese character was the traditionally well known politeness to each other. Another could be seen in railway stations where people literally pushed each other out of their paths to board local trains. Old people were not exempt from this treatment. On one occasion when he tried to board a local train an old lady was pushed over, when he tried to assist her, he was pusher to the ground. When he finally helped her to her feet she immediately pushed him back as she reentered the fray.

He had now come to the conclusion that there were two Japanese inside every body. One was the cultured, polite person and the other was the historically repressed serf who when let loose vented his frustration and anger in a frightening manner.

This reasoning explained the story he had heard in Malaya of the behavior of Japanese soldiers in Nanjing, China. As yet not fully confirmed, it told of the atrocities committed in December 1937 when Japan conquered the then capital city of China. It was alleged that over 250,000 Chinese men women and children were murdered. Many of the women were raped before being brutally mutilated. Chinese civilian men were used for bayonet training for the troops.

These thoughts reminded him of his meeting with Lord Hino the day after he arrived in Kobe. It was in the ryokan following the six hour lecture by Professor Nishikawa. Hino had said a veneer of politeness covered a coarseness in the Japanese character. A coarseness born of repression and abuse. Now he understood and this understanding caused him pain.

These realizations of the existence of this underlying coarseness and a deeply rooted antipathy towards anything not Japanese were diametrically opposed to the images he had developed in his studies of Japan in Scotland.

One afternoon he was so lost in his thoughts about his various diagnoses that he did not hear Michiko enter the room. She saw the look of anguish on his face.

"Jack my darling, what is wrong?"

He rushed towards her and held her tightly for a long time before saying, "Nothing, now that you are here."

She returned his tight embrace but persisted, "Please tell me what is troubling you."

He held her at arms length and stared into her beautiful almond shaped eyes.

"I was thinking of all the terrible things people do in war. But now that I am holding you, all I can think of is how wonderful you are and how lucky I am."

"I too, am very lucky," she said again holding him close. And although she truly did feel blessed, her face wore a worried look.

Later that night Lord Hino called to invite them to stay with him in Tokyo. Michiko was delighted.

"We shall travel the day after tomorrow which will be two days before our one month anniversary. We can celebrate this in Tokyo."

When they arrived, Michiko was shocked as she saw the haggard look on her uncle's face.

"Uncle you are so tired looking."

"Yes I have been rather busy of late but soon I can relax with both of you. You are looking radiant my niece and you Campbell are also looking well."

They had a relaxed dinner and Lord Hino seemed more cheerful. Then the telephone rang. Hino returned to apologize.

"I regret it is imperative I be away all day tomorrow and will not return until the day after. Please excuse me. I promised to spend time with you and I intend to, but not tomorrow."

"That's all right uncle, we will enjoy the tranquility of your gardens."

It was five thirty on the morning of 8th December when Jack was shaken awake. Lord Hino put his finger to his lips and motioned Jack to come with him. He put on a robe and followed him downstairs where a sleepy servant was pouring coffee.

"Great news Campbell, we have sunk much of the American Pacific fleet and have successfully landed in Thailand and Malaya."

"You attacked America?" asked Jack incredulously, his own sleepiness disappearing.

"We had no choice. We knew as soon as we pushed into South East Asia it would only be a matter of time until America declared war on us. We had to gain the advantage of a preemptive strike before they could deploy their ships. At twenty five minutes past midnight local time, we landed troops in Thailand and at Kota Bharu and one and a half hours later we attacked Pearl Harbor. Of course considering the International Date Line it is only the 7th December in America. We caught them off guard; we have gained a tremendous advantage. Naturally we do not yet have all the details but everything seems to have gone according to our plans. I recognize that look on your face; you seem to have some doubts. What are they?"

"I am sure the plans will work well. It is only that I always believed it would be your wish to have America declare war on Japan."

"Why so?"

"From everything I have read the American people are against a war they do not consider to be directed at them. They have preferred to view this as a European affair. If America had declared war on Japan the populace would have been most unhappy with their government which would have resulted in a very reluctant combatant force. Whereas, a preemptive strike may tend to galvanize their resolve to avenge what they see as an unprovoked attack."

"Hmm, my friend Yamamoto also said we run that risk, yet he felt the only way to ensure victory was to knock out their Navy. Anyway we have a great beginning and very shortly Hong Kong and the American Airbase in the Philippines will be bombed. There can be no turning back now. My niece talked of celebrating your one month anniversary tonight, now we have another momentous occasion to celebrate. Please help yourself to more coffee Campbell, I have been up since yesterday morning and must bathe and change."

That evening Lord Hino broke out his best wines for dinner. Jack sipped them appreciatively but Lord Hino gulped his down. It was obvious to Jack that Hino had also gulped down other drinks before dinner; he had smelled whisky on his breath. There was no stopping Hino from his celebration. He had received updated reports which had increased his euphoria.

"The only regret we have is that the American carriers were not at Pearl Harbor; however, we will hunt them down and destroy them. Everything else is going extremely well."

His speech was becoming a little slurred. Jack had enjoyed tasting the delicious wines but had by no means overindulged. Somehow he could not work up anything close to the enthusiasm of Lord Hino. He had used his sips to tip his glass toward Michiko and toast the one month anniversary of their marriage. At the end of dinner he noticed Lord Hino's eyes start to close. Michiko noticed this too.

"Uncle you have had very little sleep for the past week, perhaps you should retire early."

"Yes, yes Michiko you are right."

He paused for a moment focusing his now bleary eyes on her.

"This is a great day for our country my niece, a great day. I am sorry you cannot return to Kobe at present. Let's see how things develop in the next few months. Shall we?"

"Of course, uncle."

Earlier he had told Michiko he did not consider it prudent to have Jack be seen in either Kobe or Tokyo. Now that hostilities had broken out there was too much of a risk of uninformed persons attacking foreigners. He felt it much safer to relocate them to a small rural village where the local police could be told of Jack's loyalty to the Emperor and they in turn could inform all the villagers. He had found a perfect village in Tochigi Prefecture just outside Nikko. She would miss her beloved Kobe but it was much more important to safeguard her much more beloved Jack. She was grateful to her uncle for the arrangements he had made. As always she appreciated the concern this man had shown for her wellbeing and happiness.

These thoughts of gratitude were in her mind as she watched him walk unsteadily toward the stairs. Suddenly he stopped and tried to turn around, almost falling in the process. Michiko ran towards him and steadied him. She had never seen him like this. It was obvious that the combination of tiredness and a large quantity of alcohol had taken its toll. She called for a servant to help him to his bedroom. He again refocused his eyes on her.

"This is a great day my niece and you should know that things would not have gone so well without the skill and bravery of your husband. Where is he?"

"I am here My Lord."

"Ah, you are a good man Campbell. I would like to have a drink with you to celebrate."

"Tomorrow my uncle. Now you must rest. You are exhausted."

The servant arrived and helped him climb the stairs. Jack came beside Michiko and put his arm around her. She leaned her head on his shoulder as they watched Lord Hino be almost carried upstairs.

During the night she was wakened by Jack threshing about next to her. At first she was terrified and sat on a chair and watched over him. As the ferocity of his flailing subsided, she lay beside him and held him. He was still restless and muttered constantly. She was not certain what he was saying much or the time but he kept repeating what sounded like, 'The East Coast, those lovely people'.

Chapter 27

It had been decided it would be better to drive to Nikko rather than take the train. Once again, this decision was based on possible negative reaction by some people to seeing a foreigner. They took two cars; Lord Hino's Rolls Royce and a second smaller one which was to be left for Michiko and Jack to use. Lord Hino had insisted on traveling with them as he wanted to personally talk to the regional head of police who had been instructed to travel to Nikko to meet him. The three of them traveled in the Rolls Royce as it made the journey over the bumpy roads more comfortable. Also, it was now the 11ᵗʰ December and Lord Hino wanted to update them on the progress report he had received just before they left.

The report had made him ecstatic and he had been hardly able to contain himself.

"Come, come get in the car. You must hear this news. Hurry, Michiko."

As they drove off he closed the glass partition between them and the driver.

"I can hardly believe the report I was given, Campbell. Yesterday our planes sunk the two main ships recently sent to guard Singapore; the huge battleship, 'Prince of Wales' and the battle-cruiser, 'Repulse'. They were sailing just off Kuantan. Why, we do not know as the British had deserted their North East airfields the day before and this left them with no air coverage. Furthermore these ships did not use a smokescreen and left our pilots with a clear view. Can you offer any explanation for such gross negligence, Campbell?"

"Lack of leadership," said Jack contemptuously.

"Would you care to elaborate on that?" asked Lord Hino.

"They simply refused to believe an attack would happen and therefore did not prepare adequately for it. I met junior officers who bemoaned the lack of determined training for an attack. The problem lies with the senior officers, it was their responsibility and they have failed their troops and the Malayan people."

"I must say you do sound bitter, Campbell."

"It's the helpless civilians I feel sorry for. They will suffer due to those idiots' incompetence."

Lord Hino looked intently at Jack facial expression. Michiko did the same and could almost feel the pain her husband was suffering. She thought she now understood the reason for Jack's nightmare. He truly cared for the people he had met in Malaya. This deep caring for helpless, innocent people gave her one more reason to love him. Lord Hino realized that he had misjudged Jack in one aspect of his character. He was not as cold hearted as he thought. He certainly hated the British system of class structure with its consequential snobbery; however, the depth of his feelings for the common man had not registered on his normally astute analytical mind. He resolved he must take time to carefully review his new insight into Campbell.

There had been silence in the car for some time and it was not until they were almost out of Tokyo that Lord Hino diverted attention away from the prior subject by describing the area where they would stay.

"Undoubtedly you will have read of Nikko, Campbell; I know Michiko understands its importance in the history of our nation."

"Actually I have read very little on Nikko. It was not a major topic of study."

"Ah well you will enjoy it all the more. You may recall the first shogun to unite Japan was Tokugawa Ieyasu and he died in 1616. He was buried at Nikko in accordance with his wishes. He had carefully specified the buildings which were to surround his burial place; however, the first buildings completed the next year were modest. His grandson Tokugawa Iemitsu decided to rectify this situation and began the construction of the present buildings in 1634. It required two years and 15,000 artisans to complete this work. It is estimated that 2.5 million sheets of gold leaf were used."

"When you walk around the shrines and the temple you will understand why we Japanese think of this place as special. The intricate carvings and the attention to detail are stunning."

It took almost three hours to reach Nikko. They had stopped for a light lunch in the town of Utsunomiya which was the closest town to the village of Nikko. The driver had purchased lunch and they ate it in the car.

"Utsunomiya is famous for its gyooza which are dumplings made of pork and vegetables. I hope you like them Jack," said Michiko.

"They are very good and have lots of garlic, but I may have taken too much of the spicy sauce to dip them in."

"Add more soy sauce and vinegar to dilute the spice."

"I would not advise you travel to this town to enjoy this food again Campbell. There is an aircraft factory and a munitions factory here, and the authorities would probably arrest you on sight. So you had better order another plate while we are here."

They all ordered more.

It was two o'clock when they arrived at the house which was to be their home. It was large compared to others in the village but much smaller than Michiko's home in Kobe. It sat back from the road and the rear had a surprisingly large garden which overlooked a fast flowing river. All around were rice fields. It was quiet, very quiet.

Lord Hino went off to Nikko to meet the regional head of police. Jack looked at Michiko and was afraid she might be upset at the thought of having to live here, but she surprised him by hugging him and saying, "Our first home, my darling."

"If this is not acceptable Michiko, I shall tell your uncle we will take the risk and go back to Kobe."

"No Jack!" she said emphatically. "I want to be here with you; just the two of us."

She was again quite categorical. Then she added, more uncertainly, "If that's all right with you Jack."

"I think the solitude will suit me fine and having you all to myself sounds like heaven."

She threw her arms around him and he kissed her tenderly.

"My uncle was aghast that I would not bring even one of my maids here. They will look after my house in Kobe. I expected this house to be small and thought it better we are by ourselves. He does not believe I can cook."

"Can you?"

"Yes I can, as you will find out."

"Anyway he has arranged for a lady from the village to show me where to shop and she will also cook occasional meals for us if we desire. She used to have a small restaurant in Nikko and has been a widow for five years. Her name is Mrs. Suzuki. We will meet her tonight as she is bringing dinner."

"Your uncle seems to have thought of everything."

"He is a very thorough planner. He can be exasperating at times. I love it when he makes a small mistake, it upsets him so much."

"Michiko I am shocked," said Jack and they both burst into laughter.

Lord Hino returned in twenty minutes with the police chief. Michiko had found that a few provisions had been put in the kitchen and had made tea which she offered to them.

"Is Mrs. Suzuki here?" asked Lord Hino.

"No uncle, I can make tea," she hissed in his ear.

It was not long before they both left. Lord Hino had to get back to his important work. He had hoped to have a telephone installed in their new home and was chagrined that it had not been possible. A cable would have to be installed from Nikko and this would take several more months. Jack was pleased as he did not wish to get daily reports on the state of the war. Michiko said mischievously, "I thought you could arrange anything uncle."

He griped at the telephone company's inattention to this matter and vowed that someone would hear about it.

If someone had asked them what they did for he next two months they would have found if difficult to answer. Time flew by.

They had both learned much more about Nikko and loved to stroll around its wonderful treasures. They had also discovered the beauty of Lake Chuzenji which was in the mountain above Nikko. And were in awe the first time they saw the waters from Chuzenji spectacularly tumble three hundred feet at the Kegon waterfall.

They both found the winter climate a challenge. The days were reasonably warm with clear blue skies; however, these clear skies resulted in freezing temperatures at night. In a basically wood and paper house the temperature was as cold inside as outside. There was not sufficient power available to fuel even the smallest electric heater so they used paraffin heaters which they turned off before bedtime in case of fire. It was a race to get under the thick layers of covers on the futon after turning off the last heater. Once under the covers it was very cozy except for their faces. In the nights following their arrival, Jack had a few bad dreams but gradually they had all but disappeared and except for his cold red nose he was at last contented in bed.

It was 15th February when a local policeman cycled to their home to say that Lord Hino would arrive next day. That night after dinner Michiko said, "I am glad my uncle is coming as I need to ask his help."

"What help?"

"I should visit a doctor in Tokyo."

"My Darling, why didn't you tell me you were ill?"

"I am not ill, Jack but I believe you are going to become a father."

He was staggered and for a few moments could say nothing.

"You are not angry are you Jack?"

"Angry? No my darling Michiko I am pleased beyond description. But are you feeling all right?"

"Yes, you must not worry my darling, everything will be all right but it will be wise to see a doctor."

The next day Lord Hino almost leapt out of the car.

"Campbell I have the most wonderful news. We have taken Singapore."

He stopped, puzzled by the lack of reaction, "Well don't you have anything to say. This is the crowning glory of all your work."

"What we have to say is even more wonderful, tell him Michiko."

"I am going to have a baby uncle."

Lord Hino put his arms around her.

"Congratulations my dear, that is indeed wonderful news."

He then turned to Jack and extended his hand.

"Congratulations to you too, Campbell. Let's go inside and have some of this champagne I brought. It was to celebrate Singapore but it more appropriate to celebrate your good news."

Jack was quite surprised at lord Hino's reaction to their news. It was one closer to absolute elation than just happiness.

Michiko returned with her uncle to Tokyo to consult a doctor who confirmed her pregnancy. She made several other trips to visit the doctor, all without Jack. He had protested the very first time but Lord Hino had persuaded him to stay.

"I know how much you want to be with my niece, but consider this; what happens if a group of irate people attack you and Michiko gets hurt in the melee?"

That convinced him to stay behind. Lord Hino sent his car and driver for each visit. About one month before the baby was due Michiko was advised to move to Tokyo and stay at her uncle's house. This time Jack went too. When Michiko was ready to go to the hospital Jack said he was going with her and when Lord Hino protested vehemently, Jack reminded him of the disguise he used for his bodyguards in Glasgow. Lord Hino smiled in resignation and so Jack went to the hospital with his face bandaged.

Robert William Campbell was born on 15th September 1942.

Michiko and Jack agreed they would call him by the name Rob. Michiko said he looked exactly like Jack. How one could possibly see a resemblance to an adult in this little crinkled mass baffled Jack. As he sat for hours cradling his baby son, Jack could still not discern a likeness.

It was a week before Michiko left hospital to return to Lord Hino's home and she was happy to see Jack's face without bandages again. Everyone wanted to hold the baby, including all the servants and to Jack's utter amazement, Lord Hino. Jack would take his son for long walks around the estate and talk to him constantly. Finally one day Lord Hino asked Michiko, "What does he find to say to a baby for such a long time?"

Michiko smiled through tears of happiness and replied, "He isn't talking to a baby, he is talking to his son."

Rob seemed to grow every day and although Jack could still not see the resemblance that Michiko could, there was no doubt he had Caucasian features. They stayed in Tokyo until mid November before returning north to their home and were happy to do so.

Jack had felt sublime happiness when he was with Michiko and could never have believed he could be happier, but he was. He had difficulty analyzing why this was. Of course he had a son; yet it went deeper than that. It took some time for him to realize that some dormant emotion had been released. The unity of a family had touched a deep spiritual passion that he had not recognized existed within him. He realized throughout his life he had yearned for a family life.

Not remembering his father then having his mother taken away from him had left a hole in his being, the depth of which could not be measured. Into this chasm had pored hatred and bitterness. What had grown in this virulent maelstrom was undying determination for retribution. Now it seemed as though some huge vacuum had sucked all of these poisonous, corrosive emotions out of him and this hole was, in some miraculous way, being rapidly filled with peace, love and contentment.

As the months passed his sensitivity picked up on a change, one which troubled him. Since coming to the village he was struck by the friendliness of the people. At first he thought, cynically, it was due to the dire warnings of the police; however, although there was an initial element of that in the men, the women were friendly from the outset. Now Rob was an attraction to everyone but when the three of them went into the village it seemed to Jack the warmth of the villagers had cooled by a few degrees.

One day when Rob was about six months old, they were shopping in the village. Michiko was in one of the shops and Jack wandered into the one next door with Rob. Michiko left the shop looked up and down the street and turned the opposite way to look for them. Jack saw her leave and was about to follow when he heard four women talking in the shop Michiko had left.

"Isn't it a pity, he's such a nice baby."

"What do you mean?"

"Well, where will he stay when he grows up? He can't stay here. He's not pure Japanese."

"She should have thought of that earlier. She should know better."

"That's right, you don't expect the foreigner to understand these things, but she should."

Everyone continued to be polite but Jack knew that beneath this veneer lurked insularity and chauvinism; even here in the depths of the countryside.

When Rob was almost a year old Michiko took him for a periodic check up to the doctor in Tokyo while Jack stayed at home. The roads were becoming more and more congested so it was decided she should spend the night with her uncle. She was upset when she saw her uncle. He was obviously working very long hours and looked gaunt. After dinner and when Rob was sleeping they sat down to talk.

"Unfortunately the war has not been going well in the Pacific. We still have some moments of glory but recently we have more of unhappiness. I was hoping the contingency plan I devised five years ago would not be necessary but alas I fear it may be required. There is still a chance our troops will be victorious and we will continue to talk optimistically. However I know I can express my inner doubts to you. I tell you this in confidence my niece you must not mention this to anyone."

"Of course uncle."

"Not even to your husband."

"I understand uncle."

The next morning Lord Hino delayed his departure to his office to see Michiko and Rob leave in his car.

"Good bye uncle, I hope it is not too long until we meet again."

"Good bye Michiko. Give my best wishes to Campbell."

"I will uncle. Jack will be so happy to see Rob again. He cannot stand being parted from him."

He watched the car drive away with a very thoughtful look in his eyes.

Jack was waiting at the door as the car pulled up. Rob leapt into his open arms and he kissed them both.

"What did the doctor say?"

"He is in perfect health. My uncle sent you his best wishes. He does not look well Jack. I think he is the one who should have seen a doctor."

As she entered the house she saw pieces of paper lying around.

"What are you writing Jack?"

"I will tell you later," said Jack gathering them up. "Right now I just want to be with my wife and my son. I missed you both."

That night when Rob was asleep he told Michiko what he had been doing since she left.

"I decided to write down my family's history as best I can remember. You know how much I enjoyed Malaya so I will add notes on my experiences there. Also I want to add notes on the fellows I met and really liked. Hans will be one of them. Most importantly I will write notes on how I met you my love and on our life here."

"Why are you doing this my darling?"

"For Rob, it will be a chronicle he can refer to when he is a man. Who knows, he may even revisit the places I've been to and be able to compare his reactions to mine."

"But surely you can tell him all these things yourself?"

"I hope so, but nothing is certain in life and I have lots of time to write these things while they are still fresh in my memory."

She looked concerned as she said, "Are you bored, Jack?"

He brought her to her feet and held her tightly.

"No, my darling, I am not. I am so happy that it sometimes frightens me. I cannot believe how lucky I am to have you."

"Well you have me and will be stuck with me for ever," she said in mock sternness. She clung tightly to him, trembling.

"What's wrong?" he asked.

"Please do not talk of the lack of certainty in life. We must not tempt fate."

He was about to laugh at this but her continued trembling told him how serious she was.

"I promise Michiko. Let's say I am an inveterate diarist and want to record my life story. OK?"

"OK."

That night they made love. Michiko waited until Jack was sound asleep before she began crying.

Chapter 28

It took Jack two months to finish his 'diary'. He spent another few days editing his notes before he was satisfied and then he carefully bound all the pages. Remembering how upset Michiko was two months ago when he first discussed his diary he was wary of broaching the subject again but he knew it had to be done. He waited until later that day while Rob was napping.

"Well at last this is finished," he said brandishing the bound manuscript.

"Will you not add to it as the months pass?"

"The historic part of my family is complete; perhaps I will add more in a year or so."

He looked at her intently, "I don't want to upset you my darling but there is something I must ask you."

She looked anxiously at him and said, "What is it Jack?"

"I would like you to read these notes to assure yourself there nothing written against the Emperor."

Now she looked very apprehensive as she whispered, "I do not understand Jack?"

"I want you to give these notes to Rob on his twenty-first birthday and to show them to no one until then."

Tears flowed from her eyes, "Why are you speaking this way again?"

"Please don't cry. I know how much this upsets you. Let me try to explain. As I wrote these notes I began realizing how much I missed having a father as I grew up. Apart from the occasional stories from my mother and my granny I had nothing to connect me to my father.

I am sure nothing will happen to me and we will give these notes to Rob together; however, in the one in a million chance something did happen, this communication links me to my son for ever. It is very important to me Michiko and apart from you and Rob I do not want anyone else to read it. I understand your devoted allegiance to your Emperor which is why I cannot ask you to make this promise without having you be clear in your mind that it does not impugn nor potentially harm the Emperor."

She held his face in her hands and brought her face close to his.

"I will read your notes; but only because you have asked me to. I know I do not have to read them to promise you I will not show them to another person and I will give them to our son on his twenty-first birthday, with you at my side."

"Thank you Michiko but please remember no one else must read this."

She not only heard the intensity in his voice but saw it in his eyes. She stroked his cheek and through tears said, "Do not worry my love, I promise it will be as you ask."

A rekindled feeling of unease stayed with her over the next week but gradually subsided as they approach the end of the year.

Lord Hino visited them on 2nd January to wish them a happy new year. He was looking healthier but not enough to satisfy Michiko and she told him so.

"Campbell, you have turned a respectful Japanese lady into a badgering Scottish housewife."

"Not I," said Jack. "You are the one who said there were horns below that wedding headdress, remember?" then he ducked as Michiko laughingly threw a dishcloth at him.

Lord Hino watched with thoughtful interest as Jack played with Rob. It seemed they could play games endlessly. But when his mother prepared his lunch he deserted his father in favor of food. Lord Hino stayed for lunch but had to leave immediately after he finished.

Jack was pleased the weather in January was not as cold as the previous year for Rob's sake. They enjoyed their normal walks around Nikko. Rob seemed to like some of the carvings especially the one over the Royal Stable of the three monkeys; 'Hear no evil, Speak no evil and See no evil.'

The weather turned much colder towards the end of January and they had to bundle up when they went out. They were coming back from a shopping trip to the village when they spotted the Rolls Royce parked outside their house. Michiko gasped thinking there must be a problem with her uncle and hurried towards the car. She was relieved when Lord Hino emerged from the car looking quite healthy.

When they had unbundled the layers of clothing inside the house Lord Hino said, "I am sorry to arrive unannounced but an unexpected situation has arisen and we desperately need you help Campbell."

"What is it?"

"As in all these matters, you will only receive your briefing immediately prior to your departure. Can you come to Tokyo the day after tomorrow?"

"I thought all my work was finished."

"As did I. This assignment is of the highest importance and is one that needs your special talents."

"Is it dangerous?" blurted out Michiko.

"It is top secret and cannot be discussed, my niece, but I don't think it involves much danger. You should be back in about two weeks Campbell. I am sorry but I must rush back to Tokyo. It is damnably inconvenient that a telephone could not be installed here. However it appears the cost and more important the divergence of talent for the three months it would take was not justified. This message was too confidential to pass through the local police, so I had to come here. I will send my car for you at about noon."

"The war must not be going well," said Michiko. "I have never seen him so mournful."

"Yes, he certainly seems to have a lot on his mind," said Jack pensively.

The next day was very difficult for everyone. Michiko tried to be brave. She knew if she cried it would upset both Jack and Rob. Jack tried to be nonchalant about it, but deep down he felt there was something wrong about the whole affair. Something about Hino's demeanor troubled him. Rob must have inherited his father's sensitivities as he was querulous all day.

Next day the car waited at the door while Jack hugged and kissed Rob.

"Now you be a good boy and take care of your mother 'til I return."

Rob smiled at him.

"I will be back as soon as I can my love. My body may be gone but my heart is here with you, always with you."

"Please be careful Jack. I need you and love you so much."

He waved cheerily as the car pulled away but once on the main road he had a more serious look on his face.

Chapter 29

As they entered Tokyo Jack looked around but did not recognize the area.

"Are we going to Lord Hino's home?"

"No sir. You are to meet My Lord in a ryokan."

The ryokan was in a park which was completely blacked out. As they approached and he could see the inn he noticed it looked very high class. He was met at the door by a solitary greeter and led along a deserted corridor to the end room. Jack entered the room. Lord Hino was kneeling on a cushion on the tatami at a low lacquered table. He motioned Jack to sit.

"Good evening Campbell."

Jack also adopted the kneeling position.

"Good evening My Lord."

Hino offered Jack sake then took a sip of his own and began speaking in his beautiful English.

"You now have some understanding of a few parts of our intelligence organization, Campbell. Do not delude yourself by believing you know everything. You most certainly do not. Just as a geisha's kimono is designed to show only the powdered part of her neck to entice her customer, all you have is a tantalizing glimpse. Even you Campbell, with your superior intellect and insatiable curiosity, cannot comprehend the vastness of our operations around the globe. We have the greatest political and military intelligence network the world has ever seen."

Lord Hino's tone was curt, his voice strained, as though he was trying hard to keep some other emotion under control. A sense of unease crept over Jack, yet he could not identify the cause. It seemed as though a fine mist prevented his mind forming a clear picture.

"I have watched you progress and I know you, unlike most foreigners, do not draw the usual incorrect conclusions about the Japanese. Yet, even you Campbell tend to make one mistake."

'That's the second time he has used that expression' thought Jack. The repetition of 'even you Campbell' increased his discomfort and this only served to make the mist in his mind more dense. He knew there was an important truth hidden by this mist but try as he might he could not see it. He turned his attention back to Hino.

"All foreigners are confused by some aspects of our way of life and culture. Their method of handling this confusion is to generalize. We are not a mixed race like Americans and British. We are a homogeneous race and most foreigners think we are basically all alike. I do not insult you by saying you make that mistake. However, you like all others believe we must have consensus or orders from a superior before we take significant action. This may be our preferred course in many situations, but consensus should not be confused with uniformity .We are individuals and because of that we can have differing points of view. The fact that we can subsume these views for the greater good of the majority gives us a unique strength."

"However, and this is of paramount importance, groups can debate and finally come to a compromise, but only an individual can create a vision. Today I will tell you of my vision for Japan."

"Our superior intelligence organization and our successes in Korea and China have led us to believe we can achieve our proper place in the world through military force. Those who propose this may be correct but I have created a different vision to achieve our rightful role in the world. My vision differs from my colleagues. I see a future they do not begin to imagine."

"You know our history. How we developed from an oppressive feudal system to a somewhat democratic one under Emperor Meiji. Later how we grew an industrial base and consequently grew in military strength and competence. You have seen how we expanded our Empire under the Greater East Asia Co-Prosperity Sphere. And now we are engaging the Western powers in this war. Our destiny is to be a dominating force in the affairs of this world."

Hino paused to sip his sake. Jack saw the glow in his eyes and recognized the fervor of a zealot.

"We will fulfill our destiny, Campbell but not in the manner my colleagues believe. They still believe in the invincibility of our military .That belief is based on an accurate assessment of the capabilities of Britain, France, Russia and Australia. Unfortunately, they do not have an accurate enough assessment of America. The resources of America are vast, even greater than the Americans themselves realize. Their problem has always been an inability to concentrate and focus these resources. I fear we have now given America that focus by our attack on Pearl Harbor."

"The other flaw in the thinking of my colleagues is more subtle. The vision they have is based on the past. One cannot perceive the future if one focuses on the past. No country can militarily rule a far-flung empire in tomorrow's world. Those days are gone."

"In the past it was relatively simple. You won a war, annexed the land, subjugated the people, put your own people in to rule and most importantly, you did all this in an absolutely ruthless manner. You allowed no external interference from any other country. Today Japan and perhaps Russia have the mental toughness to do this, but we, Japan, do not have the resources. We do not yet have a sufficient number of leaders with the skill to manipulate other peoples. We know how to impart brutal repression but that alone will fail in tomorrow's world."

"So, Campbell, if domination by physical presence is not practical, what do we do? We need more land, more food production especially rice, and more raw materials to manufacture goods. Our islands are inadequate for all our future needs and we will not be held to ransom by other nations over the supply of these essentials. The answer is; we go to war!"

Lord Hino paused to sip his sake and to savor the confused look on Jack's face.

"Ah I see you look perplexed. Yes indeed we go to war but not conventional physical war with ships and tanks and aeroplanes. The war of tomorrow will be an economic war .The vision I have for Japan is to have the most effective economy in the world, amassing huge currency reserves and have other nations dependent on our strength."

"We cannot do this as a purely trading nation. We must develop other skills to create a sustainable superiority. Our historic skills lie in the crafts related to our culture. We will build on this, preserving our pursuit of perfection, but adding a capability to do so at much more competitive cost through the use of technology. This strategy requires two things. First, a highly educated workforce: And second, the ability to persuade others to provide us with their current best technology while we develop our own."

"To achieve this we must educate our children to a level higher than any other nation, a level unimagined by today's world. And not just the children of the rich, every child in Japan. Plans are already underway for this education program with its particular emphasis on mathematics and science. Of course the people administering this agenda have no idea of my vision. They fully understand the urgency the nation has placed on this program but believe this to be an end in itself, a social priority."

"Perhaps you doubt the advantage we will gain by such an initiative. You may believe other countries will also have better educated children. They may demonstrate some improvement, but not to the degree or the intensity of our new system. Following the war the western countries will have different priorities and they will be distracted by social unrest."

"Let me explain this aspect of Western culture to you Campbell. When this war is over Europe and to a lesser extent America, will be financially debilitated but more important their people will be mentally and physically exhausted. They will want a better life and they will demand it immediately. They will feel they deserve this life, one that their governments will be unable to instantly provide. They will become restless and demand immediate gratification of pent up desires for recently unavailable things. In their minds they will have sacrificed too long."

"The Occidental timeframe always has been much shorter than the Oriental. In some areas this is not an advantage; in this case it will guarantee our success."

"You are probably wondering where we will find the money to develop such an education system and still fund our economic one. We will be aided by the victors. Not the British, the Americans. One of their more endearing national characteristics is that they like to be liked. Believe me they will be of considerable assistance to Japan."

"Of course in the beginning we must license technology from the best sources and encourage powerful companies to invest in Japan. Then when we are strong enough we will gradually take control. We have time on our side. It may take two or three decades but it will happen."

"The initial phase of rebuilding will be characterized by a rushing into every opportunity given to us by the West. However, a critical success factor of my plan is that eventually we must be highly selective in the industries we wish to dominate. To do so we will create a new Ministry specializing in international business which will identify the preeminent foreign companies in the industries we have selected. Then it will select the most appropriate Japanese company to associate with each of these foreign companies. It will establish the guidelines for foreign investment including joint ventures, royalty agreements and remittance of funds out of Japan. All of these rules will be within a framework allowing us time to build our own capability before taking charge within Japan. The next phase will be international expansion where our strong domestic companies move from exporting to building our own production capability in foreign markets."

"You must have devoted a lot of time on this plan," said Jack. "One thing seems to be missing though."

"What might that be?"

"I don't think these well organized international companies will casually allow you to steal their markets without fighting back."

Lord Hino smiled, "As always your keen brain brings you to the essence of the plan. You have one of the finest minds I have ever encountered. Campbell-sama, if I had a son, I would feel blessed if he were like you."

His voice choked as he spoke and Jack now knew why he had adopted the curt tone. He was desperately trying to control a strong emotional bond he felt towards Jack. Still, Jack was startled by this compliment. The use of honorific 'sama' was traditionally used to address a much more senior or revered person. Yet this did not make him feel better in fact it increased his apprehension.

"Please have more sake. I want to answer your incisive question. I beg you not to attempt to leave nor to react in any way to what I am about to tell you."

As he spoke he pressed a buzzer which normally summoned a maid. The shoji screen doors slid open, but instead of a maid, three yukata clad men entered. Two sat behind Jack, the third to the right and slightly behind Hino. He recognized two of them from Glasgow and the boat journey from Lisbon.

"My apologies, Campbell. These men have been in my service for many years. Their presence is unfortunate but necessary."

Jack noticed Hino had reverted to the Lord addressing a commoner speech pattern. No more 'sama', not even a 'san'. He knew Hino could not afford to do so in front of his men, moreover he suspected Hino was now fully composed and would now be all business.

"They do not understand English and know nothing of what I am about to explain. In fact only four other people know the whole plan, code named Empire, of course one of these four is the Emperor."

Hino moved from the kneeling position to a more comfortable cross-legged one. One of the men fetched a 'tatami chair' from the corridor and offered it to Jack. This type of chair had no legs. It was a cushion with an attached padded back support. Jack curtly refused the offer, not changing from the kneeling position. A brief flicker of respect appeared in the man's eyes; he bowed slightly and removed the chair.

"Now to your question, inside the new Ministry I mentioned, will be a highly secret department which will handle industrial espionage. It will be known only to the Emperor, the Prime Minister and Minister in charge. Its mission will be to infiltrate the leading companies I mentioned at the highest levels and discover their strategic plans."

"That may not be easy for a Japanese to do," said Jack.

"Precisely! That is why I will use the most intelligent indigenous young people."

Jack shook his head.

"When this war is over I doubt you will find too many forgiving people to recruit to your cause. Even someone of your skill will find it difficult to overcome the reputation your army has created."

"Once again you are exactly correct which brings me to the part you and a few other foreigners have played."

Outside in the garden of the inn, the sound of the miniature waterfall had created a sense of hypnotic tranquility. A sudden gust of wind disturbed the peace and caused the clump of bamboo to rattle and the wind chime to startle into song. Clouds covered the moon. Jack shivered involuntarily as waves of coldness spread throughout his body. He sensed the information Lord Hino was about to share had to be momentous. Despite his shivering unease his attention remained riveted on Hino's face which seemed to darken with the blotted out moonlight.

Hino noticed Jack's reaction and said, "Your inner sensitivities have developed to a degree which fills me with awe. How I wish you could be at my side to complete the implementation plans for my vision."

The wind stopped as quickly as it had started. The bamboo was still and the wind chime's song ceased. The silence was more terrifying than the previous noises caused by the wind. Instantly, the mist which had clouded Jack's mind cleared, leaving a scene of stunning arctic clarity.

Jack knew he was about to die.

Again Hino read Jack's thoughts. He laid his hands on the low table, palms down and spread his fingers. He straightened his back, held his head erect and stared into Jack's eyes. His own eyes clearly showed his anguish. After a few seconds he recovered.

"My plan involved finding extraordinary young men from America, Britain, France and Germany to meet specially chosen Japanese ladies and create these young people who will work for us."

"You bastard," Jack spat out and tried to get his hands around Hino's throat. The two men behind him were exceptionally quick and strong and held him back.

"Does Michiko know about this?"

"Some parts but not all. I had the Emperor talk to Michiko and at his request she agreed that if I found a most exceptional person she would participate. She could not refuse the request of her Emperor. However when it came time she decided she could not go through with it. Then something must have happened during you first tour of Kobe because she said she would think about it. Then she fell in love with you. This was definitely not according to my plan. In no other case did the couple fall so deeply in love."

"And what happened to those children who had Japanese features or were girls?"

Hino shrugged and did not reply.

"I regret calling you a bastard. A bastard is a human being and you are not. You are a monster."

Hino signaled the man behind him to bring more sake.

"I feared it would end like this Campbell. I am truly sorry but nothing can be allowed to stop us taking our rightful place in this world and we can never disappoint our Emperor."

As the sake arrived Hino moved back from the table and his body guard sat between him and Jack. The two men behind Jack relaxed their hold to allow Jack to drink. One still held him by the collar and the other by the belt.

"As I said Michiko knows only part of the plan and truly believes you are now on a mission of vital importance."

"As a matter of interest how will you get these 'recruits' inside the right companies at the highest level?"

"An industrial trend began just before war broke out and I believe it will gather momentum after the war. It is a specialized type of consulting called Management Consulting and there are a few companies which focus on strategy. With their exceptional education our people will have no problem getting a job at these companies and over time will be working in the boardrooms of our target companies."

"I still don't understand how…how…how."

Jack's voice trailed off. His mouth was moving but no words came out.

"A drug in your last drink Campbell. You will have no pain."

Jack blinked three times struggling to retain focus. Suddenly he smiled. There in front of him were the faces of Michiko and Rob. They stayed there until his eyes closed.

Chapter 30

Jack had been gone for eleven days.

"Your daddy will be back home soon Rob. Isn't that good?"

Michiko held him as they looked out the rear window at the snow covered garden. It had snowed last night. When they awakened this morning it was as though some giant had laid a thick fluffy white carpet over the entire countryside.

"Let's go out and play in the snow."

She bundled him up and they played in the snow for over an hour. She made miniature snowmen and he knocked them down, giggling with delight as he did so. Every now and then he would stand still and stare over the fields as though listening and waiting for someone. Michiko was unnerved the first time he did this.

"What is it Rob? What do you hear?"

Then she realized it was probably what he did not hear that caused him to listen so intently. Snow tended to deaden sound and she understood it was the absolute silence that was puzzling to him. She made the last snowman and when he had demolished it she said, "How about some nice hot soup?"

Later that afternoon the silence was broken by the sound of car engines. She went to the door with Rob and saw two cars crunch to a halt in the snowy road. Her heart leaped with joy.

"Rob it's your daddy. Daddy's home."

She saw Lord Hino get out of his car and waited expectantly for Jack to follow. Then she noticed the warmly wrapped figure that got out of the second car and was hurrying along the path towards her.

258

It took a little time to recognize her; it was one of her maids. She stared agape at her maid then at Lord Hino who was now walking down the path alone, her brain unwilling to process the meaning of this.

"No, oh no, no, no, no," she wailed, falling to her knees.

Her maid slipped off her shoes and went past her to pick up Rob who was now crying, frightened by his mother's distress. Lord Hino knelt beside her and put his arms around her.

"I am so sorry Michiko, so very sorry."

"Tell me it isn't so uncle. Tell me he has just been injured."

"I am afraid that is not the case my niece. Your wonderful husband, Rob's adoring father and my dear friend is dead."

She began sobbing uncontrollably her whole body shuddering frenziedly. Lord Hino carried her into the house as the maid took Rob into the bedroom. He sat holding her until the violent shaking stopped. Her sobbing continued and through it she said, "It must not be true. I cannot live without Jack."

"You must, you have a son who needs you."

"Oh Rob, where is he?'

"He is being taken cared for by your maid. He is all right."

"How did it happen?"

"On his return from his mission his ship was attacked."

"Where did it take place?"

"I cannot reveal the location my niece. I can tell you that all reports indicate he did not suffer, it was very quick."

"When can I see him?'

"That is not possible, Michiko. His body was washed overboard and lost at sea."

Her sobbing lessened into crying as she buried her head in his shoulder. They sat this way for a long time before she said, "Excuse me uncle, I should go to Rob now."

Her maid cooked a light dinner but Michiko did not eat.

Later Lord Hino said, "I think it best if you and Rob stay with me in Tokyo for a while, Michiko. Perhaps we should leave tomorrow."

"Yes uncle," she replied woodenly.

"I asked my doctor to give me something to help you sleep tonight. Please take these pills before you go to bed. We shall take care of Rob if he wakens during the night."

"Yes uncle," she said, again with no inflection in her voice.

After Rob was asleep she went to her bedroom. Before taking the sleeping pills she brought Jack's notes from their hiding place and stared at them.

"You knew Jack," she whispered in awe. "Somehow you knew. But how did you know this would happen? How?"

She replaced the notes and took the pills. As she lay in bed she whispered, "You said your heart will always be with me, my darling. That will give me strength to raise our son."

Tears flowed over her pillow as sleep spread a balm over her wounded heart.

Michiko was late in rising next morning. The sleeping pills had been strong. When she did get up Rob had been fed, bathed and dressed by her maid.

She talked to Rob for some time. He seemed cheerful and wanted to play in the snow again. She asked the maid to take him outside and explained to her the game he liked to play. As she was putting on Rob's warm clothing the maid laid out breakfast for her, saying Lord Hino had already eaten breakfast. She protested, saying she was not hungry, however Lord Hino persuaded her to eat. When she finished she sat staring into space.

"Just take your time my niece and when you are ready we shall leave for Tokyo."

"I will pack now. It will give me something to do."

"While you pack I must check the desk. I believe Campbell returned all our manuals and code books however I need to make a final verification and I will take his clothes."

"All right, uncle"

It did not take long to pack everything. She held Rob tightly as she took a long last look at their home.

"I have looked through the desk and found nothing. Are you sure there were no other papers?"

Michiko did not look at Lord Hino as she replied. She looked into Rob's eyes when she said, "You have all of Jack's possessions. Everything else either belongs to me or to Rob."

Chapter 31

The pink tinged white cherry blossoms were gently falling to the ground. The trees were spectacularly beautiful, gracefully swaying in the gentle evening breeze. These delicate blossoms had been the inspiration for so many poets and writers in Japan. Their allure was endless; as evidenced by the many people who were moved to continue adding to an already vast list of writings.

Rob ran around trying to catch them as they floated in the air. He was giggling with delight as many of them escaped his little hands. When he caught one he would rush to Michiko and present her with it, opening her closed fingers to be sure the others were still there before adding the new acquisition, then closing her fingers again.

"Thank you Rob you are such a clever boy."

Two months had passed since Jack's death and she still cried a lot, usually at night. How she wished to see Jack playing with their son once again. Just to hear him adopt his Glasgow accent when he would say, "Come tae yer daddy ma bonnie wee laddie."

She had tried several times to say these words in the hope that Rob might remember his father. However, each time she tried she burst into tears and her crying frightened Rob and caused him to cry also. So she had stopped trying.

Lord Hino entered the garden and greeted Michiko. He watched Rob's game and said to Michiko, "He is becoming very agile and strong."

"He is like his father," she replied.

Rob approached Hino and put a blossom in his hand then thought better of it and took it back giving it to his mother.

"Yes he is like his father, cautious and careful who he trusts," said Hino.

He sat on the bench beside Michiko. They watched in silence as Rob played his game. She sensed his disquiet and asked, "Why are you so worried, uncle?"

"I was called to an audience with the Emperor."

"What did His Majesty have to say?"

"Yesterday His Majesty had a private meeting with the most trusted subordinate of my dear departed friend Admiral Yamamoto. The Emperor greatly valued Yamamoto's opinions. On many occasions Yamamoto said about America that we have awakened a sleeping tiger which will gain strength rapidly. Now, our sources report, their production of war material has progressed far beyond our expectations."

"Earlier in this war Hitler stupidly focused attention on his dream prize, Russia. That proved futile and since then he has been fighting a losing battle on his eastern front. This has given the Western Allies time to gather strength and they may well be in a position to launch an attack across the English Channel as early as this summer."

"How will this affect Japan, uncle?"

"Once the Western Allies gain a foothold on mainland Europe, America will be able to allocate more forces to Asia. It will be very difficult to stop them."

"Having reviewed all this information, the Emperor has suggested I move ahead with Plan Empire. This means we must leave Japan."

"When?" asked Michiko.

"Next week, my niece."

Tears welled in Michiko's eyes.

"I know how much you love Japan and you will be sad to leave; however, it was always part of the plan. It was not part of the plan for you to fall in love with Campbell; that was Karma. I wish he had lived to join you on this journey. He would have given you strength. Now you, like I, must find the strength to carry on."

"Surely the Emperor needs you here in Japan, Uncle. I know he values your advice."

Lord Hino smiled somewhat sadly.

"His Majesty was kind enough to say almost the same thing. But certain things have changed. Before this war with America we had the greatest intelligence network in the world and I was honored to be its coordinator. Now, many branches of the military have started their own networks;

some have even taken part of mine. There are some jealousies between these different branches and they do not wish to share their information, therefore, overall coordination is now impossible.

I detect that His Majesty realizes this and believes it a better use of whatever talent I have to ensure Plan Empire is fully ready should it be necessary to put it into effect."

"We must make a difficult sea voyage to South America. All the necessary arrangements have been made. There we will await the inevitable conclusion to the war. A few months after the end of the war, we shall travel to Hawaii. As you know Rob must be raised as an American and this has also been arranged. He will be brought up by a couple of Scottish descent, Jane and John McNeil. Documents have already been prepared showing them as Rob's aunt and uncle."

"These documents show Rob as being born in California and following the tragic death of his parents in an automobile accident they are raising him. They are an older couple and are very nice. They have no children of their own but have a large home. As you know you will ostensibly be the maid they hire to take care of their nephew. You will ensure he learns our language, not just speaking but also reading and writing. But no one else must know of this."

"When the time is right Rob will be told you are his mother. This will require great sensitivity and skill; however, that day is a long way off. It will almost break your heart my niece, to see your son grow up and not to have him know you are his mother. This will demand an extraordinary effort, but at all times you must remember the future of our beloved country depends on the success of this plan."

"I did not realize it would be such a difficult task."

They sat in silence, each lost in thought. Although Michiko's thoughts were sad ones, his were sadder.

'How I detest misleading you my dear niece' he thought. 'But you could not bear all he bad news I have. Your heart was broken when you lost Campbell and now you have the added grief of leaving Japan. Your only joy is your son and soon you will lose him. Not for ever even though it will seem forever to you. It is essential you stay in South America and necessary for Rob to travel to Hawaii. He must forget you. When the war is over you will join him and by that time he will have completely accepted the McNeill's as his guardians. I know he will come to love you again but for the time you are apart I must ensure you find the will to live.'

He had unconsciously been staring at Rob. Michiko noticed this and said "He is a wonderful boy, uncle."

"Yes he is, Michiko. Not only wonderful but a very special child. You have royal blood flowing through your veins, the blood of our Sun Goddess, Amaterasu. Rob has this same blood. But his blood also comes from that most extraordinarily talented Scotsman, Campbell. It is this unique combination which makes him special. He is the future key to our country rising to its rightful place as a leading international power, not through military might, but through economic supremacy."

He paused but the look of rapt attention now on Michiko's face made him continue. With a whimsical smile, he said, "It is a strange union, where you bring the sun and Campbell comes from Glasgow where the sun seldom shines. Yet together you have produced this remarkable child. Perhaps, to honor his father, he can bring some sun to Glasgow."

The whimsicalness left his smile and it broadened.

"He will be the Glasgow Sun."

About the Author

Bob Fisher was born in Scotland. He left when he was 21, soon after completing his education, to live in Japan. Since then he has visited most parts of the world.

Whether waking up one morning in Malaya to find a black panther had been trapped a few miles from his home; or, having his hotel in Vietnam partially destroyed by exploding Viet Cong hand grenades, life has never been dull.

His many years living in The Far East allowed him the opportunity to study the culture, customs and history of several Asian countries. This resonates in his writing.

He and his wife have lived in six countries. Their three children were born in three continents, Asia, Europe and South America. They now reside in the United States.

Printed in the United States
65719LVS00003B/74